WITH THE BRITISH LEGION

WITH

THE BRITISH LEGION

A STORY OF THE CARLIST WARS

BY

G. A. HENTY

Author of "With Roberts to Pretoria," "Held Fast for
England," "Under Drake's Flag," etc.

WITH TEN FULL-PAGE ILLUSTRATIONS BY WAL. FAGET

NEW YORK
CHARLES SCRIBNER'S SONS
1902

PREFACE

The story of the doings of the British Legion under Sir de Lacy Evans in Spain is but little known. It was a failure, and that from no want of heroic courage on the part of the soldiers, but from the most scandalous neglect and ill-treatment by the Government of Queen Christina. So gross was this neglect that within six months of their arrival in the Peninsula nearly five thousand, that is to say half the Legion, had either died from want, privation, or fever in the hospitals of Vittoria, or were invalided home. The remainder, although ill-fed, ill-clothed, and with their pay nine months in arrear, showed themselves worthy of the best traditions of the British army, and it was only at the end of their two years' engagement that, finding all attempts to obtain fair treatment from the Government unavailing, they took their discharge and returned home.

The history of their doings is largely founded on a pamphlet by Alex. Somerville, a man of genius who enlisted in the Legion; and the events subsequent to its disbandment are taken from the work of Major Duncan, one of the Commissioners appointed by the British Government to endeavour to see that the conditions of a convention entered into by our Government and the leaders of the contending parties in Spain were duly observed—a convention, however, that had very small influence in checking the atrocities committed by both combatants.

G. A. HENTY.

CONTENTS

WITH THE BRITISH LEGION

CHAPTER I

ENLISTED

"WELL, sir, I shall be glad to know what you intend to do next?"

There was no answer to the question, which, after a pause, was repeated in the same cold tone. "Don't know, uncle," came at last from the lips of the boy standing before him.

"Nor do I, Arthur. This is the fourth school from which I have been requested to remove you. When I sent you to Shrewsbury I told you that it was your last chance, and now here you are back again. Your case seems hopeless. By the terms of your father's will, which seems to have been written with a prevision of what you were going to turn out, you are not to come into your property until you arrive at the age of twenty-five; though, as his executor, I was authorized to pay from the incoming rents the cost of your education and clothes, and also a certain amount for your expenses at the university, and when you took your degree I was to let you have the sum of one hundred and fifty pounds per year until you reached the age fixed for your coming into the bulk of the fortune."

The speaker, Mr. Hallett, was a solicitor in Liverpool with a large practice, which so occupied him that he was too busy to attend to other matters. At bottom he was not an unkindly man, but he had but little time to give to home or family. He had regarded it as a nuisance when his elder

1

brother died and left him sole trustee and guardian of his
son, then a boy of ten years old. Arthur's father had been
an invalid for some years before he died, and the boy had
been allowed to run almost wild, and spent the greater part
of his time in the open air. Under the tuition of the grooms
he had learned to ride well, and was often away for hours
on his pony; he had a daily swim in the river that ran
through the estate, and was absolutely fearless. He had had
narrow escapes of being killed, from falling from trees and
walls, and had fought more than one battle with village boys
of his own age.

His father, a weak invalid, scarcely attempted to control
him in any way, although well aware that such training was
eminently bad for him; but he knew that his own life was
drawing to a close, and he could not bear the thought of
sending him to school, as his brother had more than once
advised him to do. He did, however, shortly before his death,
take the latter's advice, and drew up a will which he hoped
would benefit the boy, by rendering it impossible for him to
come into the property until he was of an age to steady down.

"I foresee, Robert," the lawyer said, "that my post as
guardian will be no sinecure, and, busy as I am, I feel that
I shall not have much time to look after him personally;
still, for your sake, I will do all that I can for him. It is,
of course, impossible for me to keep him in my house. After
the life he has led, it would be equally disagreeable to him
and to my wife, so he must go to a boarding-school."

And so at his brother's death the solicitor made enquiries,
and sent the boy to school at Chester, where he had heard
that the discipline was good. Four months later Arthur
turned up, having run away, and almost at the moment of
his arrival there came a letter from the principal, saying that
he declined to receive him back again.

"It is not that there is anything radically wrong about
him, but his disobedience to all the rules of the school is
beyond bearing. Flogging appears to have no effect upon

him, and he is altogether incorrigible. He has high spirits
and is perfectly truthful; he is bright and intelligent. I had
intended to tell you at the end of the half-year that I should
be glad if you would take him away, for although I do not
hesitate to use the cane when necessary, I am not a be-
liever in breaking a boy's spirit; and when I find that even
severe discipline is ineffectual, I prefer to let other hands
try what they can do. I consider that his faults are the result
of bad training, or rather, so far as I can see, of no training
at all until he came to me."

At his next school the boy stayed two years. The report
was similar to that from Chester. The boy was not a bad
boy, but he was always getting into mischief and leading
others into it. Complaints were continually being made, by
farmers and others, of the breaking down of hedges, the rob-
bing of orchards, and other delinquencies, in all of which
deeds he appeared to be the leader; and as punishment seemed
to have no good effect the head-master requested Mr. Hallett
to remove him.

The next experiment lasted eighteen months, and he was
then expelled for leading a "barring-out" as a protest
against an unpopular usher. He had then been sent to
Shrewsbury, from which he had just returned.

"The lad," the head-master wrote, "has a good disposition.
He is intelligent, quick at his books, excellent in all athletic
exercises, honourable and manly; but he is a perpetual source
of trouble. He is always in mischief; he is continually being
met out of bounds; he is constantly in fights—most of them,
I am bound to say, incurred on behalf of smaller boys. His
last offence is that he got out of his room last night, broke
the window of one of the masters, who had, he considered,
treated him unfairly, and threw a large number of crackers
into his room. He was detected climbing up to his own
window again by the house master, who, having been awakened by the explosions, had hastily gone round to the boys'
rooms. After this I felt that I could keep him no longer;

discipline must be sustained. At the same time I am sorry at being compelled to say that he must leave. He is a favourite in the school, and has very many good qualities; and his faults are the faults of exuberant spirits and not of a bad disposition."

"Now, to return to my question," continued Mr. Hallett, "what do you mean to do? You are too old to send to another school, even if one would take you, which no decent institution would do now that you have been expelled from four schools in succession, winding up with Shrewsbury. I have spoken to you so often that I shall certainly not attempt so thankless a task again. As to your living at my house, it is out of the question. I am away the whole day; and your aunt tells me that at the end of your last holidays you were making your two cousins tomboys, and that although she liked you very much she really did not feel equal to having you about the house for six weeks at a time. You cannot complain that I have not been frank with you. I told you, when you came home from your first school, the provisions of your father's will, and how matters stood. I suppose you have thought, on your way from Shrewsbury, as to your future? You were well aware that I was not the sort of man to go back from what I said. I warned you solemnly, when you went to Shrewsbury, that it was the last chance I should give you, and that if you came back again to this place I should wash my hands of you, except that I should see the terms of the will strictly carried out.

"Of course, your father little dreamt of such a situation as has arisen, or he would have made some provision for it; and I shall therefore strain a point, and make you an allowance equal to the sum your schooling has cost. According to the wording of the will I am certainly not empowered to do so, but I do not think that even a judge in the Court of Chancery would raise any objection. I have ordered your boxes to be taken to the Falcon Hotel. You will find there a letter from me addressed to you, enclosing four five-pound notes. The same sum will be sent to you every two months to any address that you may send to me. You will, I hope, communicate with me each time you receive your remittance, acquainting me with what you are doing. I may tell you that I have determined on this course with some hopes that when you are your own master you will gain a sufficient sense of responsibility to steady you. At the end of two years, if you desire to go to the university you will receive the allowance there which would be suitable for you. I have thought this matter over very carefully and painfully, Arthur. I talked it over with your aunt last night. She is deeply grieved, but she agrees with me that it is as good a plan as can be devised for you. You cannot go to school again; we cannot have you at home on our hands for two years."

"Thank you," the lad said; "I know I have been a frightful trouble to you, and I am not surprised that I have worn out your patience."

"I wish you to understand, Arthur, that the course has been made easier to your aunt and myself, because we are convinced that with all your boyish folly you can be trusted not to do anything to disgrace your father's name, and that these two years of what I may call probation will teach you to think for yourself; and at its termination you will be ready to go to the university to prepare yourself for the life of a country gentleman which lies before you. If you will let me advise you at all, I should say that as a beginning you might do worse than put a knapsack on your back and go for a walking tour of some months through England, Scotland, and Ireland, after which you might go on to the Continent for a bit. I don't like to influence your decision, but I know that you will never be content to stay quiet, and this would be a way of working off your superfluous energy. Now, lad, we will shake hands. I am convinced that your experience during the next two years will be of great value to you, and I ask you to believe that in what we have decided upon we have had your own good even more than our comfort at heart."

"I will think it over, uncle," the lad said, his face clearing up somewhat, "and will write to tell you and my aunt what I am going to do. I suppose you have no objection to my saying good-bye to my aunt and my cousins before I go?"

"No objection at all. You have done nothing dishonourable; you have let your spirits carry you away, and have shown a lamentable contempt for discipline. These are faults that will cure themselves in time. Come by all means to see your aunt before you go."

Arthur Hallett left his uncle's office in somewhat low spirits. He was conscious that his uncle's indignation was natural, and that he thoroughly deserved it. He had had a jolly time, and he was sorry that it was over; but he was ashamed of the trouble he had given his uncle and aunt, and quite expected that they would not again receive him. His only fear had been that his uncle would at once place him with some clergyman who made a specialty of coaching troublesome boys; and he had determined that after the liberty and pleasant life at Shrewsbury he could never put up with that. But upon the way by coach to Liverpool he had read a placard which had decided him. It ran as follows:

"Smart young men required for the British Legion now being formed. A bounty of two pounds and free kit will be given to each applicant accepted. For all particulars apply at the Recruiting Office, 34 the Quay, Liverpool."

"That is just the thing for me," he said to himself. "Till I saw that, I had intended to enlist; but there is no chance of a war, and I expect I should get into all sorts of mischief in no time. This legion, I know, is going out to fight in Spain. I read all about it some time ago. There will be excitement there, and I dare say hard work, and possibly short rations. However, that will make no odds to me. It will be something quite new, I should think, and just the life to suit me. At any rate I will walk down to the quay and hear what they say about it."

Going to the hotel to which his luggage had been sent, he ordered a meal at once, and then, having eaten it, for he was hungry after his long journey, he strolled down to the wharf. He was shown into a room where the recruiting officer was sitting.

"I am thinking of enlisting, sir."

The officer looked at him sharply. "Have you thought what you are doing?" he said.

"Yes."

"You are not the style of recruit that comes to us. I suppose you have run away from school?"

"I have been sent away," Arthur said, "because I shoved some fireworks into one of the masters' rooms. It happened once or twice before, and my friends are tired of me. I have always been getting into rows, and they will be glad to be rid of me."

"You look more cut out for an officer than a private. How old are you?"

"I am past sixteen."

"It's young, but we are not particular as to age if a fellow is strong and active. The pay is rather better than the line here."

"It is not the pay, but the life that I want to see," the lad said. "My guardian has washed his hands of me for the present. I have neither father nor mother. I have never had a day's illness, and I fancy that I am as strong as the majority of your recruits will be. I shall come into some money when I am of age; and I don't know any way of passing the time till then that will suit me better than enlisting when there is some chance of fighting."

"There will be every chance of that," the officer said grimly. "We have got nearly our number on board a hulk anchored in the river, and shall sail in two days. I myself go out in command of the party. You give me your word

of honour that you have neither father nor mother who
would raise objections?"

"Yes, sir. I lost my mother when I was two years old,
and my father when I was ten."

"Well, lad, I don't see any reason why I should not take
you. We have a miscellaneous body: a few old soldiers, some
broken-down tradesmen, a few clerks, a dozen or so runaway
apprentices, a couple of dozen young agricultural labourers,
and a few young men who have come to grief in some sort
of way. They are a rough lot, but they will soon be licked
into shape. Our colonel started three days ago from Leith,
and we shall join the rest of the regiment somewhere on the
Spanish coast. Even I do not know where it will be until I
open my letter of instructions. I may tell you that if you
behave well there is every chance that you will get a commission in a couple of years. However, I will not swear you
in now. I will give you the night to think over it."

"Very well, sir; but I don't think that I am likely to
change my mind."

Leaving the recruiting officer, Arthur spent the afternoon
in strolling about the docks and watching the shipping, always a favourite amusement of his during the holidays. He
had done a good deal of rowing at Shrewsbury when there
was water enough in the river, and had learnt to sail in the
holidays; and until he saw the advertisement for men for the
British Legion, he had hesitated whether to enlist or to ship
before the mast. On his way back to the hotel he bought a
pamphlet explaining the causes of the war in Spain, and
sitting down in a corner of the coffee-room he read this attentively. It told him but little more than he already knew,
for the war going on in Spain excited considerable attention
and interest.

The little girl Isabella had been recently left fatherless,
and was but a cipher. The affairs of state were in the capable
hands of the regent, her mother Christina. Don Carlos had
on his side the northern provinces of Spain, especially the

Basques. These provinces always enjoyed peculiar privileges, and Don Carlos had secured their allegiance by swearing to uphold these rights. He had the support also of a large body of the clergy. The provinces of Aragon and Valencia were pretty equally divided, and fighting between the two factions was constantly going on. Madrid and the centre of Spain was for Isabella. The royal forces were superior in number to those of the Carlists, but the inequality was corrected by the fact that the Carlist generals were superior to those of the crown. The Basques were sturdy fighters and active men, capable of long marches, carrying no baggage with them, and effecting many surprises when they were believed to be a hundred miles away. In England and France the Carlists had many sympathizers, but the bulk of the people in both countries were in favour of the little queen; and although the British government took no open part in the struggle, they had permitted the legion, ten thousand strong, under Colonel de Lacy Evans, to be raised openly and without hinderance for the service of the Spanish sovereign.

Arthur Hallett went to bed and dreamed many improbable dreams, in which he greatly distinguished himself, and in the morning went down to the recruiting office and signed away his liberty for two years.

"Do you want any part of your bounty now?" the officer asked.

"No, sir; I suppose we shall get it before landing?"

"Certainly."

"Do we go in the clothes we stand in?"

"Yes; the uniforms and arms will be supplied to you on landing."

"Must I go on board the hulk now?"

"No; the recruits in general go off as soon as they are sworn in, but as you have not asked for any part of the bounty there is no occasion for you to do so."

"Very well, sir; I will not come on board till to-morrow

evening. I have got to get rid of my clothes and portman-
teaux."

That afternoon he went up to his aunt's. He told them
that he was going to leave Liverpool; his plans were not
settled yet, but he was certainly going to travel. His aunt
and cousins were both greatly affected at his leaving.

"My dear aunt," he said, "I have nobody to blame but
myself, and I have to thank both you and uncle for the
manner in which you have borne with me; and I believe
and hope that when I come back I shall have sobered down.
Uncle said that I might come up and say good-bye to you
before I started, and in a few days you shall hear from me.
I shall not burden myself with much luggage: just a couple
of flannel shirts, a couple of pairs of vests and drawers,
stockings, and a spare pair of boots. That won't make a very
heavy kit. My other things I shall sell; they will be of no
good to me. And I shall get a rough shooting-coat instead
of this jacket, for which I am already growing too big. It
is all very well at school, but a shooting-coat with pockets
is much handier for walking in."

His cousins, who were girls of thirteen and fourteen, both
cried bitterly when he said good-bye to them, and his aunt
was also in tears.

"If you are ever short of money," she said, "write to
me; I will manage to let you have some."

"I don't think I shall be short, aunt. I shall be able to
live very comfortably on my allowance; if I don't, it will
be my own fault. I have been on walking tours before, you
know, and I am sure I can do on the money."

He went off after staying for an hour.

"That is all done," he said, as he walked down the town.
"If the war goes on for seven or eight years I shall be of
age when I come back, shall have my thousand a year, and
shall have sown my wild oats," and he laughed. "I have
certainly made a mess of it so far. Unless the Spaniards
have changed from what they were twenty years ago, their

promises are not worth the paper they are written upon, and I expect that we shall often go hungry to bed. Well, I think I can stand it if anyone can."

The next morning he called on a second-hand clothing dealer, who examined his clothes. Arthur was obliged to allow that most of these had seen rough work. However, after great bargaining he got three pounds, a rough shooting-coat, and a good supply of shirts and underclothes for the lot, including the portmanteau. He kept his stock of books, and packing them up in a box, directed them to be sent four days later, if he did not come for them, to his uncle's house. He had already bought the knapsack, and found that he could get all his remaining belongings into this. At five o'clock he went down to the quay and was taken out in a boat, with some twelve other recruits, to the hulk. As he reached the deck he regretted for a moment the step he had taken. A crowd of recruits is not at the best of times a cheering spectacle. Here was a miscellaneous crowd of men—many of them drunk, some lying about sleeping off the effects of the liquor, which had been the first purchase they had made out of their bounty money.

Others were standing looking vacantly towards the land. Some were walking up and down restlessly, regretting, now that it was too late, that they had enlisted. Others were sleeping quietly, well content that their struggle to maintain life had for the present ended. A few men, evidently, from their carriage, old campaigners, were gathered together comparing their experiences, and passing unfavourable comment upon the rest, while forward were a group of country yokels, to whom everything was strange. Here and there men with dejected faces—failures in trade, men for whom fortune had been too strong—paced up and down. A few young fellows had escaped the general contagion, and were laughing uproariously and playing boyish tricks upon each other. These thought more of their freedom from their taskmasters, and pictured for themselves their fury on finding that they had escaped from their grasp. A few, for the most part old soldiers, walked up and down with a military step and carriage. These were glad to be in the ranks again—glad to feel that they would soon be in uniform again. It was the sight of these men that reanimated Arthur. These men were soldiers; they knew war and rejoiced at it, and he pictured that in a short time this motley group—these drunken specimens, these careworn men—would be turned into soldiers, their past misfortunes forgotten, with carriage active and alert, ready to face their enemies.

"They are a rougher lot than I expected," he said to himself; "but many of them must, like myself, have come to this through their own folly. I looked for a rough time of it, but scarcely so bad as this."

One of the soldiers, struck by his appearance, stopped in his walk to speak to him. "Well, young fellow," he said, "you look to me one of the right sort. Got into a scrape, and run away from home, eh? Well, your sort often make the best soldiers. What shall you do with your kit? Well, whatever you do with it, don't let it out of your sight for the present. If I am not mistaken, there is more than one jail-bird here. You will be safe enough when we once get under way; but eight or ten have already jumped overboard and got away, and you can't count on keeping anything till we are clear out at sea. Look at those boats round the hulk. Half of them have got friends on board, and are waiting for the chance of getting them away in spite of the sentries. There are twenty or thirty of us, all old hands, who will probably be non-coms. when we are landed.

"At present we are told off on guard, and there are four of us always on sentry duty. I guess you won't be long before you get stripes too. You have only to keep yourself steady to get on. We have got half a dozen officers on board —at least they are called officers, though they know no more of soldiering than those drunken pigs in the scuppers. That is where our difficulty will be. We call them the politicals.

They are most of them men Colonel Evans has appointed for services rendered to him at Westminster. Some of them look as if they would turn out well; but others are sick of it already, though they have only been two or three days on board, and are heartily wishing themselves back in their homes. However, one can't tell at first. They may turn out better than we expect. What is your name? Mine is James Topping."

"Mine is Arthur Hallett. I am much obliged to you for coming to speak to me, for I was beginning to get rather down in the mouth."

"You mean at the look of the recruits, I suppose? They are a fair average set, I think; only one doesn't generally get so many together. By the time we have been in Spain for a fortnight, they will have a different look altogether. I wish we had a few more country chaps among them. But there are not twenty here with full stomachs, except those who are drunk with beer. They have the making of good soldiers in them, but just at present they are almost all down in the dumps."

"How much longer are we going to stay here?"

"I believe we tranship to-morrow into the vessel that is to carry us, and sail next day. I shall be precious glad when we are off. Now, come along with me and I will name you to a few of the right sort. Bring your kit along with you. It won't be safe to leave it about."

He went up to a party of four men of his own stamp. "Mates," he said, "here is a young fellow of the right sort. I wish we had a few more dozen like him."

"Ay, ay!" another one said, looking approvingly at the active figure and the pleasant face of the young recruit. "He will make a good soldier, there is no doubt; one can see that with half an eye. He is well filled out, too, for a young one. You ought to be in the cabin aft, not here. And you will be there before long, unless I am mistaken. Don't you think so, mates?"

There was a chorus of assent.

"I did not join with any idea of getting promotion," Arthur said with a laugh. "I have come out for the fun of the thing, and I mean to make the best of it. I expected it would be rough work, and I made up my mind to stick to it."

"I reckon it will be," one of the men, who was older than the rest, said. "I joined as a youngster just before Vittoria, and if I had my choice I would rather campaign in any other country. The Spaniards are brutes, and there was not one of us that would not have pitched into them rather than into the French. However, I served my full time and got my pension; but when I saw that there was a chance of service again and no questions asked as to age, I was only too glad to put my name down for it, and was promised my old berth as sergeant-major."

"I should have enlisted for the cavalry," Arthur said, "but they seem taking recruits only for the infantry."

"I don't suppose they would be able to find horses for cavalry. Well, I don't know which has the best of it. It is easier to ride than to march, but you have heavier work, what with patrols and night guard. I hear that there are ship-loads of men going from Leith and Dublin and the Thames, so I dare say there will be enough of your sort to make up a squadron if they decide to form a cavalry corps." He drew out a pocket-book. "I will put you into the 25th mess, in which there is one vacancy. Your mates are a decent set of young fellows. I picked out those that I thought would get on well together."

"Are you salted yet?"

"Salted?" Arthur repeated.

"Yes; accustomed to the sea."

"No, but I have done a good deal of sailing, sometimes in rough weather, and I don't think I shall feel sea-sick."

"Your mess is the last on the right-hand side aft. Supper will be served in a few minutes, so you can take your kit down there. I don't think anyone will be likely to touch it there—in the first place, because it is rather a dark corner, and in the second place, because we have got sentries posted at each hatchway, and no one is allowed to bring anything up on deck; so I think you will be safe in leaving anything there."

"Thank you, sergeant. I will go down at once, and put my kit there and look round."

"I will bet that he has run away from home," the sergeant said, as Arthur disappeared down the gangway. "I wish we had got a few more of that sort. I will put a tick against his name. He is young—not above seventeen, I should say —but he has the makings of an officer about him. There is one cavalry officer aft. If I get a chance, I will say a good word for him. He is just the lad for the cavalry, not too much weight, active and cheery. He seems to have all his wits about him, which is more than I can say for most of the officers, as far as I have seen of them. Still, they will lick into shape presently, though I foresee that the officers will be our weak point. They may be the right stuff, but they don't know their duty at all. There is a captain among them who doesn't know his drill, and one doesn't expect that in a captain. It is the same with many of the others; they are nearly all raw. However, I hope that the majors know their duty, and will be able to get them into shape soon. It was the same with the great war. Whole regiments were ordered on service who were fresh to it, but they soon learned to take their place with the best of them. It is astonishing how quickly men pick up their work when there is an enemy in front of them."

Arthur groped his way below. It was already growing dusk, and only two or three ports were open. Picking his way along, to avoid tripping over men lying hopelessly drunk on the floor, he reached the spot that the sergeant had indi-cated to him, and placed his kit in the corner. In a few minutes the men began to pour down, some of them descend-

ing to the deck below. Lamps were lighted and hung up
to the beams, and under the orders of the old soldiers they
took their places at the tables.

Arthur was not hungry, as he had had a good meal before
coming off, but sat down and looked round at the five men
who were to be his associates during the voyage. Two of
them he put down as clerks. One of these was a pleasant-
faced young fellow who had evidently just thrown up his
situation to take to a life of adventure; the other was thin
and pale, and he guessed him to be a man who had for some
reason or other lost his employment and had enlisted as a
last resource; the other three were respectable men of the
small trader class.

The meal, which was the first that had been served since
midday, consisted of a bowl of soup each and a large hunch
of bread. After the first spoonful or two they began to
talk.

"Well," the young man facing Arthur said, "this is not
so bad as being quite starved, for I came on board just after
dinner was served. I suppose we, are going to be together
for the voyage. My name is Roper, Jack Roper. I hated
the desk, and so here I am."

"I got into a row at school and am going to see a bit of
the world," Arthur said. "My name is Arthur Hallett."

"I had a little business, but it was so little that I could
not live on it, so I thought that I would try soldiering. My
name is John Perkins."

"I left, gentlemen," another man said, "because I was
married. I come from Manchester. By nature I am a peace-
able man, and like quiet. I could not get either peace or
quiet at home, and I don't suppose that I shall get either
here. Still, I would rather put up with anything that can
come than with my life at home. My name is John Hum-
phrey."

"I preferred the risk of being shot to the certainty of
being starved," the other clerk said. "This basin of pea-

soup is the first food I have tasted for two days. My name is William Hopkins."

"I," said the last man, "am a tragedian. Tragedy did not suffice to keep me alive; the country did not appreciate me, and I came to the conclusion that I would be an actor in this tragedy in Spain. My name is Peter Mowser."

"I hope it is not going to be a tragedy as far as any of us are concerned," Jack Roper laughed. "I don't expect that we shall have a great deal of fighting to do."

"I don't know," Arthur said. "The Spaniards did not fight well in the Peninsula, but I think they will do better against each other. I rather hope they will, for we shall find it very dull if they don't. I shall be really obliged if you will take my soup," he went on, speaking to the half-starved clerk. "I had dinner before I came on board, so I can't touch this. As you came on board without dining, you must want it."

"I do want it," the other said, gratefully accepting the offer. "They did not pay me my bounty till I came on board, and I was really faint from hunger, and it seemed hard to be starving and to have money in my pocket without a chance of buying anything to eat."

When they had all finished, one of the old soldiers came round. "One of you by turns will take the plates and spoons of the rest and wash them."

"I will begin," Jack Roper said.

"Well then, you are Number One," and he numbered them off as they sat. "You will change after dinner to-morrow. It will be your duty to fetch the rations from the cook-house and to wash up. Anyone who is badly sea-sick can defer his turn," and he passed on to the next table.

The iron legs supporting the table were folded up under it, and the table itself shut against the side of the ship. They learned that no one would be allowed to go up, so sitting in a group they talked over the life before them. Arthur was glad to find that Roper would also enlist in the cavalry if a regiment were formed, he having been brought up in the country.

"I was a fool," he said, "ever to leave it. My father was a farmer, and gave me a fair education. I had two elder brothers, and they both remained on the farm, while I was sent to a desk in Liverpool. I stood it for two years, and even if I leave my bones in Spain I shall not regret the change. I should have enlisted long ago in the army, but things are everywhere quiet now, and I did not see that life in barracks would be much more lively than a stool in an office."

While they chatted in this way a great noise was going on on both decks. In spite of the efforts of the old soldiers to keep order, some of the men shouted and sang. Others, who were just recovering from drunkenness, sat with their hands to their heads. Quiet men shrank away into corners. Some parties of jovial fellows produced packs of cards, and sitting down under a lantern, sat down to play.

At nine o'clock the lights were extinguished, and the men, wrapping themselves in blankets that had been served round, lay down, and in half an hour quiet reigned.

CHAPTER II

IN SPAIN

AT six o'clock all hands were called on deck and ordered to have a wash. For this buckets were utilized. A few stripped only to the waist, but many, among whom were Arthur and Roper, undressed and poured water over each other, feeling the need of it after the night in the close and crowded cabin. With the fresh morning all were inclined to take a more cheerful view of things, and at eight o'clock enjoyed breakfast. Then they went up on deck again, and those who smoked lit their pipes. As before, boats came up round the ship, and those which had provisions were allowed to come alongside, and sell their goods to the men who had money. Most of those on board had already got rid of their small advances, but the new-comers had all a few shillings in their pockets, and freely spent them.

Arthur and his companion each bought two dozen hard-boiled eggs and a dozen buns. Others bought spirits for a final carousal. A few stood looking mournfully at the shore. A little farther out were boats containing friends or relatives, and three or four men at different times jumped suddenly overboard and struck out for them; then half a dozen of the non-commissioned officers jumped into a boat lying alongside and gave chase, and there were fierce battles—the weapons being oars, pieces of coal, and other missiles. In all cases, however, they succeeded in bringing the deserters back, and these were at once ironed and sent below. The officers remained on the poop smoking and talking. They were all in uniform, but most of them did not attempt to exercise their new functions. One or two, however, who had served before, went about among the men chatting with them, pointing out to them that they had enlisted of their own free-will, that it was no manner of use for them to kick against the pricks, and that they would find things much better when they had shaken down.

One of these came up to Arthur and Roper when they were talking together. "So you have put your name down for a cavalry corps if one is raised," he said to them, as he looked at the list of his men; "and I can see that you will both make good soldiers in a short time. Keep away from spirits, lads, and don't take much of the native wine, and you will soon have stripes on your arms. I shall keep my eye on you both, and push you forward if you deserve it." Having then ticked their names on his list, he went on.

As they finished their dinner the steamer which had been chartered for their conveyance to Spain came alongside.

The old soldiers formed the others up in line, and they went on board. Their scanty belongings were all stowed away, and the officers then came down and inspected them. The vessel was larger than the hulk, and they were not packed so closely as before. The ports were open and the deck fresh and airy, and even the most downcast of the force cheered up.

"They are a curious-looking lot," one of the newly-appointed officers said to the cavalry captain, glancing contemptuously at the motley group on deck.

"They will look very different when they get their uniforms," the cavalry man said sharply, "and are a pretty fair sample. As far as I can see, I have no reason to grumble at my lot. There are eight or ten countrymen among them, and as many fellows from the town who have had experience in handling horses. One is a particularly smart young fellow. He is rather young yet, but, unless I am mistaken, will turn out a capital soldier. He is a gentleman, evidently. I should say that he had got into some scrape at school or at home and bolted. He is the best-dressed man on board, and, if I am not mistaken, he will not be long in winning his promotion. He is well-bred, whoever he is. I shall be glad to have him as one of my subalterns. That is the man chatting with another against the bulwark. The other will turn out a good man too, but he is not of the same stamp. The sergeant-major spoke to me about the first this morning when he went through the list with me. I should say that he was a public-school boy; you can seldom mistake them."

Next morning the vessel started at daybreak. As soon as they were out of the river some sail was also got on her.

Late the evening before, Arthur had handed a letter to the recruiting officer as he went on shore, asking him to post it for him in the morning:—

"My dear Uncle and Aunt,
            "This is written on board the steamer bound with recruits for the British Legion in Spain. It seems to

me that a couple of years' soldiering will do me more good
than merely strolling about the country with a knapsack on
my back. I had made up my mind to enlist in this force as
I came up to Liverpool. It seemed to me by far the best
way of keeping me out of mischief. I shall see a new country
and new life, and no doubt shall have some rough work to
go through. I thought it as well not to mention my intention to you, but I hope that you will not disapprove of
it. They are a miscellaneous lot on board, but a few good
fellows seem to be among them, and I have no doubt that
I shall get on very well. I don't know much about the
rights and wrongs of this quarrel in Spain, but I suppose
that as the Legion is supported by the government, I am
on the right side.

"At any rate, the little queen is a child, and there is
more satisfaction in fighting for her than there would be
for a king. We don't look like fighting men at present,
but I suppose we shall brighten up presently; and as a first
step they have served out to each of us a slop dress, which
gives us a uniform sort of appearance, and we certainly look
more respectable than we did yesterday when I came on
board. I expect we shall take to fighting presently. I am
making fun of it, because I suppose it is my nature to do
so; but for all that, I am really very sorry that I have given
you so much trouble, and I expect to be steadier by the time
I come back again. I have enlisted for two years, but if I
like the life I shall keep on at it till I come of age—that is,
if I do not get cut off by a bullet. I shall send you letters
when I get the chance, but you must not expect them regularly, for I fancy we shall have very few opportunities for
posting them. Please give my love to the girls, and say
I will bring them home some Spanish mantillas and things
when I come back. "With much love, I remain,
                              "Your affectionate Nephew."

The voyage was without incident. The sea was never
really rough, but the greater portion of the men were des-

perately ill. Arthur, however, felt perfectly well, and enjoyed the voyage; laughing and chatting with the old soldiers, helping the sick as well as he could, and relishing his food—only Roper and himself being able to partake of the meals. On the fifth day after starting the steamer came in sight of land. The sick men were now beginning to recover, and all came up on deck to look at it, and cheerfulness succeeded the late depression. At mid-day they entered the creek upon which stood the town of Santander, and crowded boats assembled round the ship as she dropped anchor three miles higher up at the village of Astellero. Before the force landed, muskets and bayonets were served out, together with belts.

The next day drilling began, or rather was supposed to begin; but as the men had all got their bounty, and some of them the money for which they had sold their clothes, most of them spent their time in the wine-shops, and a large proportion of them were helplessly drunk. Their regular uniforms had now been served out to them, but it was only this that showed them to be soldiers. Arthur and his companion were among those who for the first few days attended drill. They were both put in the same company; and as their captain was an old officer, and did his best to get his men into order, they very quickly picked up the rough drill, which was at present all that could be expected; and before they had been there a fortnight they were both appointed corporals. By this time most of the men had spent all their money. The drill therefore became well attended, and the motley crowd began to have the appearance of soldiers. Two or three other transports had now come in, and the number in camp had swollen largely.

Insubordination was punished severely by the unstinted use of the cat, and this caused the men to appreciate the fact that they were no longer their own masters. Even the sergeants were able to sentence evil-doers to four dozen lashes, and as they were always moving about among the

men, these comparatively minor floggings had more influence
in sobering them than the very severe sentences inflicted by
the regular court-martials. The colonel, Godfrey, was an
excellent officer for the post. He could, when necessary, be
very severe, but his manner was mild, and he avoided punishment unless it was absolutely necessary, in which case he
showed no mercy. He was liked by the men, who generally
spoke of him as " Daddy."

Ten days after landing a steamer came in to fetch the
troops to the town of Bilbao. Coming near the mouth of
the Bilbao river, it was found dangerous to enter. A heavy
swell was running, and a large barque was at the time
going to pieces on the sands. The steamer was therefore
sent back to Castri, twelve miles away. Here the force was
landed and quartered in a convent, and the next day a company of the 9th Regiment came down to escort them through
the mountains, as ammunition had not yet been served out,
and Carlists were known to be in the hills.

The people of this place were civil and friendly, and the
men enjoyed their short stay. At daybreak next morning the
troops were roused early, and soon they were collected outside the town. When they got to a difficult gorge they were
halted for an hour, and the brigadier-general, Colonel Shaw,
told them that the Carlists were in their neighbourhood, and
that they must be perfectly steady and quiet if fire were
opened upon them. However, they met with no enemies, and
after a march of about twenty miles they got to Portugalete,
where they were to stay for some time. The work was hard,
the drill continuous. The natives here were hostile, and
several of the men were stabbed in the streets.

The people throughout Northern Spain were, as a rule,
bitterly hostile; the province was semi-independent, with a
republican form of government, and the peasantry entirely
under the control of their grandees and priests. They cared
little about the succession, but a great deal about their privileges. The government wished to deprive them of some of

these privileges, and to make them contribute a fair share toward the revenue of the country. Don Carlos, on the other hand, had promised to support their ancient rights, and for these they were all ready to fight. He had also a certain following in the southern provinces, for the ancient law in Spain prevented females from ascending the throne. Ferdinand had before his death abrogated this law, and appointed as his successor his little girl Isabella, but Don Carlos, who was the next male heir, protested against this change of law, and claimed the sovereignty himself.

To add to the confusion that reigned throughout the country, the government of the regent was hopelessly corrupt. The ministers had all their own hangers-on—their generals whom they wished to push forward, their own avaricious schemes to realize; and the consequence was that, so far, the Carlists had more than held their own.

The latter were thorough fighters, able to march long distances, and to strike heavy blows where they were least expected. Their leader, Zumalacarreguy, had so far baffled Mina, and inflicted heavy losses upon him. The war was conducted with terrible ferocity, little quarter being given on either side, although the British government had intervened, and induced both parties to sign a convention by which they agreed to conduct the war on more humane principles. Zumalacarreguy had but some eight thousand men, but was able in case of need to add largely to these. The queen's party had twenty-three thousand, but of these nine thousand were locked up in garrison towns. Mina was thwarted by the ministry of war at Madrid, and hampered by the fact that the Carlists had spies in every village, who reported the movements of his troops to the enemy. His cruelty, too, drove numbers of those who would otherwise have remained neutral, to the Carlist side.

From the day on which he landed at Santander, Arthur had devoted every spare moment to the study of Spanish, and he found that his Latin helped him considerably. He had made the acquaintance of an Irish priest, who was glad to add to his scanty stipend by teaching him Spanish, for which purpose Arthur had drawn a small sum from his store.

The time passed slowly at Portugalete.

" It is all very well for you, Hallett," Jack Roper said, " to be grinding away at Spanish, but I don't see that it will do us much good. I know that you have made up your mind to get a commission as soon as you can. I should not care about having one even if I could get it. As far as I can see, the berth of a non-commissioned officer is as comfortable as that of a colonel. He has no responsibility as long as he does his work all right, and he has none of the anxiety that the officers experience. I never was any hand at learning, beyond reading and writing, which were necessary to me as a clerk. I came out here for the fun of the thing, and mean to get as much amusement out of it as I can; though I cannot say that the fun has begun yet. This beastly convent is like an ice-house, and we don't even get good rations. No wonder the men are going sick in dozens."

" No; we might do better there certainly. I suppose it will be all right later on, when we get a little straight. At present there is no doubt that there is a good deal to be desired."

Even to his chum, Arthur had not mentioned his reserve of twenty-five pounds. He thought it probable that the time would come when it would be of great use to him, and he resolved to keep it intact as long as he could. When not busy at drill, or working at the language, Arthur maintained his high spirits, and he and his chum took a large share in keeping the men of their company in a good temper. Ten days after arriving at Portugalete the regiment moved up to Bilbao with the 10th Regiment, and both were quartered in a huge convent which had been abandoned. The view from here was magnificent, rich pasture covering the lofty hills to their summits.

General Evans had now arrived. He was the beau ideal

of a soldier, handsome, with a dark complexion and black moustache; his face was thoughtful in repose but bright and animated in movement. Five feet ten inches in height, and well built, he rode good horses, and always placed himself at the post of danger. Unfortunately he had too much kindness of manner and tried to please everyone. As a rule he mitigated sentences of courts-martial, and objected to the shooting of anyone; but he suffered his soldiers to die in thousands rather than importune the Spanish government.

The force now marced to Vittoria, and reached that town without serious fighting, though they had a little skirmishing by the way. Here they were fated to remain for some months. The life was monotonous, the town crowded with troops, the arrangements of all kinds detestably bad. Sickness began to attack great numbers, owing to the bad food and the insanitary condition of the quarters assigned to them. The whole Legion were assembled at Vittoria, and for some weeks, beyond marching out and back to the town, they had no employment. One day, two months after their arrival there, the officer who had spoken to Arthur when he first went on board the ship at Liverpool sent for him.

"Hallett," he said, " I have watched you closely since you joined. Your conduct has been excellent. I have spoken to the colonel about it, and he in turn has spoken to General Evans. A number of officers have already either gone home sick or died, and he has been pleased to grant you a commission, to which I am sure you will do credit. I will take you now to the colonel, who will formally acquaint you with the change in your position, and I am glad to know that you will be appointed to my company. I hear that you have been working hard at Spanish, and that you can already get on very fairly with it. This will, of course, be a great advantage to you, and I recommend you to continue the study until you can speak the language fluently."

"I am greatly obliged to you, sir," Arthur said. " I can assure you that I will do my best to deserve your kind recommendation."

"Not at all. You have fairly earned your commission. That you were a gentleman, I saw at once when I first met you, and noted you down for promotion when a vacancy should occur. I shall certainly be a gainer by the transaction, for Mauleverer was practically of no use to me; and I was not sorry when he went off. Now, if you will come with me to the colonel, who has himself noticed your smartness and activity, we will get the formal part of the business over."

Colonel Godfrey was in the room with the majority of his officers.

"I am glad to say, Mr. Hallett," he began, "that General Evans has bestowed a commission upon you. I am sure you will do credit to it, and we shall all gladly welcome you among us. A man who has proved himself so attentive to his duty on every occasion should certainly make a good officer. You will be attached to Captain Buller's company."

The officers all shook hands with their new comrade, and his own captain expressed great satisfaction at his promotion. "Although," he said, "I myself shall be a loser by it."

"By the way," Captain Buller said, "fortunately for you young Barkley died yesterday, and the best thing that you can do is to take over his uniform. There are no means of sending it down, and no one will dispute the possession of it with you. Certainly it will be of no use to his friends, and you may be sure that during the next twenty-four hours it would be stolen. I will go with you at once, and order Peter, his servant, to hand it over to you.

"He had a very good horse too. You may as well take possession of that also. I will advance you, if you like, five pounds, which you can give to the paymaster, who will hand it, with his arrears of pay, to the poor fellow's relatives. It is as well to put the thing on a legitimate footing."

"Thank you very much, Captain Buller, but I have money enough to pay for it."

"All the better," the officer said.

The captain went with him and saw that he got the uniform. "I should think you could not do better than take on the servant. He is a good man, and, between ourselves, too good for the poor fellow who has gone. He is an Irishman."

He opened the door and called "Peter!"

"Peter," he said, "Mr. Hallett is now one of my ensigns, and he will take you on if you like."

"Sure and I would like it, your honour. I was wondering if I should have to go into the ranks again, and it is rather a dale I'd stop as I am."

"Mr. Hallett has arranged to take over your late master's things, and to buy his horse, and will of course occupy his room, so that you will find no difference in your duties."

"Well, sor, it will make no difference to me, and what difference there is will be for the better. Lieutenant Barkley was a kind gentleman, but he was very soft, sir, and was always ailing. I have no doubt that Mr. Hallett will be a good gentleman to serve under, for there is no man better liked in the regiment."

Left to himself Arthur at once changed his uniform. His new one, he found, fitted him as well as if it had been made for him. Then he went down to the stables and looked at his purchase. It was in somewhat poor condition, but a fine animal.

"See that he has plenty of forage," he said to the soldier. "He evidently wants more than he gets. You had better buy him some in the town every day till he gets into good condition."

"He is just wearying for work, your honour. Mr. Barkley was not famous on horseback, and when he had to march he generally led his horse a good part of the way; and he was not out on him more than half a dozen times since we landed six months ago."

Then Arthur went out to the convent yard. Roper at once came up to him and saluted. "So you have gone up, sir. I felt sure you would."

"Yes, Roper, and I wish you would come up too."

"It would never have done, sir. I make a pretty good non-commissioned officer, and manage not to get drunk till I am off duty, but I am not fit to be an officer, and should have said so at once if they had asked me. I shall miss you badly, but I shall probably see you every day, and I mean to make an exchange into your company if I can manage it."

"I will speak to Captain Buller about it. I have no doubt he will be willing enough to exchange you. However, whether or not, we can always be friends."

"You may be sure of that, sir."

It was now lunch time, and Arthur went into the mess-room, where he received hearty congratulations, and soon settled down in his place.

That evening he wrote a long letter to his aunt telling her of his promotion. "I think," he concluded, "that it will not be long before we move. We have a fairly large body of troops here now, Spanish as well as ourselves. Why we have not moved before this, is more than I can make out, but I suppose the big-wigs know. When we do begin, I hope we shall go on in earnest, for this delay is very trying. The hospitals here are all full of sick, and nothing would do us so much good as to have a sharp brush with the enemy."

Most of the officers found life at Vittoria terribly dull, but to Arthur the time passed pleasantly enough. He spent two or three hours a day working hard at Spanish, and he went every morning to a teacher of fencing, reasoning that as the sword was now his weapon he ought to be able to use it. Some of the officers were inclined to laugh at the time he expended on study and exercise, but he retorted that it was a good deal more pleasant than sitting in cafés trying to kill time. But, indeed, there was plenty to do. The hardships suffered by the troops were extreme; no pay was forthcoming; the amount of rations served out was barely sufficient to keep life together. The quarters assigned to them were bitterly cold, and they suffered terribly throughout the winter. Hundreds died; thousands were so reduced by illness that they had to be sent down to the sea-port, where very many more died; large numbers were invalided home, and but a comparatively small portion ever took their places again in the ranks of the Legion.

The officers did all they could to mitigate the sufferings of the men, but they, too, received no pay; and, except in the matter of quarters, were as badly off as the others. Some of them who were men of fortune were able to get little comforts for the sick; the rest could only show their sympathy by visiting them, and talking cheeringly to them. And, indeed, the disgust and fury of the men were so great that, had they received orders to do so, they would joyfully have set out on the march south, cut their way through the Carlists and Christinos alike, and made at least an effort to overthrow the government that had broken all its engagements to them and left them to die like dogs. What still more enraged them was, that while all this time they were left to starve, the magazines of the Spanish troops were full, and the men well fed and clothed.

With spring there was a slight improvement in matters. The remonstrances of the British general and the British government had had some slight effect. A small amount of pay was issued, and rations were served out with a little more regularity.

There was joy in every heart when it became known that the long period of inactivity had come to an end, and that a move was about to be made. As long as they formed part of the force commanded by the Spanish general, Cordova, they felt that nothing could be done. The Carlists occupied the hills round Vittoria, and at times sent parties almost up to the town, but nothing could arouse Cordova from his lethargy, or induce him to make any serious efforts to dislodge the enemy. He was, it was reported, going to co-operate with General Evans by attacking the rear of the Carlists, while the Legion was to attempt to drive them

back from the strong positions they occupied outside San
Sebastian; but both officers and men scoffed at the idea that
Cordova would move out of Vittoria, and the general opinion
was that the Legion would do better if it relied upon its own
fighting powers rather than upon any Spanish co-operation.

By this time the mob of men who composed the Legion
had been, by incessant drill, converted into soldiers, who only
wanted a baptism of fire to take their place side by side with
veterans. In point of appearance they were not much to
look at. The clothes in which for nearly six months they
had lived and slept were almost in rags, but their bearing
was erect. Suffering had set a stern expression on their
faces, and General Evans, as they marched out from Vittoria,
felt that they could be thoroughly relied on. Many who had
just recovered from sickness were still thin and feeble, and
really unfit for work, but all who could possibly accompany
the force had obtained their release from hospital, and were
the envy of many hundreds of their comrades who were incapable of moving, and of whom the greater part were des-
tined never to leave Vittoria.

As the Carlists lay between Vittoria and San Sebastian,
the force was compelled to march down to Santander. The
men enjoyed the change; the fresh warm breezes of spring
reanimated them. Many, it was true, were forced to lag
behind, but most of these afterwards rejoined, though some
were murdered by the peasantry, who were, to a man, hostile.
A strong rear-guard, however, moved slowly behind the
column, collecting those who had fallen by the way, and only
arriving at Santander twenty-four hours after the rest. As
soon as the head of the column reached Santander they were
taken on board ship. There was only sufficient transport to
carry half the Legion, but the distance was short, and in
four days half the force were assembled at San Sebastian.

All felt that the change from Vittoria was a pleasant one.
San Sebastian stands at the extremity of a low sandy tongue
of land washed on the east by the Urumea, and on the north

and west by the Bay of Biscay, and attached to the mainland
only on the south by a narrow isthmus. It was strong both
by nature and art, being defended by walls and bastions, and
almost free from the possibility of attack on the sea or river
faces by the fact that, except at low tide, there was scarce
room for troops to be landed near the foot of the walls. The
town had been almost destroyed by being fired by the French
in the memorable siege of 1813, when it cost the British
nearly fifteen thousand men in killed and wounded to capture
it. The fire had been a great advantage to it, for the narrow
streets and alleys had been swept away and replaced by broad
streets and well-built houses. The inhabitants here were
divided in their sympathies, the mercantile classes being with
the Christinos.

The heights beyond the end of the low peninsula were
occupied by the Carlists in great force. Their motive in
thus wasting their strength when they might have been better
employed in the field was not very clear to Arthur and his
brother officers. It was certain that they could not carry
the place by assault; and as the sea was open to its defenders, it was equally impossible for them to reduce it by
hunger.

The place showed few signs of being beleaguered. The
town was full, as it contained many refugee families from
the surrounding country. The shops were well filled with
goods. In the evening the promenades were thronged with
well-dressed people, who paraded up and down to the strains
of military music. The cafés were crowded, and everywhere
there was an appearance of life and animation. The people
viewed with astonishment the ragged appearance of the regiment as they landed, and many small kindnesses were shown
to them. The effect of the sea air and the bright sun did
much for the troops, and in a week after their arrival they
had so far smartened themselves up that they made a decent
show. The officers fraternized with those of the ships of
war, and although its numbers were sadly thinned since its

arrival in Spain, the Legion had recovered much of its jauntiness and self-confidence.

"This is a glorious change," Arthur said to one of his comrades, as they leant on the battlements and looked out over the sea. A good many ships were in the port, some of them transports, others laden with stores; and the sounds of music in the town came to their ears. "One begins to feel that after all one did not make a great mistake in entering the Legion—not that I have ever greatly repented the step. I have been most fortunate in getting promotion. I have come to speak Spanish decently, and I have certainly learnt how to fence."

"I don't see that the last part is likely to be of much use, Hallett. When one does get into a hand-to-hand fight I don't expect one has much time to think of the niceties of fencing. One just hits out as one can."

"Yes, if one is not a thorough good fencer; but if one is not, he finds it more natural to strike a downright blow than to thrust. Besides, I don't know that I have learnt fencing so much in order to defend myself as because it is a fine exercise in itself. It strengthens all one's muscles amazingly, and at Vittoria it enabled one, two or three hours a day, to forget all the misery that was being suffered by the men. Last, and I may say not least, of its advantages is that it will enable one to fight. I am not thinking of fighting battles, but of duels. I observed from the first a great many of these Spanish officers seem to treat us in a very cavalier sort of manner, which is a thing that I do not feel at all inclined to put up with. I believe most Spanish gentlemen learn to fence as a matter of course. I don't know whether it is so, but so I have been told, and I was determined to be able to give any one of them a lesson if he attempted any impertinence towards me. My master at Vittoria said, before I came away, that I had become a very strong fencer—as strong, indeed, as any pupil he had ever had, and that it was quite astonishing that I should have learned so much in the course of four or five months. I have already engaged another master here, and I mean to stick to him till I feel that I can hold my own with anyone."

"If you can do it in skill, I should say that you could certainly do it in strength, Hallett; you look as if you were made of whip-cord. You have got height, a good pair of shoulders, and any amount of activity. You have broadened out amazingly since I first saw you, and I should certainly say that you would be an awkward customer to any of these dons, who are, for the most part, in spite of all their swagger, an undersized lot."

"Yes, they have certainly not much to boast of in the way of strength; with a few exceptions, I would not mind taking on any two of them with one arm tied behind me."

"I wish I had given up three hours a day, all the time we were at Vittoria, working at their language, Hallett. I see that you have gained a lot by it. You are able to chat away with the Spanish officers and chaff with the Spanish girls, while most of us are no better than dummies. Of course, we have all picked up a few phrases—some complimentary, but for the most part quite the reverse—as a medium in our conversation with the natives, but they don't go far in polite society, though they do assist us a bit when we want to sharpen up some of these mule-drivers or men with the waggons."

"Why don't you begin to learn fencing? It will occupy your time anyhow, though I don't say that you would find it as useful as Spanish."

"I will think of it, Hallett, as soon as this fight has come off. They say we shall attack the enemy's lines before long. I shall not have time to learn much before that, and I may as well take it easily till then, as I may not come out of it alive. I was looking at the enemy yesterday from the other side of the town. They seem amazingly strong. I can see by my glasses that they have covered the whole face of the hill with entrenchments and loopholed all the houses, and

I think these Carlists are obstinate fellows and will fight hard."

"Well, I do hope that Evans will attack as soon as the whole Legion comes up, without waiting for Cordova. He is a hopeless brute, and I have not the least expectation of his setting his troops in motion to help us."

"I am wholly with you," his friend said. "As far as we have seen hitherto, it is evident that if there is any fighting to be done we shall have to do it. These Christino commanders seem to have only one idea, and that is to avoid an engagement. We have heard that Zumalacarreguy has been marching about capturing towns, collecting spoil, and playing old gooseberry wherever he has gone, and dodging successfully any efforts the Christinos have made to bring him to a fight. It is just the same thing round Vittoria. That brute Cordova stops there in the big house that he has taken possession of. He eats, drinks, and enjoys himself, but as for marching out to fight the Carlists, the idea seems never to have occurred to him. Well, it is time we were turning back, for it is the hour for the promenade; and I must say that I like looking at the señoras even if it is beyond my power to talk to them."

CHAPTER III

AN ADVENTURE

ARTHUR found his knowledge of Spanish very useful to him at San Sebastian. He soon made the acquaintance of many of the young men of the town, and was invited by them to feasts and dances at their houses, where he became a general favourite by his frankness and the enjoyment with which he entered into the amusements. Although he could converse very fairly on ordinary subjects, he had not as yet learned the language of compliment, and his blunt phrases greatly amused the Spanish girls. He was indeed far more awkward with them than with their brothers or husbands. Except with his own cousins, who were a good deal younger than himself, and whom he had never thought of complimenting in the smallest degree, he had never known anything of the other sex. He had the usual boyish contempt for girls, and had almost regarded them as inferior animals. Consequently he was quite at sea with these laughing, black-eyed señorettas, with their fluttering fans, their pretty gestures, and their black mantillas.

"Señor Inglese," one of them said with a smile, "do you know that you are a very rude man?"

"I am shocked to hear it," he said. "How am I rude? I admire you all, but I can't go about telling you so."

"We don't all wish to be admired, señor; there would be no satisfaction if you admired every one; but we do all expect pretty speeches nicely and delicately put, speeches which without meaning much would imply that you are wholly at our service."

"I am afraid, señoretta, that it will be a long time before my Spanish enables me to do that sort of thing. If it came to the question of putting my arm round your waist and giving you a kiss, I could manage it, but to pay you all sorts of compliments is quite beyond me."

"It would not do at all for you to behave so rudely as that, señor," the girl laughed; "that would be quite an unknown thing. It is respectful homage that we require, and such homage can be rendered by the eyes alone without its being necessary to speak it."

Arthur laughed. "But my eyes have never been trained to that sort of expression, señoretta, and I should no more know how to do it than how to fly. When I was a boy I kissed girls under the mistletoe, but that is only a sort of romp and goes for nothing. I do not think that I have ever paid a girl a compliment in my life."

"What do you mean by the mistletoe, señor? I have never heard of such a thing."

Arthur explained, as well as he could, the mysteries of this vegetable.

"What!" she exclaimed. "You kiss a girl in sight of other people! But it is dreadful—it is barbarism! No Spanish girl could suffer such a thing."

"I fancy you would, if it were a Spanish custom," he laughed. "I own that I could never see much fun in it; still, it was one of the things that you were expected to do at Christmas. However, I can assure you that I have no idea of introducing the custom here; and I will promise you that if I do kiss you it will not be in public."

"But you must never think of such a thing," the girl said, horrified. "It would be terrible! No girl permits a man to kiss her unless he is affianced, and then only very, very occasionally."

"I will take note of that, señoretta, and will wait till I am affianced before I begin."

"And will it be an English girl, or a Spaniard?"

"An English girl," Arthur said bluntly. "I do not say that the Spanish girls are not very nice, but their ways are not our ways, and they are not of our religion, and their friends would disapprove; in fact, there are all sorts of objections."

"You think them prettier than we are?" the girl said, with a toss of her head.

"No, señoretta, I do not say that. I have seen many Spanish girls quite as pretty as English girls, but it is a different kind of beauty—one that we are not accustomed to, any more than you are accustomed to the appearance and ways of an Englishman. The two races are like oil and water: you may stir them about as much as you like, they never really mix."

"I suppose that is so," she said, more seriously than she had spoken before. "They say that Englishmen make good husbands, and that they are not jealous, as Spanish men are, all of which must be very nice; still, of course there are drawbacks to them. Well, señor, we must talk this over another time, for here is my cavalier coming to claim me for the next dance."

Arthur was chatting with a young Spanish officer whose acquaintance he had made, when the latter said:

"I wish I could go up those hills to-morrow. I have an uncle living up there. He is a Carlist, and he has a pretty daughter who is to be married to a Carlist officer to-morrow evening. I would give a good deal to be able to be there, but I don't see how it is to be managed. I might get there easily enough, for I could borrow a small boat and row up the Urumea after dusk, land beyond their outposts and make my way round there; but, of course, I should be known when I got there. I am sure my uncle would be very glad to see me, but I should be recognized at once by some of his friends."

"You might disguise yourself," Arthur said. "Put on a big pair of false moustachios, and of course dress as a civilian."

"I dare say it might be done," the young officer said, "if I had somebody to go with me."

"It would be a great lark," Arthur said, "and I don't suppose there could be much danger in it. Even if you were detected they would hardly make a row at a wedding."

"No, I don't suppose I should be hurt, but the feeling between the two parties is very strong; and, as you know, quarter is very seldom given on either side."

"Yes, your methods of war can hardly be called civilized, señor."

As they stood looking at the hill, Arthur turned the matter over in his mind. He knew that the general was very anxious to obtain some knowledge of the Carlist trenches and fortifications. If he were to volunteer to accompany this officer he might be able to obtain a good deal of information on the subject. To do so he would be obliged, after the wedding, to make his way straight down the hill instead of coming back to the boat, but this, he thought, would not be so very difficult. While anyone coming up the hill would be closely questioned, it was hardly likely that so much care would be taken in the case of those walking down, for the Carlists would be constantly going up and down to get provisions from the villages. There should be no difficulty in getting down to the trenches at the foot of the hill, but from there one would have to run the gauntlet. Still, the chances of being shot in the dark would not be great, and the information that he might obtain would be invaluable.

After thinking it over for a minute or two, he said to his companion:

"I have never seen a Spanish wedding, señor, and should certainly like to do so. If you would take me with you, I should be very glad to accompany you."

"Would you?" the young fellow said. "Well, you know, it would be a dangerous business. If I were suspected, I have no doubt that my uncle would protect me: he is a colonel in their service. And if the worst were to happen, I should be made a prisoner. But if they were to find you out, I fear that they would show you no mercy, and that even my uncle would not be able to save you."

"I don't think they would find me out," Arthur said. "I can talk well enough to pass muster, if I did not enter into any long conversation, which I could take care not to do. I should, of course, keep very much in the background, as you yourself would do, I suppose. At a wedding like this would not a good many officers and others attend who are not intimate friends of the family?"

"Oh, yes; my uncle's house will be virtually open to all comers. I shouldn't speak to anyone but my cousin, who is a great friend of mine, and I should manage to get close enough to her to whisper in her ear who I am, and give her my good wishes. No, I don't think the risk can be very great, and if you are quite in earnest I should be glad of your company. Mind, if there is a row you will have to take care of yourself, and I shall look after myself."

"Certainly. I understand that I should go in with you and do as you do. I should keep in the background, and go quietly off at the end of the evening. If by any chance I am discovered I should simply make a bolt for it. The nights are dark, and as I am a pretty good runner I don't think the risk of being overtaken would be great."

"Will you arrange about the boat? And if you will tell me where it will be lying, I will meet you there to-morrow evening at any time you like to name."

"It will be quite dark by seven, and we will start at that hour. But can you row? I own that I cannot."

"Yes, I can row," Arthur said. "Now, what disguise would you advise me to take?"

"Certainly the best disguise would be that of a Carlist officer, but I don't know how it will be possible to get it. There has been some fighting between their men and ours, and a good many have been killed on both sides. The dead are generally stripped by ruffians of the town, and I have no doubt that in some of the shops in the poorer quarters some Carlist uniforms may be found. Of course, they are not likely to be exhibited for sale now; the shopkeepers will be reserving them till the Carlists come in, which they are sure to do sooner or later. My soldier servant is a smart fellow. I will send him down this afternoon to forage about, and I have no doubt that he will succeed in getting one of medium size for a tall man. But if you come down to my quarters this evening you will see what he has got; and if it is not large enough for you, I have no doubt it can easily be altered to fit you properly."

"That is a capital idea," Arthur said, "and would suit me admirably. Then I will come down, as you say, this evening, and see how your man has succeeded."

"It will be a rare adventure," the young Spaniard said.

"I told my cousin months ago that I would dance at her wedding, and as things were growing black then, she laughed in my face and laid me a wager that I wouldn't. It will be great fun letting her know that I have won."

When Arthur went to the Spanish officer's quarters that evening he found him examining two uniforms laid out on his table.

"My man has just brought these in," he said. "One of them will fit me well enough, but I am afraid that the other will never meet across your chest."

The coat was a little short for him, but this was not very noticeable. It met round the waist, but was three inches too small round the chest.

"I can get that altered easily enough. Do you think you can borrow a sword from one of your comrades? You can make some excuse that yours has gone to be repaired, as the blade has come out of the hilt. You see, the pommels of our swords are so different from yours that if I were to carry mine it would lead to our detection at once."

"Yes; no doubt I can borrow one, and I will get a belt from another on some other excuse."

"I will take the uniform now. Will you bring the sword and belt down to the river?"

"Yes. I have arranged for a boat; it will be at the San Nicola steps at seven in the evening. Fortunately, the tide will be running in at that hour, so that we shall be able to drift past the Carlist outposts, and of course it will be running out again by the time we come back."

"Capital!" Arthur said. "Everything seems to be with us, and it will be an adventure to laugh about for a long time."

"It will indeed!" the other said gleefully. "How the fellows of my regiment will envy me when I tell them where I have been! But how about our faces? Do you think we can buy moustaches?"

"I have no idea," Arthur said. "If we can't, I intend to

buy a piece of fur with long hair, or a piece of fox skin would do, and cut out a pair of moustaches and glue them on; I am sure they would stand any casual inspection. And I should darken my face and hands a little: I am rather too fair to pass observation. As no one would know me, I don't see how I could be detected. But of course you would have to alter your face as much as possible."

"Yes. Well, you see, I had always worn my hair long, and now I have cut it quite short. I have not got much eyebrow, and I will put a few dabs of fur on, so as to make them heavy; draw a line up each corner above the nose, so as to give myself a scowl; and I should get my man to make a line or two across the forehead. I think like that I should do. People don't stare much at each other on such occasions; their attention is principally occupied with looking at the bride and bridegroom, and the ceremony."

"Very well, then. To-morrow evening at the stairs of San Nicola."

On the following evening Arthur made his way down to the river. He was dressed in the simple uniform of the Carlist officers, which consisted of a tunic and a red Basque cap, with breeches or trousers according to the fancy of the wearer. He was first at the rendezvous, but five minutes later his friend Sebastian Romero arrived.

"You have not been here long, I hope?" the latter said. "I was kept talking by the major just as I wanted to disguise myself."

"No; I have only been here a few minutes."

"The boat is tied to a stake. I don't think the tide has reached her yet."

"No; I went down to see her directly I got here. She will be afloat in a few minutes."

In five minutes they were off, Sebastian sitting in the stern as Arthur took the sculls.

"I will row across to the other side at once," Arthur said; "by keeping close to that bank we shall not run the risk of

being detected by their outposts on this side. I can row for
the first mile, then as we shall be nearly opposite them, we
can drift up for as much farther; by that time we should be
beyond their lines, and can cross the stream and land."

"Yes, I think so," the other agreed. "We have to get
well past the hill, for certainly they have works right up
to the top. Of course we can see them through our glasses,
but the ground is so broken with walls, gardens, and houses
that we can't exactly see where their strong points are, and
certainly not where the Carlists are most strongly posted.
We hear such different accounts from the country people
who come in, that we cannot believe them in the slightest,
especially as we know that they are Carlists almost to a man,
and would naturally try to deceive us."

With steady strokes Arthur rowed along, keeping close
under the bank and taking care to avoid making a splash.
Presently they could hear a murmur of talk on the opposite
bank, and he stopped rowing. The stream was running up
hard, and in less than half an hour they were well beyond
the Carlists' lines. Crossing the river then, they landed at
a spot from which a path led up the hill. Sebastian said
that his uncle's house was situated about a quarter of a mile
from the top.

"When we are once in the house, Sebastian, I think we
had better not keep near each other; then, if one is by any
chance detected the other can make a bolt for it."

"Yes; I think we might as well keep apart. I am more
likely to be detected than you, but the risk of discovery
would be greater for you than for me. As a relative, it
would be thought natural that I should wish to be at the
wedding. I might be shot by the Carlists, but my uncle
would take my part, and at any rate it would be evident
that I did not come as a spy; whereas, if you were caught
it would be very awkward for you, though of course I should
say that you came as my friend, and had no idea of entering their lines. Still, it would be very awkward; and if you

should see that I am taken, I advise you to slip quietly off
at once."

Arthur, however, had no intention of remaining any time
at the house and waiting till his companion was ready to
leave, for the latter would certainly object to share in his
own plan of making his way down through the Carlist lines.
And as he was going in a way as Sebastian's guest, he could
not very well leave him. The house was but a quarter of a
mile, his friend had said, from the upper line of the works;
and, even if detected, with the advantage of a surprise he
could easily get there before being overtaken. Not, indeed,
that he expected to be pursued. His intention was to slip
away quietly soon after getting to the house, and to stroll
down to the lines, where it was improbable in the extreme
that he would be challenged.

"If by any chance I should not turn up, Sebastian, when
you want to come away, you had better go down to the boat
and wait there for a quarter of an hour, and then push off.
You may not be able to row much, but you could certainly
manage to get over to the other side, and then you would
only have to let her drift."

"Yes; but there can be no reason why we should not come
away together."

"Well, you see, one or other of us may be suspected, and
it may be necessary to slip off. I don't say that it is likely at
all, but there is nothing like being prepared for all emer-
gencies."

After a quarter of an hour's walk they reached the house.
It was, as they had expected, full of officers and friends.
The ceremony had just been concluded, and many were going up to the bride and bridegroom offering their congratulations. Music was being played, and servants were handing
round refreshments. Sebastian joined those clustered round
the newly-married pair, while Arthur mingled with those
standing in groups round the room. He had scarcely been
there a minute when he noticed that the eyes of two or three

of his neighbors were fixed upon him curiously. Wondering why their attention should be attracted to him, he put his hand up to his face, and to his horror found that half his moustache was gone. He had become warm when rowing, and this had doubtless moistened the gum with which he had fastened them on to his lip.

He at once made for the door, but as he left the room he glanced round and saw that three or four of the men who had observed him were speaking together and making after him. The moment he was outside he started to run. He had gone but twenty yards when there was a shout behind him. This unexpected discovery had altogether upset his plans. He had calculated on being able to stroll quietly down into the Carlist lines. Now he would have to exert himself to the utmost to get there before his pursuers, who were close upon him. He ran at the top of his speed, looking round once or twice as he did so. He gained on his pursuers, who, now convinced that there was something wrong, exerted themselves to the utmost to overtake him. As he neared the brow of the hill he could hear talking and laughing in front of him, and soon he came upon a line of fires round which soldiers were gathered. His pursuers now, though he could no longer see them, began to shout loudly, "A spy, a spy! Seize him!"

For a moment or two the talk by the fire ceased, and the men stood listening to the cries. They were therefore unprepared for action when Arthur dashed through them—he had no time to choose a place—and knocked over two or three who endeavoured to grasp him. In a moment he was running down the hill with a hundred men in pursuit. Presently he saw a high embankment ahead of him, which he knew must be the highest point of the defences. He ran up it, and, when he reached the top, jumped. It was a fall of some fifteen feet, but the ground was soft where he alighted, and picking himself up he ran on. He had not gone fifty yards when a musket was fired from the top of the embankment. This was followed by a dozen others, and the fire grew into a roar. Evidently the Carlists, in their bewilderment as to what had happened, were firing at random. Presently he came to a wall, which he vaulted over as a number of men ran up.

"What are they firing about?"

"Don't you see it is a Christino surprise?" he said. "Open fire at once, or they will be upon you."

Instantly the men obeyed his orders. Others ran up and joined them, and Arthur strolled quietly away. He met numbers of men running up.

"Hurry up, hurry up!" he said. "The Christinos have attacked us from behind and carried the upper line. Run on! I am on my way to fetch up all the men."

In five minutes the fire ceased. Evidently some officer had come down from the upper trenches, and passed word along the lines that the alarm was false. By this time, however, Arthur was some distance down the hill, and had little fear of being discovered. No one, indeed, paid any attention to him. The Carlists were all discussing the meaning of the heavy firing and its sudden cessation. Some officers who had come down from the second line explained that it was all a mistake, and that no one could say how it had arisen. All that they had been able to gather was that someone had run down, that a sudden alarm had been given by somebody, and that the troops had fired wildly. They were enquiring into the matter at the top of the hill; at present it was all a mystery. Arthur spent a couple of hours gradually making his way down, examining the defences and noting their position, seeing in what strength the various loopholed houses were held, until at last he came to the lowest line, a deep trench with a high embankment, and salients thrown out to take any attacking force in flank. Here, as everywhere, he was questioned; but always replied that, as far as he knew, it had been a sudden panic, possibly an attempt by the Christinos to draw their attention to that point while an attack was made below. He therefore enjoined them to be on their guard. He sallied out at an opening in one of the angles made for the outlying pickets to run in, if attacked. He now proceeded very cautiously, and a hundred yards down he saw two figures ahead of him. He walked up to them.

"Is all well?" he asked.

"Everything is quiet in front of us," the men said, "as far as we have heard. But some thought that they heard heavy bodies of men marching this way."

"I am going out some little distance to find out. Be sure that you don't fire at me as I come back."

Without waiting for an answer he went on. He heard one say to the other: "He talks queerly; didn't you notice it?"

"Yes, I thought his language seemed strange. But, you see, he did not speak in Basque, and we don't know much Spanish. Anyhow, we cannot do anything now. We will question him when he comes back again."

Highly satisfied with his success, Arthur walked on until he was challenged by a sentry ahead. He answered in English "A friend!" for he detected at once that the challenger belonged to the Legion.

"And who are you at all?" came from the sentry.

"I am one of your officers," he said. "Lieutenant Hallett, I have been in the Carlist camp."

"Come on, then, and let's have a look at ye. It is a mighty noise that they have been makin' up there."

"Yes; they have been having a scrimmage among themselves." He had now come up to the sentry.

"Well, sor, I can't see yes," the man said; "but it is clear that you are English, and that is good enough for me. Whether you are Lieutenant Hallett or not, I don't know; but I shouldn't be any wiser if I did see you, seeing that I don't know the gentleman. There are half a dozen of the boys down the hill with the sergeant at that house you can just make out fifty yards away. You had best go down to them and explain."

"All right, and good-night!" and Arthur walked on.

Arthur was passed without difficulty through the outposts, and when he reached the town he found that Sebastian had already returned to his own quarters.

"My dear friend!" the latter exclaimed, springing to his feet, "I am delighted to see you. I have been in a terrible state of alarm as to your safety. I had just whispered to my cousin who I was, when there was a sudden uproar, and many of the guests ran out of the room suddenly. I looked round in vain for you. There was a general confusion, and five or six minutes later there was the sound of heavy firing, and all the rest of the guests made off in a great hurry. Of course I went out too, and waited till some of the company came back. None of them seemed to know exactly what had happened, but all were of opinion that a spy of some sort had been discovered at the wedding. He had been pursued, had run down through the lines, and a heavy fire had been opened upon him, and none doubted but that he was killed. Curiously enough, the men of the second line of defences had opened fire on those in the upper one. Why, no one knew. It could only be supposed that they believed that a Christino force had captured the upper line of trenches. I did not stop to hear later news, but made off to the boat in hopes of finding you there. I waited a quarter of an hour, as you told me, and then got in and floated down the river. I could not keep her to one side, as you did, and found that it was better to let her go as she liked. Fortunately there was such a stir in the Carlist camp that I passed down the river unobserved, and managed with a good deal of difficulty to get the boat ashore here. I have been back now about half an hour."

"Well, I managed to get through without much difficulty," Arthur said, "and found out a good deal about their defences."

"Now, you had better have a glass of wine and a piece of bread. That is all I can offer you. But as I suppose you did not get any refreshments up there, you must be hungry."

Arthur remained for half an hour, and then left. On the following morning he went after breakfast to his colonel, and told him of the adventure of the previous evening.

" You have done wonderfully well, Hallett, and the information you have gained will be of the greatest importance to us. You had better come across with me to the general at once."

The colonel at first went in alone, but presently he came out again and called Arthur in. " So you have been into the Carlist lines, Mr. Hallett?" the general said. " It was a very plucky action. Please tell me all about it."

Arthur related how, when a Spanish officer had said that he should like to go to the wedding of a cousin, the idea had struck him that if he accompanied him he might obtain some information as to the Carlist lines, and so had encouraged him in the project. He had intended to slip away unnoticed, but unfortunately he was betrayed as soon as he entered the room by the loss of a portion of his moustache. He then recounted the whole adventure, and handed in a full report of the Carlist defences which he had that morning written.

The general looked through it. " This is of the greatest importance to us, Mr. Hallett. It is the first authentic information we have received of the position and strength of their lines, and will be of the utmost utility when we attack them, which we shall do before many days. You have certainly used your eyes to advantage. I shall study your report at leisure, and it will be of the greatest use to me in making my dispositions for the attack. I shall certainly not forget the service you have rendered us. It shows that you have a head to plan, and courage and determination to carry your ideas into effect. It shows also that you have made the best use of your time, and have acquired a sufficient knowledge of Spanish to be able to pass as a Spaniard in a short conversation. You have done very well, sir; very well, indeed! And if you go on as you have begun, will certainly rise in the profession you have chosen."

Arthur retired much gratified by the general's commendation. When he told his adventure to his comrades they could at first hardly believe it, until the colonel himself mentioned the fact, and held Arthur up as an example of what even a young officer could accomplish if he chose to go out of the beaten path to devote himself to the study of a language, and to keep his eyes open and take advantage of any opportunity that might present itself. He charged them, however, to say nothing of this outside the regiment, for San Sebastian was full of spies; and if it were known that a British officer had made his way through their lines, they might set to work and make such alterations in their dispositions as would altogether destroy the result of Arthur's observations. Several of the young officers took resolutions to follow Arthur's example and begin the study of Spanish forthwith, but the greater portion said that the chance would probably never occur again, and that it was not worth while to work like niggers when the odds were so great against any good coming from it.

Already, indeed, the greater proportion of officers in the Legion had made up their minds to return home at the expiration of the two years for which they had been sworn in. The treatment the Legion had received—the unnecessary hardships they had to encounter, the breach of faith of the Spanish government in not supplying them with food and keeping them for months in arrear with their pay, and thereby causing a loss of more than a third of their number before they had fired a shot—had sickened them of the whole business. They were ready to fight, but they were not prepared to starve; and had ships of war come to take them home, they would have accepted their release with joy. But few of them had enlisted because they had any great interest in the cause of Queen Isabella. They had joined the Legion

from the love of adventure and excitement, so dominant in
every Englishman. The six months of delay and neglect had
roughly disillusioned them, and most of them regretted bitterly the comfortable homes and the many pleasures they
had left behind them. Nevertheless, for the moment they
were satisfied. Their sufferings and those of their men had
been quickly forgotten, for they had the enemy in front of
them, and it was certain that before very long there would
be a great fight; and none felt much doubt that, in spite of
the strength of the Carlist position, and the number of its
defenders, they should get the better of the Spaniards when
they came to close quarters.

The prevailing sentiment was: "The beggars have never
fought well against either the French or us, and it is not
likely that they will begin now. They seem to have fought
fairly sometimes against each other, but that is quite a different thing from fighting against us. They are only half-
drilled, and our fellows now are almost as well drilled as our
line. They don't look much, poor chaps! but they will fight.
They are just in the humour for it, and would go at the
Christinos just as readily as at the Carlists. They have
come to the conclusion that Spaniards are brutes, and the
recollection of what they have suffered at their hands will
make them fight furiously. It was just the same thing in
the Peninsular War. The Spaniards never kept their promises, and our fellows were starving when their men had an
abundance of everything. The result was that our troops
hated them infinitely worse than the French, and behaved like
demons at the capture of Badajos and Ciudad Rodrigo."

The month's stay at San Sebastian did wonders for the
Legion. The sailors in our warships, who were filled with
pity and horror when they embarked at Santander, never
came on shore without bringing presents of tobacco and portions of their own rations for them. The shops were well
supplied, and the small amount of pay that the men had received enabled them to buy many little luxuries. As the

Legion was at the time supreme there, General Evans was
enabled to obtain from the stores a fair amount of food, and
the men speedily recovered from the effects of starvation and
illness. At last all the preparations were made. From the
manner in which the staff-officers rode to and fro with orders,
the serving out of ball cartridge, and other preparations, it
became evident that the time for attack was approaching,
and the troops rejoiced that they were at last to be called
upon to play their part as men.

CHAPTER IV

THE FIRST FIGHT

FOR some days previous to the 5th of May, plans had
been formed for an attack on the enemy's lines. The
Carlists had a double line of fortifications. The first of these
was half a mile from San Sebastian, and on the heights behind were numerous others, formed principally of steep
banks or deep lanes, and breast-works of earth. Behind
these, and separated by deep hollows, were other heights similarly fortified but more strongly entrenched, and armed with
several batteries. The main road from San Sebastian to
Aranez ran through the ground, and was strongly barricaded
at various points.

The general's force consisted of five thousand British and
fifteen hundred Spanish. All his own troops had not yet
come up, and more Spanish troops from Santander were expected; but the general, having seen the manner in which
Cordova mismanaged matters, and not being able to depend
upon him as a tactician, determined to attack by himself.
The evening before the attack was to be made, the various
commanding officers addressed the men. All was bustle that
night. By three o'clock the whole of the troops moved out

of the town. The Light Brigade, under General Reid, consisting of the Rifles, the 3rd, and an irregular Spanish corps called the Chapelgorris, advanced against the enemy's lines near the river. The Irish Brigade, consisting of the 9th, 10th, and 11th under General Shaw, moved against the centre. General Chichester's brigade, comprising that morning the 1st, two companies of the 8th, and eight hundred Spaniards—the 4th, with the remainder of the 8th belonging to this brigade, not being yet landed—attacked the left of the enemy's lines.

The three forces had marched together as far as the convent of St. Bartholemy, and there separated in the directions they were to take. The officers were all on foot, for over such ground it was impossible to advance on horseback. Two hundred yards in front of the convent lay the Carlist pickets, but so noiselessly were the operations carried out that the various divisions reached the posts assigned to them undiscovered.

As Arthur marched along in the darkness he gave a hand in passing to Roper. "Good-bye, old fellow!" he said, "if we are not to meet again; but we may hope to do so in the morning." A squeeze of the hand was exchanged, and he passed on.

It was an anxious time. The red glare of the enemy's picket-fires could be seen in the distance. The morning was dark and wet, and there was perfect stillness as they took up the places assigned to them. Suddenly a Carlist gave a shout of "Qui vive!" which was answered by a shot from one of the Chapelgorris; then there was a shout of "Forward!"

Instantly volleys broke out from the various Carlist pickets. General Evans was in front of the advancing line. His orders were that the men were not to fire, but to advance well up and then charge. The first houses were cleared, and the out-pickets driven in. Then, for daylight was now breaking, the troops began to see the formidable nature of the

work before them. The 7th Irish advanced almost without
firing a shot. Volley after volley was poured into them,
and, though they dropped fast, they went steadily on with
their colonel at their head. Sweeping forward, they gained
the long building called the Windmill Battery, though five
hundred Carlists garrisoned the loop-holes. A great number of the enemy fell in and about these houses, refusing to
surrender as prisoners, but fighting to the last till they were
finally driven out. As General Evans came up to them he
exclaimed to the 7th, " You are doing nobly, Irishmen!"

On the enemy's right equally severe fighting was carried
on; and while the 7th carried the Windmill Battery, the
Light Brigade succeeded in establishing themselves near, and
driving the enemy from other posts of similar description.

Colonel Tupper was shot through the arm while gallantly
leading his regiment, but, lest his officers and men should be
discouraged, he threw his cloak around him to hide it, and
held on with his regiment two hours longer. When he was
again facing a heavy fire, he was shot through the head. On
the left, the 1st and two companies of the 8th, under General
Chichester, assisted in the assault, but without much help
from the Spanish regiments. Colonel Fortescue, of the
Rifles, was very conspicuous, being frequently engaged hand
to hand with the Carlists; cutting his way through bushes,
over walls and other obstacles, and dragging his men through
when they were sinking in the dirt and mud. The 7th and
9th were repulsed three separate times, but a party of the
10th came up and joined them, led by Colonel Fitzgerald.
A stone wall was in front of them, and over this Colonel
Fitzgerald sprang with a riding-whip in his hand. Volley
after volley was poured upon them, and the men fell as fast
as they got over. All the officers who crossed the wall with
him fell, but he stood still and ordered his men to come on.
His last words were heard by an Irishman, who sprang over
the wall saying, " Ye'll not die by yerself, old Charlie!"

There was a rush by the others, and the position was won.

The second line of defences had now given way, the only position of importance remaining being the fort of Lugariz. Here the enemy were massed. Men tried to climb up the slippery slope to its foot, but fell or slipped back again. Until nine o'clock the troops were baffled. At this moment the two vessels with the 4th and 8th entered the bay. The boats were instantly launched, and the men brought ashore. As they landed they threw their knapsacks down on the sand. The two ships of war opened a storm of ball and shell at the fort. Colonel Godfrey, as soon as he arrived with the two regiments, at once rushed into the thick of the combat. The batteries continued to fire until they were at the foot of the wall. A breach was made and the troops rushed in, but the Carlists for a time still kept up a heavy musketry fire from the rear.

The 3rd made at the same time a determined charge on a fort that had been resolutely defended for a long time. The fight here was very stiff. Fortescue and Swan were both wounded, and Brigadier Reid was shot through the breast. Fourteen field-officers and captains, and double that number of subalterns, were either killed or wounded.

At last all opposition ceased. The Carlists drew off sullenly. The bugles rang out the recall, and the scattered and exhausted troops gathered together in regiments. They had good reason to be proud of themselves. Older soldiers could not have fought more bravely than these men, none of whom had been under fire before. The 6th and 7th Regiments suffered the greatest loss, the number of killed and wounded amounting to more than a quarter of their entire strength. The total loss was seventy-five officers and eight hundred and forty-eight privates. Many of the wounded died after the engagement. Four pieces of artillery were taken.

When the fight was over, Arthur Hallett leant against a wall panting and exhausted. It seemed to him almost like a dream, and he could hardly believe that he had come through the desperate struggle without a scratch. Excepting only when for a time it was brought to a stand-still by Fort Lugariz, the regiment had been incessantly fighting. Now pushing forward, now falling back, now broken up into parties, now gathering together again; sometimes loading and firing as quickly as possible at the walls and houses, from which flashed shot as quickly in return; then dashing over walls and across gardens, storming houses, and driving all before them. There had been an anxious time when they could not struggle up to the foot of the fort, but were forced to lie quiet, to shield themselves as they best could from the fire from its summit until the vessels of war beat down an angle of the wall to make an entrance.

It seemed to him well-nigh impossible that he could have come out of the turmoil alive. He was soon, however, aroused. The bugles were ringing out, and the unwounded men formed up in order that their names could be taken, after which the work of collecting the wounded began in earnest.

"I am glad to see you have come out all right, Hallett," Captain Buller said. "Poor Prince is killed, and I should think pretty nearly half the company. It is the sharpest fight I ever went through. If it had been much sharper there would not have been anyone left to tell the story."

"I am sorry to see that you are hurt, sir."

"My wound is not serious; it was a thrust with a bayonet through the arm. However, I have got my majority. You had got five or six steps before, owing to men being sent home. I should think there must be at least seven or eight vacancies now among the lieutenants. One's only consolation is that it is an ill wind that blows no one good."

As soon as the roll was called, the work of carrying down the wounded began, and Arthur had time to go and look for Roper. To his great satisfaction he found that he also was uninjured. They exchanged a hearty hand-shake.

"We are very fortunate to have both got through it, Roper."

"I am glad indeed," the other said. "I wondered several times how you were faring, but there was very little time for thinking."

"No; we must talk it over with each other when we have leisure. We must help to get all these poor fellows down before we can think of anything else. Well, it is satisfactory that we have had a good fight at last. I had begun to have great doubts whether we were ever going to fight at all."

"Yes; they cannot say any more that the Legion is of no use for fighting. It has been our first chance, and I think we have made the most of it."

Then they separated; and it was late in the afternoon before the work of collecting all the wounded was finished. In the meantime a number of townspeople had been hired to dig graves, and by nightfall all the dead were buried. Some of the troops slept on the ground they had won, the rest marched down into the town; rations were served out, and as soon as these were cooked and eaten all went to sleep. Arthur's regiment was one of those that remained on the hill, and the officers all gathered in one of the houses that had been carried by storm. The bodies of the dead Carlists had been carried out, and fires had been lighted. After they had eaten a meal, Arthur and two other officers started on the rounds to see that the watch were vigilant, for the Carlists had not fallen back far, and might at any moment make an attempt to recover the lost ground. Each of them had two orderlies, and these carried lanterns. The night was dark, and it was next to impossible to make their way about over the broken ground, which was still thickly strewn with dead Carlists. They were heartily glad when, an hour later, they were gathered by the fire.

As they would have to turn out again in another hour they agreed that it was of no use to sleep, and they chatted in low tones of the events of the day. All agreed that it had been worse than they had expected, and that the enemy had fought with great bravery.

"They are sturdy fellows and not to be despised," a captain said. "I certainly did not think they would fight so well. If they had fought like that against the French there would have been no occasion for us to send an army to help them. However, we have a right to be proud of the Legion; they have done gallantly. It is a pity that we have lost something like three thousand men by sickness. It would have made a vast difference if we had had our full force here."

"Anyhow, it was lucky," Arthur said, "that the other two regiments came up in the middle of it, for they had fairly brought us to a stand-still. Well, I suppose it is time for us to turn out again. At any rate it is a consolation that we shall get some sleep to-morrow."

Next day the general sent for Arthur. "I must thank you again," he said, "for the information you gained for us, Mr. Hallett. But for it I don't think we should have managed to win our way so far, for we learnt from it the weak and the strong points, and were able to take several of their most formidable redoubts, which would otherwise, I think, have been more than we could manage. I shall have pleasure in mentioning your name in my report of the action, and shall remember you if anyone is wanted for special service."

"Thank you, sir. I can assure you that I have never thought of such a thing, and only carried out my plan in the hope that I might gain some information which would be useful to you when the time came to attack. I have already been extremely fortunate in obtaining a commission although altogether without interest, and can only hope that in future I may again be able in some way to be of use to you."

Arthur afterwards went to have a chat with Roper. "Well, Roper, we have had our first battle; what did you think of it?"

"I had no time to think about it at all. It was just load

and fire, and ' Go at them, lads! ' then falling back, and then trying again. It was certainly a good deal worse than I had expected. I don't think that I was frightened. My one idea was that I wanted to get at them."

"That is a good deal like what I felt, Roper. I know I wondered occasionally that I lived through such a storm of musket balls. Sometimes it seemed as if nothing could exist in it."

"All the time I was astonished at the courage the Carlists showed. We had so made up our minds that they would not stand against us for a moment that I was quite taken aback when I found that they were fighting just as hard as ourselves."

"Not quite so hard, Roper," Arthur said. "They fought hard, I admit, but when we got among them with the bayonet we always had the best of it. The beggars could stand bullets, but they did not like steel."

"We lost heavily, sir."

"I am sorry to say that we did. We lost particularly heavily among the officers."

"Yes, sir. Everyone was saying how gallantly they showed the way. I hardly expected some of them to do so well. Of course one has no means of knowing; but there is a sort of general idea that an officer who doesn't look after his men, or seem to take any interest in them, is not the sort of fellow who would lead them well in a fight."

"I don't see why that should be so, Roper. A man may be very kind-hearted, and yet not extraordinarily plucky; while, on the other hand, a pretty hard sort of man may have any amount of courage."

"I suppose that is so, sir; but somehow one seems to think that a man who is a good fellow one way will be a good fellow another."

When off duty some of the officers would often go out for a sail, and one day four of his friends asked Arthur to accompany them.

"I don't think the weather looks very settled," he said; "still, there mayn't be any change till we are back. Anyhow, I am ready to go."

"That is right. You know you understand managing a boat, and that is more than can be said for the rest of us. We don't propose to be out more than two or three hours."

"Well, it makes a change, anyhow. After drill is over, there is little enough to do in the town till the evening; it is all right then. The better class seem to sleep during the day; at any rate, they don't show outside their houses. And though they are friendly enough when you meet them on the promenade, they are very chary of asking you to call, or anything of that sort, except when they have regular receptions."

Accordingly they went down and hired a boat, and put out. A sail was hoisted, and as the wind was dead behind them they ran out merrily. They passed within a quarter of a mile of the men-of-war.

"There is a man on that ship waving his arms and shouting," Arthur said. "I rather think he is shouting to us."

"No; I expect he is shouting to someone on the other ship," one of the others replied.

They thought no more of it, and kept their course. When they had gone five miles Arthur said: "I think we had better be making for home again. We shall have to beat all the way, and the wind is freshening; besides, I don't like the look of the clouds coming up over the hills."

The others, who were enjoying themselves, said: "Oh, we will go a bit farther; it would be a pity to cut our trip short."

They held on for another couple of miles, and then Arthur said: "I am sure we had better turn. You hardly recognize how hard the wind is blowing; we are running before it, and she keeps on an even keel. You will find matters altogether different when we have once put about."

"Well, turn if you like, Hallett. It really seems a pity."

"Well, before I bring her into the wind we had better let the sail run down and put two reefs into it. I fancy we shall have to reef it close down before we have done."

The others saw by the serious expression on Arthur's face that he was thoroughly in earnest, and they lowered the sail and reefed it. As soon as this was done, Arthur put the helm down and the boat came up into the wind. As she did so, she heeled over so far that one or two of the others grasped the gunwale fearing that she was going over.

"She is all right at present," Arthur said, as she started off on her new course; "but I wish we were five miles nearer the land. I can see she won't look up very near the wind, and we shall have a long beat before we get in."

Half an hour later the sail was close-reefed, but even under this small spread of canvas she heeled over till her lee-rail was close to the water.

"You were right, Hallett, and we were fools not to follow your advice," one of the others said. "I don't know much about sailing, but I understand enough to see that we have a very tough job before us; and the wind is getting stronger every moment."

Five minutes later Arthur said: "There is a black squall coming across the water. We had better lower the sail altogether till it has passed. I have no very strong hopes, however, that it will be over for some time. There is no break in the clouds, and I have quite lost sight of the shore."

His advice was taken. The mast was lowered and the sail rolled up, and two officers got out oars.

"You had better get them all out," Arthur said; "it is as much as we shall be able to do to keep her head to the storm. Now, all row quietly. The squall will be on us in a couple of minutes; when it comes, you will have to put your whole strength into it. It is fortunate that I am steering with this short oar. If she had had a rudder we should never have kept her straight, for she will be hardly moving through the water."

There was a sudden splash of rain, then a pause, and then it came down in bucketfuls, while the wind literally howled. For a time the exertions of the four rowers, and of Arthur at the steering oar, kept her head straight; but after a quarter of an hour the rowers, unaccustomed to prolonged exertions, began to flag. Arthur changed places with the stroke oar, and the boat again made a little way; but the advantage gained by his strength was more than counterbalanced by the want of skill of the helmsman, and at the end of five minutes' rowing the boat's head fell off, and the wind caught it and whirled it round.

"Oars in!" Arthur shouted. "I will take the helm again. You four had better sit down in the bottom of the boat. A big sea will be getting up very soon."

"How long is it going to last?" Sinclair said, when they had all crouched at the bottom of the boat.

"It may last two or three days, and the wind could not be in a worse quarter. If it shifts, we might make either the coast of Spain or France; but it is a south-easter, and will blow us right out into the bay. It is lucky you brought those two bottles of wine and that loaf of bread with you; we shall want them badly before we see land again. I wish to goodness we had run in to that man-of-war. I have no doubt at all now that the man was hailing us, and that they were going to caution us against going out farther. However, wishing is useless; we have got to grin and bear it."

"We were fools not to take your advice earlier, Hallett."

"I don't think it would have made much difference," Arthur said. "If we had turned then, we could not have got back before the squall struck us, and we should have been blown out just as we have been now."

He was now sitting in the bottom of the boat also, still holding the steering oar. There was, however, but little to do with it, the boat was running straight before the wind.

"What pace do you think we are going through the water?" Sharman shouted, for they could scarcely hear each other speak.

" About six or seven knots, I should say."

" Then if it goes on for three days we shall be something like five hundred miles out ? "

Arthur nodded. " I hope it won't keep on blowing as long as that. Besides, there may be some shift in the wind that would enable us to make either France or Spain. If not, we have only one chance, and that is, we may be picked up by some passing ship."

There was little more talk. They were all sitting close together in the stern, as Arthur said that by so doing the greater draught aft would enable the boat to keep her course dead before the wind without steering. Each felt that it was more cheerful being thus close together, even if there was nothing to talk about.

Sinclair proposed that they should have a little wine to warm themselves, but Arthur at once said: " We must not think of such a thing. We have all had breakfast, and it must last us till to-morrow morning. We may have to eke out the wine for a fortnight; those two bottles are of vital importance to us. As long as it keeps on raining we shall not suffer from thirst. By the way, it would be a good plan to shake out the sail and spread it on the seats with the oars over it, lashed into their places by the sheet. In that way we shall be able to catch the water that runs off it in the baler."

" There is a lot in the bottom."

" Yes, but it is principally sea-water. You had better shift a bit forward. The waves are beginning to break over her stern, and we must keep her more on an even keel."

Night came on. The gale was blowing with unabated force, and the sea was high, but the boat rode easily over it, for she was a large craft, and would have required double the number on board to take her down to her bearings. Fortunately the water was warm, so that while there was not a dry thread on them, they did not suffer from cold. As night came on, they rearranged their sail. They put one of the stretchers across the boat with its ends resting on the gunwale some five feet from the bow. The oars were lashed to this, sloping downward into the bottom of the boat, and over them the sail was fastened, thus making a sort of tent sufficiently large for them all to lie under. All were worn out by the buffeting of the wind, and in spite of the tossing of the boat, the hardness of the boards, and their drenched clothes, they fell asleep before long.

Morning was breaking when they awoke, and there was no change, except that the sea was running much higher. The first thing they did was to bale out the boat. Then a bottle was opened, and a little wine measured out carefully into the wine-glass that had been brought on board. The loaf of bread had been placed in a locker. This had fortunately kept dry. A slice of it was cut off and divided into five portions. It was but a meagre breakfast, but all felt better after it. Pipes and cigars were then lighted, and they began to talk.

"What chance do you think there is of a vessel picking us up, Hallett?"

"I really can't say; but there ought to be a fair chance if the wind is blowing in the same direction as when we started. It would take us out, I should think, pretty well into the course of ships going south. There are, besides, vessels making for Bordeaux and other French ports. It will be hard if we don't run across some of them; and as we have four oars and a sail we should be able to cut them off as they come in. Yes, I think our chances are good. But even now one of us ought always to keep on watch."

The rain had ceased falling, but the air was still thick, and heavy clouds were passing overhead. At one o'clock, however, these began to break, and two hours later the sun shone out brightly.

"That is a comfort," Arthur said. "In the first place it will dry us, in the second place it will cheer us, and in the third it will enable us to see a long way."

He stood up and looked round. "I can see nothing at present," he said. "It is only when we get on the top of a wave that we can see any distance."

About five o'clock in the evening they made out a sail, but it was a long way off, and was already to the west of them; and it was seen at once that it would be absolutely useless to try and row after the ship, as she was running rapidly along, although under a very small amount of canvas. Still, the sight of the vessel cheered them. They had seen one, and there was no reason why they should not see more. They now knew that the wind was blowing more from the south than it had done, and that they were therefore running to the north. This was an advantage, for they would be making rather towards than away from the French coast, and when the wind fell, might hope to reach it.

The next morning the wind had dropped a good deal. The day was bright and clear, and they allowed themselves a double portion of wine and bread. Then they got the mast up, undid the lashings of the sail, and hoisted it half-way up, making holes in the canvas by which they could put an extra reef in. Under this very reduced canvas they were able to sail comfortably, though all of them had to sit up to windward. The wind had come still more round to the west of south, so they were able to lay their course due east.

"How far are we off land, do you think, Hallett?"

"Well, we have been about sixty-six hours out. By the course we ran the first twenty-four, we made, at six knots an hour, about a hundred and forty-four miles, which would put us, I should say, something like seventy to the nearest point of France. The next twenty-four hours we were running nearly north, so during that time we must have kept about the same distance from the coast. Last night we must have been approaching rather than running away from it. Well, we are now going about four knots through the water. If the wind falls more, and we can put up more sail, we shall walk along a little faster; but until the sea goes down, I don't think we can calculate upon making above five knots. But if we are now, as I suppose, nearly in a line with the mouth of the Loire, we may not be more than thirty or forty miles from the shore; for, although I don't pretend to be particularly well up in geography, I know that the French coast runs out a good deal west till it gets to Brest."

At twelve o'clock Sinclair stood up and looked round. "I can make out a dark line," he said, "over there to the left; it looks to me like land. We should have seen it before but for the sail."

Arthur was as usual steering, but the others all went forward to have a look, and Sinclair took the helm for a minute to allow him to do so.

"That is land certainly," he said. "I should say that it is stretching out towards Brest; but I think we had better keep straight on. It may take us a few more hours to get to shore, but it would save us a lot of travelling if we were to strike the mouth of the Loire instead of Brest. At any rate we are safe now, and can venture upon a slice of bread each and a full glass of wine—a glass and a half in fact; that will still leave us with half a bottle for breakfast tomorrow morning. We may fairly calculate upon being close to land by that time."

The others were rather in favour of running to the land they saw.

"Well, look here," Arthur said, "don't you think that it would be a great deal easier to travel a hundred miles in this boat than to tramp the same distance? Besides, the coast, I believe, is very rocky all the way along there, and we might find a difficulty in landing. My own idea is, that when we do make land, we must go ashore and find out where we are, lay in a good stock of provisions, and start south again. With the wind as it is now, we could very nearly lie our course, and we could certainly do so if the wind goes round a point or two farther. I don't know what money you fellows have, but I have only a dollar or two in my pocket."

All examined their store, and the total only amounted to thirteen dollars.

"Thirteen dollars would go no distance towards taking us down through France. It would not pay for a conveyance a quarter of the distance, to say nothing about food. Even if we walked it, it would hardly pay for our bread and cheese, and we should have to sleep in the open. Then, too, we might have a deal of difficulty in getting into Spain without passports; and if we did get in we should find it almost impossible to make our way to San Sebastian, as several places on the frontier are in the hands of the Carlists. Therefore I shall certainly stick to the boat. If you prefer to tramp you can do so; but I know that before you have gone more than a day's march, you will begin to feel very sorry that you did not take my advice."

"There is a lot in what you say, Hallett," Sharman said, "and I for one shall certainly stick to it."

The others at once agreed to the idea. Arthur, being the only one who knew anything of sailing, had throughout the voyage acted as captain, and the fact that he had carried them through the storm safely had given the others great confidence in him.

"I should say," Arthur went on, "that when we make land we may as well stop for twenty-four hours. The people will probably treat us hospitably as shipwrecked mariners, and put us up and feed us. We shall all be glad of twenty-four hours' rest; and by the time we are ready to start again, the sea will have gone down, and we shall set out like lions refreshed. With a wind anywhere north of east or west, we shall be able to lie our course comfortably; and even if the wind is light we ought to make eighty or a hundred miles a day, and three days will take us easily to San Sebastian."

The sun was just setting when they saw land ahead of them, and by ten o'clock they were close to it, and could

make out that it was either an island, or a cape running
out into the sea. They sailed to the north side of it. The
sea was smooth, so running the boat ashore they got out
on to a low beach. Walking inland for some distance they
threw themselves down in a field, and as the ground was soft
in comparison with the boards at the bottom of the boat,
they were very soon sound asleep. In the morning they
finished the loaf and the wine, and then returned to the
beach. Ascending some rising ground, they saw that half
a mile along the shore there was a village standing at some
little distance from the sea. Towards this place, therefore,
they made their way.

As they entered the village they were regarded with looks
of astonishment by the natives. They were not in uniform,
but their clothes had shrunk considerably in their long
drenching. Sharman had lost his cap. All looked faded
and bedraggled, and three days' short rations had left its
mark on their faces. Sinclair fortunately spoke a little
French, and was able to make the villagers understand that
they had been blown off the coast of Spain in a storm, and
had landed late the previous evening half a mile away. The
curé of the village at once took them in, and in short time
they sat down to a hearty meal, to which they did full justice. They told the curé that they intended to start next
morning to sail down the coast, and learned from him that
the place where they had landed was the island of St. Nazaire,
and that they were some twenty miles from the mainland.

" I think you could not do better than sail along the coast,"
he said. " Once you make the mainland you will find villages and little ports at short distances. At these you can
buy anything you want. Of course you will always keep
within sight of land, except when you cross the mouth of
the Gironde. I don't know how you are off for money, gentlemen, but I shall be happy to supply you with some, which
you can send to me when you have an opportunity."

" We are very much obliged to you, sir," Sinclair said,

"but we have thirteen dollars between us, which will buy us an ample supply of things for our voyage. We do not intend to land, but shall sail on night and day. Two of us are quite sufficient to manage the boat, and we can sleep by turns."

"Thirteen dollars will be quite enough if you have fine weather and fair winds, but it would not go far if you have to stop."

"I don't think there is any fear of bad winds. There would hardly be two storms one after another at the end of the month of May; but indeed I do not think we should run short of money were we to be eight or nine days on the voyage. The wine is only, I suppose, about sixpence a litre, and if we reckon a litre a day each of wine, and allow half a franc each for bread and as much for meat, our victuals will only cost us a dollar and a half a day, and we could treat ourselves to a franc's worth of fruit and still have enough money to last us a week."

The priest smiled. "Well, sir, at that rate you can no doubt do it comfortably, and I admit that your thirteen dollars will be ample if you make the run in five days, which you certainly will do, unless you get the wind right in your teeth."

They dined at the priest's house, and he provided beds for two of them, and found accommodation for the others in some of the cottages. They did their shopping that afternoon, and arranged to start at daybreak the next morning. This they succeeded in doing, after thanking the good priest very heartily for his hospitality. Many of the villagers had been down on the previous day to look at the boat that had lived through such a gale, and some of the others had now come to see them off. They headed east so as to make the shore as soon as possible, for they agreed that as they would have nothing to guide them in case of thick weather coming on, it was best to make the mainland, and then follow it down at a distance of a mile or so. The wind was blowing now from the northwest, and, spreading their full canvas, they ran down rapidly past the island, and three hours after saw the French coast ahead.

They were now in high spirits. They had made a wonderful voyage, and were able to chat gaily over the talk there would be at San Sebastian concerning their disappearance.

"I only hope there won't be another fight before we are back," Arthur said; "that would be horribly annoying. If I were certain of that, I should feel quite happy over our adventure."

The weather continued fine throughout their voyage. The wind was somewhat light, but sufficient to take them along at between four and five miles an hour, and on the evening of the third day after starting they saw the highlands of Spain rising in front of them. On the following morning they ran into the harbour of San Sebastian, where they were hailed as if returning from the grave by their companions, who had given them up for lost.

"We certainly should have been, if it hadn't been for Hallett," Sinclair said. "He kept his wits about him the whole time, got us to rig a shelter, and stuck to the helm as long as steering could do us any good."

The general himself sent for them and heard their account of the voyage.

"Well," he said, "all is well that ends well, and I congratulate you on your marvellous escape. Moreover, you have lost nothing, for there has been no more fighting since you left."

CHAPTER V

A FURIOUS STRUGGLE

THE time passed slowly. Skirmishing went on constantly. Both parties worked at their entrenchments. Shots were exchanged by the batteries from time to time. The soldiers were in better spirits, as a certain amount of the pay due was handed to them, and for a time even the grumblers were contented. Drilling went on regularly, and was done smartly and well. Sunday was the great day of the week. Spanish colours were hoisted early, and cannon fired a salute. The church bells began to ring, and every Spaniard, male and female, rich and poor, started by six o'clock for the Cathedral, which was so crowded that very many were forced to kneel outside on the plaza in front of it, the other churches being all taken up as magazines and storehouses. At seven o'clock the service was over, the shopkeepers began to open their stores, and country people and others thronged the great square.

Although firing went on as usual, sports were held down on the sands. When the market was cleared away, the plaza was soon filled with dancers, principally girls, who danced to the guitar. In the crowd were Spanish and English officers, grave dons, all the better class of the town, the women in their black silk dresses and mantillas, peasants, beggars, soldiers, and sailors. Many would stroll to the ramparts and watch the firing till eight o'clock, at which hour the Spaniards all went to bed, and the streets were quiet save for an occasional drunken soldier and the patrol parties.

Then there was another long interval without pay, which caused serious disaffection. Several of the regiments broke into open mutiny, and absolutely refused either to obey orders or to leave their barracks. Some of these mutinies lasted for a fortnight, and were caused partly by want of pay and partly because many of the men believed that they had enlisted only for a year, and now that the period of their service was drawing to an end, considered that ships should be arriving to take them home.

The officers were greatly puzzled what to do. It was extremely doubtful whether any of the regiments that were still obedient would, if called upon to do so, fire upon the mutineers, and it was morally certain that if they did so the disaffection would be so great that the whole Legion would fall to pieces. The officers went about among the mutineers trying to get them to return to their duty. Some of the regiments were pacified by distributing small sums of money among them, others were reduced by stopping the supply of all rations, and gradually things settled down again.

The desultory fire that had been going on for so many weeks was succeeded, on the 1st of October, by a series of attacks by the Carlists.

Heavy firing broke out at three o'clock in the morning, shot after shot falling in the town, and so well aimed were they that none doubted but that the gunner was one John Wilson, a deserter from the Legion, who had once been in the Royal Artillery. There had been many desertions from time to time, and the Carlists were constantly shouting invitations to our men to come over to them, promising them good pay and good treatment—offers very enticing to men on small rations and no pay.

As the fire broke out columns of Carlist infantry advanced, driving the pickets before them. Some of these threw themselves into houses, and defended themselves against overwhelming numbers. The 3rd Regiment and the Rifles were the first to reach the scene of action, many of them running up in their shirts, or with their tunics all unbuttoned, having leapt to their feet, seized their rifles, and hurried off without a moment's delay. Drums were beating and bugles sounding all over the town, the non-commissioned officers turning the men out as fast as they could.

The officers were riding about and getting the men to fall

in. As they arrived they were formed up behind walls and other shelters. The 3rd and the Rifles had checked the Carlist advance. As the 8th Regiment formed up, a cannon shot from the Carlist fort on the Ametza Hill fell close to a group of officers, many of whom were knocked down by the stones thrown up, and then went through the column, killing one man and knocking down half a dozen others. The men, however, laughed and joked among themselves. The next ball went right through the horse of a mounted officer, killed two soldiers behind him, and a woman who was out looking for her husband's body, having just got news that he had been killed.

Our artillery had now come on the scene, and, directed by Colonel Colquhoun, an admirable and scientific officer, soon got the range. He himself levelled one of the cannon at a column of Carlists a mile distant. The ball burst just at the right moment and committed great havoc, and the gunners of the other pieces in the battery, under his instructions, opened such a terrible fire upon the column that it broke and disappeared. He then laid three guns on the Ametza fort. They were fired simultaneously, and to the delight of the soldiers they burst on the parapet, carrying death and confusion among the gunners, and killing, among others, the deserter who had given them so much trouble. Up till ten o'clock the Carlists maintained the offensive, but at that hour the Lancers came on to the field. They charged in gallant style on the south-east side of the Ametza hill, and the Carlists gave way and ran until they reached their breastworks. Here it was impossible for the cavalry to follow, and they at once drew off under a very heavy fire. They then charged again and again at the various parties scattered over the plain, moving in as perfect order as if on parade, and doing great execution. But for the fact that the Spanish entrenchments were so extensive as to afford shelter for the scattered fugitives, the loss inflicted upon them would have been extremely heavy.

The special object of the Carlist attack had been the village and fort of Alza. This was defended by two Spanish regiments, one of the Legion, and a battery, and these repelled the attack with great slaughter.

A dog belonging to the Legion, which had taken part in every fight, always marching at the head of the regiment, distinguished himself greatly in this battle. Strangely enough he never barked except in face of the enemy. He had been twice wounded, and on this occasion, in company with a Spanish friend of his own species, advanced and retreated with the Lancers. They had gone on for some distance, where the balls were flying thick, but during one advance the Spaniard tumbled over and came back hopping on three feet. Briton looked back, but would not retreat, and stood barking his defiance at the enemy. Presently a ball slightly wounded him in the throat. He returned to his companion, who was hobbling away, and tried to turn him, and repeatedly offered to lead another charge by advancing a short distance himself. Presently he got another wound on the head. The men lying in shelter called to him, and he came in and got his wound partially dressed, and then at once set off again. His Spanish friend had in the meantime been killed, and Briton having in vain tried to make him rise, came back to the men and endeavoured to get them to go out and carry his friend in.

The National Guard of San Sebastian turned out well. They had no regular uniform, but carried a bandolier filled with cartridges, and their rifles; and many of their women, who came out with the men, took shelter in the woods and assisted in carrying in the wounded.

General Evans rode about with the greatest coolness through the heavy fire, but although hundreds of bullets were aimed at him he was only hit once through the ear.

So the fight continued all day until night put an end to it. No attempt was made to storm the Spanish position. As General Evans mentioned in his despatches, this could not have been effected without the loss of at least five hundred men, and the capture of the entrenchments would have been dear at the price.

After this battle there was an interval of quiet. Arrangements had been made by General Evans with the Spanish commanders that he would not take the offensive until they were ready to co-operate with him. The force was therefore again set to work to entrench, and as the men received a pint of wine and threepence three-farthings a day in addition to the usual twopence halfpenny, the service was a very popular one. The extra pay sufficed to keep the soldiers from grumbling, and the extra food that they were able to purchase put them into better condition.

One of the well-known figures in the town was General Jauregui. He had been in turn a shepherd, half soldier, and half guerilla; but when the war broke out he raised a body of volunteers for the queen, and soon attained the rank of general. He was not liked by the officers under him, many of whom were nobles, but he was beloved by his men. He had many relations in the ranks, and was not ashamed to sit down and eat and talk with them. He possessed the rare peculiarity in a Spaniard of being fat.

Months passed; and not until the 9th of March did it become known that the advance was to take place the next morning. No secret was made of it, as the general's desire was that the Carlists should gather to resist him, for he wished to strike a heavy blow. Each man was given a peseta (equal to tenpence halfpenny) to buy tobacco and other necessaries, and the shops of the town were crowded all day with British soldiers. A good deal of the money was invested in chocolate, for it was thought probable that the battle would last more than one day, in which case rations would not be served out.

There was no going to bed that night. Fires were kept blazing everywhere, and cooking-pots were hung over them. Extra flints were served out, and new shoes for those in need

of them, and men exchanged with each other the addresses
of their relations in order that news might be sent to them
if they were killed. All night the men sat and joked, until
an officer went round and ordered them to fall in quietly.
The Spanish regiments had already turned out and taken
up their places, some on the glacis and some in close column
behind one of the batteries.

As day broke the men were called to attention, and almost
simultaneously the batteries opened fire. A column marched
against the Ametza with such resolution that its garrison
evacuated it hurriedly, leaving many thousands of rounds of
ammunition behind them. The fighting was desperate all
along the line. One rocky hill was taken and retaken five
times during the day. The terror of the scene was added to
by the fact that the furze on the hills caught fire from the
explosion of the shells, and many wounded were burned to
death. Many of the places were thickly dotted with the red
coats of the Legion.

The fight continued all day, and the troops lay down and
slept on the ground they had won. Upwards of a thousand
had fallen; and the Carlists must have suffered much more
severely, for they had been exposed to the fire of artillery
while they themselves had no guns in action. The next day
passed quietly, the artillerymen being occupied in getting
their guns up on to the height they had won. On the second day after the battle, in spite of a pouring rain, the advance began again. The artillery cleared the way, turning
the Carlists out of the houses they occupied; the troops
crossed the river by a bridge of boats, and moved on without
serious opposition, and were glad when the order came to
halt and occupy the houses of the deserted village.

A little beyond the village there was a hard fight the next
day, but at night the troops fell back to the houses they had
occupied in the morning. The rain still came down. On
the following morning at twelve it cleared. The Carlists
lay concealed until the columns got very near to them, and

then opened a tremendous fire. At three o'clock the engagement had become general. Some of the troops fired away all their ammunition and then charged with the bayonet, before which weapon the Carlists always fell back, although they would stand against the heaviest musketry fire. The strongest point of defence of the Carlists was the Venta Hill. Round this the battle raged all day, and in the afternoon it was decided to make a final attempt to take it.

The 8th Regiment of the Legion was in camp, and was about to start on the attack when General Evans rode up.

"You cannot go on with your one regiment, Colonel Hogg," he said; "there will be some more up very shortly."

"Oh, allow me, general, to go on," Colonel Hogg said. "I am sure we can get through the breast-work;" and then turning to the regiment, which was in close column, said: "Men, would you rather go on by yourselves or wait for others to come on to help you? We have a chance here that we will not divide with another regiment."

The men answered with a tremendous cheer.

"Go on, then, brave fellows!" General Evans said, and the regiment advanced. The artillery were hard at work, and the scream of the rockets sounded over the din of the musketry and guns. The regiment with a loud cheer emerged from the cover which concealed them, and as they did so a blaze of fire ran along all the enemy's defences. The four mounted officers galloped at their head. Every man cheered as he ran down into a road and then up again through hedges and across broken ground. A storm of bullets swept through them, and the guns on the heights played upon them with grape, but fortunately most of the missiles went overhead. They reached the first barricade. The colonel was the first to mount it, and some others climbed up; but the majority were so out of breath with their shouting and the pace at which they had run, that they were forced to pause. The barricade was built of turf, and was too steep to be climbed, but the men set to work to tear it down with their hands, and soon made a passage through which they could pass.

There was no active opposition here, for our guns sent their shells so thickly among the Carlists that it was impossible for them to withstand them. As the 8th poured through, they found the ground nearly covered with dead. The bugles now sounded a halt, but the men were not to be restrained, and eagerly pressed forward till they reached the top of the hill, which the Carlists had evacuated as they neared it. Here a battery of four guns was taken, and the flag flying above them hauled down. In the battery were found two barrels, one of wine and the other of spirits, and a tremendous rush took place. While the men were frantically fighting, there was an explosion and a shout of " There is a mine underneath!" and a frightful rush to get away from the spot took place. In the midst of this a soldier calmly walked forward and filled his canteen and that of two of his comrades. This action considerably reassured the others, and the panic soon abated when it was found that there were no more explosions. It turned out afterwards that the man who had shown such coolness had not been able to get near the casks, and had quietly taken out some of his ammunition from his cartridge box, laid it on the ground under the feet of those fighting to get at the liquor, and shaken out the fire from his pipe on to it. However, the contents of the casks were soon finished. The regiment was then re-formed, and as it was dark they lay down in the fields. They had won their way thus far, but they had reached their limit.

The news of the fighting had been carried by active men all over the country. It was evident that the further advance of the Legion would place them in possession of the main road to France, and reinforcements were called up from all sides. Already Evans was opposed by a force far more numerous than his own, and when the news of his advance arrived every Carlist within fifty miles was on the road. Espartero, who was with his army round Bilbao, had promised to march, and General Saarsfield, who commanded another royal army, was also to have moved, so as to occupy the enemy's attention, but neither had done so. The Carlist army had been, a week before, withdrawn from before Saarsfield, and during the night of the 15th, ten thousand men slipped away from the force facing that of Espartero and crossed the mountains to assist their friends.

Espartero himself had ridden, when he heard of the progress that Evans was making, to see with his own eyes how matters were going on. The fighting had again begun, and the Carlists had already been driven back into the town of Hernani, when Don Sebastian, one of the sons of Carlos, arrived with ten thousand infantry and three hundred cavalry. These marched out, column after column, and the vast superiority of numbers enabled them to not only show in force in face of the allied army, but to threaten both its flanks. For a time the Legion and its Spanish allies held their ground firmly, but they had considerably more than twice their number opposed to them, and the flanks were gradually driven in towards the centre. The Rifles, who were on one flank, had fought with obstinate bravery; and on the other, two Irish regiments stubbornly faced an overwhelming force of Carlists, and were engaged in a hand-to-hand fight with them. Colonel Cotter, of the 9th Cork, was conspicuous for his gallantry. Alone he rode repeatedly into the leading Carlist ranks, until he was completely surrounded and fell fighting to the last.

The 6th, 7th, and 8th Regiments, who were in reserve, were soon drawn forward into the fight. The 6th were first called up. The whole of the Carlist cavalry dashed forward to attack the leading company, which alone was available to meet them, but were received with such a tremendous volley that they were driven backward in great confusion, with immense loss. Two howitzers of the Marine Artillery sent showers of grape among them, and of the fine regiment which had advanced, a shattered group of fugitives returned. The Carlists, working round, threatened the artillery, and these were only saved by desperate charges of the Lancers and the staunchness of two companies of the 6th. The Spanish regiments fought but badly, and by their retreat exposed the Legion to a heavy cross-fire, which compelled them to fall back. The 8th, the last regiment of the reserve, who had been lying concealed in a hollow, were then called up. Two hundred of the wounded had been left behind in a large house, and these, as the Carlists advanced, were bayoneted to a man. The 8th went boldly forward, and answering nobly to Colonel Hogg's call upon them to charge, rushed under a tremendous fire to a wall, on the other side of which a strong force of the Carlists stood, while many were already crossing it.

The 8th dashed forward and bayoneted all who had crossed the wall, and for a time fought the Carlist battalion crowded behind it; but other troops were pushing on both to the right and left, so, threatened on both flanks, and with an overpowering force in front, the 8th sullenly fell back. Broken up into parties, they still fought desperately, and were only saved by a furious charge by the Lancers. The Carlists, unprepared for cavalry, broke in confusion, and thus the survivors of the 8th were able to draw off. The regiments of Chapelgorris had distinguished themselves during the day. They had refused to be brigaded with the other Spanish regiments, but fought by the side of the British with the most desperate valour; they were indeed almost annihilated. Nevertheless, the few survivors of these and the 8th nobly beat back an attack of the Carlists. There was a regiment of Royal Marines on the ground, but these were prevented by Lord John Haye, who commanded them, from taking any prominent part in the fight, and they lost but eighteen men wounded and none killed, while the Legion had lost very many hundreds, two or three regiments being almost wiped out. The retreating force passed the height of Venta, which they had so gallantly won four days before, and only halted when they reached the lines they had occupied previous to the 10th.

Arthur had borne his full share in the incidents of that terrible day. He had fought as fearlessly as the best, and had brought the remains of his company out of the fray, his captain being among the many officers who had fallen. So great had been the slaughter that he found himself at the end of the day high in the list of lieutenants. He had received three wounds, but all were slight. He had broken his sword in a hand-to-hand encounter with a Carlist officer, but had ended the fight by striking his opponent full in the face with the pommel, and stretching him senseless on the ground. When they reached the lines he went across to Roper's company, and to his great pleasure found that his friend had escaped with only a bullet through his arm.

" This has been a dreadful day, Mr. Hallett ! "

" A terrible day, Roper ! Three to one against us, I should say there were."

" But we made a stiff fight of it, sir; and the Legion has a right to be proud of itself. If the Spanish regiments had not given way, I think we might have held our own with them."

" I doubt whether we could in any case, Roper. They were altogether too strong for us. Still, we should have done better if the Spaniards had stood, and might at any rate have retired in good order to the Venta Hill, and held that against any attack the Carlists might have made. I hope I shall never see such fighting again."

" The same here," Roper said. " I think a thousand of us can do fairly well against two thousand of the Carlists; but when it comes to twenty thousand against about four thousand, the odds are too great altogether, for no one can say that the Carlists don't fight well. It was lucky, sir, that the Lancers arrived when they did, for I don't think any of us would have got away alive if it hadn't been for them. I quite made up my mind that we had all got to go down, when they came thundering up."

"It was indeed a most fortunate thing, Roper. During the last part of the day I had been fighting with a musket among the men, for I broke my sword, and pistols are of no use in a fight like that. Well, I am going off now to see if I can be of any good in the hospital; the surgeons must have their hands more than full."

Arthur's offer of aid was thankfully received, and he worked all night, assisting the surgeons by holding the patients while the amputations were being carried out, handing them sponges and hot water, and generally aiding them in their operations. When morning came he was so fatigued that he made his way with difficulty to his quarters in the town, where he flung himself down to snatch a few hours' sleep.

There was a great hush over the camp during the day. Then only, as the men wandered about asking questions concerning missing comrades, did the full extent of the disaster that had befallen them make itself felt. The gaps in the ranks were terrible. Their missing comrades were all gone, for the Carlists had given no quarter. Even if not seriously wounded, all who fell into their hands were either shot or bayoneted by them. It was hard, after having fought their way victoriously for three days, that such a misfortune should befall the Legion! Their one consolation was that every man had done his duty, not one had turned his back to his foe.

The gaps among the officers had been terrible. Several of the regiments had lost all their field-officers; others had suffered greatly. Deep were the execrations upon the Spanish generals, who should have detained the Carlist armies facing them, but who by their lethargy had allowed some twenty thousand men to slip away and join those with whom the Legion had been so successfully engaged; and not a few of the men would willingly have obeyed an order to attack the

Spanish regiments, who had deserted them as soon as the fighting began.

At first it was anticipated that the Carlists would take advantage of their success and attempt to capture San Sebastian, and there was a general hope that they would do so, for all felt confident that they could resist any attack that might be made. The entrenchments were very formidable, and a number of heavy guns were mounted upon them. The guns of the ships, too, would give their support.

But the Carlists were well satisfied with their success. The greater portion of the troops that had come from Durango, and the force opposed to Espartero had marched away again, leaving only a sufficient number to oppose any further attempt on the part of the defenders of San Sebastian to take the offensive.

Of this, however, there was but little prospect. Scarce three thousand five hundred out of the ten thousand men of the Legion were fit for service; disease and battle had accounted for the rest. Besides, of the two years for which they had enlisted there were but a few months to run. Had they been treated well, by far the greater portion would willingly have remained. At first they had felt but small interest in the struggle in which they had enlisted. Most of them were ne'er-do-weels—men who had been glad to accept any offer with the prospect of giving them a living; the Christinos were no more to them than the Carlists. Now the case was altogether different—the Carlists had become their personal enemies. They would not have come to hate them for their doings in a fair fight. But the fact that they massacred every man who fell into their hands, whether wounded or not, had raised in the minds of the soldiers a feeling of undying hatred and a burning desire for revenge. They had not received the treatment they had a right to expect. They had never been properly fed since they landed; they were still months in arrears of their pay, and then only irregularly received the wretched pittance of twopence half-

penny a day. If the Spanish government had deliberately
set themselves to drive the regiments into mutiny, they could
not have gone about it better, and it was certain that when
the time expired few indeed would consent to remain any
longer in the ranks.

The officers were no less indignant than the men. Their
pay was nine months in arrear, and those who had no means
of their own had only subsisted by the assistance of others
better off than themselves. Considering what they went
through, it was almost a matter for surprise that the whole
Legion did not embrace the offers of the Carlist emissaries,
who were constantly at work trying to sap their loyalty to
the Christino cause, and go over in a body to the Carlist
lines. After the reverses that had befallen them, the
Spanish government seemed more indifferent than ever to
their sufferings; only very occasionally, ridiculously small
amounts were sent to them, sufficient to pay the soldiers a
few pesetas apiece. In these circumstances it was not surprising that the drill became slack and discipline relaxed.
The officers, deeply indignant, could not bring themselves
to be severe upon the soldiers, who suffered even more than
themselves, and so took no notice of minor acts of insubordination.

Shortly after the battle Arthur had received his usual
quarterly letter from his uncle. "My dear Arthur," it ran,
"herewith I enclose order as usual on Messrs. Callao, of San
Sebastian, for thirty pounds. We are all very glad to find
that you have passed through the last battle without serious
wounds. You have been most fortunate in that respect.
Your term of service will end in a few months' time, and we
trust that at its conclusion you will return home. I am
afraid that after the life you have been leading we can
hardly hope that you will resume your studies—indeed, it
would not be reasonable to expect it. Still, you might travel
or otherwise employ yourself a great deal better surely than
in getting yourself shot at, and that in a cause which—al-

though no doubt you now feel some interest—cannot affect
you in the same way as if you were fighting for your own
country.

"According to other accounts, and from letters I have
seen from other members of the Legion, you must have been
suffering great hardships. No doubt at San Sebastian these
have been less cruel than they were at Vittoria; still, they
have been severe. You tell us very little about them, and,
as I say, it is from other sources that I form this opinion.
We are all obliged to you for always writing directly after a
battle, for we are in a state of considerable anxiety until we
hear from you, as of course no details of casualties are pub-
lished; and in the interval between the first report of the
fighting and the receipt of your letter we are all very unset-
tled, and your cousins'. studies are greatly deranged.

"We all talk and think of you very frequently, and I am
afraid that we are inclined to pride ourselves on having a
relative who has won his commission and distinguished himself in Spain. Still, my dear lad, I do hope that if the
term of service of the Legion is to be extended—and I think
that it probably will be—you will not be among those who
remain in the service. The risks appear to be enormous.
More than half the Legion are by this time either dead or
invalided home. I ask you, what can compensate a man
for running such risks, especially when, as in your case, he
is not driven by straitened circumstances to incur it? You
have done well; you have, so to speak, won your spurs. It
will be something to look back upon all your life. Surely
that is good enough. Your first enlistment was, to my mind,
a wild and foolish business; but I own that, annoyed as I
then was, I should be still more so were you to repeat the
mistake.

"Pray think over this seriously. Remember, pecuniarily
you have no need whatever to remain in the Legion. You
tell me that you have still most of the money I have sent you
lying by. You have but three more years to wait till your

majority, when you will receive three hundred pounds a year, and, if necessary, I can add something to this amount.

"Your cousins insist that you must be now almost a man, as you say that you are over six feet, and no doubt the life that you have led must have aged you a good deal and, I hope, taken some of your foolish recklessness out of you. They have asked me to say that they hope you won't bring home a Spanish lady as a wife, and I have assured them that, although I consider you capable of many follies, I feel convinced that you will not commit such a crowning one as that. They and my wife all send their love, and their earnest hopes and prayers, in which I join, that you will come home safe and sound to us.

"I remain, my dear Arthur,
"Your affectionate Uncle."

To this Arthur replied:—

"My dear Uncle,

"Many thanks for your letter and remittance. As to what you say about my continuing my term of service, in the event of the Legion as a whole re-enlisting for a further term, I cannot promise to take any particular course at present. You say that I can have no interest in the cause for which I am fighting. I can assure you that we have a very vivid interest in it. I grant that that was not the case at first, and that we looked upon it in the mere spirit of adventure; but that is all changed. The Carlists are not like civilized enemies; they behave rather like wild beasts. They give no quarter, and every poor fellow who falls into their hands—officer or soldier—is shot or bayoneted at once. Even the wounded are slaughtered ruthlessly.

"Now you can very well imagine the state of fury and hatred excited by such doings. The war has become a war of revenge, and men, when they go into battle, hope that if they are hit it will be by a fatal shot, and not by one which will lay them helpless on the ground, with the certainty of being shot or bayoneted in cold blood unless the Carlists are beaten, and we hold the ground on which we have fought. I don't say that this is entirely the fault of the Carlists, for in the early part of the war the Christinos were just as bad, from what I hear. However, that is the state of things now; and if the Legion were but well treated, I think there is scarcely a man who would not willingly extend his term. The fact that I have been promoted is another reason why I might be tempted to go on. Of course, it will make no difference to me afterwards whether I hold the rank of lieutenant or colonel at the end of the war; but now that I have gone into the thing I want to see the end of it.

"However, I do not think that you need feel uneasy on that score, for I am convinced that, when the term has expired, the greater part of the Legion will take their discharge. Their treatment has been so scandalous that I believe that if the order was given for the Legion to march to Madrid, fight their way through all obstacles, and hang every member of the government, they would receive it with joy.

"As to what the girls say about a Spanish lady, assure them that though I am really a man in stature and strength I am still a boy at heart, and am no more affected by the pretty graces of some of the Spanish girls than if they were dolls. They are very jolly to chaff with, but certainly, in my case, nothing to make love to. I hope that by the next time I write I shall be able to tell you I have got my company. With love to you all,

"Yours affectionately,
"ARTHUR HALLETT."

CHAPTER VI

A CAPTIVE

"HAVE you heard that Maltravers is missing, Hallett?" Sinclair asked Arthur one morning as he came out of his quarters.

"Missing? No; how is he missing?"

"That is what nobody seems to know. He was on duty last night, and went along the line a certain distance, and then he seems to have disappeared. An enquiry is being made among the men on duty, but so far there does not seem to be any explanation. He certainly was not shot, for there are no signs of his body. One idea was that he might have been taken suddenly ill, and turned off to come into the town to report himself. I believe a search is being made now on the ground that he would cross, to see if he has fallen there. Of course no one thinks that he could have deserted."

"I should think not," Arthur said. "There are men who grumble so continuously that one would hardly be surprised to hear that they had taken other service, but that was not at all Maltravers' way; he always made the best of everything."

"Well, it is very strange."

The most exhaustive search failed to bring anything to light respecting the missing officer. The sentry at the last post he had visited had observed nothing singular in his manner. The next post was three hundred yards away, but, although it was a dark night, the officer could not have missed his way. There was a sharp drop in the ground beyond the line that he would traverse, and as the route was the same that had been used for many months, it was scarcely possible that anyone could miss it. The idea that Carlists could have come down from their entrenchments, the nearest of which was four hundred yards away, and captured him, without the sound of a struggle reaching the ears of the sentries to the right or left, seemed hardly possible. Some suggested that he might have gone suddenly out of his mind, and wandered down into the town or to the bank of the Urumea, and there fallen in, but this seemed to all to be wildly improbable.

The officer's letters and papers were examined, but nothing whatever was found that could in the slightest support the idea that he had committed suicide. There was nothing to do but to enter his name upon the list of missing, and hope that he would yet turn up some day and explain the mystery.

"It is your turn for the night duty, Hallett," Sinclair said to him three days after the strange disappearance of Maltravers.

"Yes, I know that my turn for duty begins this evening."

"Well, keep a sharp look-out, old fellow; we don't want any more mysterious disappearances in the regiment."

"No; one is more than sufficient; I have been over the ground half a dozen times during the past three days in the hopes of finding some sort of clue, but without the least success. Perhaps as I go round to-night some bright idea may strike me. Of one thing," he said with a laugh, "you may be perfectly sure: that is, that if I don't turn up in the morning it will be neither desertion, suicide, nor insanity."

"No," Sinclair said; "I should certainly never suspect you of any one of the three."

The others laughed. "You certainly did your best to save your life on board that boat, so we will put suicide out of the question. As to desertion and lunacy, I think they may be equally barred. If you are missing, I shall say that the pixies have carried you off."

"Yes; I think you can safely put it down to that."

After mess was over, Arthur took his pistols and sword and started to the house that was used as the rendezvous of the officers on duty for the night, made his usual visit to the outlying posts along a portion of the line some three-quarters of a mile in extent, and returned. A few minutes before twelve he again started on the same tramp, his companion on duty going in the other direction. Nothing unusual happened until he was half-way along; then, as he passed a ruined hut, he suddenly fell, stunned by a heavy blow from behind. He knew nothing for some time, then he felt dimly conscious that he was being carried along. Reviving consciousness showed him that there were two men at his arms and two at his legs, and that a cloak or some other woollen garment was wrapped round and round his head, and something thrust into his mouth. All this was taken in little by little, for his head buzzed and ached from the blow that had fallen upon it.

It was some time before his brain began to work in earnest. Then he gradually came to understand that he was in the hands of the Carlists. These four men must have stolen quietly down from their entrenchments and hidden among the ruins of the hut, struck him to the ground, probably with the butt-end of a musket, and were now carrying him off. Doubtless, this was the manner in which Maltravers had also been captured. He knew that to struggle would be absolutely useless; and indeed, from a murmur of talk that went on around him, he judged that he was already in the Carlist lines. He could feel that he was being taken up the hill. After what seemed a very long time, his bearers came to a stop. A door was pushed open, and he was carried through and dropped on the ground. Then he heard the door close and the lock turn. He sat up, and took the muffler from his head and the gag from his mouth. His head ached as if it would split, so, knowing that there was nothing to be done, he rolled up the muffler and, using it as a pillow, dozed off after a time into a heavy sleep. When he awoke, he heard talking outside.

" This is the second five dollars each we have made, Pedro; if we go on like this we shall soon get rich."

"I don't see why we shouldn't," the other said. "As long as the nights are dark, we can always be sure of making our way down unobserved. We may reckon on snatching two or three more before there is a moon, and even then we shall be able to do it when there is rain."

"I don't suppose we can catch many more that way," the other said. "When they find officers keep on disappearing they will send three or four of the men round with them, and then, of course, there will be an end of the business. Still, if we can catch half a dozen more we shall not have done so badly."

As soon as day broke, Arthur sat up and looked round. He had still a splitting headache, and there was a lump as big as an egg where the blow had fallen. His cap lay upon the ground near him, having apparently been thrown in there by the men who had carried him up. His arms had been taken away, and he had no doubt that nothing had been left behind that would leave any indication as to what had befallen him. The hut, which was about twelve feet square, had evidently been inhabited by a peasant. It contained two or three broken pieces of rough furniture, and the floor was littered with odds and ends of old garments, broken crockery, &c. Two little loop-holes, about six inches square, admitted a certain amount of light when the door was closed. Looking out of these, he saw that the hut stood on level ground, evidently at the top of the hill. Numbers of Carlists lay on the ground wrapped up in their cloaks.

Two or three small huts and houses were dotted here and there on the plain, the nearest of them being about two hundred yards away. This one had a garden round it, and looked as if it was still inhabited. Like the hut in which he was confined, it was built of stone, and was roofed with slabs of the same material, but was larger and apparently had an upper story or loft.

Having seen this much, he sat down until, by the stir around, he knew that the camp was awake. It was not until, as near as he could guess, nine o'clock—for his watch had been taken away from him—that anyone came near him, though he knew by the talking that there were two sentries at the door. Then he heard the key turn in the lock, and an officer, who by his uniform, he thought, was a colonel, entered. Arthur rose to his feet.

"You are English, sir?" the colonel said.

"I am."

"Why do you fight on the side of the Christinos? We know that you are badly treated by them: you are half-starved and you get no pay. Well, sir, you are a prisoner in our hands; and I need hardly say what your fate will be if you do not accept our terms. If you will enter the service of Don Carlos, you will be well-fed, well-paid, and welcomed as a comrade. It can make no difference to you on which side you fight—Christino or Carlist. You have learned what to expect from them, neglect and suffering; with us you will have neither. We are certain to win in the long run. You will get promotion and honour—the alternative is death! I will leave you till this evening to think over the matter."

He went out, and in a quarter of an hour two soldiers entered bearing a dish of meat and beans, and a large jug of water. Arthur had no appetite; but he took a copious drink, poured some water over his cloak, which he rolled up as a pillow, and lay down on his back, with his head upon it. Its coolness eased the throbbing of his wound. As he lay he thought over his position. "The case is a very bad one," he said to himself. "Certainly I am not going to turn traitor; that needn't be thought of. I have no doubt that the threat of shooting me, if I refuse, will be carried into execution. The question is, whether it will be carried out at once on my refusal, or put off till to-morrow morning. Surely they will give me another twelve hours. If they don't, there is an end of it. There is no possibility whatever of escaping in the daylight; I don't know that there is much chance at night, but there may be a chance. At any rate, I have all day to think it over."

He lay there for some hours, sitting up occasionally to pour more water upon his pillow. The throbbing of his head subsided somewhat, and at one o'clock he sat up and forced himself to eat. " Escape or no escape," he said, " I must keep up my strength." When he had finished his meal he stood up. His head still throbbed, though the pain was much less acute. First he went to the door and examined it: the hinges were strong and rough, the lock was sunk in the woodwork; it was evident that it could not be forced.

" Now," he said to himself, " I have the option of trying to get the screws out of the hinges or cutting round the lock." He felt in his pocket for his knife, and gave an exclamation of disappointment when he found that it was gone. This was a bitter blow. He spent some time looking about the floor in the hopes of finding some piece of iron which he could use for getting out the screws, but although he searched the place most carefully, he could find nothing that would serve his purpose.

The walls of the hut were far too solid to admit of his making a way through them. It might, he thought, be just possible to burrow under them; but he quickly dismissed this idea, for there was no great depth of soil on the rock, and it was almost certain that the foundations of the wall would be carried down to it. He went to one of the little windows, and stood there gazing out vaguely. Presently he saw an old woman come out of the nearest house, cut some vegetables, and go in again. He wondered what they were, and what she was going to have for dinner, hardly knowing what current his thoughts were taking. As he roused himself and looked round a fresh idea struck him. The walls could not be attacked, the door would defy any efforts that he could make, the floor was altogether unpromising—but there was the roof! A new hope sprung up in his breast as he looked up.

The roof was simply composed of slabs of stone, and although these had been roughly plastered, the lines where one had been laid on another showed clearly. The slabs were from an inch to an inch and a half thick, and about two feet square. The walls of the cabin were about eight feet high, and Arthur could just touch the lowest range of slabs with the tips of his fingers; but he saw at once that the materials within the hut would enable him to reach it easily. There was a rough stool some two feet high; one of its legs was gone, but by propping it against the wall it would stand. He placed it there and mounted upon it. It was a bit shaky, but it held his weight. The top of his head was now but a few inches below the slab, and he had no doubt whatever but that he could raise it. The two sentries, as far as he could tell, were both in front of the cabin, and considering its structure it was very improbable that there was one behind. Thus, then, if they gave him until the next morning he could well hope to make his escape.

He was so delighted at this that he hardly felt any longer the pain in his head. It would of course be no very easy matter to make his way down through the Carlist lines; but as he had done it before, he might well hope to do it again. "At any rate," he said to himself, "nothing can be done till night, and I may as well sleep till then."

He laid himself down again, this time going to sleep so soundly that he did not hear the guards come in and put some more food down. About six o'clock he awoke, and at once took another meal. Half an hour later the colonel again came in.

"Well, sir, what is your answer?" he said.

"I do not like to turn traitor," he said. "Certainly I have no reason to be very grateful to the Christinos, and if the offer were that I should resign the service I should certainly accept it; but I do not like to fight against my old comrades."

"You would not be called upon to do so," the colonel said;

"you would be attached to one of our other armies. We have had a good many deserters from your lines, but we cannot utilize them because they understand so little Spanish and no Basque. We want an officer to lead them. There are plenty to make a strong company, and I will promise you that you shall have their command and shall not be employed here."

" Give me till to-morrow to think it over, sir. You have already taken one of our officers, may I ask what reply he gave? "

" The obstinate fool chose death," the officer said. " I was sorry; but, of course, it had to be done. I trust that you will not be so foolish. At any rate, I will give you till to-morrow morning; but unless you are by that time prepared to accept my offer, your fate will be the same as his."

So saying, he left the hut. Thankful for the respite, Arthur went to one of the little windows and looked out. Numbers of fires were burning, and the Carlist soldiers were gathered round them, some cooking their food, others smoking and talking. The hours passed slowly. Arthur waited to choose a time when the camp was growing quiet, but when there were still some sounds that might deaden any noise he might make. At last the moment arrived when he thought he could attempt to get the stone off, though he did not intend to try to escape till all were asleep. He placed the stool against the wall again, and climbed up, and then pushed with all his strength under one of the slabs. It gave a little. He tried again, and it yielded. Working very carefully, he got the upper end out from underneath the slab above it, then raised it, turned it sideways, and lowered it into the hut.

The talk of the guards outside went on uninterruptedly, and it was evident that no sound had reached their ears. Arthur sat down and waited. Hitherto he had felt no nervousness, but his anxiety now became intense. One of the guards might enter the place. There were no special grounds for fear that this would happen, as hitherto the sentries had only opened the door to bring in his meals; still, they might do so. Again, a soldier who had been chatting with his comrades at one fire might move off to sleep at another, and notice the hole caused by the removal of the slab. This was certainly very improbable on so dark a night; still, the thought of the possibility of one or other of the two events taking place kept Arthur's nerves on a strain.

At last everything seemed quiet. The night was perfectly still, save that he could hear an occasional sound of talking and laughter in the trenches lower down the hill, where doubtless a considerable number of the Carlists would remain on watch. At last he felt that the moment had come for making the attempt. He again leant the stool against the wall, put his hands on the edges of the two slabs by the side of the hole, and pulled himself up. Very noiselessly he raised himself higher and higher till he could get his legs over the wall; then he turned, lowered himself by his arms, and dropped. As he did so he rolled over, and with difficulty refrained from uttering a groan. Instead of dropping, as he had expected, on even ground, one of his feet had come on a rough stone lying against the wall, and in the fall he had badly wrenched his ankle.

He did not attempt to move for a time. The chance of passing down through the Carlist lines was at an end. For fully ten minutes he lay there; then his mind was made up, and turning over on to his face, he began to drag himself along towards the house he had been looking at during the day. It was his only chance. If he could conceal himself there he might be safe. When his escape was discovered in the morning it would be supposed that he had made his way down through the lines, or had gone out through the rear of the camp and taken to the mountains until he could work his way back to the town. There would certainly be no search for him close to his prison.

It took him nearly half an hour at that slow rate of progression to make his way to the house. When he reached it, he raised himself on to his sound foot, noiselessly lifted the latch, and went in. He closed the door behind him, and sat down against it. Knowing nothing of the interior arrangements, he dared not move for fear of waking the inmates. He therefore remained there motionless, dozing occasionally, until the first dawn of day enabled him to obtain an idea of his surroundings. The room in which he was was unoccupied, but an open door at the back showed where the old woman and whoever might live with her were sleeping. A rough ladder in the opposite corner of the room led up to an open trap-door leading evidently to a loft. This was what he had hoped for, and making his way across to it he pulled himself up the ladder, and found, as he expected, that he was in a low loft. It was half filled with hay and faggots, and climbing over these he laid himself down behind them and lay listening.

In an hour he heard cries of alarm, followed by a great hubbub in the camp, and had no doubt that his escape had been discovered. Presently he heard a stir below, and, listening, made out two voices—one, which was, he had no doubt, that of the old woman whom he had seen, and the other apparently that of an old man, probably her husband. He had taken a long draught of water the last thing before leaving the hut, and had put the remains of the food in his pocket. He now bandaged his ankle as well as he could, and then slept the greater part of the day. Beyond the quiet voices below he heard nothing, which showed that no suspicion existed that he was hidden so close. He was troubled only by the heat during the day, but suffered a good deal from this.

At daybreak the next morning he made his way to the trap-door and looked down. On the table a large jug of water and half a loaf were standing. He crawled down the ladder, took them both, and returned to his hiding-place. An hour later he heard angry talk below. He did not understand Basque, one of the most difficult languages to acquire, but he guessed that the owners were railing over the loss of the jug and bread, and doubtless putting it down to some soldier who had entered after they had gone to sleep and stolen them. The loss could not have been a heavy one, but the old couple did not get over it all day, but continued to grumble at intervals. To him the proceeds of his theft were invaluable. He was able to keep the bandage round his ankle bathed with cold water, and he calculated that the bread would, with care, last him three days, and that the water would hold out as long.

This proved to be the case. The old man came up once during that time with a large bowl, which he filled out of a sack containing lentils; otherwise, Arthur was altogether undisturbed. At the end of that time the pain in his ankle had abated, but he could feel that it was still very weak, and that he dared not yet attempt to walk on it.

That night he went down and refilled his jug from a pail, and carried off a loaf of bread from a cupboard. After possessing himself of these things, he very carefully drew back a bolt of the door. When the old couple awoke he heard them engaged in a furious quarrel. They had missed the bread, and finding the door unbolted, the old woman had charged her husband with neglecting to fasten it, while he was stoutly maintaining that he had done so, and that she saw him do it. The quarrel lasted with more or less acerbity the whole day. Had Arthur possessed any money he would have placed a copper coin or two on the table to pay for the bread he had taken; but both pockets had been turned inside out by his captors, and he was absolutely penniless.

The loaf lasted for four days, and when it was finished he determined that, although his ankle was still very weak, he would attempt to get away. He was very reluctant to again help himself from the old people's store. It might be at least three days before he could enter the town, although he hoped to be able to accomplish it in one. Still, if his foot should give him trouble he might have to lie up in shelter.

However, he contented himself with only taking half a loaf, and at eleven o'clock at night, when everything was quiet, he opened the door and went cautiously out. His object was to get down to the Urumea, which was but a mile and a half off, so, going back from the brow of the hill, to avoid falling in with any sleeping Carlists, he started.

He had gone but a short way when he felt his foot beginning to pain him badly. At first he tried hopping, but he found that the jar of each jump hurt him as much as if he were using the foot, and as he had no knife he could not cut himself a stick. He therefore sat down, and swung himself along on his hands. This was a slow method of progression, and he had to stop frequently to rest his arms and wrists. He soon gave up all idea of being able, as he had hoped, to reach the river and to swim down past the Carlist lines before morning. He kept on, however, till the dawn had begun to break. By this time he could not be more than a quarter of a mile from the river. Crawling into a thick clump of bushes he lay down, and being thoroughly tired out with his exertions he slept till mid-day. When he awoke he ate a large hunch of bread, and then waited until it became dark enough for him to make another move. As soon as night fell he set off. It took him nearly an hour to cross the quarter-mile of broken ground; but at length, to his satisfaction, the bushes ceased and he saw the river twenty yards in front of him.

He had, soon after starting from the cottage, taken the boot off his injured foot and tied it to his waist. He now took off the other and fastened it by its fellow; then he stepped into the river, and found to his satisfaction that the tide was running out. Had it not been so, he must have sat down and waited until the ebb began. After wading for some little distance, he struck out for the centre of the river; then he turned on his back and let himself drift, turning occasionally on to his breast and striking out carefully for a time, so as to get a change of position. Luckily the water was quite warm. Presently he heard the sound of talking, and perceived a glow of light on the stream. He swam across close to the other shore, and saw, as he floated down, the fires of the Carlists stretching in zig-zag lines along their entrenchments, rising one above another.

He was confident that, plainly as he could see everything there, the sharpest eye could not discover him so far beyond the circle of light. Still, he did not attempt to swim until he was well beyond the fires; then in a quarter of an hour he knew that he must be within the lines of the Legion. He thought, however, that it would save trouble if he were to land abreast of the town, so he swam on until he reached the bridge that had been thrown across the river. Then he went ashore, having been about two hours in the water. The water appeared to have benefited his ankle, for he found that he could now limp along slowly. Making his way to his quarters he went quietly up to his room and opened his door. A candle was burning there, and Roper was sitting at the table with his head in his hands. He looked up as Arthur entered, and then sprang to his feet with a shout of joy.

"Thank God, you are back! Thank God! I have never quite given you up, sir, although everyone else has. Every evening when I have been off duty I have come and sat here, as I knew that when you came back it would be after dark."

"I am glad indeed to see you, Roper! I have had a very narrow squeak this time—I never want to have as narrow. I will tell you all about it presently."

"Your clothes are all wet, sir."

"Yes. I must change them at once. When I have done that, you must go up to the colonel and report my return. I sprained one of my ankles, and can only just hobble along, and I don't want to put any more strain on it than I can help; so when I am undressed I will turn in. By the way, I think before you go off you might cook me something, if there is anything to be had."

"There is nothing here, sir."

"While I am undressing, you might run out and buy
me something; cold meat of any sort will do. I have had
nothing but bread since I went away, and not much of
that."

Arthur was in bed by the time Roper returned.

"I have got some cold meat, bread, and a bottle of wine,
sir."

"Thank you, Roper. Put them on that table and draw it
to the side of the bed. When you have done that, please go
and report my return, and explain why I can't come and do
it myself."

He had scarcely finished the meal when the colonel came in.

"Welcome back a thousand times, Hallett! We have all
been in a terrible way about you. I hoped for the first two
or three days, and insisted that whatever had happened to
you, you would get out of it, if there was but the remotest
possibility of escape. Now, let us know all about it. I supposed you were carried off, as Maltravers was. How it happened we could not find out, but since that time every officer
has made his rounds with four men with him, and as a consequence we have had no more disappearances. Now, please
tell me all about it."

Arthur told the story at length.

"By Jove, you have done wonderfully well!" the colonel
said. "It has been one of the narrowest touches I ever heard
of; and if you hadn't sprained your foot you would have
been back among us within twenty-four hours of your
capture. It was lucky, indeed, that you had particularly
noticed that cottage and its occupants during the day, and
that the thought struck you to shelter in it. Well, I won't
say anything more now; it is ten o'clock, and I am sure you
must want a good night's sleep."

"I shall be glad, sir, if, the first thing in the morning,
you will send the surgeon round to me. My ankle is not
nearly as swollen as it was, and I have no doubt that the
few hours I spent in the water did me a lot of good. At

the same time, I shall be very glad to have it bandaged, and don't want to be kept in bed by it. Of course, I shall be able to ride, but that would be no good for my company work."

"You must leave your company work alone for a week or so. I shall be glad, if you find that you can ride, if you will come round to my quarters at ten o'clock, and I will take you to the general."

The next morning Arthur lay in bed until the surgeon came. While the latter was bandaging his ankle, he had to give him a short account of his adventure.

"Well, you got through it well," the surgeon said, "but I should not advise you to try that sort of thing again; you may not be so lucky next time. You have given your ankle a very awkward wrench. I should advise you to avoid any attempt to walk for at least a week or ten days. If you do, you may have to lie up for six weeks."

Roper came in to help Arthur to dress, and to make his breakfast for him. Arthur's servant had been killed in the last fight, and since that time Roper had, whenever he was off duty, installed himself in his place. After breakfast he brought Arthur's horse round, and the latter mounted and rode to the colonel's quarters. That officer's horse was at the door, and he came out at once before Arthur had dismounted.

"Don't get off, Hallett," he said. "Dr. Spendlow has been round here since he left you, and said that you must on no account use your leg for another ten days. He said that if you would obey his orders you might be fit for duty in a fortnight, while if you did not do so, you might be laid up for a long time."

They rode to the general's quarters, which were a quarter of a mile away.

"You must walk in here," the colonel said; "but lean on my arm, and I will take the weight off that foot."

On the colonel sending in his name he was at once admitted. "General," he said, "we are stronger by one officer than I thought we were. Mr. Hallett has returned."

"I am indeed glad to hear it," the general said warmly, and coming up he shook Arthur heartily by the hand.

"He must sit down, sir," the colonel said; "at present he has only one available leg."

"Now, Mr. Hallett," the general said, when Arthur was comfortably seated, "please give me a full account of what has happened; it may throw light not only upon your disappearance, but on that of Captain Maltravers. Before you begin your story, I should like to ask whether you have seen or heard anything of him?"

"Yes, sir. I am sorry to say that I did not see him, for he was murdered by the Carlists. The choice was given him to desert to their side or to be killed, and he nobly chose the latter alternative."

"I am sorry indeed," the general said. "He was a fine young fellow, and he died a hero's death. What a terrible war this is—a war to the knife! Indeed, it seems to me more cruel and pitiless every month, in spite of the efforts Colonel Wylde, the British commissioner, is making to persuade both parties to desist from these atrocities. I am afraid that one side is almost as bad as the other. Both declare that they commit these murders by way of reprisals, and I am bound to say that in the early stages of the war the Christinos were nearly as bad, if not as bad, as the Carlists. Since then, however, they have been somewhat better, and have really tried, I think, to keep the Convention, to respect the rules of war and to spare prisoners. They have, it is true, shot a great many, but it has been by way of reprisals for the brutality of the Carlists, and especially of those of Cabrera, who has several times shot women as well as men.

"And now for your story, Mr. Hallett."

Arthur again told his story at length.

"I compliment you highly on your quick-wittedness, Mr. Hallett; it certainly saved your life. And in such a cell as you describe, with two armed guards at the door, it is not one man in fifty who would have thought of escaping through the roof. Not less sharp was it to take at once, crippled as you were, to the only place that offered you shelter. Altogether, it was a remarkably well-planned and well-carried-out affair; and be assured that if any opportunity should occur, I shall take advantage of it to utilize your services. Now, I hope you will obey the doctor's orders and go back to your quarters, and stay there till your ankle is quite well."

This Arthur did; and for the next three or four days held a sort of levee in his quarters, almost all the officers of the Legion coming in to see him and to hear his story, which he became perfectly tired of telling long before the visits were over. His companions in the adventures in the boat were especially pleased to see him, and came in every day to have a chat with him.

"You seem fated to get into adventures, Hallett," Sinclair said, when he first heard the story. "You get nearly caught as a spy, and manage to make your way through the enemy's lines with a lot of valuable information; you get blown out to sea, and you save us and yourself; and now you get carried off, and threatened with death in twenty-four hours, but make your escape and rejoin. My dear fellow, I am afraid you will at last come to a bad end. It is evident that neither water nor bullet has power over you, and that your exit from this world will be hastened by a collar of hemp."

"I hope not, Sinclair; I shall do my best to avoid it. Hanging seems to be an uncomfortable sort of death, to say nothing of its being strictly unfashionable."

"Well, we shall see," Sinclair said; "but I cannot help thinking that that is what will happen to you. Now, what is your next adventure going to be?"

Arthur laughed. "I must leave that to fate. Two out of my three adventures were certainly not brought on by myself. I was blown out to sea owing to your obstinacy in refusing to turn back when I wanted to. I was certainly carried off this time by no will of my own. So that only what you call the spy business was of my own choosing. I can assure you that I have had enough of adventures, and shall not get into another if I can manage to avoid it."

Ten days later Arthur was reported fit for duty, and was very glad to resume his regular work.

CHAPTER VII

A GREAT CHANGE

ONE day Colonel Godfrey sent for Arthur. " General Evans is going to send Major Hawkins to Madrid, and has asked me to recommend a young officer to accompany him as his assistant. I have mentioned your name to him, as you speak Spanish fluently, which very few other officers can do. He will probably remain there for some time, and will act as the accredited representative of the Legion. I know that I have undertaken a certain amount of responsibility in recommending so young an officer; but from what I have seen of you, and from the distinguished service you rendered by going into the Carlist camp and obtaining information concerning it, I feel convinced that you will acquit yourself well. You will receive the temporary rank of captain."

" I am greatly obliged to you, sir, for recommending me. I fear that I am very young for such a position."

" You are young, certainly; but a year of campaigning has added some years to your appearance. And as far as height goes, you are half a head taller than the majority of Spaniards. General Evans has asked me to bring you over to him, so we will go at once. Major Hawkins is now with him."

They walked across to the general's house.

"Good-morning, Captain Hallett," the general said. "I am glad to see that your leg has quite recovered. Your knowledge of Spanish has been of service to us, and now it will be of advantage to yourself. Colonel Godfrey has, I suppose, told you of the mission which I propose for you, namely, to accompany Major Hawkins as his assistant. You will, of course, be under his orders. He also speaks Spanish, but not so fluently as you do. In case of his falling ill or of his being incapacitated, you will carry on his duties. The post will be to some extent a permanent one. The Spanish government pay no attention to my letters, and it is therefore absolutely necessary that I should be represented and my requests urged strongly upon them. My troops are half the time on the edge of starvation, and can get neither pay nor rations. I have written in the strongest manner to them. I think it will be as well for you to go as an officer on my staff. The Spanish think a great deal of dress; Captain Forstairs is going home on sick leave, and will, I have no doubt, be glad to dispose of his uniform for a trifle. If it will be any inconvenience to you to buy it, I will have any sum you require handed over to you from the chest; of course, like other officers, you are some months in arrear with your pay. And indeed, in any case, an allowance will be made for your uniform, unless you should afterwards become a member of the staff."

"Thank you, sir; but I am well supplied with money, and can purchase the articles myself. Should I only use the uniform for a short time, I will, at the conclusion of my mission, hand it into store."

"You will take a servant with you, as it is necessary to keep up a good appearance. Major Hawkins will give you all necessary instructions. He proposes to start to-morrow."

Greatly pleased at his appointment, Arthur first went to Captain Forstairs' quarters and purchased his uniform, getting it complete for a five-pound note. He then went to Roper.

"I am going away on a mission, Roper, and may, for anything I know, remain for some time at Madrid. As you know, my servant was killed the other day, and I want another who can ride."

"I shall be very glad to go with you if you will take me," Roper said.

"But you see you are a non-commissioned officer."

"Oh, I would give up my stripes readily enough if you will take me. I am not very fond of the captain of my company."

"Then in that case I will go across with you and ask him to let you give up your stripes. You are quite sure that you would like it?"

"Quite sure; I am heartily sick of San Sebastian. I am accustomed to riding, and should enjoy the trip greatly."

They went away to the house where the captain was lodging, and Arthur had no difficulty in getting him to consent to the sergeant's resignation, and to give him permission to accompany him. Arthur then bought for Roper a serviceable horse. This done, he went to the major's.

"I have got the uniform, and shall be ready to start in the morning, sir," he said.

"I am glad that you are going with me, Captain Hallett," said the major, who having been in the Legion since its formation, knew Arthur well. "I am sure we shall get on well together; and as I am rather shaky in my Spanish, it will be of great assistance to have you with me. I may tell you that I am the bearer of a note from General Evans saying that unless money is sent for the pay of his troops he will engage in no further operations. The Spanish army is regularly paid, and there can be no reason why we should not be. More than that, he will withdraw into San Sebastian. We have shown brilliantly enough that we can fight, and we have done more with our small force than Cordova has with his big army. I am convinced that our threat to retire from the struggle will wake them up. At the same time, we must not be too sanguine about our getting through. We shall take the road by Bilbao to Vittoria. So far it will be plain sailing, but after that I expect we shall find some difficulty, for the Carlists are strongly posted a few miles from the town. I expect we shall have to hire a guide to take us across the mountains. However, we shall have plenty of time to think of that when we get there."

Arthur now went down to the camp of the Lancers, who had arrived a few weeks before. They had had two or three deaths since they came, and on making enquiries Arthur found that he could purchase for a few shillings a Lancer's suit. This he handed to Roper, whom he had taken with him, and he told him to carry the suit back and put it on.

"Your clothes are not fit to be seen in," he said, "and this suit is a very fair one. If you give it a good cleaning to-night it will be quite respectable, and you will look much smarter in it than in that ragged thing."

"It looks pretty bad, certainly, sir, and is none the better for having lost all its buttons; there is hardly a button left in the regiment. When they are hammered down, the natives here take them as coins. They know nothing about money, and I expect these buttons will be passing about as cash long after we have all cleared out of this. I sha'n't know myself in my new rig-out. The man it belonged to has evidently taken care of it. There is only one thing you have forgotten, sir, and that is the saddle."

"Yes, I have forgotten that. Here are three pounds—you had better buy one."

The party started early the next morning and went by boat to Bilbao, slept there, and rode the next day to Vittoria. Here they halted for a day, and going to head-quarters obtained the services of a guide to take them across the mountains. On starting on the following morning they at once left the main road, and presently struck up into the hills. The road was extremely bad, and they were forced to go at a walk; the guide, who was mounted on a mule, rode on ahead. They halted for the night at a deserted hut some distance down the descent. Here they took shelter, congratulating themselves that another day's ride would take them to Burgos, where there was a strong garrison. They had brought provisions with them, and having made a hearty meal lay down for the night. Next morning they continued their journey, and were near the plains when they saw a party of men hurrying towards them.

"They are Carlists!" the major said. "It is of no use turning back or going up the hill; they would run our horses to death. Look here, Captain Hallett, they will cut us off, that is evident; but we may make our way through them. I will put my papers in my holster. If I fall, snatch them out and carry them on. Now, let us gallop."

Setting spurs to their horses, the four men dashed forward. Half a dozen of the Carlists reached the road before them, but drew back before the impetuosity of the charge, firing their rifles as they did so. Without a halt the little party dashed on at full speed. For a time the Carlists attempted to keep up with them, but were soon left far behind.

"I am done for!" the major said, swaying in his saddle. "They hit me as I passed through them. Take the papers and ride on."

"I cannot leave you, sir." And leaning over, Arthur caught the major as he was falling, and lifted him on to the horse before him. He rode on for another half-mile, by which time the Carlists were out of sight. But his burden had become more and more heavy in his arms, and when he drew his horse up, he found that the major had breathed his last.

"I am hit, too, sir," the major's servant said; "I have a bullet in my hip."

"We are not more than ten miles from Burgos now. I am afraid there is no chance of obtaining help until we get there. Roper, bring the major's horse up against mine," for the animal had followed its companions. "That's it.

Now tie that head-rope round the major and ride on one side of him, and I will ride on the other. We shall have to walk for the rest of the distance."

It took them three hours to reach the town. Arthur went at once to the citadel and saw the governor. "I have brought with me a major in our army," he said. "He was the bearer of a despatch to your minister of war. We were attacked by a party of Carlists nearly ten miles away, and he was shot. I beg that you will give him a military funeral, as he fell in the cause of your queen. I have also a trooper with me who is severely wounded. I will, with your permission, leave him here in hospital."

"Certainly, sir. The officer shall be buried to-morrow morning. I am grieved indeed that none of my men went up the road this morning. They go up every other day to prevent bands of Carlists from raiding over the country."

The governor invited Arthur to stop in the castle. The body of the major was laid in a room close by, and on the following morning he was buried with military honours.

"I will take the major's horse with me, Roper," Arthur said, when all was over; "it is a good horse, and a spare one may be useful. At any rate we may as well keep him."

Accordingly, after thanking the governor for his courtesy, they proceeded on their way, Roper leading the spare horse.

"We have begun badly," Arthur said, as they rode from the town. "The major was a brave fellow and a good soldier. It is sad indeed that he should have been killed in a skirmish like this. It leaves me in a very awkward position. However, I must deliver the letter. There are two or three British commissioners out here, and if one of them happens to be at Madrid I shall ask him to present me and to help me on a bit."

"I hope we are not likely to meet with any more of these Carlist chaps."

"I hope not, Roper; but really I don't know anything about it. We got no news at San Sebastian of what was

going on elsewhere, but they can hardly be wandering about
on the flat country. I fancy they are almost all infantry,
in which case they will not care to expose themselves to an
attack by cavalry."

They arrived at Madrid without adventure. They put up
at the Hotel Principes, and to Arthur's relief found upon
enquiry that Colonel Wylde, the chief British commissioner,
was at present staying at the hotel. He at once went to his
room.

"I have called, sir," he began, after introducing himself,
"to ask you if you will be good enough to give me some information as to how I had better proceed. I started from
San Sebastian as assistant to Major Hawkins of our Legion.
He was the bearer of a letter from General Evans with complaints about pay and provisions. Both officers and men
are many months in arrears. Major Hawkins was instructed
to inform the ministers of war and finance that unless the
money were sent immediately, the general would withdraw
the whole of his force into San Sebastian, and take no further part in the fighting. He has sent remonstrance after
remonstrance without success, and feels that matters can be
allowed to drift no longer. The men are in rags and are
half-starved. On our way down we were attacked by Carlists
and Major Hawkins was killed. I carried him into Burgos,
where he was buried with military honours. I only received
my appointment as his assistant on the day before leaving,
and beyond the fact that I was to remain here to assist him
generally in acting as General Evans's representative, I know
nothing of the duties. Considering the importance of the
mission, and the absolute necessity that money shall be sent
without delay, I have ventured to ask that you will introduce
me in the first place to the two ministers to whom I bring
letters, and if you will, as far as you can, support his application."

"I will gladly do so, Captain Hallett. Indeed, it is my
duty to aid you. I am not charged in any way to interfere

with our Spanish Legion, but incidentally anything that is of importance to the general cause would of course be of interest to our government. We may at present be called benevolent neutrals. I am well aware that General Evans has sent repeated applications, and that practically no result whatever has come of it. I will therefore not only go with you, as you ask, but I will myself urge upon them the importance of the application, pointing out that by refusing the necessary means to General Evans they are in fact breaking the terms upon which that Legion was raised; and that being so, the general would be acting with perfect propriety in withdrawing the troops from the field, and giving permission to all who may choose to leave at once, which would of course mean a complete break-up of the Legion.

"They will not wish that. It was humiliating for the Spanish to be forced to hire foreign soldiers to assist them, and no doubt that feeling has driven them to treat the Legion very badly; but at the same time they have themselves been continually in want of money. A considerable proportion of the country is in arms against them, and their resources have been greatly diminished in consequence. This, however, after all, is no excuse for them. They offered certain terms to men to fight for them, and the bargain should have been kept. It was the same in the Peninsular War. We went to fight their battles, and they threw every impediment in our way, starved our men when they themselves had a superabundance of supplies, and so created a hatred far greater than our men felt for the French.

"They are behaving in exactly the same way now; but, so far as our troops are concerned, there is one broad difference. In the first war we fought partly, at any rate, from feelings of patriotism; whereas in the present case, although a few may have gone into it from a feeling of sympathy for the little queen, the great proportion of the Legion are neither more nor less than mercenaries, and would have enlisted as readily for Don Carlos as for Isabella. And now, sir, I will go across to the war office with you. I have myself many times urged that steps should be taken to relieve the necessities of the troops, and I am not at all sorry that General Evans has at last put his foot down."

It was but a short walk across the square, for the hotel faced the war office. On Colonel Wylde sending in his name he was at once admitted.

"Well, Colonel Wylde, what can I do for you?" the minister said cheerfully.

"I have brought across to present to you, señor, Captain Hallett, who has just arrived from San Sebastian with a very important letter from General Evans. He was accompanied by an officer senior to him, but the latter was killed by a party of Carlists as they came along."

The minister looked sharply up at Arthur, who, bowing, handed him the letter. He begged them to be seated, and opened the communication. He frowned heavily, and then with a very evident effort recovered himself.

"The matter shall be seen to," he said. "You know, Colonel Wylde, how straitened our resources are, and that nothing would please us more than to comply with all General Evans's requests. No one can grieve more than I do at the delays that have taken place in complying with his requisitions."

"But, sir," Arthur said, "the Spanish troops are always well-fed, though it may be that their pay is sometimes in arrears. Our troops get neither food nor pay. They are in rags, and many of them are barefoot. No single promise that has been made to them since the day they landed has been kept. Nearly a third of their number have died of fever brought on by cold and want, and yet in spite of this they have been ready to fight, while so many of your own generals have held back. You think I am bold, sir? I am urging the cause of some five thousand of my countrymen, who have, confiding in Spanish honour, come out here to fight your battles. If you could go and look at them yourself, sir, and see their condition, you would pity them, and would marvel that they have so long shown patience. Feed them and pay them, and they can be depended upon to carry out their share of the agreement. But assuredly they cannot be depended upon if they are starved."

"I am not surprised, sir," Colonel Wylde said, "that General Evans feels that no more can be done. The officers have been now nine months without their pay, the soldiers six months. More than a third of their number have died or been invalided home; and the heavy list of their killed and wounded in battle speaks for itself of the bravery with which they fought. I must say that I approve of General Evans's decision. He owes it to the men who serve under him, and I cannot but say that the treatment they have received has been a grave scandal and dishonour to the government of Spain. I have myself been four times to Madrid to urge their claim, and absolutely nothing has been done. I consider that General Evans will be amply justified in carrying out his threat."

"The matter shall be seen to at once," the minister said, with an air of frankness. "I will consult my colleague the minister of finance, and will see that money is forwarded very shortly. You can assure your general, señor," he said to Arthur, "that steps shall be taken to comply with his request without delay."

"I will send a message to that effect. My own orders are to remain here until the treasure has been sent off; and that even when that is done I am to stay here as the general's representative to convey his wishes personally to you, until at any rate all arrears of pay have been cleared off. It is not a favour that we are demanding, but a right. I shall do myself the honour of calling upon you every day or two, to ascertain when the convoy with treasure will start. Of course you can refuse me admittance, but General Evans will know what that means."

After a few more words Colonel Wylde and Arthur left the ministry.

"You spoke out straight, Hallett," the British commissioner said with a smile.

"I could not help doing so, sir. The state of the men is pitiful in the extreme. They are scarecrows; they have practically no uniform whatever save their greatcoats, and they are in rags. I should have liked to take the little man by the neck and shake him."

"They are in a bad way themselves," the colonel said. "The court is a perfect nest of intrigue. There are something like half a dozen parties, each with their own nominees to push and their own interests to serve. Large sums are wrung from the people, but they are for the most part absolutely wasted in jobbery. If it were not that the British government have taken the part of Isabella, I should recommend them to stand aside altogether and let the factions fight it out. There are a few honest men on both sides, and the Carlists indeed know what they are fighting for. To the other side it is a matter of indifference who wins, provided they themselves can feather their nests. They are not fighting for the poor little queen, but for their own private interests.

"Well, I know a good many people here now, and shall have much pleasure in introducing you to their houses and making things pleasant for you; for it is evident that if, as you say, you have to stay here until all arrears of pay are received by the Legion, you will assuredly wait for an indefinite time. I am going to a reception this evening at half-past nine, and I shall be very glad to present you there if you will call for me ten minutes earlier."

"Thank you very much, sir! I should be very glad to make the acquaintance of some of the people."

Soon after his return to the hotel Roper came up. "I have seen the horses fed, sir; what is the next job?"

"The next thing will be to get a meal, Roper; I am going to do the same."

"Oh, I have done that, sir, and it was the best meal I have had for some time, I may say since I left England."

"Well, I sha'n't want you any more at present, so I should advise you to take a turn round. Some of the soldiers are sure to get into conversation with you, and as we are likely to be here for some time it is just as well that you should make some friends. You know enough Spanish to get on with; I expect a little will go a long way."

"Is there any chance of our getting our money, sir?"

"I expect we shall get some. Now that the Spaniards see that they have got to do something or let the troops go home, they will pay up enough to keep them quiet for a time. I don't suppose it will be much, but sufficient to keep the wolf from the door at any rate."

"Well, sir, will you mind if I go out in mufti. I picked up for a few shillings some clothes belonging to a Spaniard, who died before I came away. They are respectable sort of clothes, and I thought, if I were going to stop here, that you would let me wear them. In this uniform I should be a sort of show. Everyone would be wondering who I was."

"Certainly, if you like, Roper, and I think it is a very sensible idea. You would be able to stroll about in them without attracting any attention, but at the same time, you know, you would not be able to make friends with the soldiers."

"Oh, I shall get into talk with them, sir; a glass of aguardiente will go a long way with those chaps, and of course I shall let them know that I am a soldier myself."

"Yes, Roper, and there will be the advantage that with you in plain clothes, I can walk about with you, which will be a good deal more pleasant for both of us; so if you will change your things while I am at dinner, we can take a turn together afterwards."

"Thank you, sir; I should like that very much. It is a biggish town; I shall feel quite lost in it for a bit."

A few minutes later the bell of the table d'hôte rang. Arthur went down to it. The table was full, and he speedily became engaged in talk with people sitting next to him, who were much interested on finding that he was a British officer. They asked him many questions as to the state of things in the north, about which there were all sorts of contradictory reports. He, on his part, learned something, for he heard that it was generally expected that Cordova was going to be made war minister. After dinner two or three officers came up and spoke to him, and when they heard that he was on General Evans's staff, said that they would be glad if he would smoke a cigar with them. He answered, however, that he was engaged for the evening, but would be very glad to do so on some other occasion. Then he went down and joined Roper, who was standing at the door of the hotel, and walked about with him for a couple of hours.

"What hands these chaps are for cloaks!" the latter said. "In the north I used to think that they wore them to hide their shabby clothes, but it can't be the same here. There is a cold feel about the air, and I should not be sorry to have on one myself. This is evidently the time they stroll about most. The square looked quite empty this morning, and now it is full of people walking up and down."

"Well, Roper, I must be off, for I am going as I told you, with Colonel Wylde."

It was a large house, and the rooms were very full. When they entered, the colonel at once took Arthur up to the hostess and introduced him.

"What is your news from the front, Captain Hallett?" she asked.

"There has been nothing doing for the past month," he answered. "San Sebastian is very full. The Carlists look at us from a distance, and we look at them."

Then he passed on as another guest came up. Colonel Wylde introduced him to several ladies and gentlemen, and then left him to talk with a personage who was evidently of importance. There was no dancing going on. The refreshments served were of the lightest description.

"This is a change indeed to me," Arthur said. "It seems

to be another world almost; to say that we have been living roughly would be but a faint idea of the state of things."

"And how are things getting on up there?"

"It is dull work except when there is a fight, and we know nothing whatever of what passes elsewhere."

"Are all your officers as young as you are?"

"No, madam. I have been exceptionally fortunate, and owe my promotion largely to the fact that I have, since we landed, spent all my spare time in learning Spanish."

"You speak it very well, Captain Hallett."

"I speak it well enough for all practical purposes, señora, and should speak it better still if it were not that the language up in the north differs very widely from that spoken here."

Several cards were left on the following day for Arthur. In the majority of cases these mentioned which day their owners received visitors. On the second day he called on the minister of war, and was told by him that every possible effort was being made, and that he hoped in a few days to send off a portion at least of the sum due.

Arthur then wrote a despatch to General Evans telling him of Major Hawkins's death, and relating his interview with the minister. "I think," he said, "that some money will be sent, but I anticipate that the sum is likely to be exceedingly small. From what I hear, I believe that the government are really very short of money. The minister was evidently much alarmed at your threat to disband the Legion, and he will make every effort to induce you to alter that determination. I shall endeavour to see him every other day, and shall continually repeat my assurances that you are in earnest on the subject. Colonel Wylde is also using his efforts in the same direction. He has been very kind to me, and introduced me to many people."

It was three weeks, however, before a month's pay was despatched, with promises that more should speedily follow.

By this time Arthur had become quite at home in Madrid.

He knew many officers to speak to. Some of these belonged
to the garrison; others seemed to have no good cause for
being there, but kept up the pretence of being engaged on
important business. One of them said to him one day, " We
seem a very united family, do we not? "

" Yes; no one would dream from the appearance of Madrid
that a civil war was going on."

" And yet society is split up into a number of sections,
each working secretly against the others. Outwardly there
is no sign of this; everyone goes to the receptions and looks
smiling and pleasant. Practically everyone doubts everyone
else; and there are numbers of well-known Carlists, but they
hold their tongues, at any rate in public, and rub shoulders
with the men whom they would gladly kill. It is funny,
when you are able to look behind the scenes a little. I have
no doubt you will be able to do so before long. I saw you
chatting, for example, with Señor Durango, a very nice
young fellow. There is no doubt that he and his family are
all Carlists; but they are well connected, and have plenty
of friends among the Christinos.

" I believe two-thirds of the people you meet don't care
a snap which party wins. If they are here, of course they
profess to be Christinos; if they are away in the provinces,
they hold correspondence with Carlists that they may keep
themselves safe whichever side wins.

" Altogether, I consider that the Carlists are more in
earnest; the Christinos are the more numerous, simply because they hold the capital and the government. If the
Carlists were to gain one great success, it would be the other
way. It is a game of self-interest; Don Carlos and Christina are merely counters. Some want governments, others
titles, others posts in the ministry, others commands—there
is nothing real about it from beginning to end, except for
the poor devils of soldiers who have to fight. You will see
that in a short time Cordova will retire, and that Espartero
will probably take the command; that would be certainly

welcome to the army. He is a fine fellow, and if he were allowed he would be able to do great things; but he would no sooner be appointed than a dead-set would be made at him, and he would be hampered in every way. Well, I must be going. I dare say you are wondering what is my motive in staying here. Well, I am trying to get the command of a regiment, and a regiment, if possible, stationed here in the capital. Adieu!" And throwing his cloak over his shoulder he sauntered away.

Arthur sat some time thinking. "Well, if the Legion breaks up, which I expect it will do before long, I think I shall stay out here. If I take a lodging and live quietly, I can do on my one hundred and twenty pounds a year. There will be a lot to see, and probably no end of fun. I have got eighty pounds now, so I can a little exceed my allowance. I should certainly like to have some fun again; I have had little enough, goodness knows! since I left England. Besides, if I were to go home now I should have thrown away all the time that I have spent in getting up Spanish. It is funny how they all take me for at least five- or six-and-twenty."

The month's pay had some effect. For a short time the troops were somewhat better off. Arthur had received a letter from General Evans thanking him for obtaining a small proportion of the sum due, and urging him to continue his work. Then he heard that there had been some more fighting, that Irun had been captured by storm, and that several other towns had either been taken or had surrendered. Two months later he received another letter from the general saying that he was going home, and that the Legion was about to be disbanded.

"A small body of about eight hundred men have agreed to remain here to form a new Legion; this may succeed for a time, but I have little doubt that they will be treated in the same way as we have been. However, it will be open for you to join it if you are willing to do so, or you can make

your way down to Cadiz and come home by ship from there.
I enclose an order on Madrid for forty pounds for yourself
and fifteen pounds for your man, which has been lying in
the hands of the paymaster here until you should return.
Should you wish it, you can, I have no doubt, enter the
Christino army with your present rank."

"That is something out of the fire anyhow," Arthur said,
as he put the order into his pocket-book. "Well, if the Legion failed, it was not from want of pluck. Out of about
six thousand, we have had over two hundred killed and
wounded officers and over two thousand three hundred rank
and file; so though we have not achieved anything, we certainly need not be ashamed of our fighting. Besides, at least
two thousand five hundred have died in hospital, so that half
our strength is accounted for."

Roper shortly afterwards came in.

"The Legion is disbanded, Roper, and it is open to you
to go north and embark with the rest, or to go down to Cadiz
and take a passage home from there."

"What are you going to do, sir?"

"I am going to stay here in a private capacity; I want
to see the end of the thing. I shall make this my head-
quarters, and shall ride about and see what goes on. I know
a good many officers now, and they can give me letters of
introduction to others; and as I have fought for them, no
doubt I shall be well received in their army. At any rate,
I have no wish to go home at present."

"Can't I stay with you, sir?"

"I should like to have you with me certainly, but I can't
afford to pay your wages."

"Well, sir, my food would not come to much, and I like
the place, and I like the life, and above all, I like being
with you. You must have someone to look after your horse.
I don't want to go home empty-handed, and I would certainly a great deal rather not do so, but stop here if you
would keep me."

"I would keep you willingly enough, Roper, but the only question is—can I? I must move out of this lodging and find a smaller one. One certainly could live cheaply enough here at the cafés; no one seems to take anything but coffee or chocolate, and a cup seems to last them for hours. From the large number of people one meets at the cafés and sees nowhere else, I should say that they must dine at some cheap place or at their homes. However, we will think it over."

A few days after his arrival at Madrid, Arthur had written home.

"My dear Uncle,
            "You will be surprised to see by the heading of this letter that I am at Madrid. But my first piece of news is, that I am now a captain, nominally upon the staff of General Evans, but actually on detached duty, a duty which is likely to keep me here for some time—in fact, until the Legion is disbanded. Therefore you need feel no further anxiety as to my safety. I am here to endeavour to worry the government into sending stores and pay for the Legion. To this end I call upon the minister of war every few days. The first time he saw me; since then he has always been too busy. I have also called upon the prime minister, and have spoken to him with what he considered indecent warmth, and I don't expect to do much good in the future. However, here I am.

"I am at present in an hotel. The food is good, the bed is soft. I have with me my good friend Roper, of whom I have spoken to you in almost every letter I have written. When the good fellow found that I was coming here, he threw up his sergeant's stripes to accompany me as my servant; it is a great comfort having him with me. I have been made a member of the principal club here, and have already made several acquaintances, so I have no doubt that I shall have a pleasant time. I am not going to tell you about Madrid, because you can, if you choose, find a much better description of it in books than I can give you. Please send the next remittances, which will probably be the last, to some mercantile house here.

"You will be glad to hear that though I failed in getting the arrears of pay for the Legion, I have been informed that I can draw monthly for the pay due to me while here. As living at an hotel is not dear, this and my allowance will suffice very well for my requirements. I have seen Colonel Wylde, the British commissioner, who is a very charming man. Of course he has been doing the very best he can for the Legion, but he is very frequently away with the army. I will explain how it is that I am in charge here on a mission of real importance. Major Hawkins, who was chief of the mission, was killed in a skirmish with the Carlists that we had on our way down. He was a very nice fellow, and I was very sorry at his death. I don't, of course, know yet whether they will send another field-officer to take his place or leave me in charge. I rather hope they won't send one. I don't think they would be wrong to leave it to me, for cheek is very useful in this sort of work, and I flatter myself that I shall stir them up a good deal—more than an older man would be likely to do. Certainly I shall not be inclined to take 'No' for an answer. I will write shortly again.   "With love to you all,

"Your affectionate Nephew."

CHAPTER VIII

A DESPERATE ADVENTURE

AS Roper's desire to stay with Arthur remained unchanged, the latter gladly accepted his offer. One of the horses was at once sold, and they removed into smaller lodgings, consisting only of a tiny kitchen, one sitting-room with a fold-up bed in a corner, and a closet just large enough to hold a bed for Roper. Arthur was obliged to buy a suit of dress clothes, some white shirts, and two suits of ordinary clothes. They lived on terms of perfect equality when indoors, except that Roper carried out their simple cooking at breakfast and supper, while in the middle of the day they went to a quiet trattoria in the suburbs; and after a week's experience Arthur found to his satisfaction that, even with the hire of stables and the horse's forage, they were living well within his income.

There was, of course, some surprise among his acquaintances at the substitution of civilian clothes for his uniform. It made no difference, however, in the cordiality of his reception, for he had become by this time a popular character, especially with the ladies, who appreciated his frank boyishness and freedom from formality, so unusual among their own people.

Colonel Wylde had taken a great fancy to the lad, and said to him one day: "I have been thinking over your case, Hallett. Of course I was not empowered to offer you any specific position, but I am permitted to despatch messengers to any point where I may be unable to go myself. I wrote a month since to say that operations were being carried on over so wide a field that I found it impossible to give attention to all points. I stated that an English officer named Captain Hallett had come down here as General Evans's agent. You were now unemployed, and would, I was convinced, prove a valuable assistant; and I asked that I might be permitted to appoint you as my aide, with the same rank as that which you held under General Evans in the Legion. I said that you were well mounted, and that the expense would be so very slight that I strongly recommended your appointment, as I was sure you would gladly act under me without any extra appointments except the pay of your rank and forage allowance for your horses, and the other usual field allowances, which will altogether make your pay about one pound a day. I have to-day received a reply authorizing your appointment with the rank of a captain in the army."

"I am indeed obliged to you, colonel!" Arthur exclaimed in delight. "I would most gladly have placed myself under your orders even without the pay, though I do not say that that will not be acceptable. But I could not get work that I should like better. I cannot tell you how much I am obliged to you."

"I feel that I spoke for myself as well as for you, Captain Hallett. It is impossible for me to keep my eyes everywhere, and you will, in fact, double my utility. There are only two other commissioners out here, a number altogether insufficient to cope with all that is going on. Indeed, very many regrettable things occur owing to a want of supervision. When one or other of us happens to be present, we can insist upon the articles of the Convention we brought about between the parties being observed; but if we are not there, a great deal of shooting in cold blood still takes place. You will, of course, have to provide yourself with an undress staff uniform. You can send a tailor here to see mine. It would not do for you to use your own; that is known to be a Christino one; and as you may have to go into the enemy's lines, you must therefore be easily recognized as one of us. You had better get high boots and breeches, and, of course, a cocked hat. These will not cost you anything like so much as they would at home; people work much more cheaply here. By the way, I have larger stables than I require, so you may as well keep your horses there."

"I suppose I may put my man into uniform too, sir; it is more convenient, and would look better."

"Yes, I think so. My own two orderlies belong to the 13th Dragoons; if you like, I will accept him as a recruit in that corps and put him on the pay-sheet; but you must get his uniform."

With renewed thanks Arthur took his leave and hurried back to his rooms.

"I have great news, Roper," he said. "Colonel Wylde has obtained permission for me to act as his assistant, and you are to enlist in the 13th Dragoon Guards so as to ride with me in uniform. So we can shift out of these little lodgings again, and needn't look upon every penny before we spend it."

"That is good news indeed!" Roper exclaimed. "And I shall be more useful to you now, for during the past four months I have learned to talk Spanish quite well, from having been so much in the barracks with the soldiers."

"Well, in the first place we have to be measured for our uniforms, and we are to send the tailor to Colonel Wylde to see the patterns. Then we will look out for lodgings. The two horses are to be taken to the colonel's stables, so that we shall save that expense. The whole thing is entirely his doing, and I am tremendously obliged to him."

Three days later the arrangements were completed; comfortable lodgings were taken, and they had shifted into them. The uniforms had come home and been found satisfactory, and Arthur had reported himself as ready for service.

"I shall be going up to the north again myself," the colonel said. "When I do so, you had better start out for the east. The war is being conducted with great ferocity there, and it is much to be desired that the Conventions agreed to last year shall be enforced, or at any rate, that an effort should be made to enforce them. Cabrera is a brave and skilful commander, but his cruelties are abominable. He was always cruel; but the atrocious action of Nogueras, in causing his mother to be seized and shot, has closed his heart to all feeling of mercy. He shoots women who fall into his hands as well as men; and on one occasion he shot no fewer than eighty-five sergeants in cold blood. I fear greatly that no remonstrances would be of any avail with a man who seems to revel in bloodshed. I do not say that he has not had terrible provocation; and if he were to get hold of Nogueras, I should not blame him if he cut him into small pieces. I do not think, therefore, that it will be of any use your trying to influence him. You may, however, attempt to persuade the various Christino chiefs in Aragon and Valencia. I know that their position is difficult. They are urged by the friends and relatives of the men murdered by the Carlists to make terrible reprisals when they get the opportunity, and in consequence the war is becoming one of extermination. I have no hope that you will be able to do much, but you can at least try. I shall be glad to be able to report, even in one or two instances, that efforts have been made by the Christinos to mitigate the horrors of the struggle."

The next day Arthur again wrote home.

" My dear Uncle,

"I have a wonderfully good piece of news to give you. I told you in my last letter that, now the Legion was disbanded, I intended to stay here for a time on my allowance and savings. Now all this is changed, for Colonel Wylde has obtained for me the appointment of Assistant British Commissioner, with the temporary rank of captain in Her Majesty's service. Isn't that splendid? There is excellent pay and allowances, so I shall be able to live like a fighting-cock. This will be my head-quarters, but I shall generally be with one or other of the armies in the field; and it will be, I know, a satisfaction to you all that I shall not be called upon to take any part in the fighting, but shall be merely a spectator of the fray. Now, even you will think that I am not doing wrong in staying in Spain. I am very much at home here, and have many friends and acquaintances, for you know by this time I speak Spanish really like a native.

"The family I am most intimate with is that of Count Leon de Balen. He is a young man of about five-and-twenty, with three young sisters, the eldest of whom is about the age of sixteen. Leon has been in England and speaks

English fairly, and is very English in his ways, and doesn't keep his sisters bottled up, as most of these Spaniards do; and I visit there just as I should at any English house where I was intimate. Roper is of course with me. He has been nominally enlisted in an English dragoon regiment, and wears the uniform. I am having an English staff uniform made for me, and were you here you would see me swaggering down the streets as if they belonged to me; I really feel as if I were somebody. I hope to hear that you are all pleased, and that even you agree that I could not possibly do better for myself than remain here till the end of the war. How long that will be, goodness only knows! I shall be in no hurry, for it is just the life, of all others, to suit me. Love to all.

"Your affectionate Nephew."

In due time the answer arrived:

"My dear Arthur,
        "We are all delighted at the receipt of your letter. We should, of course, be extremely glad to have you back with us, but at the same time we cannot but recognize that you could not do better for yourself than you are doing. I do not know that personally I am extraordinarily gratified that you should be holding a commission as captain in Her Majesty's service, and as Assistant British Commissioner in Spain; but I am bound to say that your aunt and cousins seem to be filled with an altogether excessive pride in the position you have gained. The girls have been going about among their friends crowing like little gamecocks, and even your aunt, ordinarily a tranquil and quietly disposed woman, appears to be quite puffed up.
        "However, joking aside, we are all highly gratified—I certainly admit that I myself am highly gratified too—and feel that you could not do better for yourself than remain for three or four years, by which time, I hope, the war will be

finished. You will, as you say, see what is going on without running any serious risks; and when you are in Madrid I can quite imagine that, with your official position, you will lead a very pleasant life. I almost feel, Arthur, that you are getting altogether beyond advice, and are now able to go on your own way. I can only say, therefore, that we shall be all very glad to have you back again with us, and I hope that every trace of the unpleasantness which necessarily resulted from our last interview will be altogether forgotten.

"Your affectionate Uncle."

That evening Arthur called at the house of the young Count Leon de Balen. It was one of the houses at which he had become most intimate. The count had little of the reserve and hauteur common to most Spanish nobles. He had from the first taken a great fancy to Arthur, and had made the latter at all times welcome to his house. It had been one of the first to which he had been invited after his arrival at Madrid, and was one of the few which were always open to him.

"I have been taken to task several times," the young man said one day with a laugh, "for inviting a man, and that man a foreigner and a heretic, so familiarly to my house. Two years ago I was for a few months with our embassy in London, and I came to like your ways very much. It was very pleasant to be able to make calls at houses without ceremony, and I made many friends. It seemed to me in all respects better, for young people get to know each other and to like each other. Young men and young women in your country meet and talk and dance together, and are good friends, without thinking of marriage; whereas here girls are for the most part shut up until a marriage is arranged for them. Of course I hold, as other people do, that young ladies should not go out alone, and should always be accompanied by a duenna; but in their own house, and under their parents' eyes, I can see no occasion for strictness. I might have some hesitation in giving a young Spaniard a general invitation to my house, because he would not understand it, and would think that I wished to introduce him as a suitor to one of my sisters; but with an Englishman it is different. You laugh and talk with them as if they were your own, and I think it is very good for them, and that they are as pleased to see you as I am."

When, therefore, Arthur had no other engagement he very often went in for a chat in the evening to the young count's, and he was naturally one of the first he told of his new appointment.

"I congratulate you most heartily," Leon said. "I have been wondering, since I heard that your Legion had been disbanded, what you were going to do. I am leaving, as I told you, for one of my country estates near Albacete, with Mercedes, and shall be away about a couple of months. If you chance to be coming that way, I need not say how glad I shall be to see you. Of course you don't know yet where you are likely to go, but it may as well be there as in any other direction. Perhaps you will be back as soon as we shall? I hope so sincerely."

On the day when Colonel Wylde left for the north, Arthur started for Mercia. When out of the town he called Roper up to his side.

"I am heartily glad to be at work again, Roper."

"I am not sorry myself, sir. I have nothing to say against Madrid, but one gets tired of having nothing particular to do, and especially as for the past three or four days, since I have been in this scarlet uniform, everyone has stared at me in the street. I shall get used to it in time, of course, but it is rather trying at first."

"I dare say it is," Arthur laughed. "Of course, I don't feel it so much. There is not so much difference between officers' uniforms as between those of private soldiers, at any rate not between undress uniforms. I am a good deal more comfortable in my present dress than I was before, for I could not but see myself that it was getting very small, and I had almost given up wearing it."

"Yes, you keep on growing so. You were a good bit taller than I was when you joined the Legion two years ago, and now you are pretty nearly a head taller. You must be over six feet now, and I see these little Spaniards look up to you as you walk along."

"Yes, I have been rather disgusted at shooting up so. I don't suppose other people notice it; but as I was wanting to look six or seven years older than I am, it was annoying that I should keep on growing. Well, I think I have pretty nearly done now."

They travelled by comfortable stages down to Mercia. Arthur had several interviews with the general in command of the forces there, and received assurances from him that every care should be used to mitigate the horrors of the war, but that such a passion of rage had been excited by the massacres perpetrated by Cabrera that it was all but impossible to keep the people in hand.

"It is to Cabrera himself that you should address yourself, señor," the general said. "We are anxious to prosecute the war in the spirit of civilization, but as long as he persists in carrying it on like a demon it is plainly impossible for us to fight in kid gloves."

"I will go to Cabrera," Arthur said; "even he ought to have satisfied his vengeance for the murder of his mother. Were I in his place I would hunt Nogueras through the country until I found him, but it is simply monstrous that he should continue to take vengeance upon innocent people."

After remaining four days at Mercia, Arthur therefore turned his horse's head north. When he neared Albacete he heard that Cabrera had been making a raid from the Sierra de Val de Meca, and had swept down nearly to the city, harassing the country and carrying off much booty. Arthur was told that Cabrera had attacked and taken the Palazzo of the Count de Balen, so half an hour after entering the town he rode out to enquire after his friend. As they approached the house they saw smoke still rising from it. Putting their horses to a gallop they speedily arrived in front of the house, only, however, to find that it was a mere shell. As Arthur alighted a man, whom he knew by sight, came out from a small outhouse.

"What has happened? Are the count and his sister safe?"

"Alas! no, sir," the man said. "The Carlists burst into the house yesterday morning. The count opposed them and was struck down desperately wounded. Donna Mercedes was carried off by them. They sacked the palace and then set it on fire. Three or four of the men were killed. I was away at Albacete. I found that some of the women had carried the young count out behind the house. He is in here."

Arthur hurried in.

"My dear Leon," he said, "this is terrible news that I hear!"

"Terrible," the other said faintly. "I am wounded badly, but that is nothing except that it will keep me a month before I am fit to act; but it is awful to think that Mercedes has fallen into the hands of that ruffian Cabrera. Thank God you have come! I know you will do all you can for me."

"Assuredly I will. In the first place, do you know which way the villains have gone?"

"Yes; they have gone up by La Roda. They will doubtless sack that place, and Minaya, and Villar Robledo."

"Have you fresh horses?"

"No; they have driven every horse off."

"That is unfortunate, for I made a good long journey to Albacete. When I arrived I heard a rumour that your place had been sacked, so I rode straight here. At any rate I must give the horses four hours' rest, and then I will push on. Tell me how it all happened?"

"I was at breakfast yesterday when the servants came run-

ning in with the news that a large body of horsemen were
coming up at a gallop. I ran down with Mercedes, but it
was already too late to get to our horses. They rode up,
and their leader, who was, I believe, Cabrera, ordered the men
to seize my sister. I drew my sword, but I was cut down
almost before I had struck a blow. I knew nothing more
until some hours later, when I found myself lying here,
where, it seems, the female servants had brought me, and
saw that the house was on fire from end to end, and that the
Carlists had gone and taken Mercedes with them. I think
I was nearly out of my mind till nightfall, then I slept for
some hours, overpowered by exhaustion. I found when I
awoke that Monte had returned in the evening and had been
sitting by me all night. I sent him off at once to Albacete.
He returned at mid-day with a message from the command-
ant there to the effect that Cabrera's force was too strong to
be attacked, and that he expected to have to defend himself.
I cannot say that I was surprised. Cabrera is so dreaded
that it requires a strong man to attempt to make head against
him, and indeed when I once got over my fury I recognized
that as Cabrera might be fifty miles away by the time my
messenger got to Albacete it would be hopeless to attempt
to pursue him."

"I will set out as soon as the horses have had a rest.
Fortunately, I have not been hurrying myself so far, and
they are both in good condition. I will see Cabrera himself, and will do all in my power to rescue your sister."

"I fear your journey will be useless, Hallett. The wretch
has become a wild beast since the murder of his mother; but
I know you will do all you can. If I were but able to travel
I would go with you and would stab him to the heart if he
refused to release her, but it will be long before I shall be
able to sit on a horse again."

"I should think the best thing you can do, Leon, is to
have yourself carried on a litter to Albacete, where your
wounds can be properly seen to."

"So far I have no one but these women to carry me. They tell me that the whole of the men were driven off the estate and made to enter Cabrera's ranks."

"Well, he did not go much farther than this, and there must be men to be had from some of the villages a few miles away. I will send your man off at once to get half a dozen of them to carry you."

"You must want something to eat, too. Will you call one of the women in here? What have we to eat?"

"We have got some green corn, señor—some of the fields set on fire were too green to burn—and we caught some chickens wandering about."

"Then cook some for the señor and his servant."

Leon now lay for some time without speaking. He had lost a great deal of blood, after the departure of the Carlists, before the women ventured to go near him, and although he had roused himself on Arthur's arrival he was now too exhausted to talk further. After a stay of four hours Arthur started again. It was already dark, and he would have preferred waiting till daylight had not the count's anxiety been so great that he thought it would be better to go, at any rate for a few miles. After travelling for two hours they arrived at a farm. An old woman was the only occupant; as the men had gone willingly enough with the Carlists, the house and its belongings had not been interfered with. The horses were put up in a shed, and the two men sat down by the fire talking.

"I have very little hope of getting Donna Mercedes out of Cabrera's hands by fair means; it is like asking a tiger to give up a kid. My great hope, Roper, lies rather in rescuing her myself. Of course, I do not know where she is confined, or how she is guarded. It is not likely that they would place a very strong guard over her. You and I together ought to be able to get her away. Of course, I can form no plans until we see the place. There will be risk in the business; that can't be helped. I have got in and out of my bedroom at school many a time, and can back myself to climb anywhere. It will be your business to bring the horses round in readiness when I get her out. If you can possibly get hold of a third animal it will be a great advantage, for we shall have to reckon upon being pursued."

"I am ready for anything, captain. The count was always very civil to me when he called upon you, and he never came without making me a present. No doubt he knew by our lodging that things were not very flourishing with you. It is just the sort of business I should like. We have done no fighting for the past nine months, and I shall be right glad of a skirmish."

"I expect it will be something worse than a skirmish. If this brute Cabrera won't give the young lady up, it will be a serious job to take her, even if you can get another horse; for good as ours may be, it is probable that there are better ones in his camp. However, it is all so vague at present that it is useless to try and form plans. One thing, I am sure, we can say: fewer than six won't take her from us once we have got her. We must not deceive ourselves that they will respect our uniform. Cabrera respects nothing. And if we stand between him and his vengeance we need not flatter ourselves that he will let us go."

"Well, sir, a man can't die better than in trying to save a woman; that is how I look at it."

"Quite right, Roper; it is the death of all others that I would choose. However, I have faith in ourselves, and I fancy that we shall get through somehow, though I am pretty sure that it will be a very close shave. I think we had better lie down till daybreak. You have given the horses a good feed, have you not?"

"Yes, sir; I have put down half a sack of beans between them. They will be fresh enough in the morning; till yesterday we have not travelled more than fifteen or sixteen miles a day, and they had a week's rest at Mercia. They could not be in better condition."

They started as soon as it began to be light, and on reaching La Roda heard that Cabrera had rested there on the previous day, and had gone on that morning to Banada and Villar de Navado. On arriving at Banada they found that Cabrera had ridden on half an hour before to Villar de Navado. This place they reached at eleven o'clock. The place was full of Carlists. Arthur alighted in front of the principal house. He was looked at scowlingly by the men thronging the streets, but nothing was said to him.

"I wish to see General Cabrera," he said. "Will you say that I am one of the British commissioners?"

After being kept waiting for two or three minutes he was asked in. Cabrera was a powerful man with a face full of strength and energy.

"To what am I indebted for this visit, señor?" he asked as Arthur entered.

"I have called, sir, to implore you to respect the Conventions entered into between both parties and signed by them, and on the part of the British government by Colonels Wylde and Lacy."

"I have nothing whatever to do with it," Cabrera said. "The Christinos have committed great atrocities; it is my intention to revenge them whenever possible."

"But at least, sir," Arthur said, "you do not war against women?"

"I war against my enemies, men and women. My own mother was murdered by them, as no doubt you are aware, and for each drop of her blood I shall take vengeance."

"But, sir, the lady whom you carried off the day before yesterday was not the wife of a Christino general, nor in any way connected with the war."

"Her brother was a well-known Christino," Cabrera replied, "and all the enemies of Don Carlos are my enemies. It is well that these young nobles at the court should learn that by supporting the government against the king they are as much our foes as if they were fighting in the field. I make war in my own way; other generals may do as they like. I refuse to have my hands tied, and I intend to inflict a heavy lesson upon these politicians of Madrid. Against the young woman herself I have no special quarrel, but as a member of a leading Christino family she is an enemy, and as such she will be shot to-morrow morning. There, sir, it is useless to talk further. My mind is perfectly made up; and if you wish to remain till the morning to witness the execution, you are perfectly at liberty to do so. In fact, I should prefer it, for I wish it to be known that prisoners who fall into my hands will be shown no mercy."

Arthur rose. "Well, sir, in taking my leave of you, I beg in the name of my government to warn you of the consequences of making war in defiance not only of all its rules and usages, but of humanity."

Cabrera simply waved his hand in scorn, and Arthur, turning, strode out of the room.

"Find some place in the outskirts of the village and put up our horses," he said to Roper; "there I will talk with you."

A hut, from which its inhabitants had fled on the approach of the Carlists, was soon found.

"You have brought a good allowance of beans with you, have you not?"

"Yes, sir; I have nearly half a sack."

"Give the horses a good feed, and then we will talk matters over."

He sat down on a broken chair. "As I expected, Roper, the villain is not to be turned from his purpose: the lady is to be shot to-morrow morning. It seems to me that there are between three and four thousand men in and around the village. Of these, as far as I could see as we rode in, only a hundred or so are mounted. We may take it that our horses are better than the average; they have not been doing such long marches, and they are really good animals. I don't know which is the best; but I should fancy that if we get a fair start not above thirty will keep up with us, perhaps not above twenty. That is the number we may have to cope with. The first thing we shall have to find out is where Donna Mercedes is confined, and how she is guarded. It is unlikely that they will have placed more than two or three sentries over her; they would know well enough that she could not escape by herself.

"I should say that there will be one sentry outside the door, and perhaps two inside. If there is a door or a window at the back of the house, we need not bother about the man in front. I must do for the two men inside. You bring the two horses round within a hundred yards of the back of the house, and we will drop out of the window, if there is one, or walk out of the door. First of all, we must find out the house; then it will be your business to stroll round and choose a horse in such a position that you can lead it off without disturbing others. You must get it behind the side of the street on which our house stands, so that you will not have to lead it across the street, but simply bring it and place it with ours."

"All right, sir; I think I can answer for that part of the business. I suppose you will not begin until half-past ten or eleven; they will be pretty nearly all asleep by that time."

"No, I sha'n't begin before that."

They waited for a couple of hours, and then strolled out into the village. The Carlists, knowing that they had had an interview with their chief, paid no great attention to them, and presently Arthur seized the opportunity of asking a woman who was standing at her door which was the priest's house.

"It is the last house in the village on this side of the street, señor."

Arthur continued his stroll to the end of the village, and then turned back and walked to the other end. It was the heat of the day now, and most of the men were lying down asleep in the shade of houses and trees, and there were but

few in the street. Stopping at the priest's house, he knocked
at the door and entered.

"I am an English officer, father," he said to the priest,
who was a tall, thin old man. "My errand here is to save
the life of the young lady who has been carried off and
brought here, and whom Cabrera is going to shoot in the
morning."

"It is terrible, señor!" the priest said; "it is terrible!
but what can we do? I have already seen this man, and
warned him of the consequences of so dreadful an action.
He told me to mind my own business and that he would
mind his, and I was thrust bodily out of the house protest-
ing vainly."

"Well, father, then I take it that if you had the power
you would have the will to save this poor young lady?"

"Assuredly, my son; but I am old and feeble, and what
can I do?"

"You can do much, father. I wish you to go again to
Cabrera. Say that, as a man of God, it is your duty to receive this young lady's confession, and to stay with her,
pray with her, and comfort her during the night, and demand that he give you an order to do so."

"He cannot refuse such a request," the priest said. "The
worst malefactor has the right to have the attendance of the
clergy before his death. But how would that benefit her
save by my spiritual help?"

"You will have no more to do with it, father. You will
bring me the order here, and then as soon as it gets dark I
should advise you to leave the village and walk some twenty
miles away, and wait until Cabrera has left the neighbourhood, which he doubless will do to-morrow; the rest of the
business will be my affair."

"But do you mean——" the priest began.

"I mean, father, that after it is dark I shall put on your
robe and hat, if you will lend them to me. I shall present
myself at the door with the order, and when I am admitted

and the door is closed again, I shall proceed to knock on the head any men who are inside. I don't think there will be more than two. Having done that, I shall go to the young lady's room and lower her down through the window. My man-servant will be waiting behind with horses, and, if we are lucky, we shall get a long start of them."

" I will do it," the priest said; " even if I were to be killed I would do it. Even this monster cannot refuse to allow a priest to visit one about to die. Possibly he might, if alone, but the very peasants under him would call out at his refusal. Shall I go at once? "

" No; it would be best that you should go to him just as he has finished his dinner; doubtless six or eight of his officers will be with him. You had best write out the order before you go, so that it will only need his signature. I rely upon your eloquence and authority to induce him to grant it to you."

" I will obtain it," the priest said; " even the worst malefactor has a right to the consolation of a priest."

" Thank you, father. You will have the satisfaction of having saved an innocent girl's life. Now, in the next place, will you tell me in which house she is confined? I have not liked to ask the question."

" She is in the house next to that in which Cabrera is quartered. There is a sentry at the door."

" What sort of a house is it? "

" It is like the others, except that the lower windows are all barred."

" Are there windows behind? "

" Yes; I believe there are."

" Do you know whether there is a sentry behind? "

The priest shook his head. " I do not know, sir."

" Well, I must ascertain that," Arthur said. " At eight o'clock, señor, I will be here, and you shall give me your robe and hat, and the order. Then I should advise you to leave at once. Do you know which way they are going to march? "

" They are going east; they will take refuge again in the mountains."

"In that case, father, you will not have to walk more than eight or ten miles, and can take shelter in the nearest village. Adieu! Surely you will never regret the good action you are doing."

He went out into the village again, and meeting Roper, said to him: " You see that house next to the one where Cabrera is quartered? In that house Donna Mercedes is confined. You see, there is a sentry at the door. I want you to stroll round carelessly behind that side of the village, and ascertain if a sentry is posted there also. If so, I shall have to leave you to manage him. You won't be able to bring up the horses so close as you would otherwise do. You must leave them a short distance away, steal up to that fellow, and silence him. The safest way will be to stab him to the heart. It is unpleasant to be compelled to take such a course, but extreme measures are necessary; for if he had time to shout we should have the whole camp on us in five minutes."

" I will do it, sir. I would rather not, but I see it has to be done."

" I have arranged everything else. The priest is going to get an order to pass the night praying with Donna Mercedes. He will hand it to me, and I shall enter the house disguised in his robe and hat. I don't know how many men there will be inside, but I should certainly say not more than two. Those two I have got to silence. I hear that the house has bars to the lower windows, but the upper ones will not be so carefully guarded, and I shall lower the lady down to you. Just before half-past ten crawl up close to the sentry, and as the clock chimes, strike. Then go back and bring the horses up as near as possible, and come yourself underneath the window. I shall go in as the clock strikes, and shall be ready for you when you come up. I think we ought to get away before an alarm is given, and if we have anything like luck we shall have a long start. It would be well if, when you are going round now, you would observe closely where the men are bivouacked, so that we can, if possible, get through without disturbing them in any way."

CHAPTER IX

THE ESCAPE

AT five o'clock in the afternoon Roper rejoined Arthur in the hut.

"Well, what is your report?"

"The house looks all right, sir. There are no bars on the upper windows. There is a sentry sitting down against the wall; as far as I could see, he was asleep. I don't think it will be possible to get the horses up close; but as each man seems to sleep just where it suits him, I think it would be easier for us to make our way through them on foot than to get the horses through. I don't think there will be any difficulty in getting the third horse. Do you think the lady knows how to ride, sir?"

"No; I think it is quite possible that she does not; but if we take another horse I can ride double with her by turns. I would risk a great deal rather than go with only two horses."

"We will get one somehow, sir. When shall I move the horses?"

"You had better take them down to the river just after dusk. Wait with them there for a quarter of an hour, and then walk away with them to some quiet spot—of course, as near as possible to the house. Then lie down beside them; no one is likely to notice what horses they are. Probably Cabrera's horses are behind his house."

"Yes, they are, sir."

"Well then, get them as close to those as you can. You might wait a short distance off till it is time to make a move, then take them as close to his horses as possible. Loosen the foot-ropes of one or two of his horses, so that when the time comes we can easily take one, and perhaps two, of them. We can each lead one; that will give us two changes."

At eight o'clock they went out from the cottage, each leading a horse. Already the number of men in the streets had begun to thin.

"Are you going?" more than one asked Arthur as they passed.

"Yes," he said; "I have tried in vain to induce your chief to spare the life of the lady he took prisoner, and finding my entreaties of no avail, I am going."

"It is a pity," the man said; "but the general will have his way, and who can blame him?"

They went down to the river, watered the horses, and then Roper took the two bridles and started to walk some distance down the bank, so as to be able to approach the back of the village as if he had been grazing the horses in the fields. Arthur, on his part, went to the priest's.

"I have succeeded, my son. At first he would not do it, but it was evident to him that those with him were shocked at the idea of refusing to let the lady have the last ministrations of the Church. 'Here is the paper,' he said when he signed it. 'You may go in to her, father, but I will have no goings in and out. You may enter, but you will remain with her till she is brought out for execution at daybreak.' I said, 'So be it.' Here, my son, are my hat and soutane. May God's blessing light upon your brave effort to rescue her, and may you carry her off to safety! It seems to me a desperate enterprise, but you are young and vigorous, and doubtless accustomed to strife. You had best leave this house when I have gone. The Carlists are for the most part faithful friends of the Church. Several have been here to-day to confess their sins, and more are to come this evening, and it were best that they should not find you here. If they find the house empty, they will suppose that I have gone to the church or on some other mission."

"I thank you for your suggestion, father, and I shall act on it. I fear I shall not be able to restore your things to you; therefore, I pray that you will accept these five pieces of gold in order that you may replace them."

The old man hesitated. "I need no reward for doing my duty," he said.

"Nor should I think of offering it to you, but I know how very poor you village curés are, and that it would be perhaps a serious trouble to you to replace these things; and as I am well provided with money it is but just and right that I should enable you to replace the goods you have given me. For your aid I can only give you my heartfelt thanks; and I doubt not that, when all this trouble is over, the Count de Balen will make a handsome offering to you for the use of your poor."

"Here are the hat and soutane, my son. Take them and my blessing. May God enable you to carry out your noble object."

The priest then put on a biretta, and went out at the back of his house. Arthur rolled up the dress and put the hat under his arm, and also went out behind and sat down against the wall of the house. When he heard the clock strike a quarter to ten, he put on the priest's robe and large three-cornered hat. He took up a lantern which the priest had placed on the table, went through the house, and out at the front door; then, imitating the quiet walk of the priest, he went up the now deserted street and paused before the sentry.

"Benedicite, my son!" he said. "I bear an order, signed by your general, authorizing me to pass the night with this poor child. Here it is;" and he held the paper up to the lantern. The man glanced at it. He could neither read nor write, but he knew Cabrera's signature by sight, having seen it on many proclamations. He knocked at the door.

"Open," he said; "here is one with a permit to enter, signed by the general."

The bolts were drawn, and the door opened. A rough-looking man stood by it, another was sitting at a table; he stood up as the apparent priest entered. The first man shot the top bolt, and as he stooped to fasten the bottom one Arthur drove his dagger to the hilt between his shoulders; and then, turning, sprang upon the other man and seized him by the throat. Taken wholly by surprise, the man could offer no resistance. Arthur flung him back across the table, retaining his grip upon his throat until the man became unconscious; then he thrust a piece of wood he had brought with him between his teeth, and tied it there, securely fastened his hands and legs, and tied these to the legs of the table. He had thought this all out: one man must be killed, the other he had hoped to overcome and silence by surprise. Then he took a candle which was burning upon the table and went up-stairs.

A key was in the door. He turned it and went in. Mercedes was lying upon a bed. She sprang to her feet as he entered. "Hush!" he said, as he removed his hat. "I have come to save you, Donna Mercedes. Hush, I implore you!" for he saw that the girl was on the point of uttering a scream of joy; "your life depends upon your keeping silence."

She dropped back upon the bed and burst into a passion of tears, which he permitted for a few minutes. Presently with a great effort she checked herself. "This is the first tear I have shed since I saw Leon killed."

"He is not killed, Donna Mercedes; he is grievously wounded, but will, I hope, recover."

"Are you sure?" she exclaimed incredulously, rising to her feet and laying her hand on his arm.

"Quite sure; sure, at least, that he was well and sensible

when I left him, and was to be carried this morning down to Albacete. He was only anxious about you, and I told him that I would bring you safely back to him. I have got my man with me; by this time he will have slain the sentry beneath your window, and we must be going. Now I will let you down. I will take hold of your hands and lower you as far as I can reach; it will not be more than a foot or two to drop. First, I will blow out this candle; possibly the opening of the window would be noticed were it alight."

He spoke in a quiet, matter-of-fact way so as to steady the girl's nerves, blew out the candle, and opened the window. "Now," he said, "I will let you down." He lifted her through the window, and then, holding her wrists, lowered her as far as he could reach and then let her go, and swinging himself out dropped beside her. "We must wait now," he said, "till my man comes to fetch us to the horses. It is as well that your eyes should become accustomed to the darkness before we move."

In three minutes Roper came up.

"It is all right so far, Roper; here is the lady beside me. Now for the horses."

"They are not fifty yards away, sir. You must be careful how you walk, for there are many asleep in the garden. I have noted all their places, and if you keep your hand upon my shoulder I can lead you through."

Placing the girl between himself and his follower, his hands on the latter's shoulders, Arthur moved quietly along. He could vaguely make out a dark figure lying down here and there. It was an intensely anxious time, but all seemed perfectly quiet. They reached the end of the garden, and going through a hole in the fence, came presently upon four horses. Arthur dropped his hat and soutane, and threw his cloak, which he had brought with him, over his shoulder.

"Shall we mount here or walk?"

"I think we had better walk a bit, sir."

Arthur took the bridles of two of the horses, and telling

the girl to keep close behind him, followed Roper, who led the other two horses. They walked for four or five minutes, then Roper stopped.

"I think we are well beyond them now, sir," he said. "I have been over all this ground five or six times this evening, and I am pretty sure that none of them are beyond us."

Arthur put on his cocked hat, which he had previously carried, as, if they had been noticed, its outline would at once have provoked curiosity. Then he mounted one of the horses, and lifted Mercedes into the saddle in front of him. They went at a walk for some little distance, and then broke into a canter.

"We are safe now, are we not?" Mercedes asked.

"I hope so. The only question is the hour at which they change the guard. My man killed a fellow who was under your window, and of course this must be discovered when they do so; that was the only thing that I could not calculate upon. However, when they discover that we have escaped it will be some time before they mount; and as they won't know which way we have gone, the betting is strongly against our being overtaken. I think, upon the whole, we may consider ourselves pretty safe."

They rode along by the side of the river, crossed it at a ford at Banada, and just as day was breaking arrived at the ruins of the palace. Arthur had twice changed horses, but few words had been spoken on the journey.

"You must not think, Don Arthur," the girl had said once, "that I do not feel grateful because I cannot tell you so; it is because I feel too grateful to express it."

"Do not trouble yourself, señorita. I know perfectly well how you must be feeling, and it is not at all necessary for you to tell me; you must have gone through a terrible time indeed."

"I thought more of my brother's fate than my own," she said. "It did not seem to me to be so hard to die. It was of Leon, my dear brother, that I thought so much, and grieved for. I could hardly think that that terrible man really meant to kill me, and yet he seemed altogether without pity."

"He was. The good priest, whose dress I wore and whose place I took, had endeavoured in vain to turn him from his determination. I myself saw him, and denounced the crime as being contrary to the Conventions; but he would not hear me, and declared that, come what might, you should be shot the first thing in the morning. And it was only when I found that the case was absolutely hopeless that I determined to set you free at whatever risk. The priest aided me. He obtained from Cabrera an order to spend the night with you, in order to prepare you for death. He passed me the order, and went away himself so as to escape the vengeance of that scoundrel, and I and my man between us managed to get you out."

"But there were two men below, were there not? I heard them talking."

"Yes; I had to kill one of them, and the other I gagged and tied up. I don't suppose he will be any the worse when they find him in the morning. Now, we will change horses, and then I hope you will try to sleep. You cannot have closed an eye since you were captured, and we shall have plenty of time to talk later on." The girl did as he told her, and remained quiet in his arms, but he could see that her eyes never closed.

"I wish I could ride," she said once, "so that I might relieve you of my weight."

"Your weight is nothing," he said; "and each time we change horses I put you on the other side, and so rest my arm."

As they drew up at the shed from which he had ridden thirty-six hours before, the women ran out and cried with joy.

Arthur handed the girl down to them.

"Take her inside," he said, "and give her something to

eat, and then let her lie down for a bit; she must be desperately tired."

Then he himself got down and shook hands warmly with Roper.

" This has been as good a night's work, Roper, as you are ever likely to do, if you live to be a hundred."

" It has been a good business, sir, and I enjoyed it all except the stabbing of that sentry. It went badly against the grain, but I knew it had to be done, for it was our lives against his."

"I had to do just the same thing; but, as you say, it was a matter of necessity, though I wish heartily that it had been Cabrera himself. However, the thought will not trouble me. If men choose to follow a ruffian like that, they must take the consequences. Those are two good horses you got hold of."

"Yes; that one is Cabrera's own. Fortunately he was standing at the end of the line. I had noted his position before it got dark, and was mightily pleased that I could get at him, for I thought it would rile the scoundrel nicely to lose not only his prisoner but his horse. The other is a good one too."

"Well, give them a good feed all round; and then you must see what we can get to eat ourselves, for we only had a piece of bread all yesterday and not much the day before. We can get some beans anyhow, and, I expect, a chicken, and I will tell the women to boil one down for Donna Mercedes. We may be sure that she has eaten next to nothing since she was taken."

A woman presently came out from the hut and said that the lady had dropped off to sleep, and that one of their number was sitting with her. They set to work at once to carry out Arthur's instructions. Two chickens were killed, dipped into boiling water to take the feathers off, and then cut in two and put over a wood fire. Some beans were baked on a girdle, and another chicken was put into a pot to simmer.

"Boil it down till there is only about a pint of liquor left," was his order; "then strain it, and keep it hot for her till she wakes. Have you heard how the count bore the journey?"

"Yes, sir; some of the men came back in the evening and said that he had slept a good deal on the way."

Five hours later Donna Mercedes awoke, and having drunk the broth prepared for her, came out.

"Now, if you feel strong enough we will ride on to Albacete at once," Arthur said. "Your brother must be in a terrible state of anxiety about you, and your appearance will do more for him than the doctors can do."

"I am ready," she said brightly. "The sleep and a wash have done wonders for me."

Roper at once put the saddles on the horses.

"No," she said; "I will ride now. I never have ridden, but I am sure that I can do it, and you can fasten a leading rein to my horse."

"It is not easy without a side-saddle, señora; but the pommel of this saddle is high, and if we go gently you will be able to hold on."

"At any rate I will try," she said.

The stirrups were arranged the proper length and Donna Mercedes lifted into the saddle.

"I shall manage very well," she said, as she settled herself on it. "I will learn to ride after this. I won't be so helpless in future."

Before mounting Arthur attached a leading rein to her horse's bit, and they started at a gentle canter, Roper leading the other horse. Three hours' riding brought them to Albacete. They put the horses up in the stable, and then enquired where the count had been taken. It was to the principal hotel, and there Arthur went at once with Donna Mercedes. They went up to the room together, and Arthur opened the door, let the girl pass in, and then closed it behind her and went down-stairs. A quarter of an hour later a servant came down and said that the count wished to see him.

"Ah, my dear Arthur!" Leon exclaimed as he entered, "how can I thank you enough, for my sister and myself, for all that you have done for us! She seems restored to me by a miracle."

"It is not much of a miracle, Leon; it required only a little invention and a little pluck, and the affair was managed. I felt that it was very hard if I could not get your sister out of the hands of that scoundrel, and our success can scarcely have afforded you more pleasure than it has Roper and myself."

"It is all very well to say so, but the fact is not changed. You have rescued her from certain death, have carried her off from the centre of four thousand men. My sister tells me that you did it in the disguise of a priest."

"Yes, and the good man gave me every assistance. I have not been ill-paid," he said with a light laugh, "for I have got hold of two very valuable horses. Now, you will have to take care of each other. Your sister has been splendidly brave, but she will need rest and quiet for a while, she could not have a better thing to do than to look after you; and it will do you good to be cared for by her. I shall wait here for a couple of days, for the horses have had four long days' work. I suppose you have not seen anyone here yet?"

"No; a good many gentlemen of my acquaintance have left their cards, but the doctor said I was not to see anyone at present. He thinks it will be nearly a month before I can move; and he said this morning that he was afraid I should get into a high state of fever if I agitated myself. However, I have no fear of that now. You have done me more good than all the doctors in Spain could do. Now, Mercedes, you must lift your head up from that pillow and stop crying."

"No one could have been calmer or cooler than your sis-

ter was, Leon; and now that it is all over, and she has
found that you are doing well, you must not be surprised at
her breaking down a little. I can assure you that from the
time I entered her room till we rode fairly away she was as
quiet and composed as possible; in fact, she did not speak
a single word from the moment I lowered her down from
the window till we were able to put our horses into a canter.
To me it was just like a school adventure. I was always
getting into scrapes at school, and master after master refused to keep me—it was for that reason that I enlisted in
our Legion—and it really seemed to me the same sort of
thing, only with a little spice of danger and the pleasure
and satisfaction of doing some good.

"And now, Donna Mercedes, if you will take my advice
you will go straight to bed. You will want all your strength
to nurse your brother. You have gone through frightful
anxiety, and have made a long and very fatiguing journey,
and before you install yourself at your brother's bedside you
want a long rest. If you do not take it, you will be breaking down badly. You see for yourself that he is doing well,
and now that he has got you back again there is no fear of
his having a relapse. He himself can have slept but little.
Therefore, I trust that you will at once lie down and have
a good long rest, and that he will do the same, then this
evening you will be able to have a quiet chat for a couple
of hours. I shall be quite willing to take my own prescrip-
tion and lie down till this evening."

"Arthur is right," Leon said. "We have all gone through
a painful time, and we shall be more ourselves after a sleep.
I don't think I have slept five minutes at a time since we
were attacked. At any rate, we must both obey orders. It
is one o'clock now, we will meet here again at eight."

Arthur at once went down-stairs. He found Roper in the
stables, he having just fed the horses.

"Now, Roper, you had better turn in at once; I have
arranged for a room for you. I shall not want anything

more to-day. You had better settle with one of the stablemen here to feed and water the horses this evening."

"I will come down again, sir, later."

"Well, you can do it if you wake, Roper; but I expect that when you once shut your eyes you won't open them again till to-morrow morning. At any rate, you can arrange that the horses shall be attended to if you should not come down. I feel very uncertain myself about waking."

Arthur gave orders that he should be roused at eight o'clock, and in a very few minutes was fast asleep. He could hardly believe that he had been six hours asleep when there was a knock at his door. However, he jumped out of bed, washed as well as he was able with the very scanty supply of water deemed sufficient for his ablutions, and then went down to Leon's room.

"You look better, Leon," he said as he entered.

"I feel better. Indeed, I have slept like a dormouse, and did not wake till the servant came in a few minutes ago. The doctor said that I was quite a different man from what I was this morning."

"I feel ever so much better too, and should feel better still if I could have had a bath. I hope your sister won't wake; she would be all the fresher for a complete night's rest."

"She told me she slept a good deal on the ride."

"Yes; I think she dozed. No wonder! She must have had a terrible time of it, poor girl! It was a fearful position for her, and I quite expected that when I got to her I should have found her completely prostrated."

"I expect she will get up. I know she wants to hear how you have managed it all. She has told me that she had not asked you anything. You appeared suddenly, dressed as a priest, and after you had got away she had felt so happy in being safe, and yet so bewildered at it all, that she had scarcely spoken at all, and I can quite understand her feelings."

"So can I, perfectly, and on our ride to this place I could see that she was thinking of nothing but meeting you. I don't think she credited my assurance that you were not mortally wounded, and was yearning for a sight of you. Ah, here she is!"

"You are looking better, Leon," she said, as she came up to the bedside.

"I am feeling a hundred per cent better. The doctor says that I am quite a different man, and that whereas when he saw me this morning he did not feel at all sure that I should get over it, he has no fears whatever about me now. So you see, Arthur, you have saved both our lives."

"Well, don't let us say anything more about it, Leon. The affair has turned out all right, and there is no more to be said on the matter."

Leon smiled. "That is all very well for you, but it is not quite so satisfactory to us. Now, you must tell us all about it. For the present I only know that you got a priest to help in some way, and I want the full particulars."

"Well, I will tell you the whole story."

And he gave a full account of the events from the moment of his arrival in the village. "I would have given a good deal," he said, after describing the scene with Cabrera, "to have got the scoundrel in a quiet place by myself, though I am bound to say I doubt whether I should have been found the better man. The fellow, to do him justice, is uncommonly vigorous and powerful, and I might have discovered that I had caught a Tartar; but I was so furious with him that I would willingly have taken my chance. Of course I can make every allowance for a man whose mother has been murdered in this war, and I can understand his showing no mercy to men of the other party who may fall into his hands; but to take revenge upon women, who had nothing whatever to do with the wrong he has suffered, is monstrous. He should know by his own feelings what their friends would suffer. However, as he was not to be moved

I felt that I must depend upon myself, and I decided that
the only way to get at the señora would be by the assistance of the priest, or at any rate that that was the first
plan to attempt."

He then related his interview with the priest, and the
manner in which the latter had at once agreed to aid him,
the various steps he had taken to ascertain the position of
the Carlists lying about the village, and to secure a spare
horse, and how he had carried out his plans.

"I was sorry," he said, "to have to kill one of the men
in the hut, but I could see no other way of disposing of
both of them before an alarm could be given. Of course if
I had not been able to obtain the priest's disguise I should
have had to kill the sentry at the door too, but even then
the men inside might not have opened the door to my sum-
mons, probably they would not have done so. Still, I own
that it went desperately against the grain to have to stab
that man; that was really the only unpleasant part of the
business. All the rest was simple, and Donna Mercedes was
very brave and very quiet. Roper had obtained an accurate
idea of where the Carlists were all lying, so that there was
not a single hitch in the affair. If it hadn't been for your
sister I should have almost preferred a chase and some excitement, but as it was, I was of course very thankful that
everything went so perfectly."

"I will take care," Leon said, "that the priest is made
comfortable for life. I can, at any rate, show my gratitude in that quarter, though I must always remain in debt
to you. What are you going to do next?"

"I am going to stop here for a couple of days, and if I
can get a good price for two of the horses I shall sell them.
I shall keep that one of Cabrera's. It is a splendid animal;
and I think of the others the best is the one that belonged
to Major Hawkins. The other two are both good animals,
and worth, I should say, from thirty to forty pounds apiece."

"I will give you that for them gladly. Of course, Cabrera's people carried off all mine, and I must have two for riding back to Madrid, so I shall be really glad to take your two off your hands."

"Very well," Arthur said; "I certainly did not want to saddle you with them, but as you say you really want them I would rather sell them to you than to anyone else."

"Then that is settled. I shall get Mercedes to write to-morrow for two of my servants to come here; the men who accompanied us were both killed. Besides, I must get Donna Martha, her duenna, and her maid to join us to keep her company. It would not be seemly for her to be here alone while I am laid up."

Arthur laughed.

"By the way, Mercedes, you will have to write to Don Silvio, telling him what you have gone through."

The girl looked earnestly at her brother, but made no answer, and he turned again to Arthur.

"But you did not say what you were going to do?"

"I hardly know. My instructions were to go to Mercia and see the governor there, and to endeavour to impress upon him the importance of observing the Conventions strictly. I was not altogether successful. He repeated his desire to do so, but pointed out to me that Cabrera so persistently refused to observe them in any way, and committed such atrocities, that the people were roused beyond control. However much, therefore, he might wish to carry on the war humanely, public opinion was too strong for him, and the friends of the people murdered by Cabrera naturally clamoured for reprisals. It was my intention, when I arrived, to proceed to Cabrera's camp and endeavour to persuade him to carry on the war less ruthlessly. Well, I have been to him, and see that remonstrances are not of the slightest avail. I shall now go to Madrid and request the minister of war to send a formal despatch to him calling upon him to conduct the war more humanely, and saying that unless he does so, all his followers who fall into the hands of the royal troops must be put to the sword, however painful it would be to him to give orders to that effect. I don't suppose such a communication would influence him in any way, but it might influence his followers, who can scarcely like to fight with, as it were, halters round their necks. It is extraordinary to me that people of one nation should fight so ferociously, and should refuse quarter to each other. Against a foreign invader one can imagine such a spirit, as, for example, when you were invaded by the French; but that people of one blood should, on a mere difference of opinion as to who should be king, hate each other so venomously beats me altogether."

"I cannot give any reason for it," Leon said. "I am in favour of Christina, and should not mind doing a little fighting, though, as I am not a soldier I don't feel called upon to take up arms. Still, it seems to me that the matter might be as well settled by everyone giving a vote one way or the other, and the minority then yielding gracefully."

They chatted for some time, the conversation being principally kept up by Arthur. Mercedes scarcely opened her lips, but sat by her brother's side holding his hand. At ten o'clock his nurse came in and said that he must now be quiet for the night, and the others again went off to their rooms. After breakfasting by himself, Arthur went down to the stables.

"I have sold those two horses to Count Leon."

"Yes, so he has been telling me."

"Oh, you have seen him, have you?"

"Yes, sir; he sent down for me half an hour ago. He looks a deal better than when we left him three days back."

"Yes; he will do now. He has lost a lot of blood, and it will be some time before he gains strength again; but the doctor said yesterday that he had no fears whatever as to his getting through."

"Well, he has quite taken away my breath this morning."

"Has he? In what way?"

" Well, sir, he has told me that when he gets to Madrid he will make me a present of five hundred pounds."

" I am glad indeed to hear it, Roper. You have done him an enormous service at a good deal of risk. I have always understood that he is a wealthy young noble, and I have no doubt he can very well afford to do it."

" I told him, sir, that really I had nothing to do with it, and that I had simply done what you had ordered me, never having seen the young lady myself. But he would not allow that that made any difference. I had assisted in saving his sister's life, and he was very pleased to be able to make such an acknowledgment of my services. I should not mind how many ladies' lives I saved on such terms."

" Well, I am heartily glad, Roper. It always has been a source of annoyance to me that I was not able to do more for you when we have been such friends together."

" That is all right, sir. We were friends together for a time, but I was in my right position and you were not. That, of course, was soon put right, and we have stood ever since in the proper relation towards each other. I am only too glad to work for you, and now you have put me in for a very good thing. If I were to go home now, everyone would say that I had done mightily well for myself, and I should go in for farming again; I made a mistake in leaving it."

" Well, when we get home, Roper, I will see that you have the first farm that is vacant on my estate."

" Why, I did not know that you had an estate," Roper said in surprise.

" Yes, I have an estate, and, I believe, a pretty good one; but I am not to come into it till I am five-and-twenty. I think my father saw that I was a harum-scarum sort of chap, so he settled it in that way. But though I am not to come in for it till I am twenty-five, I have an uncle who manages it for me, and I can certainly persuade him to give you the first farm that is vacant. I had intended to do so before, but I thought there might be some difficulty about it, because you would require capital to work it, but this five hundred pounds would give you a fair start on a small farm."

"That would be splendid, sir! That will give me something to look forward to. As long as you stay out here I shall stay with you, if it were for another ten years; but it makes all the difference having something to look forward to afterwards, for I have wondered sometimes what on earth I should do when I went back again, I should feel so strange. I have thought, too, sometimes about you, and what you would do when this affair had come to an end. Well, I am as glad to know that you will be all right as I am about myself."

Arthur went upstairs. As he entered the room Mercedes got up from her brother's bedside and went out.

"I am a little upset, Arthur," Leon said.

"Are you? What is the matter? you are not feeling worse, I hope?"

"No; it is nothing about myself, it is about Mercedes. You know that three months ago she was betrothed—not formally, you know, but the matter was arranged—to Count Silvio de Mora. It was a suitable match in all respects. He was some fourteen years older than Mercedes, and a worthy cavalier. Of course he asked her hand of me, and I gave my consent, and she offered no more objection than a well-brought-up maiden should do. Now she turns round and tells me that she has resolved not to marry; that after being so near to death and saved as by a miracle, she is resolved to live single. She does not wish to enter a convent or anything of that sort, but at any rate to live single for some years—in fact until I marry, and then she will probably go into a religious house.

"Well, it all seems so unnatural, because she has always had very high spirits and been fond of gaiety. I have asked her to think the matter over, but she declares that nothing can influence her, and implores me to let her have her own

way. I can understand her feelings. Of course, she is
greatly shaken by what she has gone through; I hope though
in time she will recover her spirits. But she has declared
that nothing will move her; and after such a terrible experience as she has had, I feel that at present, at any rate,
I must let her have her own way. I cannot hold a pen yet,
and I shall be greatly obliged if you will write in my name
to the count. The thought of this engagement evidently
preys upon her mind. She says she did not sleep all night,
and I see that she will have no peace until I carry out her
wishes."

"Of course, I will do as you wish, Leon, and will write
from your dictation. It seems to me natural, poor girl,
that she should be terribly shaken by what she has gone
through."

CHAPTER X

A GOOD SERVICE

THE letter took some time to write. It began with an
account of the attack upon the chateau, and the manner in which the count and his servants were struck down
and Donna Mercedes carried off. It then described how Cabrera had sentenced her to be shot, and how, a few hours
before the sentence could be carried out, she was rescued by
Captain Hallett and brought safely to Albacete, where the
count himself was lying wounded.

"My sister is greatly prostrated by the terrible trials that
she has passed through. She considers that she has been
preserved by a miracle, and that she must dedicate her life
to good works. She has expressed to me, my dear count,
her irresistible repugnance to the plans we had formed, and
has implored me to ask you to relieve her from her engagement to you.

"I have argued with her in vain, and I beg of you not to take it amiss that I should ask you to release her. She is profoundly shaken, and will not, I am sure, for a long time be fit to be at the head of an establishment like yours; and, indeed, as I have said, she talks of entering a religious house. I trust, my dear count, that this unfortunate circumstance will not cause any breach in our friendship or the long-established good feeling between our families. With assurances of my deep regret at this severance of a tie to which we had both looked forward, and of my regard and appreciation, I sign myself yours most cordially."

Here Leon took the pen in his own hands and feebly added his signature.

"Between ourselves," he said, "I am not altogether sorry that the engagement is broken off. I have a great esteem for Don Silvio, but I am not sure that he and Mercedes are quite suited to each other. He is somewhat grave and is in the thick of politics, and I fancy that Mercedes has a little resented the small share of attention he has paid her. However, undoubtedly the affair would have gone on in its usual course had it not been for this matter."

Arthur took his departure on the following day. It seemed to him that Donna Mercedes shunned her brother's room while he was there. He thought it natural that she should be embarrassed by the feeling that she owed so much to him, and that, as the letter he had written for Leon showed, she should be profoundly affected by the events through which she had passed. It was, too, natural that she should desire to be alone with her brother, as at present she was without a maid or companion, and would of course wish to act as his nurse. He therefore said good-bye to them in the evening, as he intended to start early.

"I hope I shall see you in the course of a month or so, Leon," he said.

"Yes, I hope so."

"And I trust, Donna Mercedes, that you will be looking

more yourself, and will have shaken off the effects of the trial you have gone through."

The girl put her hand in his, and looked as if she would have spoken, but she was evidently too much moved for words. So he turned and left them.

"I should hardly have thought that she would have felt it so much," he said to himself as he went up to his room; "though, of course, it has been a most terrible trial, what with the anxiety about her brother and herself. However, I hope she will soon shake it off. I know she has plenty of spirit, and nothing could have been more plucky than the way in which she behaved until we were fairly away from her prison. No doubt she feels it more now that it is all over and she has nothing to keep up for. I wonder how the count will take her breaking off the engagement? I am not sorry she has done it. He is extremely courteous and, I suppose, attentive, but he was always formal, and did not seem to me to really care for her. Not that I know anything of such matters; still, I think myself that if I were engaged to an extremely nice girl I should not content myself with pressing the tips of her fingers. However, that may be the Spanish custom. How my cousins would have laughed if I had treated them in such a ceremonious sort of way!"

It was nearly a month before Arthur returned to Madrid, for he was with the Christinos when they were defeated by Cabrera with great loss near Tortosa. He had taken no actual part in the fight, though he had ridden with the Christino general, and as soon as he saw that the battle was lost he rode away.

"It is quite evident, Roper," he said, "that the Christinos do not fight so well as the Carlists. They seem to be plucky, too, but the Carlists fight with greater fury. They have much less discipline, but they hurl themselves upon their foes with such a disregard for death that there is no withstanding them. Now, our fellows beat the Carlists at their own game; they were equally ready to go at the enemy, and had a good deal more discipline. It is evidently useless for us to remain here. Cabrera won't observe the Conventions, and kills every officer who falls into his hands. The Christinos would be quite willing to show mercy, but they don't often get the chance of doing so. We will go up to Madrid and report to Colonel Wylde, who will, I dare say, be back by the time we get there."

"I sha'n't be sorry, sir, for it is not pleasant being with troops who always get licked. It seems to me, sir, that the Carlists are likely to win in the long run."

"I don't think so, Roper. You see, they will never remain long in the field. Their villages are everywhere in the mountains, and they can't be kept together any time, for there is the difficulty of provisions. They rush down, defeat or avoid the Christinos, and collect a considerable amount of spoil, and then go off to their homes again. They are a sort of semi-organized guerillas, and although guerillas can maintain warfare for a long time, they must in the long run be defeated. They have been fortunate in having wonderfully active leaders. They first of all had Zumalacarreguy, and now they have Cabrera, both of whom have the faculty of inspiring their men with an intense enthusiasm and a willingness to endure all hardship. But neither of these generals has succeeded in introducing anything like discipline, and though splendid guerilla chiefs, they are not the men for moulding a whole people into regular soldiers."

Two days after his return to Madrid, Arthur was delighted to see Leon enter his room. He still looked pale and thin, but his expression was bright and cheerful.

"Well, old Paladin," he exclaimed, "here I am, well and getting strong again. We have travelled by easy stages, and taken ten days to come from Albacete."

"That is right. I felt sure that when you had nothing to do but eat and drink you would soon pick up again. And your sister, I hope she has recovered also?"

"Partly, not altogether. I hope she has given up the

idea of becoming a religieuse. It would be a thousand pities if she were to shut herself up in a convent, and I am sure she would bitterly regret it afterwards. She has had a great shock, of course, but the effect will pass off in time. I could see that it was a great relief to her when she received an answer from Don Silvio releasing her from her engagement. It was written in excellent language, and was really irreproachable in tone; but between ourselves I don't think his feelings were very deeply touched. She has certainly picked up faster since she received it. She broke down a good deal when we arrived to-day, and she had her sisters and Donna Martha to cry over and coddle her. I won't ask you to come to us this evening. I think she had better be quiet. What have you been doing since you left us?"

Arthur gave an account of his journeying.

"I am thinking," the count said, "of raising two companies from among the tenants of my estate near Seville. I shall not be happy until I have crossed swords with that fellow Cabrera."

"I can understand that. But, you see, Cabrera is not a fellow to be found so easily; he is here to-day and gone to-morrow; strikes a blow in one place, and then two days afterwards falls upon a column a hundred miles away. I think, Leon, if I were you I would give up the idea. You have everything that one can wish for; you are rich, and popular, and happy in your family. It is all very well for people who want the pay and position of generals to go into the army, but you have nothing to gain by it. And at any rate, as long as your party hold their own against the Carlists, I don't see that you have any business to put on a uniform."

"Every word you say is as applicable to yourself as it is to me. This is no affair of yours. It doesn't matter a snap of the finger to you whether Don Carlos or Christina reigns in Spain."

"That is true enough, but I have got my living to get. I like the life and excitement."

" That is well enough at present, but this war is not going to last for ever."

" No; and if it were, I should not remain out here. I have some years to kill. When that is over, I shall go home and live on my own land."

" Oh, I didn't know you had land; you never told me so."

" No, Leon, I am not given to talk about my own private affairs. I was wild as a boy, and my father thought it was well that I should not come into my fortune until I arrived at years of discretion, and he very wisely tied it up so that I could not touch it until then. I don't mean that I shall ever be a great magnate as you are, but I shall have a very nice estate, which will be all the larger for having waited fifteen years for me."

" I am very glad to hear it, very glad; though it does seem to me very hard that you should be kept so long out of it. Still, I am the last who ought to complain, for if you had not been obliged to become a sort of knight-errant I should have lost my sister."

" Nor have I anything to grumble at, though I do wish I had remained at school a couple of years longer and finished my education."

" Education!" Leon laughed; " you must have done with that long ago."

" I am not so old as I look," Arthur said.

" Well, you look as old as I do, anyhow."

" I am not so old by a good many years. I won't tell you how many, for I don't want to be treated like a little boy."

" I don't think I should do that if you said that you were only ten."

" Well, I can tell you, as a great secret, that I am more than ten."

" Well," Leon said, getting up with a laugh, " now I must be off. Mercedes, who has developed into a regular tyrant, only gave me leave to come out on condition that I would not stop more than five minutes, and if it had been anybody but yourself she would not have let me come at all; not, I think, even if the Queen Regent had sent for me."

"She is quite right, Leon, though I should like to keep you here; but I am sure that after riding in here this morning you ought not to have moved out again. Well, I will walk with you back to your own door."

Arthur, on calling on the following morning, was received with great enthusiasm by Mercedes' two younger sisters, with whom he had become a great favourite, and also by the young count. Mercedes, however, seemed painfully shy with him.

"I don't think I shall ever feel comfortable with you again, señor," she said with a great effort. "I feel quite over-powered with the sense of what I owe you."

"Then, señora, you will oblige me to regret that I ever interfered in your behalf," Arthur said with a smile. "The sooner you get that idea out of your head the sooner I shall feel comfortable again. It was a great pleasure to me to be of service to you, but you will take the pleasure out of it altogether if you are going to be unnatural with me."

"But I can't help it," she said.

"Then I sha'n't rescue you another time when you get into a scrape. Once I picked a young cousin of mine out of the water. The ice was thin, and I had no right to take her on; but as I scarcely ever did what was right I took her, and she went through. Of course I went in after her, and we were both nearly drowned. Well, I did not hear the last of that for a long time; it was always being thrown up in my teeth, till I declared that I would never take a girl out skating again. And now it seems that you are going to make it just as disagreeable for me."

The girl laughed.

"Well, I will really try hard not to. I will tell myself that anyone else would have done just the same as you did, and that there was no danger in it, and that it was altogether a most commonplace affair."

"Good!" he said. "That will make us both much more comfortable."

"And how old was this cousin of yours?"

"Two years younger than I was. That was the last time we had a bit of fun together. My aunt entertained the idea that I was making the girls into regular tomboys, and I don't think they ever went out with me again afterwards. I am afraid I was not so sorry as I ought to have been at losing their society, for I was getting to the evil age when boys think girls rather nuisances."

"And what age may that be, señor?" one of the younger girls asked with a laugh.

"Well, in England I think it begins about fourteen and lasts till about twenty."

"Oh, then we may flatter ourselves that you will not regard us as nuisances."

"No; you are very well-behaved little girls, and you don't expect me to play with you."

"Play with us, indeed!" the girl said scornfully; "I should think not. Why, I am fifteen."

"A very grave and reverent age, señorina. I have not got my hat on, or I would take it off to you in token of my respect, not to say veneration."

"How different you are from Spaniards!" the girl said. "A young Spanish gentleman would lift his hat courteously if he passed us in the street, but, unless he were very, very intimate, would hardly think of speaking to us even in the house, whereas you actually laugh at us and make fun of us. I have to laugh sometimes when I think I ought to be very indignant."

"You should practise looking indignant before a glass, señorina, else I am afraid it would be a failure and I should not be properly impressed. Now, Donna Mercedes," he said, turning to her, "I hope you have found Leon a very good patient."

"He was very good the first fortnight, but after that he

was by no means so easy to manage. I had very often to appeal to Donna Martha, and sometimes he absolutely set her at defiance."

"At any rate he has done credit to your nursing."

Then they settled down for a quiet talk, and Arthur heard how they had at first travelled by very short stages, and had gradually increased the length of the journeys.

"It was very tedious," Leon said, "and I could have come a good deal faster if I had been allowed. And now about yourself: I suppose you came back a fortnight ago?"

"No; I only came back the day before you. I changed my mind and went down to Tortosa, as I heard that a battle was imminent there, and to my disgust I saw the Christinos utterly routed by Cabrera. Fortunately the Carlists were not strong in cavalry; if they had been, the Royalists would have been entirely destroyed."

After chatting for some time longer he took his leave. In half an hour he returned.

"I have just heard very bad news. I can assure you it is very serious. You know that Don Carlos completely defeated General Buerens at Herrera, killing ninety-two officers and inflicting a loss of two thousand six hundred men killed, wounded, and prisoners. Espartero hurried up to rejoin Oraa. The Carlists affected to retreat, but really joined Cabrera, gave Espartero the slip, and are this morning within four leagues of Madrid."

An exclamation of dismay broke from his hearers.

"And we have no troops here!"

"None but the Urban Guards, who have just been called out; but I should say they could not stand an hour before a Carlist attack; and, moreover, there are, as you know, a large number of Carlist sympathizers who will be certain to rise as soon as they attack the walls."

"Then I had better send the ladies off at once," Leon said, rising to his feet; "if they leave the other side of the city they may get away."

"I think it would be safer for them to stay here; the Carlist cavalry may be round the town in a couple of hours. They might be cut off, so that they would certainly be safer here. It is true that Cabrera is with Don Carlos, but he will not be supreme, as the latter would, I am convinced, restrain his cruelty. He would know well enough that nothing could be worse for his cause than for his entry into his capital to be marked by scenes of bloodshed. I think the greatest danger will be from a rising of the mob before the Carlists enter, and I should strongly advise you to arm all your men, to barricade all the windows not protected by bars, and prepare to beat off any assault. The house is very strong and solid, and the mob would hardly be able to capture it in the face of a firm resistance, for we may calculate that Don Carlos will enter the town within an hour at most after any disturbance breaks out here."

"I will have it done at once."

"I would certainly set about it. It is scarcely likely that Don Carlos will be before the town till to-morrow morning, which will give you ample time to make your preparations. How many men have you?"

"With the stablemen and all, I have eighteen."

"That should be sufficient. I will help you to set them to work, and will then go out into the town and bring you in the latest news."

The men were at once collected. Leon sent some of them out to buy some crowbars, and set them to work to get up the paving-stones in the hall and the yard, and with these to block up all the windows on the ground floor. When they had fairly begun Arthur went out, and finding Roper, asked him to saddle the horses; and, having done that, rode out to see the state of things prevailing. The streets were in an uproar. Some of the people appeared almost out of their minds with fear, and the dreaded name of Cabrera was on everyone's lips. A large mob had assembled before the headquarters of government, and with many gestures abused the ministers for leaving the capital undefended. Others among the crowd with difficulty concealed their exultation. Many of the public offices were pelted with stones. A deputation of influential citizens went to the palace and had an interview with Christina, who maintained a firm countenance, and told them that Espartero with his army was following hard on the track of Don Carlos, and that the city would at most have to resist for a few hours.

Presently there was a rush to the walls, and the Carlist cavalry could be seen galloping towards the town. Arthur mounted his horse and, followed by Roper, rode to the gate towards which the horsemen were approaching. A regiment of the Urban Guards was drawn up here. He rode up to the colonel, who was personally known to him. " Colonel," he said, " may I suggest to you that if you were to lead your men outside, they could drive off the Carlist cavalry? They could not stand against infantry, and would probably ride off after a short exchange of shots; and the result would greatly raise the spirits of the townspeople, and perhaps lead them to decide upon their making a resistance. Of course I have not a shadow of authority, but as one of the British commissioners I feel it my duty to point out to you the very great advantage of such a step. I am ready myself to ride out with you and take my share in the fighting."

" I will do it, sir," the colonel answered. " I see the truth of what you say."

He addressed a few words to the men, and then, ordering the gates to be thrown open, marched out leading the regiment, Arthur riding beside him. The cavalry were but four hundred yards away, and as the infantry marched out they formed up in companies and opened fire upon the horsemen. The latter answered in a straggling and undetermined manner, and then in two or three minutes turned and rode off.

" I congratulate you, señor," Arthur said. " I think it is quite probable that you have saved the capital. The troopers will carry back word that the garrison are determined to resist. This is sure to cause hesitation in the councils of Don Carlos, and we may feel certain that at least for to-day nothing will be done, and every hour that passes will bring Espartero nearer to our assistance."

The regiment were enthusiastically cheered as they returned to the city, and they received a great ovation as they entered the Puerto del Sol, the great square of the town. The minister of war himself came down and thanked the colonel, and bestowed upon him the rank of general. The latter generously said that he had acted in accordance with the advice given him by the British commissioner, that he would not have thought of taking the step but for that advice, and that the British officer had ridden out with him. Thereupon Arthur, who had, when he entered the city, gone off to his lodging, was sent for, and received the formal thanks of the minister. This incident seemed to greatly inspirit the defenders; the noisy crowds now dispersed, and preparations for the defence were carried on vigorously.

After leaving the Ministry Arthur went back to aid the count in his preparations. Already a great deal had been done, and by evening the house was placed in a position to make a stout defence against any attack by an undisciplined force.

In the afternoon the count went out for a short time, and on his return said to his sisters: "Young ladies, you will please salute the hidalgo, Captain Arthur Hallett, as the saviour of this city. He told us he had been out through the gate with a regiment that went and fired a few shots at the Carlist cavalry; but it now appears that it was he who advised the officer in command of the regiment to go out, and that he gallantly rode with the colonel at their head, for which service he has been publicly thanked by the minister of war."

"Yes, and I was ashamed of being thanked," Arthur said. "I went to have a look at the Carlist cavalry. Seeing a regiment of infantry at the gate, I suggested to the colonel that it would be a good thing to go out and drive them off, as even a little thing like that would tend to restore confidence; so we went out and fired half a dozen volleys. The Carlists fired a few shots in return and made off. There is the beginning and the end of it."

"At any rate, Arthur, everyone at the club agreed that it has had a great effect in restoring confidence. The crowd demonstrating in front of the various Ministries dispersed. Many of the men who had absented themselves from the muster of their companies have now joined them, and it seems probable that if Don Carlos attacks us to-morrow, which everyone supposes he will do, a stout defence will be made."

"Well, I dare say it may have had that effect, Leon. That is just what I expected when I suggested the move, but it is nonsense to make such a fuss about it; and it was as much as I could do not to laugh in the minister's face when he talked about it as a very valiant business."

"I think, seriously, Arthur, that the affair may have a good deal of consequence. Probably the cavalry were sent on to ascertain the disposition of the town, and see whether it was likely to surrender without a blow; and the fact that this little sortie was made will give the idea that we are prepared for a desperate resistance. Everyone knows that Don Carlos is a man who can never quite make up his mind, and several men at the club agree in thinking that it is quite possible he may march away again without attempting anything."

"If he does, Leon, it will be a death-blow to his own cause. By throwing Espartero off his track, effecting a junction with Cabrera, and marching within striking distance of the capital, he has got an opportunity that he will never have again. He ought to have attacked to-day. The news that he had captured Madrid would have roused his partisans to great enthusiasm, and brought all the doubters over to his side; whereas, if he throws away this opportunity he will disgust the men who have come so far from their homes, will certainly infuriate Cabrera, and will show that he is utterly unfit to be the head of a well-nigh desperate cause."

All night the work of preparation went on. Cannon were got out of the arsenal and mounted in commanding positions. The gates were blocked up with stones, ammunition piled on the walls, and the whole population toiled at making preparations for defence. In the morning every point from which a view over the country could be obtained was thronged in anticipation of seeing the enemy advancing, but to the general delight the plain seemed to be absolutely deserted. Very speedily a party of mounted gentlemen sallied out from one of the gates, and rode out to reconnoitre the country. Arthur went with them. They rode to within two miles of the Carlist camp, but no signs of movement were discernible. They watched for three hours. At the end of that time they saw the royal tent and those around it lowered, and an hour later could make out the whole army drawing off. With exultant shouts they mounted and rode back to the city, where their news excited a wild enthusiasm. The fickle crowd shouted and applauded the ministers as furiously as they had the morning before denounced them. Leon had, to his great disgust, to abandon the idea of joining the party riding out, and had awaited at home the return of Arthur with the news.

"They have gone!" Arthur exclaimed as he ran upstairs.

"Gone?"

"Yes! horse, foot, and baggage."

"Exit Don Carlos!" the count shouted. "Yesterday he literally had the game in his hands, to-day he has thrown it away. There, girls, please each make a curtsy to Don Arthur, he has saved Spain."

"What ridiculous nonsense, Leon!" Arthur said almost angrily.

"It is good sober sense, and not nonsense at all. Don

Carlos had no doubt been assured that he had only to elude the armies in the field, and show himself before Madrid, when the town would open its gates to him, and the authorities come out to surrender the capital. The fact that the troops sallied out and attacked his cavalry has completely overthrown his hopes. I believe that the town would have surrendered without resistance if he had marched straight on yesterday. To-day it would have fought, but it could not have offered any strong resistance. The walls are rotten, and the Carlist cannon would have made a breach in them in no time. In fact, I don't suppose they would have troubled to do that, but would have carried the place by storm. Now the chance has gone, and for ever; for after this fiasco he will never be able to persuade the mountaineers to make this long march again. They may go on fighting for a long time before the thing is over, but we shall never see the Carlist army before Madrid again. Call it a happy inspiration if you like, my friend, but it was a happy inspiration that saved the Christino cause."

An hour later a royal messenger came to the house, saying that on calling at the English officer's lodging he was told that he should probably find him at Count de Balen's, and, that the queen regent desired his attendance at the palace.

"I have led my first and last sortie," Arthur exclaimed in a tone of despair. "As far as I am concerned, the Carlists may occupy Madrid without my moving from my rooms to prevent them. Was there ever such a fuss made over such a ridiculous affair? Still, I suppose I must go."

"Of course you must go," Leon said. "Don't be foolish, Arthur! You can insist on getting off being thanked by Mercedes and me, but there is no getting off being thanked by the queen."

With a shrug of the shoulders Arthur went down-stairs and, mounting his horse, rode by the side of the mounted messenger to the palace. Here he was at once escorted to the apartment of the queen regent. A number of her ministers were gathered there. By her side was the little Queen Isabella, a child of between five and six years old. Her minister of war stepped forward, and taking Arthur's hand, led him up to the two queens.

"Your majesty," he said, "I beg to present to you Captain Arthur Hallett, one of Her Britannic Majesty's commissioners. I have already had the honour to inform you that to him it is due that Colonel, now General de Layer, conceived the idea of leading out on his own responsibility his regiment, which was on guard, against the Carlist cavalry. He accompanied the colonel at the head of his regiment, and they drove off the Carlist cavalry with loss. It is doubtless largely due to that proof of the courage and resolution of her majesty's troops that the Pretender abandoned his idea of attacking the town, and has marched away with his force—a confession of defeat which will undoubtedly have a very desirable effect in establishing your daughter on the throne, by animating your faithful followers throughout the country, and by dispiriting those of Don Carlos."

Queen Christina held out her hand to Arthur, who, not being sure of what was the right thing to do, knelt on one knee and kissed it. "Give this gentleman your hand," the queen said to the child; "he has done you a very, very great service."

The child did as she was told, and said: "Thank you; I think I shall like you very much."

"I am told also, Captain Hallett," Christina said, "that you performed an act of extreme valour which is at present the talk of our court, namely, that you went alone into the camp of Cabrera and effected the rescue, from that ruthless leader, of the sister of Count Leon de Balen, who had been condemned to death by him—an act which in itself stamps you as an officer of the most distinguished bravery. Taking into consideration that act, performed on behalf of a sister of a nobleman of our court, and the service you have now performed for us, I have pleasure in handing you the Cross of the First Class of San Fernando and Knight of Isabella the Catholic."

"I thank your majesty most deeply for the honour you have been pleased to bestow upon me, and which I feel I have done little indeed to deserve."

"That is for my counsellors and for myself to judge, Captain Hallett," she said graciously. "I trust that we shall see you sometimes at our court."

Arthur then retired, the court chamberlain having placed round his neck the sash and insignia of the Order. "I suppose I must wear this thing," he said as he went back, "but it is really too ridiculous. I don't say that the action had not an effect, no doubt it had; but there was nothing in the doing of it."

He had promised Leon to return and tell him what the queen said to him, and he went up to the drawing-room with quite a rueful expression on his face. The girls were still there with their brother, and as he entered with the decoration all clapped their hands.

"It is all very well for you to applaud," he said, "but it makes me feel downright ridiculous. If I had done anything worth doing, I don't say that I should not feel gratified at such an honour, but for merely saying 'Let's come out and fire a few shots' it is absurd."

"It is you that are absurd, Arthur," Leon said, laughing. "Now please tell us exactly what her majesty said. Exactly."

"Well, she said that I had done her great service, and then that she had heard also about my rescue of Donna Mercedes, and that for that service, performed for the sister of a nobleman of her court, and for the service done to herself, she bestowed this honour upon me."

"I am glad," Mercedes said in a tone of delight. "You would not let us thank you, but you have been thanked by Queen Christina. I am pleased more than I can say."

"So am I," Leon said, shaking hands heartily with him.

"It is very good of you to say so, Leon," Arthur said in a depressed tone; "and I don't say that I shouldn't value the honour immensely if I had really done any exceptionally brave thing. Thank goodness! I shall only have to wear this ribbon and star on very special occasions."

"Yes; but you will always have to wear the rosette, you must remember that. In this country you are now the Cavalier Arthur Hallett, with a right of entry to the royal court at all times, and many other privileges, concerning which I will make enquiry and inform you."

Arthur laughed uneasily. "It is all very well for you to joke about it, Leon, but I can assure you that I find it rather a heavy infliction."

"You should not," Leon said earnestly. "It is a real honour, and, let me tell you, a high one; and to us it is a special and very great pleasure that the service you did us has been considered in the bestowal of it upon you."

"Well, I won't grumble any more, and will specially regard it as a souvenir of the service I was enabled to render to your sister, which it will be one of my greatest pleasures to remember all my life."

"That is well spoken," Leon said; "and, like yourself, I can assure you that it is an immense pleasure to us that although we are powerless to show the gratitude we owe you, the action has been recognized by our queen."

"And now, Leon," Arthur said, to turn the conversation, "you have all the work of putting down your pavements again."

"Yes. As I don't think we shall hear Don Carlos knocking at our doors again, I have already set the men to work, and we shall soon have things tidy once more."

"Well now, I will be going, Leon."

"Well, don't forget that you are engaged to dine here today. We shall have quite a gathering to celebrate our return."

CHAPTER XI

A THWARTED PLOT

ESPARTERO marched in on the following day, and after spending three days in resting and refitting his army, started on the 17th of September in pursuit of Don Carlos, and, pressing upon his rear, obtained the welcome news that Cabrera, utterly disgusted with his irresolution, had left him with his command and gone back to the mountains. Colonel Wylde had returned on the day after Espartero arrived.

"I hear you have been doing good service, Captain Hallett," he said, when Arthur called upon him.

"The service was really nothing, sir; it was not worth talking about. Some Carlist cavalry came galloping up against one of the gates, and as there was a regiment of the Urban Guards drawn up there, I advised their colonel to go out and drive them off. He took my advice, and went out and fired two volleys, and the Carlists bolted."

"Yes, I quite admit that the affair was unimportant in itself; but there can be equally no doubt that it had very wide consequences. No doubt Don Carlos sent on his cavalry in hopes that the town would open its gates to him, as we may be sure his partisans had promised to do. When they were so roughly received, he imagined that he had been altogether misinformed, and that he would meet with a desperate resistance. Knowing how close Espartero was behind him, he concluded that he would not be able to capture the place before that general arrived, and so drew off. There can be no doubt that his hesitation at this critical moment has sealed his fate. He will never get the Basques to come down from their mountains again. I am told, also, that you did a very gallant action down in the south, and it was that as well as the affair here that induced Christina to give you the Order of San Fernando and knighthood. I shall have pleasure in recommending to the government at home that you be permitted to accept and wear the decorations, which you could not do at home without such permission."

"I certainly should not want to wear them at home. They may be very useful to me in this country, though indeed I should hardly like to wear them even here, for I have certainly done nothing to deserve such honour. I shall really be glad, sir, if you will send me off again as speedily as possible, for I shall be glad to escape from the congratulations which I shall have to receive if I remain in Madrid."

"Things are likely to be quiet for a time," the colonel said. "Espartero has applied for another army to be raised, but the ministry are so jealous of him that there is little chance that the request will be granted, and he will have to set off in pursuit of Don Carlos with but a small force. At present the real point of interest in Spain is the struggle between Espartero and the government, a body of men utterly incapable and wholly corrupt. Their weakness and unpopularity constitute the greatest danger that threatens the country, now that Don Carlos has retired. I have the honour to be in the confidence of Christina, and she feels deeply the situation in which she is placed by the intrigues and jealousies of these men. Unfortunately she is powerless in their hands, and can only endeavour to keep matters going, and to prevent an open outbreak between the various parties. However, as you want to get away, you may as well go with Espartero; I will introduce you to him to-morrow."

"Thank you very much! I would far rather be moving about than staying here, for I feel that I am drawing my pay and doing very little for it."

The colonel smiled. "It is evident, Hallett, that patience is not one of your virtues. You have just been away for two months, and only returned three days ago. However, I can understand that Madrid has no great attractions for you, and that you prefer being actively employed. I have seen Espartero this morning, and he intends to start again in two days' time, so you will not have long to wait."

Espartero received Arthur warmly when Colonel Wylde presented him on the following day, and spoke strongly of the service he had rendered in getting the regiment to go out and meet the Carlist horse. "I wish," he said, "that I had a few young officers ready to take the initiative. There is no lack of bravery among my troops; they obey orders and fight well, but I have to see to everything myself. Doubtless things will improve in time; and I think that this action of yours may have some influence in showing the officers of the army that opportunities present themselves sometimes, when even the youngest can make their mark. I shall be very glad indeed to have you with me, and I trust that you will consider yourself on my staff."

"Captain Hallett could very well do so," Colonel Wylde said; "the alliance is becoming closer between the two nations. British marines and sailors have been fighting in the north, and it is more than probable that a force of regular troops will be sent from England, only Captain Hallett must recollect that if he takes any active part in an engagement he forfeits his privileges as a British commissioner, and will certainly if captured be treated as a prisoner of war."

"I am quite ready to risk that, sir," Arthur said.

"Yes; but you must bear in mind that I must at any moment be able to recall you if I need your services elsewhere."

"Certainly, sir; I shall always hold myself at your orders."

Loud regrets were expressed by Leon and his sisters when they heard that their friend was leaving them so soon.

"You can do us good service here, Leon, if you choose."

"How do you mean?"

"Well, it is clear enough that the ministry, divided as they are on all other points, are united in their jealousy of Espartero, who seems to me the one honest and capable man in Spain. Now, if you would endeavour to get up a party to support him, and to move public opinion so strongly in his favour that they will compel the ministry either to give him adequate support or expose themselves to be kicked out, you will be doing a great service to the country. You saw yourself the condition of his force when they marched in yesterday, utterly worn out and fatigued, almost in rags—deficient in everything that makes up an army. If you speak of this on all occasions, stir up feeling among men of your own class, denounce the government for refusing to supply him with the men and means to carry on the war on a proper scale, you will be doing an immense amount of good."

"I will do so; I will become a conspirator. I thoroughly agree with you as to Espartero, and will really devote myself to supporting him. Henceforth I will become a public man, and make government tremble;" and he struck his breast theatrically. His sisters and Arthur all broke into a laugh. "Seriously, I will devote myself to the business, Arthur. I have felt for some time that I ought to be doing something for my country. I know nothing of soldiering, and cannot very well ask for a musket and go out and fight; but I do think I could be doing some good in working for the downfall of this government, for which no one but its hangers-on and followers have a good word to say. I will begin by speaking indignantly of the state of Espartero's army, and directly he openly breaks with government I will work heart and soul to second his efforts."

"Don't be in too much of a hurry, Leon; you know that men who have spoken out too loudly have been either sent to their estates or imprisoned. Begin at first by declaring that the state of the army is disgraceful; do not attack the government until Espartero himself takes the field against them. When he once does so, I am convinced that the dissatisfaction that exists will find a voice, and that the government will not dare to set themselves against it."

Two days afterwards Arthur and his follower started with Espartero. Four days later they found that Don Carlos was only three leagues in advance; and believing that his force were resting for the day, Espartero at once moved forward. But he was ignorant of the nature of the country; had he been aware of it, he could have caught them in a trap, and Don Carlos himself would have fallen into his hands. Unfortunately, as he had to feel his way down a steep defile, the Carlists discovered his approach and retired precipitately. On the 28th it was found that Don Carlos had been joined by another division, but Espartero had also been strengthened. He therefore divided his army into two corps, one commanded by General Lorenzo with fourteen battalions, while he retained the command of the other and larger division. A few days later the former force was attacked suddenly by a superior Carlist army. It defended itself with great obstinacy.

Espartero started instantly when he heard the sound of the firing, and arrived in time to save Lorenzo, and attacking the left and centre of the Carlist force, sent them flying in disorder. He was, however, unable to follow up his victory, being forced to await the arrival of some convoys of clothing and provisions. These arrived two days later, and pressing forward he picked up many deserters from the Carlist ranks. These all declared that discord and confusion raged in the Carlist army, and that the Basques and Navarrese had declared their determination to return to their provinces whether Don Carlos was willing or not. In the course of two or three days their army broke up altogether, crossing the Ebro at various points under their respective chiefs, and making their way off to the mountains. Espartero devoted the remainder of the year to organizing transport and supply, and punishing acts of indiscipline and insubordination that had broken out at various places.

As soon as the operations ceased Colonel Wylde wrote to Arthur requesting him to go down to join General Flinter, an English officer in the service of Spain, who was about to be sent down to Toledo at the request of the deputies of

Estremadura. He at once left Espartero and rode to Toledo, where he arrived on the same day as General Flinter.

"Colonel Wylde told me that he had sent you to join me, Captain Hallett, and spoke very highly of your energy and courage. I shall be very glad to have your assistance. This place is a nest of Carlism. Their central Junta is here, and although at the present moment I cannot take any steps against them while they remain quiet, it will not be very long before I shall be able to do so."

Arthur took up his quarters at the same hotel as the general, and for the next fortnight aided him in restoring discipline and order among the troops, who had been in garrison there for some time, and had fallen into a slack state. At the end of that time news was brought that a Carlist force under Basilio Garcia was approaching on a raiding expedition, and Flinter persuaded the authorities of the town to join him in declaring it in a state of siege.

"Now," he said, "I may be able to lay hands on some of these Carlist fellows, if I can but obtain evidence against them. There is no doubt that among them are some of the leading men of the province, and I am afraid that, even if I catch them, they will slip through my fingers. The government at Madrid are, as you know, very hostile to the English. Sir George Villiers, our minister, is constantly urging them to support Espartero, and is in close communication with that general, therefore they are opposed to us all. It was only because they did not see how they could refuse the request of the deputies of Estremadura that I was allowed to come here. You may be sure that, what with the personal objections of ministers to me, and the fact that these men are all wealthy enough to bribe right and left, they will take no action against them, however clear the evidence I may be able to bring forward. Still, that makes no difference in my duty, and I shall certainly lay hands on them if I can obtain anything like certain evidence."

"Who is considered the principal?"

"The Duke de Ladra."

"It is at his house they are likely to meet, I suppose?"

"Yes, I should say so."

"I will set my man to work; he is a sharp fellow, and he may be able to find out something about these meetings."

Roper had had his time entirely on his hands since their arrival at Toledo, and, being of a chatty disposition, had already made a great many acquaintances. He was a good-looking young fellow, and his scarlet uniform opened the doors of a good many houses to him.

"Roper," Arthur said to him that evening, "I know that you are constantly getting up flirtations wherever you go."

"Well, sir," Roper said, "I must do something, and sometimes it has been hard work to kill time. Did you say that for any particular reason?"

"Yes. Do you happen to know anyone in the household of the Duke de Ladra?"

"Well, yes, sir; I do know a young woman there. She went with me to a festa yesterday evening."

"Well, I wish you could find out in some way when any meetings of leading men of the place are held there, and whether they meet on any particular day."

"I know that there was a meeting last night, sir, because she said it was what she called a men's evening, and therefore she could get out."

"Well, when you see her again, Roper, you might perhaps find out when the next meeting will take place by asking her when she can come out next."

"I can manage that easily enough, sir," and he looked enquiringly at his master.

"I want to be present at it, Roper."

"You do, sir?"

"Yes. These men are Carlist conspirators. We cannot seize them without some evidence against them, and if I could only overhear their talk we should be able to lay hands upon them."

"That would not be easy, sir."

"No; I quite see that. But don't you think that if you were to say that you know a cavalero who is very anxious to be present at one of these meetings, and would willingly pay ten golden pieces to anyone who would smuggle him up a back stair to a point where he could see what goes on, she would be likely to accept the money?"

"I can't tell you, sir. Teh pounds is a large sum to one of these servants, who don't get more than two or three pounds a year. I should tell her, of course, that it would never be known who had admitted you, and you would take an oath not to betray her if anything happened. Possibly she might consent; at any rate I could sound her carefully. It would be quite a marriage dot to her; but it would be a dangerous business for you, sir, if you were caught."

"Yes; but when everything was arranged I should get General Flinter to send down a body of troops under an officer to surround the house, with a warrant for the arrest of all persons found within it. If I were discovered I should at once fire a pistol, and that would be the signal for the officer to rush in with the soldiers, and run up-stairs to the room. As soon as they heard the noise, they would cease attacking me. You might possibly be up there with me. If so, I think we could certainly rely upon holding our own against a dozen conspirators for three or four minutes."

"Yes, I should say so, sir. Half of them are likely to be oldish men, and would be so surprised and confounded at seeing us that they would lose some time before making the attack."

Two days later Roper brought news that he had met the young woman again; she was not unwilling to help, but that she held out for twenty pounds; that the meetings were held once a week, and that there was likely to be another in four days. "She is to meet me again to-morrow evening. I am to tell her whether you are willing to pay twenty pounds, and to hand it to her when she lets us in."

"Yes, I will pay that. It is worth it; for if these fellows organize a rising in the town at the same time as the Carlists attack it, we shall be in a very bad way. When you see her to-morrow, I will tell the general."

On the next evening Roper brought news that everything was arranged, and that they were to be at a certain back door of the duke's mansion at nine o'clock on the following Thursday.

Arthur then went in and told the general.

"It is a capital plan, Captain Hallett, and I am deeply indebted to you; at the same time, it is a dangerous one as far as you are concerned."

"I don't think there is much danger in it, sir. In the first place, we are not likely to be discovered, and if we are, my man and I can defend ourselves till the troops come up."

"Well, if you are ready to take the risk there is no question that the scheme is an advantageous one, and will remove a very serious danger. I will, on the morning of Thursday, draw up an order for the arrest of all persons found at the duke's, and will, soon after nine, myself bring down a hundred picked men. You may be sure that if I hear a pistol-shot I shall instantly demand admittance, and rush up to your assistance. You had better get me information as to the precise position of the room, so that we may be able to make straight for it, and not waste time in entering other rooms."

The preparations all worked smoothly. At six o'clock in the evening there was a meeting of deputies and the warrants for arrest were signed, and a few minutes before nine Arthur and Roper, both wrapped up in cloaks, and carrying pistols as well as swords, went round to a door that the woman had shown to the latter. Roper knocked three times, and the door was opened. They entered, and Arthur handed to the woman the money he had promised her.

"You follow me very quietly," she said. "There is no fear of our meeting anyone, these stairs are never used after dark. I will take you to the room, but you must arrange about your own hiding-place. Mind your promise that, whatever happens, you will not betray me."

"Do not be afraid," Arthur said, "we will keep good faith with you."

Going up very cautiously in the dark, they came presently to a small landing. "This is the door," she said. "I believe they have all arrived, and will come here in a few minutes."

She opened the door carefully and looked in. "Those curtains are the best hiding-place," she said, pointing to some drawn across the window. "I don't think there is any chance that they will move them."

She closed the door behind them, and they walked across to the window and took their places behind the curtains. It was a room of considerable size. A table stood in the middle, and at this twelve chairs were placed, with writing materials before each. They talked together in a low whisper.

"If a row takes place we will both run to the corner to the left. In that way only two persons can attack us at once, and as they will probably have nothing but knives about them, we ought to be able to keep them off easily enough."

Presently the door opened, and twelve gentlemen entered. The last to come in turned the key in the door, and one of them went to the door by which Arthur had entered and locked that also; then they sat down and began to talk. They were, as the general had thought probable, arranging a plan by which parties of men should seize the various gates. They were to wait till the major part of the troops had issued out to meet the Carlists, and then the bands were to fall upon those that remained. Each of those present gave in a list of the number of followers and friends he could answer for. The total amounted to about six hundred, but they agreed that this number would probably be multiplied by four, as it was certain that a large number of the lower class of the town would join them, though it would not be prudent to take them into the plot till the moment for action arrived.

Arthur had heard enough, and he was sure that by this time the house would be surrounded and the general ready to enter. He whispered to Roper to be ready, and then, turning round, thrust his pistol through the window and pulled the trigger. Then, as the people at the table sprang to their feet, he and Roper leapt out and took their places in the corner, Arthur saying: "You had better surrender, gentlemen! The house is surrounded, and there are no means of escape."

Several of the younger men drew their knives, but shrank back as Arthur and his follower dropped their cloaks, drew their swords, and levelled their pistols. "You will only be throwing away your lives," Arthur said sternly. "Armed as we are, we are a match for the whole of you. Listen! you can hear blows on the door below."

There was indeed a sound of loud knocking, which suddenly ceased. The conspirators spoke hastily together. One man ran to the table and caught up some of the papers, but Arthur fired at his hand. Almost immediately afterwards there was a loud knocking at the door. Shrugging his shoulders, the duke walked to it and turned the key. The general, followed by a dozen soldiers, entered. "Duke de Ladra," he said, "you are my prisoner, together with all in this room. I hold a warrant of arrest against the whole of you, on a charge of treason against the queen and government."

"I have no power to resist you, sir," the duke said, "but you will repent this outrage."

"I think not, duke. The town being in a state of siege, I have full authority to act as I have done. But the warrant is also signed by ten of the deputies of Estremadura. Now, gentlemen, I do not wish to use violence. I will allow

you all to take your hats and cloaks, and must then march
you to a place of detention. · The matter will then be looked
into, and you will be tried by court-martial."

The duke bowed coldly. "Gentlemen," he said to his
friends, "for the present we must yield to force. We shall
doubtless have a reckoning with this gentleman later on."

Quietly they walked downstairs. The general directed
four soldiers to remain with Arthur until he returned. He
marched the prisoners to the jail and placed a strong guard
over them, and then returned to the house.

"Your plan has worked splendidly," he said to Arthur,
"and it has been managed without bloodshed."

"Altogether, except that I had to put a bullet through the
hand of one of them, who was about to destroy those papers
—they are lists of the number of men that each bound himself to produce when the rising took place."

"And you heard all that was said?"

"Yes;" and he related the conversation which he had
overheard. The room was then searched carefully, and a
number of papers and letters to friends throughout the country were discovered, showing that preparations had been
made for a very formidable rising throughout the province
directly Toledo fell into the hands of the Carlists.

"It is well that we nipped the thing in the bud," General
Flinter said when he examined the papers, which were carried for that purpose to his rooms. "Now, I dare say you
think that these men will all be executed; you were never
more mistaken. We shall try them by court-martial and
condemn them to death: the government will smother the
whole thing up and release them."

"Impossible!"

"It is not only possible, but certain. These men are all
playing a double game. In the first place, they wish to keep
well with both sides; in the second place, they hate me, first
as an Englishman, and secondly as a strong adherent of
Espartero; in the third place, these men will bribe the gov-

ernment largely, and money will do anything in Spain.
However, one good thing will come of the discovery of the
plot: it will excite immense alarm among all connected with
it. Many, when they hear of the seizure of these compromis-
ing letters, will move away from their homes at once until
they think that the storm has passed over, or keep quiet,
and instead of having the whole country in a flame we shall
only have Basilio's force to deal with."

Two days later the court-martial was held, the general and
his officers sitting upon it. Arthur and Roper both repeated
what they had heard; the lists of men that would be supplied, and the work for which they were to be told off, were
brought forward, together with some arrangements that had
been made between the duke and Basilio; and the prisoners
were found guilty and condemned to death. The proceedings of the court-martial and the sentences were sent off to
Madrid for confirmation by the government.

"Now, that is off our hands," the general said to Arthur
when the tribunal broke up, "and we can turn our attention to Basilio without any fear of leaving the city un-
guarded."

Two days later, however, a messenger arrived post-haste
from Madrid saying that the proceedings had been most
high-handed, and that the prisoners were merely to be kept
in confinement for the present. At the same time half of
General Flinter's little force was at once to march for the
capital.

"What did I tell you?" the general said, as he threw the
order across the table to Arthur. "What do you think of
that for a government?"

"If I had my way, I should like to march to Madrid, seize
the whole of those scoundrels, and hang them from their
own balconies."

"Well, I have nothing to do but obey orders; but if they
think they have prepared the way for the Carlists to enter
Toledo they are greatly mistaken. I shall obey the order

and send off the troops. I shall refrain from executing these traitors; but I shall not let that part of the order be known, and so shall keep their friends throughout the country on thorns."

The conspirators, indeed, had taken advantage of the laxity of the prison arrangements to send off large sums of money to members of the government to endeavour to procure the removal of General Flinter. The government journals prepared the way by violent abuse of the general, who had maltreated harmless men, and was a brutal Englishman; and in a few days orders were issued for his removal. The Carlists, who were kept well informed of what was going on, approached Toledo and actually obtained possession of the bridge, but Flinter was still there, although he had received the notice of his removal. He had but three hundred men under his command, but with these he sallied out and, after hard fighting, drove the enemy off. He started in pursuit, and received some reinforcements as he went, and being perfectly well acquainted with the country he was enabled to continue his march all night. In the morning he came upon a large body of Carlists, and, taking them completely by surprise, fell upon them and utterly routed them.

No more brilliant act had been performed during the war. The government in vain endeavoured to belittle it, but the people were not to be deceived, and by them Flinter's victory was regarded at its true value. They pronounced so strongly in favour of him that the government was reluctantly obliged to yield, made him a Marshal de Campo, and placed him in charge of the provinces of La Mancha and Toledo. The action had a great effect upon the course of the war in Estremadura. It completely disorganized the Carlists among the mountains of Toledo, set free an important province, and robbed the enemy of a base for the operations which they had arranged should take place there during the approaching season.

Arthur had ridden out with the general to the attack of

the party who had occupied the bridge, and took part in the night march and in the concluding victory, and the general in his report spoke very highly of his courage and services, and, moreover, gave him full credit for the discovery of the plot and capture of the plotters. The government complained both to Sir George Villiers and Colonel Wylde of the share he had taken in the operations, but both replied that British officers were perfectly at liberty to take part in operations that would strengthen the Royal cause, and that the government were only too glad of the assistance of British seamen and marines in the operations in the north.

The government then endeavoured to sow dissension between Espartero and Cordova. The latter had now left the army and returned to Madrid, where he had entered the Cortes. But Cordova remained firm, and refused to be brought into these intrigues. They further endeavoured to annoy Espartero by displacing the chief of his staff, in whom he had implicit trust, without consulting him.

Arthur had, after the defeat of the Carlists by General Flinter, returned to Madrid and gone to join Espartero, who on the 28th of January arrived at Villa Nueva de Mena and found the enemy strongly posted and entrenched on the right bank of the river Cadagua. On the morning of the 30th he attacked them in three columns under a heavy fire, and after hard fighting succeeded in driving them from four villages they had occupied.

They fell back to a still stronger position in the rear, but from this they were also driven, and by one o'clock they were in disorderly retreat; but owing to the difficult country no pursuit was attempted that day. The next morning Espartero moved with eight battalions to Berron, Iriarte going to the right with four battalions. After marching half a league he found the enemy strongly entrenched, but they retreated, on his approach, to the fortified convent of Santa Isabel, where they had the support of two Biscayan regiments and four battalions of Navarrese, and occupied the

formidable heights in heavy masses. As soon as Iriarte's
column became engaged with the Carlist left, Espartero attacked the position of Santa Isabel, and in spite of a very
heavy fire with which he was met, carried it with a rush and
advanced against the heights, on which the chief force of the
enemy was posted.

Here an obstinate resistance was made; but before dark
the Carlists had been dislodged at the point of the bayonet,
and were in full retreat into the mountains. The Christinos
remained near Berron to protect the evacuation of Balma-
seda. This place was at such a distance from the base that
it was considered impracticable to hold it, as its supply of
provisions could only be kept up by means of large escorts
and at considerable loss of life. It was therefore decided to
blow up the fort and withdraw the garrison, strengthening,
however, the fort at Villa Nueva de Mena, which now became the most advanced post of the Christinos. This was
left in charge of General Latré, Espartero returning to
Logroño.

In the meantime, however, matters were going badly elsewhere. The fortresses of Morella and Benicarlo had just
fallen into Cabrera's hands, and Oraa, who was opposing
him, was calling loudly for reinforcements. Basilio Garcia
was plundering Castile. Espartero, now sickened by the
abuse which had been poured upon him by the orders of the
government at Madrid, determined to match himself against
them, and issued a proclamation giving an account of the
state of the army, the sufferings of the soldiers—who were
without pay, and often without food—and the contempt with
which the government, while wringing money in every manner from the country, turned a deaf ear to all his requests
and left the army to starve. This proclamation had an immense effect throughout the country. The people had been
so sedulously taught to believe that everything was going on
well, that the troops were well fed and regularly paid, that
this exposition by the general whom all trusted and believed

came like a thunderclap, and eventually brought about the downfall of the ministry.

From this moment they felt that Espartero was their master, and, although still putting many difficulties in his way, did not venture openly to oppose him. Espartero's next movement of any consequence was in connection with a Carlist expedition under Negri, which had been despatched with the intention of wasting the hitherto unmolested provinces of Galicia and the Asturias. It was extremely important that this expedition should be crushed; because if the Carlists were permitted to lay waste these provinces, which were both rich and well-affected to the Christino cause, there would be so great a falling off in the contributions that it would be difficult in the extreme to maintain the armies in the field. Espartero set out with nine battalions and fourteen guns, but without cavalry, while General Latré, who was to follow him by a separate route, had also nine battalions. He was in total ignorance of the movements of Negri, who entered Castile on the 15th of March at Soucillo, but he discovered on the 24th that he had gone into the Asturias. Latré came up with him on the 21st, and, although inferior in force, had the advantage. Espartero marched on Leon to prevent their entering Galicia or uniting with Don Basilio. Under a good leader the men had confidence. The Christinos were capable of very long marches, and on this occasion they travelled two hundred miles in nine days, and a short time afterwards marched ninety-two leagues in fourteen days.

While they were doing this good service, Iriarte, with a division twice as strong as that of Negri, was resting quietly at Alcobendas with the apparent intention only of avoiding the enemy. Had the Carlists remained in the Asturias after their defeat by Latré, they would have found great difficulty in escaping from the united action of that general and Espartero; but on hearing of Espartero's movement on Leon they countermarched, and on the 27th of March were at Belorado, with Latré's division—now under Iriarte—a day's march in their rear. Espartero had also returned by forced marches to Palencia, and reckoned on finding himself, after two or three short marches, in front of the enemy, with Iriarte only a short distance in the rear; but on the night of the 30th of March he received a despatch saying that another Carlist expedition had passed into Castile. This, like much of the information he obtained, turned out to be untrue, but it compelled him to march in that direction, leaving the pursuit of Negri to Iriarte.

CHAPTER XII

A FIASCO

WHILE Espartero was waiting for news that Negri was approaching, he learned that Iriarte had inflicted a check upon the Carlist leader, and that the latter had again countermarched. He at once concluded that the Carlists would make for the Sierra de Burgos, and marching with all speed in that direction, at one o'clock on the morning of the 22nd instant he came within sight of their camp-fires. They retreated, and he did not overtake them for some time. Espartero, with his staff, a few mounted officers, and a little escort of forty cavalry of the guard and twenty-five English lancers, had pressed on ahead of his troops, and fearing that the enemy would outmarch his men and get away, placed himself at the head of the little party and charged furiously down upon them.

Taken wholly by surprise at this sudden attack, and not knowing what force he had at his back, two thousand men surrendered to him without resistance. There was a scene of wild enthusiasm among the troops when they came up and saw what had been effected. It was little wonder, indeed, that Espartero's troops were so devoted to him, so ready to make any exertion when called upon to do so, and to attack any force of the enemy against whom they might be directed. Espartero possessed, indeed, all the attributes required of a great general—quick in decision, prompt in action, firm under disappointment, ready to delay until the right moment arrived for striking, or to hurl his troops impetuously at any point required; taking the greatest care for the comfort of his men, able to bear calmly the factious opposition of political antagonists, and to be patient under the repeated blunders or obstinate lethargy of the military commanders serving under him. A great and strong man in every way, the only really great man that Spain has produced for the past two centuries.

The enthusiasm excited by this daring action greatly strengthened Espartero's hold upon the people in general. The destruction of Negri's expedition was complete, for, in addition to those who had fallen in battle or who had been taken prisoners, no fewer than two thousand had deserted during the pursuit by Iriarte, or had, after being captured, consented to join the queen's service.

"It was worth while to take part in this affair, Roper. One might live a century and not have a chance of being one of seventy or eighty men who had charged an army of two thousand and took them all prisoners. It does one good to serve under such men as Espartero and General Flinter."

"That it does, sir; they are both splendid fellows and no mistake. It seems to me that the Carlists are fools to go on with this war; they are always on the run. I don't say that they don't fight bravely sometimes, but they must have lost all real hope of success. Everyone says they are sick of Don Carlos."

"Yes; he is the last sort of man with whom brave people could have any sympathy. He is surrounded by mere adventurers, holds himself entirely aloof from his own generals, and treats them as haughtily as if he were a king who could bestow all honours and rewards. I should think that they are no longer really fighting to put him on the throne. The northern provinces are still holding out for their privileges. As to Valencia and Aragon, I should say that they are fighting from sheer obstinacy. I do not see what they have to hope for. They have been struggling for four years, and so far have certainly held their own, thanks to the energy of Cabrera; but there must be an end to it sooner or later, when they will find that they have gained nothing by all their losses and sacrifices."

Espartero moved up to Vittoria, and in June laid siege to the fortified town of Alava, on the high road from Vittoria to Pena-Cerrada. This town had been taken by the Carlists ten months previously, and these had placed a strong garrison in it. He arrived in front of the town on the morning of 19th June, and was immediately attacked on the left by six Carlist battalions under Guergue. Fighting went on all day. During the night some heavy guns were placed on a battery against a strong stone redoubt. This had been lately constructed by the Carlists on a hill to the north of the town, which it completely commanded. The distance was found, however, to be too great, and in the morning Espartero, observing that his skirmishers had been allowed to approach close to the fort, determined to carry it by storm. He at once launched his troops against it. The fort was gallantly defended—grenades, stones, and other missiles were hurled on the attacking party; but numbers and enthusiasm prevailed. Espartero was looking on, and his soldiers, feeling themselves invincible, finally swarmed over the parapets, and the fort surrendered.

The town was now summoned to surrender. It had been abandoned by the governor, who left a garrison of only four hundred men to defend it. These fired upon the bearer of the message, and on the following morning the guns opened upon them. The firing lasted from seven in the morning till two in the afternoon. Many of the houses were demolished, but the losses of the besiegers were heavy, for they were all this time exposed to a serious attack on the left, led by Guergue's force, which had been reinforced during the morning by four battalions from Navarre. Espartero therefore decided upon another dashing step. Leaving half his force to continue the bombardment of the town, he formed the rest into four battalions, and with this force and his cavalry he attacked Guergue, who was strongly entrenched on a wooded height, supported by four guns. As the Christinos entered the wood they were exposed to a very destructive fire from the Navarre battalions, but advanced steadily without firing a shot. As they pushed forward, a hail of round shot, grape, and musketry swept them at a distance of three hundred yards; but they crossed a small ravine and fell upon the enemy, while Espartero launched his cavalry against the Carlist column that was opposed to him. This abandoned its artillery, and broke and fled in all directions.

The battle had lasted but half an hour. In that time the four guns and four hundred prisoners fell into the hands of the queen's troops, and a far larger number would have been taken had their escape not been facilitated by the intricate mountainous country. As soon as the defenders of the town saw that the force on which they had relied for protection was defeated, they abandoned the place and made their escape into the woods behind. A garrison was placed in the town, and the army proceeded to Logroño and prepared for the siege of Estella, and while doing so had a successful engagement with the Carlist commander-in-chief.

Colonel Wylde had joined Espartero a day or two after the capture of Pena-Cerrada, and he at once sent Arthur south to join the force with which Oraa was preparing to besiege Morella. Here he found three other English officers, commissioners of the British government, who were to report the doings of the army, and above all to urge that the Convention regarding the treatment of prisoners should be observed. Morella was a town of great natural strength. **It** lay in the very heart of the mountains, was built on rising ground, and defended by twenty guns. This town and Canta-Vieja, some twelve miles distant, formed the head-quarters of Cabrera, whose force amounted to a little over ten thousand men. Oraa had his head-quarters at Teruel, and believed that the Carlist troops would not venture to defend Morella.

Cabrera's troops differed materially from those against whom Espartero was fighting. The latter were peasants, animated by a desperate determination to defend what they considered their rights and privileges; the others were rough, idle fellows, fugitives from justice, men who preferred a life of adventure and a chance of plunder to work, but the iron discipline maintained by their leader welded them into a whole, and inspired them with vigour and bravery. Cabrera was in his way as remarkable a military genius as Espartero; but while one carried on war mercifully, the other tarnished his reputation by countless acts of cruelty and cold-blooded murder.

The force was arranged in three divisions, and the advance was planned so that all should arrive at the same time in the neighbourhood of Morella. On the 24th of July Oraa left Teruel, and was joined on the 28th by General Baltho's division, and on the following day by San Miguel. On the 8th of August he was immediately in front of Morella. The united force amounted to sixteen thousand infantry and twelve thousand cavalry. Matters began badly. Oraa was well aware that his supply of provisions was a scanty one, and yet he allowed the waste of a store of grain that would have supplied the army for some time. The wheat had been cut, but was lying in the fields, and instead of having it collected and placed under cover, he permitted the troops to take the corn to sleep on and feed their horses. Much of it was used as fuel, and all that was not consumed was spoiled, and yet there were mills on the ground and also ovens. But even from the commencement of the march, the commissariat arrangements for the troops were anything but lavish.

When the force left Teruel they were supplied with four days' bread and seven days' rice. No meat was issued to them for six days, and then they only received half a pound a man; and yet during the march the troops were ascending to high ground, the rain fell in torrents, and the temperature was much lower than that to which they were accustomed. By the 13th of August the allowance fell to six ounces of rice and two ounces of bread; and on the 17th, the last day of the siege, the troops were almost without food. The cavalry horses and other animals, numbering at least three thousand, had already been two days without forage, and had had no barley since they started, twenty-four days before. The other divisions were no better off. Even these scanty supplies had been maintained with the greatest difficulty. Five battalions had to be employed in keeping the road open. The siege artillery should have been brought up in two days, but seven were found necessary. The army being assembled moved round to the other side of Morella, having to fight hard to gain the position.

San Miguel's division did not bring up their guns till the 9th of August, the operation being conducted so carelessly that the road was left open for the Carlists, who kept up a constant fire and killed one hundred and fifty men. On the 10th the siege began. The troops took up their position, and drove a portion of the Carlist levies back on Morella. Next day, however, San Miguel was ordered to make an attack upon a position occupied by the Carlists, which interfered with the movements of a body of troops about to proceed down to escort a convoy of provisions. Cabrera reinforced the threatened point. San Miguel attacked boldly, and carried three positions one after another; at the fourth, however, he was so strongly opposed that Oraa ordered him to retreat, as he did not consider the position of sufficient importance to justify further fighting. The attack, however,

was so far successful that the force sent to escort the convoy managed to make its way down.

On the 12th the heavy artillery was taken to the places
fixed upon for the establishment of the batteries. The guns
were placed about five hundred yards away from the walls,
the mortars twice that distance. The next day was devoted
to erecting the batteries, and these opened fire at daybreak
on the 14th of August. The shooting was far from accurate, and the enemy's return was steady. The spot selected
to be breached was a gate between and flanked by two tow-
ers, known as the gate of San Miguel. Directly Cabrera saw
the point about to be attacked, he began to construct a strong
retrenchment behind it, with a parapet and ditch, defended
by *chevaux-de-frise;* and the following day, when the breach
began to be formed, he heaped up on it a great quantity of
combustibles. Although the breach was very imperfect, Oraa
issued orders for an assault on the evening of the 15th. To
the English officers with the besiegers it looked like an act of
madness, but Oraa felt that success must be instant, or the
siege must be given up on account of the impossibility of
feeding the troops.

The attacking columns were formed in rear of the batteries, where they remained for three hours, and then advanced, with bands playing, to go within a hundred and fifty
yards of the breach. The broken nature of the ground threw
them into confusion. It was midnight before they arrived
at the breach, and up to this time dead silence had reigned
in Morella. By the music, if by no other means, the garrison
were kept perfectly informed of the motion and progress of
their enemies, but Cabrera had issued strict orders that they
should remain silent until the troops had reached the foot
of the breach.

The moment they arrived there a brilliant flame darted
up from the breach, and a tremendous fire of bullets, hand-
grenades, and stones burst upon them. The red glare rose
higher and higher, and the men, enfeebled by hunger and

fatigue, stood appalled.· Many, however, rushed forward
with desperate bravery, only to fall under the storm of missiles; and at last they fell back, finding it absolutely impossible to surmount the obstacles posted there. Never were
men sent upon a more hopeless task.

That evening the earnestly-looked-for convoy arrived. It
had had to fight the whole distance up. Half the waggons
had been lost and over eighty men. The next day passed
quietly, and then it was decided to make another assault at
daybreak on the 17th, although no attempt had been made
to enlarge the breach or render it more practicable.

Fifteen hundred men advanced at daybreak in two columns, provided with ladders and sand-bags with which to
climb the bottom of the breach, where the wall had not been
destroyed. As they advanced they were received with a
heavy fire of artillery and musketry; the fire again blazed up
on the breach. The left column, on reaching the foot of the
wall and climbing the ladders, found them too short, and fell
back in great disorder. The right column in front of the
breach found it impossible to ascend unassisted, and the
space was too confined to admit of the formation of any
number of troops. At only one place, and this very narrow
and steep, was it possible to climb, and many officers and
men who tried to make their way up died in the attempt.

Seeing the absolute hopelessness of the attack, Oraa ordered a retreat, and the troops fell back, having lost two hundred and seventy-six killed and wounded. It was at once
decided to raise the siege. Without provisions or ammunition it would have been madness to persevere. The retreat
was accompanied by terrible hardships. Thr ɪ were continuously harassed by swarms of guerillas; the marches were slow
and short; the wounded were carried in hundreds on doors
and window-shutters; and when, five days later, the army
reached Alcaniz, it was found that it brought down fifteen
hundred wounded in addition to the dead left behind.

Arthur had not been present at the two assaults. He had

ridden down with the troops that left on the 12th, and when these were attacked had, at the request of the officer in command, ridden up to a small tower where twenty men were posted to keep down the fire of the surrounding Carlists. They were to have been drawn off as the troops passed, but the Carlists interposed in such great force between them and the main body that it was impossible for them to sally out.

"There is nothing to do," Arthur said to the officer in command of the little party, "but to defend ourselves here. They may leave us alone. Pardenas will be back with the convoy to-morrow, and then we shall be relieved."

"It is a pity that you did not bring your horse with you, sir; you might then have managed to escape."

"I certainly should not have left you in the lurch. I did not bring the horses with me because I knew that, as our pace would be very slow, it would be easier to go on foot. Now, we had better set to work at once; as soon as the Carlists have finished with the convoy they will come back to us."

The place was an old fortified house, now almost a ruin. Stones were piled in the doorway, and all prepared for a desperate defence. It was not long before parties of Carlists drew off from those harassing the column and approached the house. They shouted to the soldiers to surrender, but these replied with musket shots. When some two hundred men had assembled round the place the assault began. The men defended themselves bravely, and many of the assailants fell, and all drew off several times. When darkness came on, however, they crawled up to the house and set to work to pull down the barricade at the entrance. The defenders went up to the top of the house and dropped stones down upon them. For some time the fight went on, but gradually the stones of the barricade were dislodged, and a storm of fire drove away its defenders. The officer in command had fallen, and Arthur called the men up into the story above. Here the defence continued until only five men were left. The Carlists, however, had suffered so heavily that they drew back once more, and summoned the defenders to surrender."

"It is no use fighting any longer, Roper," Arthur said to his follower, who was sitting on the floor with a bullet through his leg. "What do you say, lads?"

"We have done all we can do," they said. "They have promised us our lives. We are ready to surrender. We can be no worse off even if they don't keep their word. We shall certainly be killed if we hold out any longer."

"We will surrender," Arthur called down, "if you will swear to spare our lives. If you won't do that, we will fight on; and it will cost you a good many lives before you over-power us."

There was a consultation below, and then an officer came forward and said:

"We promise you your lives if you surrender."

Arthur at once went down the stairs and handed his sword to the officer. The men followed him, leaving their muskets above, two of them assisting Roper downstairs.

"You are brave fellows," the Carlist said, "and have cost us dearly. However, you did your duty as we have done ours. How many of you have fallen?"

"Fifteen and the officer commanding."

"You have cost us double that number. Well, we will stop here for the night."

The bodies of those who had fallen were carried out of the house, and some fifty of the Carlists established them-selves there. The prisoners were ordered into the room above, and four of their captors were told off with muskets to watch at the foot of the stairs. Arthur had now time to examine and bandage Roper's leg. The ball had broken his ankle, and Arthur first put some rolls of cloth round it, and then cut some pieces of wood and put his foot into splints and bandaged them with his sash.

"I am awfully sorry, Roper. I am afraid you will have

to go through a good deal of agony before you can get your leg properly attended to."

"It cannot be helped," the man said. "I have no reason to grumble. I have been through a good many fights, and this is the first time I have been hit."

"Well, I wish we had been caught anywhere else. It would have been a nuisance being made prisoner in any other part of Spain, but I certainly do not fancy falling into Cabrera's hands again. After the way we robbed him of his prey last time, we can expect no mercy from him now. Of course, the fact that we have been taken actually fighting against him does away with any claim one might set up on the ground of being neutrals. I don't suppose they can take us to Cabrera yet at any rate, and we may have some chance of making our escape before they do. I certainly shall not try to get away unless you are well enough to make off with me. I am afraid that that is not likely to be for some time."

"No, I hope you will not think of such a thing as that," Roper said earnestly. "In the first place, your remaining here with me could do me no good; on the contrary, it might do me harm, for Cabrera will probably recognize you, and I should be sure to share your fate. On the other hand, if you were away he certainly would not know me, and I should have as good a chance as any of the others."

"I don't think that would make any difference, and indeed, if you were alone the chances are that you would be shot at once, as these men would not trouble to carry a wounded prisoner along with them, whereas with me a prisoner, they would consider that you should receive as good treatment as I until Cabrera gives some orders respecting us."

In the morning the prisoners were marched up into the mountains, and the next day the party, which was now swollen by many others, went down to the brow of a hill near Morella. The Christino prisoners were made to carry Roper, who suffered a great deal from pain in his ankle. Here they remained for a week. The greater portion of the Carlists went off every day to take part in the fighting; and on the occasion of the two assaults on the fortress all watched with intense interest the struggles at the breach, and went into ecstasies of delight at each repulse of the assailants.

When the army began its retreat a guard of ten men remained with the prisoners, and the rest went away to join in harassing the retreating foe, and it was a week before they returned. The inflammation in Roper's leg had now somewhat subsided. Arthur kept it continually bathed, and it had twice been dressed by a surgeon who came up to attend to the wounded Carlists who were also there. Two days passed, and then, just as it was getting dusk one evening, Cabrera rode in. He chatted for some time to the men, and then said:

"I hear that you have an officer a prisoner here. Let me see him."

Arthur was brought up to the light of the fire. Cabrera started on seeing his uniform, and then seizing a brand held it close to the prisoner's face.

"Ah," he said, "so I have laid hands on you at last. This is your second visit to our camp, señor Englishman. Last time you were received as a British commissioner, and you abused the permission by interfering in my plans, by killing two of my men, and by carrying off a prisoner condemned to death. I hear that you were captured this time when fighting with the Christinos, and have therefore forfeited all right to protection from your uniform. Tie this man to a tree, and shoot him at daybreak!"

His instructions were at once followed, and Arthur was fastened by a leathern thong wound tightly round and round his body.

"His servant is also here," one of the men said; "he has a broken leg."

"Put him by the side of his master. Shoot them both in the morning!"

"I don't ask mercy for myself, Cabrera. I know that it would be hopeless to do so from such a bloodthirsty ruffian as yourself; but this poor fellow has only acted under my orders, and is entitled to fair treatment."

Cabrera, who was standing by the fire a few yards away, turned round angrily.

"You dare to insult me before my soldiers?" he said furiously. "Dog of an Englishman!"

"Insult you?" Arthur repeated. "Is it possible to insult you? Do you not glory in your crimes? Is there a true man in Spain who does not spit on the ground when he hears the name of such a monster?"

Cabrera caught a musket from the hand of one of his men, levelled it, and fired. Arthur felt a stinging pain in his arm; then he felt the leathern thong that bound him slacken, unwind itself, and fall off—it had been cut by the bullet. Quick as thought he slipped round the tree and dashed off at the top of his speed. So quickly had this taken place that it was a few seconds before the Carlists understood what had happened; and he had gained forty or fifty yards before, with a yell, the whole of them started after him. But night had now completely fallen, and he was already almost out of sight. A dozen muskets were discharged at random, but he was untouched, and running at the top of his speed he began to descend the slope behind the hill. Going uphill he knew that the Carlists, sturdy mountaineers, would have speedily overtaken him, but he felt sure that downhill he could leave them; hampered by their muskets and their heavy shoes they would have little chance of catching him. He ran for a few hundred yards. The mob of men behind him were now out of sight, and when he came to a great rock he threw himself down behind it.

In half a minute the crowd of men ran past. As soon as they had done so, he got up and listened. There were none behind him, and he turned and ran up the hill again. When he reached the place he saw, as he expected, Cabrera standing alone by the fire, the whole of the men having joined in the chase. Had he been armed he would have rushed to attack him, but being without a weapon he broke into a walk, and, making a slight circuit, kept the tree by which Roper had been placed between him and the fire. Stepping very quietly he moved up to it.

"Hush, Roper," he whispered, "it is I."

Roper in his excitement had managed to raise himself up, and had worked himself round a tree, where he was standing listening to the shots in the distance.

"Put your arms round my neck," Arthur said, "and get on my back."

"No, no, sir; don't you hamper yourself with me."

"Shut up!" Arthur said, "and do as I tell you. I am not going without you."

Roper did as he was told, got on to Arthur's back, and held on with his knees and his arms.

"Get up as high as you can," Arthur said, and putting his arms under the man's knees he started off as he had come, still keeping the tree between him and the fire. When he felt that he was beyond the circle of light, he turned off and made away in the other direction. For three hours he walked on, stopping occasionally and putting Roper down, and then after a quarter of an hour's rest going on. His progress was slow, as he had to pick his way between rocks and bushes; but at the end of three hours he felt certain that he was out of sight of anyone on the hills above Morella, and he lay down in a thick clump of bushes.

"That will do for to-night, Roper," he said. "I don't think I can go any farther, and I think we are fairly safe here. We shall have to lie quiet all to-morrow, for there may still be some parties hanging about or harassing the troops. I think it has been a pretty well-managed affair."

"First-rate, sir; but I am sorry you have burdened yourself with me."

"Don't talk nonsense, Roper; we are just as likely to make

off thus, as if I had been by myself. Now the first thing to do is to put a handkerchief round my arm. That ball went between it and my body, and it is not much more than a graze; still, I fancy it has been bleeding a good deal, for I have felt weaker for the last hour or so."

He took off his coat and cut off the sleeve of the shirt, and Roper then tore it up and bound it round the wound. Then he put on his coat again, and they lay down together for warmth.

"How furious Cabrera will be when they all come back and say they cannot find me! I don't suppose they will think anything about you till the morning. They will hardly guess that I came back for you, but will think that you crawled away a short distance, and will hunt about for you in the neighbourhood. I should like to hear Cabrera's remarks when they come back empty-handed. Well, I shall not want rocking to sleep, I fancy that five minutes will do for me."

When they woke up it was broad daylight. Arthur got up, went to the edge of the bushes, and looked out.

"I see nobody about," he said; "but at any rate we must wait here till it gets dark. Cabrera will keep the men looking for me all day. There is a patch of uncut wheat a short distance away. I will go and cut an armful, it will be something for us to munch;" and he went out and broke off the heads of as much grain as he could carry, and brought it back to their shelter. They passed the day munching the wheat and talking, and sometimes sleeping.

"There is a house that looks as if it were in ruins on a rise two miles away. I will try to get there to-night. It is not at all likely to be visited by the Carlists. As we go we will cut as much wheat as we can carry in our clothes, and take up our station there."

"Well, I have been thinking, sir, that if you could cut a good strong sapling with a fork, for me to use as a crutch, I could make shift to get along."

"I can carry you very well, Roper."

"I would much rather that you made me a crutch, sir. Your arm is certainly not fit for use, and I would much rather try the other way; then if I find I can't get on, you could carry me."

Searching about among the clump Arthur found a suitable sapling. He had been deprived of his sword when captured, but his pockets had not been searched, and he had still his knife with him. He cut and trimmed a stick, and, with Roper's cloak wound round and round it, it answered well as a crutch.

They started as soon as it was dark, gathered a sufficient quantity of grain to last them for some days, and then made their way to the house. They crossed a little stream a quarter of a mile away, and there drank heartily. Arthur had gathered a faggot of dry sticks on the way, and when they arrived at the house they made a fire in a corner and sat there talking for an hour or two, then, wrapping themselves in their cloaks, lay down to sleep.

Next morning they explored the place. The roof was gone, but they found that there was a staircase leading up to a turret, and that the upper chamber of this was still intact. Here they determined to establish themselves.

"We had better wait here for a fortnight, Roper; by that time you may be able to walk. It is certain that Carlists will be moving about between here and Alcaniz, and it would be very dangerous to try and make our way down there. We shall be losing nothing, for we may be sure that it will be some time before Oraa will make another advance again. When I go out next, I will cut a couple of good clubs. If only two or three Carlists happen to drop in here, we may be able to defend ourselves; at any rate it will be a comfort to have some means of making a fight for our lives. We will carry away the ashes of our fire, so that any party that comes in will not discover that the place has been inhabited. It is not likely that anyone entering will take the trouble to come up here."

Four days passed. Each day Arthur collected sufficient faggots for their fire in the evening. As long as this burned, he kept their coats hanging against the loophole to prevent the glow from being seen from without. Every morning at daybreak, and every evening after dark, he went down to the stream and brought up with him, full of water, a broken vessel he had found. On the third evening they saw a party of twenty men approaching. They at once went up to their turret-room. Roper was now getting accustomed to the use of the crutch, and was able to make his way about with some little activity. The men came in, and Arthur, descending the stairs, heard them agree to sleep there for the night. Several went out to get wood, and presently a great bonfire was burning within, and some meat was cut from a calf they had brought in, and cooked. After eating their supper the men sat chatting around the fire. Later on one of them said:

"They say this old house is haunted. Years ago a robber lived here who preyed on travellers. They say that he once carried off a maiden in the night. Screams were heard, and the girl jumped off the top of the turret and was killed. After that her spirit haunted the place, groans and cries were heard nightly in the turret; and as even robbers would not stop here, the house fell into decay. Once or twice travellers have spent the night here, and have always been obliged to leave it owing to the dreadful noises. This was a hundred years ago."

Silence followed this recital, then one said:

"No doubt the ghost is laid by this time, and I for one vote against leaving this good fire and going outside to shiver all night."

Two or three others agreed, and the talk went on as before; but, as Arthur could detect, there was no longer the same tone of jollity, and pauses in the conversation were frequent. At about eleven o'clock the talk died away, and it was evident that the men were lying down to sleep. He went up to Roper and told him of what he had heard.

"I tell you what, Roper; I have set my mind on having some of that calf. We have been living on grain for the past fortnight, and the smell of the meat cooking has worked me up to such a point that I feel I must get a share of it whatever happens. I have been thinking it over, and I feel sure we can manage it. What they have been saying has put the idea into my head. We will give them a scare. If they hear nothing they may station themselves in this house for some days, and in the morning one of them may take it into his head to come up here. First of all, I will strike twelve heavy blows with my stick on the floor, then we will give some deep groans and shriek in as unearthly tones as we can. You may be sure that will send them flying out."

CHAPTER XIII

A DESPERATE ATTEMPT

ARTHUR struck as hard as he could twelve blows with his stick. He listened; there was a dead silence below. Then he gave three deep groans, while Roper followed with a succession of such wild screams and cat-calls that Arthur found himself unable for a minute to continue. Then he relieved himself with some loud quavering laughter, and the two kept up an almost demoniac noise for two or three minutes. They had heard a wild rush below, and Arthur, going to the loophole, heard the men shouting and running terror-stricken in the distance. Then they had a good laugh over the fright they had given the Carlists, and knew that they could now lie down and sleep till morning.

"The peasants are fearfully superstitious, and would not come near this place again to-night if they were offered fifty guineas apiece. However, I would not answer for them in the morning, so as soon as it begins to be light we will go out at that gap at the back of the house, and hide up for a bit in the bushes. They may muster up courage enough to come back, but I don't think they will."

Accordingly they went out in the morning and hid in some bushes a hundred yards from the house. Three hours passed, and as there were no signs of the Carlists, they went down to the house again. Here they found that the Carlists had left half the calf behind them, and they cooked some slices and made a hearty breakfast.

Four more days passed, and then Roper said that although he could not yet put his foot to the ground, he was quite sure that with the help of the crutch he could hobble at any rate four or five miles.

"We cannot try to get across this rough country. We must take to the road; we know it runs something like a mile in front of the house. We shall have to keep our ears open, in case any Carlists should be near; but, if we hear a party coming, as there is no moon we shall only have to go thirty or forty yards from the road and lie down till they have passed."

They slept all day, and started as soon as night fell. Roper found it harder work than he had expected, but he hobbled on, stopping every two or three hundred yards to rest. After going, as near as they could calculate, four miles, they saw a light on the road ahead of them, and felt sure that it was a Carlist outpost. They accordingly left the road, and going some four or five hundred yards to the left, lay down among some rough rocks. In the morning they could make out ten Carlists. They kept quiet all day, and during that time made a careful examination of the ground in front of them, as it was evident that they would have to keep off the road until well past the Carlist outpost, which was, no doubt, close to a spot from which it could command a view of a long stretch of the road ahead.

When darkness was coming on, they made a meal of veal, which they had cooked before starting, and corn. As soon as it was quite dark they started. The ground was rough, and Arthur had to support Roper for a considerable distance. The fire was an indication of the exact point where the outpost was keeping watch, but as two sentries might be thrown out a mile farther ahead, they did not dare go down on to the road. By morning they had not gone more than two miles, so painful had been the work of making their way along through the rocks. They could see no one on the road, and lay down in shelter with the firm belief that they should get to Alcaniz the next night. That evening they started again, and taking to the road kept on steadily all night, and to their satisfaction saw, when morning dawned, the town of Alcaniz but a mile away.

Arthur was heartily greeted on his arrival, and found to his great satisfaction that his two horses had been brought down by an English officer. "I had really very little hope of your returning. I quite gave you up when it was found that you were not with us when we got here, and my hopes faded altogether when you failed to come in after our miserable failure to take the place. Your man seems to have fared very badly."

"Yes. He had an ankle broken by a musket-shot the day we were cut off; however, it is healing nicely, though I don't think he will ever have the use of the joint again."

"Well, come into my quarters and bring him with you. I should think, probably, that you are wanting something to eat?"

"That I am. I may say that since we have been taken prisoners we have had nothing but corn to eat, till three days ago, when we were lucky enough to get some veal which we frightened a party of Carlists into leaving behind for us."

Giving Roper into the hands of an orderly, who was charged to give him something to eat as soon as possible, Lieutenant Lines took Arthur up to his quarters. In half an hour an ample meal was set before him.

"Now, tell me your adventures," Arthur's host said, as they lit their cigarettes.

Arthur gave a full account of them.

"Well, you are not born to be shot, Hallett, that is quite evident. That fight in the old house was a hard one, as you lost fifteen out of twenty, but to come out of that unharmed was nothing to your escape from Cabrera's shot at thirty yards distance. And your rescue of your man was splendid! The poor fellow must have had a bad time of it."

"Yes; and he never complained once, though I could see at times that he was suffering abominably. I was horribly afraid, as we made our way down, that he would fall among the rocks, much as I tried to steady him; and if he had done so, I have no doubt that he would have lost his foot. As it is, I hope it will not be long before he is riding behind me again. I suppose there is nothing new here?"

"Nothing whatever, except grumbling. The artillery declare that they did their work well; everyone else says that they did it badly. They declare that the infantry ought to have carried the place, which we know the best troops in the world could not have done; and the cavalry and infantry declare that every man-jack of the engineers ought to be hanged."

"Well, I don't know that they are not all right," Arthur laughed. "From the place where I was standing you could see straight into town. There was a great retrenchment behind the breach, and had they got up the breach, and through the fire at the top, they would simply have been mown down like sheep. But, after all, the man who ought to be hanged is Oraa; he blundered hideously from the moment we started. We arrived before the town without provisions, and he acted as if he had only a village with a mud wall to storm instead of a really formidable fortress. He certainly would be tried by court-martial and shot in any other European country. As it is, I hope he may never be employed again. At any rate, there is no chance of anything being done for some time. This business has ruined Espartero's plans in the north, where he was, as you know, preparing to besiege Estella; but there can be little doubt that this affair will compel him to break off his preparations and come down here. Our force is practically *hors de combat* for the present, while the enormous prestige that Cabrera will acquire will bring the peasantry flocking to his banner in crowds, and the news will be received with enthusiasm by the Carlists all over Spain. It will, therefore, be necessary to concentrate every man who can be brought up to strike a heavy blow at him. As it will probably be two or three months before Espartero can be in a position to do that, I shall leave for Madrid. I lost a good deal of blood from this wound in my arm, and for the past three weeks have had a very rough time."

"I shall leave also," the other said. "This town is one great hospital. I am especially attached to this army, and must remain near it, but I shall move off some twenty or thirty miles."

"The first thing I must do is to get a surgeon to examine Roper's leg. I don't think for a moment that anything can be done for it, but he can bandage it more skilfully and better than I have been able to do, and make it more comfortable for the poor fellow."

The next day Arthur mounted. Roper would not hear of being left behind. "I can't put my foot in the stirrup," he said, "but I can ride with the other leg only, and get a loop over from that stirrup to go under the other knee, and make a sort of sling for it; if I get tired of riding that way, I can get my leg over the saddle and ride like a woman. I will do anything rather than be left behind."

So by easy stages they rode to Madrid, where Arthur was joyfully greeted by Count Leon and his sisters. Roper's leg was again examined by a surgeon, who said that it was going on very well, but that the ankle would always be stiff.

"That won't matter," Roper said; "it will only be like

having a wooden leg with all the appearance of a natural one. It won't interfere with my riding at all, and I don't suppose I shall feel it much when I get accustomed to it."

When Arthur came to recount his adventures his friends were horrified at the risks he had run, and Donna Mercedes turned pale when she heard that he had been in the power of Cabrera.

"What an escape! What an escape!" Leon said. "To think that his bullet should have set you free! It seems almost miraculous."

"It was noble of you to go back to fetch your soldier," Donna Inez said, clapping her hands. "Oh, it was splendid!"

"He is always doing splendid things," Mercedes said. "You must promise me, Señor Arthur, that you will never run the risk of falling into Cabrera's hands again. Twice you have escaped him, but the third time will assuredly be fatal."

"It would certainly be fatal to one of us. If I had had a weapon when I went back, we should have finished our quarrel then and there. However, I will willingly promise you not to run the risk of falling into his hands again if I can help it."

"We shall be very unhappy if you go that way again," Donna Inez said; "sha'n't we, Mercedes?"

Mercedes only nodded her head, she was evidently too moved to speak.

"Well, go on with your story," Leon said. "You left us with your man riding on your back."

They laughed heartily when he told them how he had obtained meat by acting on the superstition of the natives.

"It was running a great risk, and you had no right to do it," Mercedes said.

"If you had been keeping life together on raw corn for three weeks, I think that you would think yourself perfectly justified in running a good deal of risk in obtaining a supply of meat. But really we did not consider that there was any risk at all, knowing how superstitious the peasants are; and I think, Donna Mercedes, that you yourself, after having heard that story, with such surroundings would have felt more than a little uncomfortable when you heard the gruesome noises which were made by Roper and myself—especially, I may say, by Roper."

"I am so sorry to hear of his injury," Mercedes said in a tone of great concern.

"I am very sorry too. It is a sad thing, but he makes light of it himself. There is little doubt that though he will be able to walk, the joint will always be stiff; but he will certainly be able to ride."

"Leon, you must take me round to have a chat with him. We must see if there is anything we can do to make him comfortable. Is he up, señor?"

"Oh yes, he's up, and lying on the sofa. He thinks himself that he could hobble along with a stick if he tried, but of course he will not be allowed to make the experiment."

"And how long are you going to stay here, Arthur?"

"I should think a fortnight or three weeks."

A week later, however, Roper was able to walk with a stick, and could ride again without discomfort, keeping both legs in the stirrups, but putting his weight entirely on his left leg.

The repulse at Morella had brought to a climax the indignation of the populace against the government, and the Duke de Frias had been called upon to form a ministry; but he was as much influenced by jealousy of Espartero as his predecessor, and kept Narvaez at the head of a new army of reserve he formed in the neighbourhood of the capital. All sorts of rumours were current of plots and conspiracies.

One day, a fortnight after their return to Madrid, Arthur was riding through the streets, followed by Roper, when the two queens drove past. As usual when driving about the city, they had no guards or outriders, but merely a coachman on the box and two footmen standing behind. Arthur saluted as they passed. The carriage was a closed one, and he could see that only the queen and the queen-mother were inside.

He and Roper rode out some miles into the country, and were turning to come back when four or five gentlemen rode along in a party. Arthur knew two or three of them by sight, and bows were exchanged as they passed.

"A party of pleasure, I suppose," he said to Roper, "though the weather is beginning to get cold for excursions to country mansions."

A minute later a carriage came along. The blinds were drawn; there were two footmen behind.

"I wonder what they have got the blinds down for? It is not often one sees that, even if there is no one in the carriage."

Two or three hundred yards farther back another party of gentlemen came along.

"That is curious, Roper. One would think that those two parties of gentlemen were acting as escorts to the carriage."

He rode along for another half-mile, and then checked his horse suddenly. "I have it!" he exclaimed. "Did you notice that the near horse in that carriage has a curious mark in the centre of its forehead—a sort of crescent? It seemed familiar to me, and I have been wondering where I saw it before. Now I have it. It was one of the horses in the queen's carriage that passed us to-day. It is not the same carriage, but it is certainly the same horse. There is something wrong. Why should the carriage be going along with the blinds down? Why should half-a-dozen men be riding a quarter of a mile in front, and as many more behind?"

"I tell you what, Roper; the thing looks to me very serious. The three men I knew in the first lot were generally believed to be Carlist sympathizers. It is possible that they have carried the queens off. Their disappearance just at the present moment, when things have been going so badly, would cause a turmoil throughout the country. If they were missing, Don Carlos would seem to be the only possible successor. We must follow the thing up, and find out at all risks whether my suspicions are correct. It is a grievous pity we are not in uniform, and have no weapons with us. However, we can buy swords and pistols somewhere as we go along. Probably they will change horses somewhere farther on. They may have relays at various points on the road. I don't mean, of course, that we can fight all the escort; but if we can find out for certain that they have captured the queens, we can give information at some town where there is a garrison, and swoop down upon them. At any rate we must follow them, if necessary to the French frontier, though it is not likely that they intend to go so long a distance; they will probably carry their captives to some country chateau in a retired spot, perhaps a hundred and fifty or two hundred miles away. Of course I may be wrong altogether, but if we find that they have relays it will be a matter of certainty that they are carrying off someone of importance. That mark on the horse would certainly seem to point to the fact that they have taken the queen herself. However, we may make up our minds that we have a long ride before us, Roper."

"All right, sir. I am willing to ride through Spain, though I wish my leg was all right again. I think I could go on all night on horseback, but should not be of much use dismounted."

"I don't think it is likely to come to fighting. We know that there are some twelve of them, and probably the man on the box and the two men behind also belong to the party. There will be servants and retainers at the house where they stop, and we could not think of attacking such a force as that by ourselves. What we have to do is to find out who they are carrying off. If it is the queen, we can get help; if it isn't, we may still rescue some damsel of importance."

By this time they were galloping along the road.

"We must time our pace well by theirs." They were going at a sharp trot. "Whatever we do, we must not show on the road behind them. You had better drop back and ride a good quarter of a mile behind me. If they see one solitary horseman far in the rear they would not think much of it, but if they saw two of us they might possibly suppose that we were following them. I must get a sight of them occasionally, no matter how far off, so as to be sure that they have not turned off from the main road."

Roper reined in his horse, and Arthur rode forward until he came to the crest of a slight brow, and as his head rose above this he could make out the horsemen a mile and a half in advance. The instant he did so he checked his horse and dismounted for a few minutes. When he went forward he saw that the group of horsemen were a mere black mass on the road. Feeling certain that a single figure could not be made out at that distance, he rode on at a gallop. Now and then he caught sight of them, but when he did so he always checked his horse for a time. At last on reaching the crest of a hill he stopped suddenly and dismounted, for he saw a group gathered in front of a wayside inn not more than half a mile away. He left his horse behind him, and stood against a wall so that his figure should not be seen against the sky-line.

As he looked he saw the party start again, so waiting until they were well away he followed. Five miles farther, when at some distance from a small town, he observed that they turned off, and had no doubt that they intended to make a circuit, so as to pass round it unobserved. He waited until Roper came up. "They have turned off here," he said. "I shall ride straight through the town, and post myself near the next road that comes in on this side. You follow them and watch the road closely. You can't help seeing the tracks of so large a party. Ride pretty fast till you sight them. If, as I expect, they take a turn again and come down upon the main road, you will know that I have followed them. If they turn off in any other direction you must trace them to their halting-place, and then ride to the junction of the two roads where I shall be waiting you. I shall remain there until you come, however long that may be, unless I follow them along the main road."

"I understand, sir. It is a comfort to know that as long as it is daylight we cannot miss them. It is when it gets dark that we shall have a difficulty."

"When it does get dark, Roper, we must muffle the feet of our horses and then close up until we can hear them; in that way we shall keep them in touch."

Arthur rode quietly through the town and halted a mile beyond it, where a road came in on the side on which he had seen the carriage turn off. He placed his horse behind a wall a few yards from the junction, and himself went forward until, stooping down behind some bushes, he could obtain sight of them as they passed. Ten minutes later he heard the clatter of horses. The advance-guard passed, and then he heard the wheels of the carriage. As it came along he could see that the blinds were still down. As he had expected, the horses had been changed. Five minutes after the last party of horsemen had passed, Roper came up.

"Stop there, Roper," Arthur said, standing up; "we must wait till they have gone a bit farther before we go out into the road. Well, I am more than ever convinced that there is someone of the very greatest importance in that carriage. The mere fact that they have taken the trouble to make this detour is sufficient in itself to show that. I am afraid we are in for a long ride."

"It can't be helped, sir; it is a real bit of excitement, though not quite so exciting as it was when you carried me on your back."

"No; but the excitement will come when we have to undertake the job of finding out for certain who it is they have carried off. The fact, though, that five or six at any rate of the riders are men of importance in itself points most strongly to the idea that they have carried off the queens. I have no doubt many of them have changed horses. If it is intended to take them a long distance they will all have sent off a relay of horses, probably placed in twos and threes, to small roadside inns. We shall have to change horses too somewhere. Our animals have both had easy times, and can be reckoned upon for fifty miles; but as we have no time to give them a rest, we cannot ride them farther than that. We have gone a good twenty-five miles already. At the next wayside inn we come to we will halt for five minutes, take the bits out of their mouths, and give them some bread dipped in wine, and do the same at the end of another ten miles.

"By the road they are going they are making for the Ebro, and will strike it at Alcola. I think that Medinaceli lies about fifty or sixty miles from there, but I know of no large town between this and Alcola. The latter place is only about twenty miles from Saragossa, so we can get troops from there, and from Tudela if they turn north; so I hope they will hold on as far as that. I fancy it is a little over a hundred miles from here."

It was dark when they rode into a small town, which they had seen the party ahead enter without attempting to make a detour; and waiting for a few minutes, they rode in to the principal hotel.

"Landlord," Arthur said, "a number of our friends have just ridden through the town, have they not?"

"Yes, sir; about ten minutes ago, but they made no stay here."

"We have been trying to overtake them, and our horses are done up. Can you procure us a couple of fresh ones? We are willing to pay well for their hire, but they must be good."

"Yes, sir; I happen to have a couple of good ones in the stable."

"Well, tell your men to slip the saddles and bridles on to them at once. See that our horses are well attended to. If you have something hot ready, please set it on the table at once; we have not a moment to waste."

In a quarter of an hour they were on their way again, and rode hard for the next ten miles. They had bought a blanket at the town, and now cut it into strips and muffled their horses' feet. Then they rode on again, and in another half-hour could plainly hear the sound of horses' feet ahead. All night the chase continued. They were more comfortable now, as they had no fear whatever of missing those of whom they were in pursuit, and could keep on at a regular pace. The carriage changed horses about every fifteen miles, and just as morning was breaking, and they were beginning to fall behind again, they arrived at Alcola. As they expected, the party went straight down to the ferry. Arthur again obtained a change of horses, and he and Roper took another hasty meal of boiled eggs and bread. They then rode down to the ferry, which was coming back after having taken the last batch of horsemen across.

"You are rather late, gentlemen; that is, if you belong to the party that have just crossed."

"Yes; we have stopped to change horses. However, we shall soon overtake them. Did you hear them say how far they were going?"

"I heard one of them say 'It is only twenty miles farther,' but that was all."

"Ah, that is about the distance I thought it was," Arthur said carelessly. "I suppose the roads are not very good?"

"I don't know which way they went, sir; the road by the river is good enough, the others are not much to speak of."

When they landed they went up to the village. There were some people about in the streets, and from them they learned that the party had taken the road to the north-east. They did not hurry now, the marks of the numerous horses' feet were quite sufficient guide. Arthur judged that there would be no possibility of approaching the place where they stopped before nightfall. They therefore did not attempt to lessen the start the party had obtained. After riding for about twenty-five miles they found that the tracks turned off the main road at a village, and they could see a large mansion standing some two miles away.

"That is where they are bound for, I have no doubt whatever," Arthur said. "We will stop at this little inn here."

He went in and ordered a meal to be prepared. "I shall stop here for to-day," he said to the host. "I suppose we can have a couple of rooms?"

"Yes, señor," the man said with an air of much reverence, for guests of his quality were unusual.

In half an hour the host himself brought in the meal.

"You have surely had a good many horsemen along here recently? I have noticed a great many foot-marks on the road," Arthur said carelessly; "has a troop of cavalry passed along?"

"No, señor; it was a party of gentlemen riding with the Count de Monteroy."

"Quite a large party of guests. It is not often that they have the house full at this time of the year?"

"No; it is getting late for that."

"Well, you can get our rooms ready. We have had a very long ride, and will sleep for a bit." At the place where they dined they had bought swords, and two brace of pistols with ammunition. Both were dead tired, for they had ridden something like a hundred and forty miles.

"I expect some of those men ahead must be even more tired than we are; indeed, I have noticed that the tracks are fewer this morning than they were yesterday evening."

"I noticed that too, sir. I expect they tailed off by the way and took to their beds. However, I don't suppose that will make any difference to us; there are sure to be a number of retainers in such a big house—too many for us to cope with."

"Well, I can hardly keep my eyes open. I will order dinner for six o'clock. It is just ten now, so that will give us eight hours. There is one thing in our favour: the others will be as tired as we are, and the chances are that they will most of them take to their beds and remain there till the morning."

Both slept until the landlord knocked at the door and said that dinner was served, and then after bathing their heads to wake themselves thoroughly, they went downstairs and ate a hearty meal. It was arranged that they should take the horses as near as they dared to the house, so that in case of discovery they could at once ride away, and so get a sufficient start to defy pursuit. Leaving his horse with Roper at a distance of three or four hundred yards from the house, Arthur went up to it and walked slowly round it.

The shutters in the front of the house were not closed, but the curtains were drawn. By looking between them, however, he could see that the party were at dinner. There were lights in two or three windows upstairs. It was probable that in one of these rooms the prisoners were placed. Going round the house again, still more carefully, he saw that the shutters of one of the lower windows were closed, and it struck him as possible that the captives were here and being served with a meal at the same time as their captors.

"At any rate," he said to himself, "I can try here. If the curtains are drawn and the shutters closed, they are not likely to hear me open the window."

He had no ladder by which to reach the upper windows, so he determined to take advantage of the men being all at dinner and attempt a bold stroke. It was certain that many of the guests would be strangers to the servants in the house, and that any who met him in the passages would take him for one of them. He went to the front door and tried it. It was open, and he peered in. The hall was deserted. He watched for a minute or two, and as he saw no servants pass or repass, he guessed that the kitchen was on the same side of the house as the dining-room, whereas the closed window was on the other side. He dropped his hat and cloak, slipped into the hall, closed the door, walked across, and turned in the direction of the room he wanted. He saw that two men were standing at the door, evidently on guard. He walked boldly up to them. As he had hoped, he was evidently taken to be one of the count's guests, and they drew aside and allowed him to turn the handle and enter the room. In the centre stood a table. A child was asleep on a sofa, and a lady sat beside her. The latter rose to her feet immediately.

"I thought," she said sternly, "that it was promised that no intrusion should take place on my privacy."

"Your majesty," Arthur said, stepping forward to her, "does not recognize me. I am Captain Hallett, whom your majesty graciously made a first class member of the Order of Fernando. I have followed your majesty from Madrid, keeping your carriage in sight the whole way. I had only a suspicion that it was you that had been carried off, and before I could verify it by seeing you, I had nothing to go upon. Now that I have ascertained it, I will at once leave you, for we may be interrupted at any moment. I will go to seek a rescuing force. Tudela is the nearest point at which there are troops. I have written an order in anticipation to the senior officer there, commanding him to place himself under my orders. Here is pen and ink. I pray your majesty to sign it at once."

He placed the paper on the table, and the queen at once signed it.

"I will thank you afterwards, señor," she said, "for myself and my daughter. I will not detain you for a moment now. Your life would be forfeited instantly were you found here."

Arthur bent on one knee, kissed her hand, and then without a word left her and went out of the room, saying as he

opened the door: "Your wishes shall be respected, madam."
Then he walked quietly down the passage, across the hall,
and out at the front door. In his delight he ran full speed
to the spot where Roper was holding horses.

"It is as we thought: the queen and the regent are prisoners there, and I have seen them. Now, we must ride to
Tudela—it cannot be much more than thirty miles—and we
must get the troops here by daylight if we can."

As they galloped away he told Roper how he had managed
to see the queen.

"It was a bold stroke, sir, but succeeded splendidly. I
only hope they won't ask the men on guard if anyone has
been there."

"I thought of that, Roper, but the chance of it is very
small. They could not imagine that there was anyone who
wanted to see the queens, and it is improbable that the conspirators have mentioned to anyone in the house who their
prisoners are. It is likely that the guards were only told,
when they were placed there, that the ladies were fatigued
with their journey and must not be disturbed. The secret
is too important to trust anyone with it. At the first village we come to we must engage a man with a horse to act as
our guide; we shall never find our way across country without one."

In a quarter of an hour they came to a village and stopped
at the inn.

"Landlord," Arthur said, "we want a man on horseback
to guide us to Tudela; it is important that we should get
there this evening. Of course, we shall be ready to pay well
for such service."

"What do you call well, señor?" the landlord said.

"I will give three pounds."

"Then I will go myself with you. My horse is not very
fast, but he is strong, and can do the journey easily."

"Very well, then; saddle him at once. Don't waste a
minute about it."

In five minutes the landlord rode out of the yard. He carried a couple of lanterns.

"You take one of them, Roper. I will ride between you and this good fellow."

The road was bad, and it was well that the landlord had brought lanterns, for it was a cross-road, and often nothing but a mere track. It was one o'clock in the morning before they rode into Tudela. The little town was asleep, but they roused the people at the principal inn.

"Does the colonel commanding the troops stop here?"

"No, sir; he stays at the large house fourth down the road on the right-hand side."

"Well, landlord, I want you to get supper for us, and I shall require two fresh horses in the course of an hour, and also one for this man who has come with me. I shall have to arrange with you to send these horses to the place where I borrowed them. I will pay you well for your trouble."

"I will manage it, señor," the man said, much impressed with the decided manner of his guest. "I have no horses myself, but will get them for you."

Arthur went to the house indicated, and rang loudly at the bell. He had to ring two or three times before there was any answer; then a head was thrust from an upper window.

"Who is making that noise?"

"I am a royal messenger," Arthur said, "and must see the colonel instantly."

Presently the door was opened by a man with a light. He showed Arthur into a room upstairs.

"The colonel will be in in a minute or two," he said, lighting two candles on the table.

In three minutes the colonel came down, buttoning up his tunic.

"What is it, señor?"

"I am the cavalero Captain Hallett, and I am the bearer of a message to you from the queen."

"From her majesty?" the colonel exclaimed in surprise.

"Yes. Now, colonel, before I hand you the letter I wish to impress upon you the necessity for absolute secrecy in this affair. It must be mentioned to no one, unless you have Donna Christina's permission to do so. I need scarcely say that the matter is likely to be of considerable benefit to you. Here is her majesty's order."

"This is a strange message," the colonel said, after reading it through two or three times. "It has no official seal, and is altogether unlike a document one would expect to receive from her majesty."

"That is so, colonel. Her majesty was not in a position to affix her seal, but the signature is hers, which is all that is important. Now, sir, I will tell you what has happened. Her Majesty Queen Christina and her daughter have been carried off from Madrid by a party of armed conspirators. She is at the present moment at the chateau of the Count de Monteroy, and is held a prisoner in his house. I have had an interview with her there, and have received this order from her. What force of cavalry have you here?"

"I have only fifty men, señor."

"That will be sufficient. You will at once call them under arms and start back with me. We must surround the chateau before daylight if possible, and if we ride fast we may succeed in doing so. You will there arrest the count and all his guests, who are ten in number, but who may by to-morrow morning be still stronger. You will then form an escort for the queens, and conduct them back to Madrid. I don't know what is happening there, but at any rate we will contrive to ride in after nightfall, so as to get them back to their palace unseen. After that the matter will be in her hands and that of her government."

CHAPTER XIV

A RESCUE

THE colonel, who had given an exclamation of astonishment on hearing of the outrage upon the queens, was
evidently a man of action. He ran to the door and shouted
"Thomasso! Stephano!" in tones of thunder. Two men
came running down-stairs in their night attire. "Run to
Captain Zeno, and order him to have his troop at my door
in a quarter of an hour from the present time. Tell him
that it is a matter of life and death. Don't stop to dress;
throw on your cloaks and run to him at once." Then he
turned to Arthur. "They may not be here in a quarter of
an hour, but they won't be many minutes longer. The captain sleeps at the barracks, and he will turn his men out at
once."

Another man was wakened and ordered to saddle the
colonel's horse at once. "How did this monstrous thing
happen, cavalero, if I may ask?"

"I do not know how the queen was carried off; but I was
riding on the road seven miles outside Madrid when I saw
a carriage coming along with closed blinds. Accompanied
as it was by twelve gentlemen I should have thought that
it was a pleasure-party going to some country chateau, but
that the carriage had closed blinds struck me as strange.
Still, I should have thought no more of the matter had I not
noticed a peculiar white mark on the head of one of the
horses—a mark which I had that very morning noticed on
the head of one of those in the queen's carriage. The matter struck me as being so strange that I determined to follow. I kept near them all the way. They had relays of
horses at various points on the road, and changed them
quickly. I managed also to change mine and that of a servant with me, and finally traced them to Count de Monte-

roy's. I was still in doubt as to whether it was her majesty who was in the coach, but I succeeded in obtaining a private interview. I saw her but a minute. I had prepared this document for her signature, which I was lucky enough to obtain. Now, colonel, you know as much about the matter as I do."

Arthur could see that the officer was highly delighted at the thought of the opportunity that had fallen in his way. He ran back to his room and made a more elaborate toilet. Arthur went off at once to the hotel to see if the arrangements there were going on satisfactorily. The three horses were at the door, so he sat down with Roper and ate a hasty supper.

"Now, landlord," he said, "I want you to send these two horses to this address; here are a couple of pounds for your trouble. The horse ridden by the landlord who acted as my guide here must be kept till to-morrow. He says he will come over and fetch it himself."

Hearing a clatter of hoofs at this moment he went out and found the troop just arriving at the colonel's door. He mounted his horse and rode there at once. The colonel had come out, and was in the act of mounting.

"They have only been five minutes over the quarter," the latter said. "You have done very smartly, Captain Zeno. You know the way, cavalero?"

"No; but this man with the lantern does. He guided me here."

The guide and Roper, with their lanterns, rode off at the head of the column; the colonel and Arthur followed, the former calling up the captain to his side. "I dare say you are wondering what you are called up so suddenly for, Captain Zeno; but this gentleman is the bearer of an order for the arrest of the Count de Monteroy and some persons in his house. We must ride fast, for it is important that we shall get there in time to take all in the house by surprise. It will be light at six, so I hope we shall get there by that time; but if not, it is likely that we shall arrive before anyone is stirring. It is, I understand, important that none of the people there shall escape."

"Carlists, I suppose, señor?" the captain asked.

"I don't know," the colonel replied; "there are no particulars whatever in my orders, which is simply for their arrest."

The innkeeper was now better mounted than before, and the journey was done in a little over five hours. The day had broken, but as they approached the house they could see no signs of life. The colonel posted forty of the men round the house, with orders to cut down anyone who tried to escape; then with the other ten men, their captain, and Arthur, he went up to the hall-door and knocked loudly. A minute or two later he knocked again, and it was opened by a servant, who had evidently but just risen. He started at the appearance of the soldiers.

"You will lead me at once to your master's bedroom," Arthur said. Seeing that the colonel and he had both drawn their swords, the servant without a moment's hesitation conducted them to Count de Monteroy's room. Arthur, accompanied by the colonel, went in. The count opened his eyes, and then sprang suddenly out of bed. "I arrest you, Count Juan de Monteroy, on a charge of high treason! Resistance, señor, is useless: I have fifty soldiers round the house and ten of them behind me here."

The count swore a deep oath, and then shrugged his shoulders. "So there is a traitor among us?" he said scornfully.

"No, señor; your party have all been true to you," Arthur said.

The colonel called in two men. "You will remain here with this gentleman. You will allow him to dress, but see that he touches no paper or documents of any kind. When he has finished you can bring him below, and there keep strict watch over him until further orders."

The colonel went from door to door with his men, and

arrested the whole party without resistance. There were twelve of them; those who had been left behind on the way having arrived late the previous evening. After seeing to the arrest of the count, Arthur, followed by two soldiers, ordered one of the trembling domestics, who had now come down, to take him to the room of the lady and child who had arrived the day before. Two guards stood beside it.

"Do you know why you are placed here?" he asked sternly.

"No, señor; except that we came on guard at eleven last night and were ordered to allow no one to enter the room, and to refuse to allow the lady inside to come out unless escorted by the count himself."

"Well, you are relieved from that duty now. You will go down-stairs and remain there; we may want to question you again presently."

Then he knocked at the door. It was immediately opened, and Queen Christina came out. "I was expecting you this morning, señor; and, looking out of the window, saw you ride up with the troop."

Arthur waved the two soldiers to move away. "Madam," he said, "I do not know what your wishes may be; but I thought it as well to keep the knowledge of your identity from all save the colonel."

"Come in here. The queen is dressed. Before we say anything else, señor, I must thank you with all my heart for the inestimable service that you have rendered me. I thank you in the name of the queen, of myself, and of Spain. I am obliged to you for having kept our identity a secret. I have been thinking the matter over since I saw you last night and learned that there was a chance of rescue. I should certainly prefer that we should return to Madrid as we have come, incognito. What has passed there I know not, but I think it possible that my government have kept the fact of our disappearance from the knowledge of the people, and I should wish to consult with them when I get back as to the advisability of continuing to do so. I shall, of course, take better precautions in future; but the news that I had once been carried off might lead desperate men to repeat the attempt. However, we shall have time to talk this all over on the journey. I should certainly wish to start as soon as possible."

"You can leave in half an hour, madam, and can travel as fast as you came here. There are relays of horses on the way. Your escort cannot keep up with you, as there would be no possibility of procuring remounts for so many men. There would be no occasion for an escort, because you can ride with the blinds up, and by keeping your veil down there will be no risk of your being recognized. What do you wish done with regard to the prisoners, madam?"

The queen hesitated.

"I have not thought. What do you say, Captain Hallett? You have done so much in this matter that I will trust to your opinion."

"I should think, madam, that it might perhaps be as well to send them all under charge of the colonel who has come with this troop to Tudela, or to leave them here in his charge, in either case holding him responsible for their safety. Then you could consult with your ministers as to what steps should be taken. It might seem preferable to them that their trial —if trial there should be—should take place at a provincial town rather than the capital. I should think they could be better guarded at the barracks at Tudela than here. Shall I order breakfast to be brought up here, madam, or will you take it below?"

"I would rather have it here."

"It is a quarter to seven now; shall you be ready to start at eight? May I present the colonel to you, madam, before you start? He was most zealous, and started with his troop of cavalry in an extremely short time after hearing my message. He is the only one of those here who knows of your majesty's identity."

" Certainly, present him to me. I shall, of course, see that he receives promotion."

" Does your majesty wish me to accompany you? "

" Of course I do, señor. I thought that so much a matter of course that I did not mention it. I have very, very much to say to you, for I know nothing at present as to how you came to be here."

At the appointed hour the queens came down-stairs and went into the drawing-room, where the Spanish colonel was presented to them. Christina spoke to him very graciously and thanked him for his services, which she said should be shortly recognized.

" I should wish you," she said, " to keep the prisoners in entire seclusion; let them have no communication with anyone. Let the men who supply their wants be distinctly warned on no account to exchange a word with them. I think the best plan might be for you to have a house cleared out for them, so that they can be placed in rooms apart, with a sentry at each door, and sentries round the house to see that they communicate with no one. It might be better for you to requisition the prison, and see that the present inmates are placed elsewhere. I rely upon your absolute secrecy, colonel, as to myself and my daughter having been here. I cannot say what course government will take in the matter; therefore I rely upon you to keep them absolutely apart from all communication until you receive orders from Madrid." She held out her hand to the colonel, who kissed it and retired much gratified.

The carriage was at the door. The count's coachman, who had driven them down, was placed on the box, and Roper took his place beside him. Two soldiers dressed in plain clothes took their places behind, and one other, similarly dressed, mounted one of the count's horses and led those that had been ridden by Arthur and Roper. Arthur himself had been commanded by the queen to take his place in the carriage with her.

"You know this gentleman, do you not, Isabella?" the regent said as they drove off.

The child had been gazing fixedly at Arthur.

"Yes, mamma, I think I do. He is the handsome gentleman, isn't he, who was presented to me some time ago for doing something very brave?"

"Yes, my dear; you said you liked him, you know."

"Yes I did, mother."

"You ought to like him a great deal more now, Isabella, for he has done something very great for us. You are too young yet to understand it, but I can tell you that he has done a very, very great service, one that you should never forget as long as you live. Now, señor, I have been in vain wondering how it was that you should have arrived in our room in the manner of a good fairy last night."

"It was almost by an accident, madam, and that I was there was due to the fact that the Count de Monteroy made the mistake of putting the horses out of your carriage into his own instead of taking others." He then related fully the manner in which his suspicion had been aroused, and how he had, with his man, followed the carriage. "Of course, your majesty, if I had been in any way sure that you were in the carriage, I should have closed up at the first town you came to, and called upon the authorities for aid to rescue you; but beyond the mark on the horse—and there may be more than one horse so marked in Spain—I had nothing upon which I could act. The carriage evidently belonged to the party who rode with it, but the mere fact that the blinds were drawn down was in itself no proof that any prisoner was in it. It might have been merely full of wine and provisions for the use of the party going down to stay at a chateau.

"It was, therefore, absolutely necessary for me to assure myself that you were prisoners. That might have been a most difficult thing to find out, and I had in vain, on the journey, thought over some plan. As it turned out, it was, as I have told you, simply a matter of good fortune. The closed shutters pointed out the room where you were likely to be, and from the fact that dinner was going on I was able to get to the door of your room unchallenged. Your guards took me for one of the count's guests, and thus everything was easy and simple. Of course the moment I left your majesty I rode straight to Tudela, and started with the troop on the return journey twenty minutes after I arrived."

" Well, señor, I hardly know which to admire most: your recognition of the horse, your quickness of perception that something very unusual was being done, and the manner in which, in spite of the immense fatigue of the journey, you kept in sight of us until you traced us here; or the fearlessness with which you risked your life, as you certainly did, to ascertain whether your suspicions were correct. Now, I will tell you how we were seized. Of course our coachman and footmen must have been heavily bribed. We were driving through the town when suddenly we turned in at the gateway of a house in a quiet street. I could not now say where the house was, for I was talking to Isabella, and paid no particular attention to the route by which we were proceeding to the palace.

" The moment we entered, a number of gentlemen came round, the door was opened, and one said:

" ' Madam, I must trouble you to alight.'

" I began to demand what he meant by such insolence, but he cut me short by saying:

" ' Madam, I repeat that you and the queen must alight. We have no time to spare. Unless you at once descend and enter this carriage standing here, we shall most reluctantly be obliged to use force.'

" It seemed to me that it would be useless to resist, for it was evident that these men were desperately in earnest and would not hesitate to carry out their threats; so we did as we were ordered. A lady—I believe she was a relation of

the count's, from what she said—afterwards got into the
carriage, followed by a gentleman. The blinds were then
pulled down, and the man took out a long dagger and said:

" ' If you move, madam, or attempt to pull up the blinds
or to give the alarm, I shall not hesitate to stab you and
your daughter to the heart, as our safety, and that of a score
of other people, would demand it. I should deplore the
necessity, but I should not hesitate to act.'

" After we had driven for half an hour he got out. I could
hear a horse brought up to the door, and he mounted. I
had no doubt that the carriage was accompanied by mounted
men. The woman was of powerful build, and after we had
once started I gave up all idea of trying to give the alarm,
which would, I felt sure, be fatal. When the blinds were
first pulled down I heard one of the men speak furiously because the horses were not in our carriage. Someone else
said something, and he said:

" ' What does it matter if it is half an hour earlier than
we expected? They ought to have been ready. Take the
horses out of that carriage.'

" There was a running about, and the pair of horses were
put in. Then one said:

" ' Be sure that, directly we have gone, that carriage is
broken up and burnt. There must not be a splinter of it
left—nothing to show that anyone has ever been here. You
see to it, Ferdinand; you have got saws and everything else.
Remember the safety of all of us may depend upon its being
done thoroughly.'

" Three minutes later we started. It almost seemed to me
that I was in a nightmare from which I did not awake till I
got to the end of the journey. I chatted with Isabella, but
I did not exchange a single word with the woman in the
carriage with us. From time to time when we stopped to
change horses a tray of food was handed in, and we ate and
drank, though I had little appetite; but I felt that I must
keep up my strength, for I had no idea how long this strange

journey would last, or what would happen at the end of it. That we had been captured by adherents of Don Carlos I had, of course, no doubt. I did not fear that we should be injured; but I did think that we might be kept for many years, perhaps for life, in close confinement, in which case, doubtless, all parties would at last accept Don Carlos as king. There would, no doubt, be a general search for us; there would be great troubles; but when it seemed to all that we should never be found, even our best friends would be willing to accept Don Carlos. What do you think will have taken place at Madrid?"

"I should certainly say, madam, that when you are missed every effort will be made by government to keep your disappearance a secret, while attempts will be made in all directions to find out the mystery. It will appear almost incredible that you and your carriage, horses, coachman and footmen should suddenly and mysteriously have disappeared. No doubt your captors did not ride out in a body. Some of those you saw there doubtless remained to destroy the carriage; possibly others may have waited a mile or two outside the town. Two, perhaps, would keep some distance ahead of the carriage, and two would follow. No particular attention would be attracted by a carriage, with the blinds down and apparently empty, being driven through the street at a leisurely pace."

"After the man got out of the carriage," said the queen, "we went very much faster. For a time I wondered which way we were going, and where we were to be taken; but as hour after hour went on I ceased to trouble over it, and was principally occupied in endeavouring to appease Isabella's curiosity concerning the strange method of travelling, and by telling her stories to keep her amused. As soon as it became dark she fell asleep with her head in my lap. I dozed occasionally, waking up when the horses were changed. When morning came I felt that we were being ferried across a river; then in a couple of hours we arrived here. The carriage drew up and the door was opened. Several gentlemen were standing there, and all took off their hats as we dismounted, and expressed their regret at having given us so long and fatiguing a journey.

"The Count de Monteroy assured me that every attention should be paid to our comfort, that we should be treated with every respect, and that we should be in no way intruded upon. Three times during the day servants brought in food, and we were requested to come down to dinner. I was in half a mind to refuse, but I thought it was better that Isabella should have a change, and I might learn something of the arrangement of the house. It is fortunate, indeed, that I did so, for if I had been kept a prisoner up-stairs, I do not think that even your ingenuity and courage could have enabled you to obtain an interview with me."

The coachman had been ordered to take exactly the same road as that by which they had come, and to stop to change horses at the same places.

"By the way, señor, is the servant who rode with you the same as accompanied you on the occasion when you rescued Count Leon de Balen's sister?"

"He is, your majesty. He is at present riding on the box with the coachman, as he has been lamed in a fight with the Carlists; and although his ankle, which was broken, is now nearly healed, the fatigue of the long ride has been so great that I took the liberty of placing him upon the box to keep his eye on the coachman, while one of the troopers leads our horses."

"The first time we stop I beg that you will present the brave fellow to me. He must have suffered greatly from the long ride."

"I have no doubt that he has suffered, madam, but he has said nothing about it. He rode with that leg loose in the stirrup, only using the other. However, he acknowledged this morning that he could not sit the horse going back, and said he would remain with the troops for two days, resting.

It was then I decided to put him on the box instead of one of the soldiers, as I had intended."

" Where did he get wounded, and how ? "

" If it is your majesty's pleasure I will tell you. It is a long story, and if I mistake not we shall be changing horses in a short time, so I had better leave it until we start again."

" Very well," the regent said; " the longer the story the better, for we have a long journey before us."

When the carriage stopped, Roper was called to the door.

" This is my man, your majesty, who has ridden from Madrid with me."

" I thank you most heartily," the queen regent said. " Isabella, give your hand to this brave soldier. It is he who has helped this gentleman to get us away from that house. He rode all the way behind us."

" You are a very good man," the child said, as she held out her hand to Roper, who kissed it somewhat awkwardly. " It was a very nasty, long journey for mamma and me, and it must have been much worse for you, as you had to ride all the way."

" Yes; and he helped his master to get that pretty young lady, Donna Mercedes de Balen, out of the hands of the wicked Carlists, who were going to kill her."

" I had very little to do with it, madam; I simply did what my master told me."

" I know Donna Mercedes well," the child said. " She has been several times with her two sisters to play with me. I am glad you did not let them kill her."

Roper bowed and retired.

" Is he a private soldier ? " the regent asked.

" He is a private soldier for my sake, madam. He was a sergeant in the regiment of the British Legion to which I belonged, and when I was sent to Madrid to enquire about the pay due to the Legion, he gave up his rank in order to accompany me as my servant, which was the more meritorious as we had been private soldiers together."

"But you could never have been a private soldier?" the regent said in surprise.

"I was, madam. I had got into a scrape at school, and my guardian offered to allow me one hundred and twenty pounds a year till I came of an age to become possessor of the estate of my late father; and as they were recruiting at the time for the Legion, I thought I should like to see something of the world, and therefore I enlisted."

"A Spanish nobleman would never think of doing that," the regent said.

"I was not a nobleman, madam. My father was what you would call a country gentleman, living on his estate, which was, I believe, a fair one. He died when I was only ten years old, and left me to the care of an uncle. I only propose remaining in Spain until I come of age to inherit the estate."

"At what age do you inherit?"

"We generally inherit at twenty-one, madam. My father considered, and very rightly, that I was not of a disposition to settle down, and therefore stated in his will that I was not to come into the estate until I was twenty-five."

"Then I suppose it will not be long before you go?"

"It will be some little time yet; I am a good deal younger than I look."

The regent smiled. "That is because you are so big and strong, I suppose, Captain Hallett. And are you thinking of taking a Spanish lady home as your wife? There, I ought not to have asked you," she said; "only I remember that when a certain young lady told me a story of what had happened to her, she coloured up very prettily when she mentioned your name. But there, I won't say anything more about it. Now, as we are off again, perhaps you will tell us that story of how your follower was wounded?"

Arthur told the story. Both the regent and her daughter were greatly interested, and insisted upon hearing much fuller particulars than he wished to give of the manner of his escape from Cabrera, and of his return to carry off Roper.

"No wonder the man is attached to you," Christina said warmly; "it would be strange indeed if he were not. It was a grand action, Captain Hallett, however much you may make light of it. Now, sir, I own that I feel sleepy; I scarcely closed an eye last night. Would you mind riding for a time?"

"Certainly not, madam."

They were just stopping to put in fresh horses, and Arthur was by no means sorry at the change. He glanced into the carriage at the next halting-place, and saw that the regent and her child were both asleep. Another fifteen miles and they changed again.

"We have some food, have we not, Captain Hallett?" asked the regent.

"Yes, your majesty; we have a large hamper behind the carriage."

"Then have it brought in here, and please come in yourself. How far have we gone?"

"About forty-five miles, madam."

"What time shall we get to Madrid?"

"About one o'clock in the morning, madam."

"Well, we will dine now. Then we will talk for an hour or two, and I will try to get to sleep again, for I know that I shall have no sleep to-night after I get in, but shall be up all night with my ministers. I hope all the men are getting food?"

"Yes, madam; I brought a basket of food for them too, otherwise there must have been much delay when we changed horses."

"You seem to think of everything, Captain Hallett," she said, as he moved away to get the hamper.

"I had better open it and pass the things in, madam."

"No, bring it inside; we can put it on the seat by you. It will be an amusement to open it. It is many, many years since I enjoyed an impromptu meal like this."

The carriage rolled on and the hamper was opened. It

contained every necessary for a meal. There were several
bottles of the count's best wine, cold fowls, pasties, and a
variety of sweets, together with glasses, plates, and other
necessaries. The regent and the little queen entered into
the spirit of the thing with great zest. To the former it
was a relief indeed to be eating without ceremony, and able
for the moment to put aside all the cares of state, which
weighed so heavily upon her; to the little queen it was something perfectly delightful, and both laughed and chatted
with a freedom and abandon that set Arthur quite at his
ease. The meal lasted for a long time, the regent declaring
that she had not eaten so much nor enjoyed a meal so thoroughly for years.

The queen was enchanted. "Why can't we always eat like
this, mamma," she said, "instead of having to sit up, with
three or four servants to wait upon us, and everyone staring disagreeably? I do so wish we could."

"Well, we can't have it quite like this, Isabella; but I
will make up my mind that once a week we will dine together
in my closet, and then we will have everything put upon the
table and help ourselves, and try and think that we are not
queens, or anything else disagreeable."

"That will be nice, mamma! And you won't say once to
me, 'You mustn't take this, Isabella,' or 'You must sit upright,' but just let me do as I like?"

Her mother nodded. "Yes, that shall be the agreement."

The child clapped her hands. "That will be nice!" she
said. "I am so tired of my governess saying, 'You mustn't
do that,' and 'You ought to do this.' It will be nice,
mamma! When shall we begin—this day week?"

Her mother nodded.

"And will Captain Hallett always dine with us?"

"No, my dear; Captain Hallett has other things to do;
but perhaps sometimes, when he is in Madrid, he will come
as a special treat for you."

The child nodded contentedly. " I shall be very angry with him if he does not come often," she said.

The meal lasted until they arrived at the next changing place. Here Arthur got out again, and was glad to regain his own horse. It was just one o'clock when they rode into Madrid. There were lights in the palace, and the gates were still open. They did not drive up to the principal entrance. The regent decided that she would enter at a side door, and try to make her way to her apartments unnoticed, as it was possible that the news of their disappearance had been kept from most of the servants of the palace.

" Come up with me, if you please, Captain Hallett," she said.

The door was unbolted, and after giving orders that the carriage should be taken round to the stables, and that the soldiers should put up at an inn for the night and come round for orders in the morning, she entered, with Arthur carrying the child, sound asleep, in his arms. They climbed some stairs to the first floor. Up to this time the queen had been in ignorance as to her whereabouts, but she now knew where she was, and made her way to her own chamber. Leaving Arthur outside, she went in for a minute or two, laid the child on a bed, took off her wraps, and then came out.

" Now, we will go to the council-chamber," she said; " I expect we shall find some of the ministers there in consultation."

She led the way along a gallery, and opening a door went in. Eight men were sitting there, and they leapt to their feet with a cry of astonishment as the regent entered, followed by a young gentleman who was unknown to them.

" Why—your majesty! " her minister said.

" Yes; I understand that you are surprised to see me," she interrupted. " Now, gentlemen," she went on, as she went to her seat at the head of the table, " I will, in the first place, ask you what has happened here since I have been away; after that I will tell you where I have been. Has my absence been known? "

"To very few people, your majesty. Fortunately, I was here awaiting your return. As the time passed and you did not arrive, I became anxious. When you were two hours late, I sent for my colleagues and we had a consultation, but we were unable to form any idea of what had become of you. Your carriage had not returned. It was not possible that any accident could have occurred, for if so, we should have heard of it. At nine o'clock we became seriously alarmed, and all went out to different parts of the city to make cautious enquiries as to where your carriage had been last seen, and whether a report was current that an accident had taken place. We met here again at eleven. None of us had heard of any news. Your carriage had been seen in various parts of the town early in the afternoon, but where it had been last noticed we could not find out. We set the whole police to search quietly—no one was told of your disappearance. A search was made for the carriage. In the meantime it was given out that the queen was unwell, and that you were remaining with her and nursing her. Your majesty's surgeon was called in and sworn to secrecy, and he has twice a day come to the palace. We have been, as your majesty may well imagine, at our wits' end to know what to do. To announce that you had disappeared would cause a disturbance in the city, and an enormous state of unrest throughout the kingdom. We have met to-night to consider how long the secret could be kept, and whether it would be expedient at once to offer a very large reward for news concerning you."

"Happily, duke, I am in a position to settle the matter and to relieve your disquietude."

She then related how she had been kidnapped, and how she was taken to the house of the Count de Monteroy and confined there. Many were the exclamations of anger as she went on.

"It is monstrous! Incredible!" were among the exclamations when she ceased.

"Then how, madam, did you obtain your freedom from

the hands of these malefactors? It would certainly seem that they had taken every precaution to keep the place of your confinement secret."

"Precautions they did take that would have deceived most people," the regent said, "but which, happily, failed to deceive this gentleman here. Now, Captain Hallett, perhaps you will please tell these gentlemen how it happened that you traced and rescued me. I request that you will tell it in full detail."

Thus commanded, Arthur gave a full account of the way in which his suspicions had been aroused, of his pursuit, the manner in which he had discovered that his suspicions were correct, and the steps he had taken to obtain the release of the prisoners.

"Well, sir," the premier said, when Arthur had brought the story to a conclusion, "I have to congratulate you most heartily, in my own name and on behalf of the other members of her majesty's government, upon the manner in which you have rescued the queen and the queen regent from the hands of their captors. You have shown an amount of acuteness, of steadfastness of purpose, and of courage, in venturing into this den of conspirators, that does you an extraordinary amount of credit. We can hardly imagine what would have happened had the place of confinement of the queen remained undiscovered. The whole kingdom would have been in uproar; civil strife would have been more rampant than ever. We thank you most heartily, in the name of Spain, for what you have done for her. Have you the list, señor, of the men who have been arrested?"

"Yes, señor, this is it."

The premier ran his eye over it and passed it on to his colleagues.

"It is difficult to believe," he said, "that some of the gentlemen here mentioned could have been engaged in such a conspiracy; however, we cannot at present decide upon so important a question."

"I may say, señor," Christina said, "that for my own part I should vastly prefer that there should be neither scandal nor trial. I prefer that they should be ordered to leave the kingdom at once, with the understanding that if they return they will be arrested on the charge of high treason. It would be most unfortunate if this matter should be made public. The plot has failed; but the mere fact that it has been tried might lead others to repeat the attempt. In the next place, most of these men who have been engaged in the matter bear historic names, and have wide connections. It would therefore be one of the gravest scandals ever known in Spanish history were they to be tried and punished on such a charge. This is my opinion on the subject. I submit it to your judgment, and I think that when you come to take into consideration the magnitude of the interests involved, you will agree with me that it would be advisable to let the matter pass unnoticed.

"In time, when these troubles are all brought to an end, it will be possible to extend to these conspirators the hand of mercy, and allow them to return to such portion of their estates as may be deemed fitting. And now, gentlemen, I will leave you. I have had four days of great fatigue and anxiety. I should say that to-morrow a notification should be issued to the effect that the queen has recovered from her passing indisposition, and that in the course of the day we should show ourselves in the streets as usual." So saying she rose; the members of the council also stood up, and bowed deeply as she left the room followed by Arthur.

CHAPTER XV

A CHALLENGE

ON leaving the palace Arthur went to his room, where he found supper awaiting him, Roper having confiscated to his use the contents of the royal hamper.

"I thought you would want something before you went to bed, and I was sure that I did. I have already eaten mine, but here is a fowl, sir, and two bottles of wine."

"Well, I am not sorry to have them, though it is three o'clock in the morning; however, we can sleep as late as we like to-morrow."

At twelve o'clock, however, Arthur was awakened by Leon entering his room.

"We have been quite uneasy about you, Arthur. Where have you been? What have you been doing with yourself? I came round here four days ago; the concierge said you were out. I called again in the evening, and next morning I learned that, when you left, you had said nothing about any intention of going away; that you had certainly taken no clothes with you, but had gone out with Roper in attendance, just as if you were going for an ordinary ride."

"That was just the intention with which I did go out, but circumstances were too much for me. Now, what I am going to tell you is a complete secret, and before I say anything about it you must give me your promise that it shall not, on any account whatever, go beyond yourself and your sisters."

Leon looked at Arthur in surprise, but seeing that he was quite in earnest, gave the required pledge.

"Well, you will be surprised to hear that in the four days I have been away I have ridden over three hundred miles."

"Over three hundred miles?"

"Yes. That is not bad for what was really three and a

half days' work, for I arrived here at three o'clock this morning."

"You stupefy me," the young count said. "Why, no horse could have done it."

"No, and no horse did it; I had relays about every fifteen miles."

"You travelled post? What did you carry? A despatch for Espartero, or a cartel to Cabrera?"

"Prepare yourself for a surprise, Leon. I carried in my hand the safety of the queen and the regent."

"The safety of the queen and regent! You are not joking, are you? How could you have to ride three hundred miles on such an errand?"

"Well, briefly, Leon, the queen and the queen regent were carried away a hundred and fifty miles, and I brought them back again."

Leon looked seriously at his friend.

"You are not quite well, are you?" he said; "you are a little upset, my dear fellow, about something. You are talking nonsense, you know; the queen has not been out of Madrid. She has been unwell and her mother has been nursing her."

"So you were led to believe, but the facts are as I have stated. The queen and her mother were seized when driving through the streets of Madrid four days ago. They were placed in a carriage with closed blinds, and were carried to a place some twenty-five miles beyond the Ebro and some thirty miles from Tudela. I followed them with Roper. I had the luck to obtain an interview with her majesty, rode to Tudela, and brought back a squadron of horse, surrounded the house where they were imprisoned, captured all the conspirators, and brought the queen and her mother back to Madrid at one o'clock this morning."

"You seem to be talking sensibly," Leon said, "but I really cannot take in what you say. It's a hundred and thirty miles good to the Ebro, and you say it was twenty-five miles farther; then you rode from there to Tudela and back, a distance of sixty miles, so that you have, in fact, covered some four hundred miles. Where have you slept?"

"I think I slept a little on horseback on the way to Tudela and back, and I have slept since three o'clock this morning, as I was some time at the palace. I have no doubt that in addition I dozed occasionally for some minutes in succession in the saddle during the return journey, and I had a sleep of eight hours in the daytime the day before yesterday; and if you had not come in I dare say I should have had as many more before I woke to-day."

Leon looked so serious that Arthur burst into a hearty laugh.

"That is good," he said, "and will wake me up. Now, Leon, if you will wait for five minutes I will get up and dress. Did you see Roper when you came in?"

"Yes; he opened the door to me as usual."

"Well, if you will tell him that I shall be out in ten minutes, and want some coffee and something to eat, he will make it for me; but mind, don't ask him any questions. I am not going to have the story spoilt by anyone else telling you about it; not that I think you would get anything out of him, for he is absolutely trustworthy, and I told him last night that no whisper must pass his lips of what has taken place."

In ten minutes Arthur went into the sitting-room, and as he entered Leon said: "If you are going to eat your breakfast before you tell me anything, I will go away. I cannot repress my curiosity, and I will take a ride or do something to keep my brain steady until you are ready to unburden yourself."

"I will begin at once, and tell you while I am eating.

"Now," he began, as he sat down and poured out some coffee, "the thing in a nut-shell is precisely what I told you. And now as to particulars:—I was riding with Roper, and had gone about seven miles out. As we returned I met a party of gentlemen on horseback. At some little distance behind them was a carriage with the blinds down. Again, at a distance behind the carriage was another party of gentlemen. Altogether there were twelve men. It struck me as rather curious; still, they might have been going down to spend the day at some chateau, and carrying provisions or something of that sort in the carriage. I should not have thought much more about the matter, if it had not been for one thing: as the carriage passed me, it struck me that I knew one of the horses by a rather curious white mark on its forehead.

" As I rode on, it suddenly occurred to me where I had seen a horse similarly marked: it was in the carriage in which the queen was driving when I saw her in the street, just as we were starting. Naturally this led me to review the position. Who was in the carriage? Why were the blinds down? How was it that six men were riding in front of it and other six behind it? It struck me that possibly they were carrying off the queen, and I resolved to follow and see where they went. They rode much farther than I expected, changing horses at quiet places every twelve miles or so, and going very fast, till, as I told you, they crossed the Ebro between Saragossa and Tudela, and went some twenty-five miles farther to a mansion, which I had no difficulty in learning belonged to Count Juan de Monteroy.

" Having found that out, we stopped at an inn in a village two miles from it, and had that sleep I mentioned, as it was ten o'clock in the day, and I could do nothing till dark. Then I went to the mansion and found, by looking through the curtains, that the party were at dinner. I found also that the windows of another room on the ground floor had closed shutters. The two rooms lay on opposite sides of the grand entrance. The door was open. I peeped in, and could see no one about; so I took heart, walked boldly in, and turned along the corridor to the room with the closed shutters.

"Two men were standing on guard at the door, but of course they took me for one of their master's guests, and I walked coolly past them, and found in the room the queen and her mother. I got the regent to sign an order that I had written out, for the officer commanding at Tudela to place himself under my orders. Then I rode over there and fetched a squadron of cavalry, which arrived at daybreak. We surrounded the house, took the twelve men there prisoners, started an hour later with the queens, and arrived here at one o'clock this morning."

Leon gazed at him in open-eyed astonishment.

"You are certainly a most surprising fellow, a most astonishing fellow! I don't know what to say to you. Here, single-handed, you have thwarted a plot that might have brought ruin to the country; you have saved a couple of queens; you have captured, too, the leaders of the plot; you have ridden, what with your journey to Tudela and back, four hundred miles at least, in the course of three days and a half; and here you are, telling me all this as if it had been a natural and everyday occurrence."

"It certainly was not an everyday occurrence, Leon, but it was an affair that might have happened to anyone who kept his eyes open and possessed a certain amount of endurance."

"So this is the real history of the young queen's indisposition?"

"Yes. I think the ministers acted very wisely in keeping the thing a secret."

"It is the first wise thing they have done," Leon said. "I don't see that they are a bit better than the last ministry. However, never mind that now. And about yourself? you must be fearfully stiff."

"I am very stiff, but that will wear off by to-morrow."

"And did your man perform this marvellous journey in spite of his broken leg?"

"He rode there with me, and when I went to fetch the

troops, but he came back on the box of the queen's carriage. His leg hurt him a good deal last night, but I hope no real harm is done, though no doubt he will have to keep quiet for a few days."

"Well, they ought to make a duke and grandee of Spain of you for it."

"I sincerely hope they won't think of anything of the sort," Arthur laughed. "Fancy my going back to England with such a title as the Duc de Miraflores! The thing would be absolutely ludicrous!"

"Well, they will have to do something big anyhow," Leon said. "Now, tell me the story more fully. You have got nothing to do, and may as well gratify my curiosity."

"There is really very little to tell, but I will give it to you;" and he then told the story in detail.

"Well, it is really remarkable that you should have been able to keep them under your observation during all that long journey without letting them know that they were followed."

"You see, they could have had no idea that there was anyone after them; if they had, they would no doubt have left a couple of their number to follow at a distance of two or three miles. They no doubt felt quite sure that the absence of the queen was entirely unsuspected, that no search could be made for her for at least six hours, and that assuredly no parties would be sent off in any case to scour the country till next day, by which time they would have crossed the Ebro. If, instead of taking the horses from the queen's carriage, they had waited five minutes till their own were yoked, their plot would have been successful. Their plan was uncommonly well laid, and they could hardly have conceived it possible that one of the queen's horses would be recognized in a private carriage; nor would it have been had I not happened to observe that peculiar mark that very morning."

"Well," Leon said, "I will be off now to tell my sisters."

"I shall not stir out to-day, Leon. I really feel that I

should enjoy a day's rest, and it is possible that I may be
sent for to the palace."

"That is almost certain; the ministers must have many
things to question you about, as the queen last night can
only have given them a general account of the affair."

Indeed, a court messenger rode up an hour later and requested Arthur's attendance at the palace. He dressed himself fully and went there. On his arrival he was conducted
to the council-chamber.

"The queens have not yet risen, Captain Hallett. I
should be glad if you would give us much fuller details than
the regent was able to give us last night; perhaps, too, in
addition to what you yourself know of it, you may have
heard from Queen Christina the particulars of her capture."

Arthur gave the particulars at full length, both of the
queen's capture and of his own proceedings.

"Thank you, Captain Hallett," the premier said. "It is
the most audacious attempt against the person of a Queen
of Spain that I have ever heard of; and the manner in which
you thwarted it is no less remarkable. We have already
despatched a courier with orders to Colonel Queredo, ordering him to bring the prisoners to Madrid under the escort
of the troop of cavalry, and to accomplish this with all possible speed, placing them in three carriages and keeping the
most careful guard over them, confining them by day in
some suitable apartment where they can communicate with
no one, and travelling after dark only. They will be tried
privately. I may tell you that although their lives are un-
questionably forfeited, we do not intend to carry out the
extreme penalty, as this could not be done without the whole
affair becoming known—a matter that we are most anxious
to avoid. In the first place, the men are all members of
good families, and could not be so disposed of without the
whole matter being known, and the attempt so nearly succeeded that it might be again tried. Their estates will, of
course, be forfeited, and they will be taken to the frontier

and forbidden ever to cross it again, under penalty of incur-
ring the death-sentence that will be passed upon them. And
now, sir, may we ask you what shape you would like our
gratitude to take, for this great service you have rendered?"

"I have no desire for a reward in any shape, sir," Arthur
replied. "I am an English gentleman with an estate in my
own country, and am well pleased that I have been able to
render a service to the Queen of Spain and her mother.
That is ample reward for my efforts, and I can assure you
that I shall be best pleased if nothing else is done in the
matter. I feel personally thankful to you that you have
decided not to execute the men concerned in the matter; it
would be a pain for me to know that the lives of twelve
men, who were doubtless actuated by what they believed,
however mistakenly, to be the good of their country, should
be forfeited through me. May I enquire if you have arrested the coachman and footmen? I do not ask that mercy
should be extended to them. They were of course bribed
heavily, and I do not think any punishment too severe for
men who could so betray their mistress."

"The police are in search of them, Captain Hallett. We
can hardly expect to find them for some time, for they would
naturally leave within an hour after the perpetration of their
crime, and as they have four days' start they will by this
time be far away. No efforts, however, will be spared in
tracing them. As to what you have said, we shall of course
inform the regent of your declaration, which doubtless does
you the highest credit, but which, as you must see, can hardly
be entertained by us, as it would be impossible for the queen
to remain under so deep an obligation to a gentleman, however honourable and disinterested."

"Well, sir, I can only say that I spoke in earnest. I shall
always be pleased to look back at having been able to render
a service to the Queen of Spain, who had already honoured
me by creating me a Knight of the Isabella of the first class
and a Companion of the Order of San Fernando the Catholic."

He was again sent for to the palace by the queen that afternoon.

"I have been for a drive with my daughter," she said, "and have been acclaimed by the populace, who were evidently pleased that Isabella has recovered from her indisposition; and things will now, I hope, go on as before. I feel that at present I have not thanked you as you deserve for what you did for us. Believe me, that I am not ungrateful. My little daughter is not old enough to understand the service you have rendered us, but in her name I thank you most deeply, and shall ever retain a deep feeling of obligation towards you."

"The service was one that any gentleman might have performed. The sight of that carriage with the blinds down, and the knowledge that one of the horses that was drawing it belonged to your majesty, might well have excited the suspicion in anyone that something was wrong. That idea once entertained, he would have taken steps to get to the bottom of the mystery."

The regent smiled. "I can assure you, Captain Hallett, that few of my countrymen would have troubled their heads about such a matter one way or another, or have put themselves out of the way to investigate it. The premier tells me that he has informed you of the course they intend to take as to these traitors. Has it your approval?"

"Entirely so. I am very little qualified to judge such matters, but it certainly seems to me in the highest degree desirable that this attempt on your person should not be generally known. People may guess as they choose when they hear that these men have been banished for life, but they may merely suppose that they have been concerned in some plot or other. Anything would be better than to let it be known that you had been actually carried off."

That evening Arthur paid a visit to Leon's, and was received with enthusiasm by the three girls. "Leon has been telling us all about your doings, Señor Arthur," Inez exclaimed. "So you have saved the two queens and brought them safely back to Madrid? It was splendid! You can't tell how proud we feel of you, as we flatter ourselves that we are your greatest friends here."

"That you certainly are, Donna Inez. I have no very intimate friends here except yourselves."

"As for Mercedes, she regularly cried," the girl went on.

"You should not tell such things, Inez," Mercedes said, colouring hotly. "I know that it was silly of me, but it did seem so brave and so wonderful."

"There was no bravery in it. The only time when there was ever real danger was when I entered the house and discovered the queens; otherwise, the question was only one of sitting so many hours in the saddle."

"I won't have you belittle yourself," Mercedes said, with an attempt at playfulness. "It was just the same thing when you rescued me: you tried to make out that anyone could have done it. It was altogether a splendid deed."

In a short time guests began to arrive, for it was the evening on which they entertained. Arthur could not help being amused at the talk, which turned partly on the young queen's illness, her rapid recovery, and what would have happened had her illness been a serious one.

A week later Arthur appeared at the trial of the traitors, and gave evidence as to their proceedings. Christina's account of her capture was read aloud. The prisoners attempted no defence, as the complicity of the whole of them in the affair was too evident to dispute. They were all sentenced to death, with the confiscation of their estates. The death-sentence, however, was commuted by the queen regent into banishment for life, and they were taken to the frontier and there released.

On the day after the trial the estates of Count de Monteroy were bestowed upon Arthur by decree signed by the queen regent and the queen. He went at once to the palace to receive the document, and implored the regent to take back the gift. " I have no intention, your majesty, of remaining in Spain after the conclusion of the war, and the gift would be a burden to me. I could not look after the estates, nor see to the welfare of my tenants. I hope that in time, when all these matters are settled, your majesty will be able to recall these unhappy men and replace them on their estates. Doubtless an amnesty will be granted at the end of the war, and I trust that your majesty will be able to include even these malefactors, who will, we may be sure, be moved by your clemency to become faithful servants of yours."

" But a queen cannot be ungrateful, cavalero."

" Your majesty, it is sufficient for me to know that I have your gratitude, and I shall always be proud to know that I have been able to do you and your daughter service, therefore I implore you to take back this gift."

" I cannot refuse any petition from you," the regent said, and taking the deed of gift in her hands she tore it in two; " but in some way, at least, we must manifest our gratitude."

Three days later Arthur received a business notification from a banker in the city stating that the sum of a hundred thousand crowns had been paid by royal order to his account, and five thousand crowns to that of the soldier, John Roper. He felt that he could not refuse this gift, and called at the palace and sincerely thanked the two queens for it.

" We feel, and shall always feel, that we are under the deepest obligation to you, señor; and we have been permitted to show you but a very small portion of it."

Roper was in the highest degree delighted. He had now thrown away his stick, and was able to walk fairly well.

" Well, Captain Hallett," he said, " I never thought, when I sailed on that expedition from Liverpool, that I should come home at the end of a few years with fifteen hundred pounds in my pocket; nor, when we sat down to dinner on board that hulk, that through you I was to have such good fortune."

"You must not put it in that way, Roper. It has come to you through the friendship that led you to give up your stripes in order to follow me, and for the service you did in both the affairs in which we were engaged together."

"It is mighty little I did beyond following your orders. Now, sir, I don't care how soon we go back to England."

"Nor do I, Roper; but we must see this business out. From what I hear, Maroto, Don Carlos' commander-in-chief in the north, who appears to be an unmixed scoundrel, is negotiating with Espartero for surrender. He has already seized and murdered six of the Carlists' best generals, who would, he knew, be opposed to his projects. If the negotiations do not fall through, there is an end to the Carlist cause in the north, and Espartero will be able to move with his whole force into Aragon, in which case he will speedily bring the contest to an end."

A week later Arthur was at a reception at Leon's, when he observed a man scowling at him, and asking his name from a friend, learned that he was Count Silvio de Mora. He thought no more of the matter at the time, but on the following morning a card, with the name of Don Pedro de Verderas, was brought in to him. He at once ordered Roper to show him up. A young man entered and bowed courteously, but waved his hand aside when Arthur offered him a chair.

"I have come to you, señor, on the part of my friend Count Silvio de Mora, who conceives himself to be seriously aggrieved by you."

"Indeed, sir; in what way? I have never exchanged a word with him that I am aware of, though I certainly observed that he was looking unpleasantly at me last night."

"The count's grievance is a very clear and distinct one, señor. He was, as you are doubtless aware, betrothed to Donna Mercedes de Balen. That young lady, as a consequence, he tells me, of her being captured by the Carlists, wrote by the hand of her brother to say that the shock had been so great that she was determined never to marry, but to spend her life in good works. The count, my friend, assented, though deeply troubled by the decision. The count now finds that by common report Donna Mercedes——"

"Stay, sir," Arthur said sternly, "don't let the name of Donna Mercedes de Balen be brought into this matter. The Count Silvio de Mora conceives that he has a quarrel with me and demands satisfaction. That is quite enough as between two gentlemen. I shall be perfectly prepared to give him that satisfaction. A friend of mine will wait upon you to arrange the preliminaries."

"Nothing can be more satisfactory," the Spaniard said. He and Arthur exchanged deep bows, and he went out.

Arthur sat down to think deeply. He was now twenty, with an experience that made him feel years older. Donna Mercedes was a year younger, and gradually for a long time past he had been aware of the fact that it was more than the friendship brought about by their close intimacy that he felt towards her. She was in all respects a charming girl. She was bright, pleasant, and natural; one of the acknowledged beauties of Madrid. He had often told himself that it would be wrong of him to presume, on the friendship of Count Leon, to raise his eyes to his sister, who was co-heiress with her sisters to large estates which had been the property of her mother. The queen's remark about her blushes when she mentioned him had often recurred to him, and they had suggested to him that possibly it was not mere gratitude she felt for him. The queen's gift had placed him in a better position than before, so that it would not be necessary to ask her to wait five years before he would be able to support her in the style of life to which she had been accustomed. He had been intimate with the family in a manner altogether contrary to Spanish customs, and it might well be that she had come to care for him.

"Well, I will speak to her brother about it after this affair is over," he concluded; "and now I will send word to Don

Lopez Parona. I have seen a good deal of him, and no doubt he will act for me."

He sent Roper off with a note, and an hour later the young man came in.

"Don Lopez," he said, " Count Silvio de Mora has forced a quarrel upon me, and it is necessary that I should fight him. I have sent for you to ask if you will be my second in the affair."

"With pleasure, Captain Hallett. What arrangements do you wish made?"

"Well, I have been thinking it over. I don't pretend to be a really good shot with the pistol, though I have practised a bit. Do you know whether the count is a good swordsman?"

"He has the reputation of being an excellent one."

"Well, I took lessons with the sword four years ago when I was at Vittoria, but I have never used a straight sword since. I don't suppose he is a better shot with the pistol than I am. I wish you to say that I have not touched a sword for years, but that if he will give me a fortnight to practise I will choose that weapon; if he objects to that, I will take pistols. I fenced for nearly six months at Vittoria and worked very hard, and my master said that I was really a good swordsman, and had learned as much as a Spaniard would in two years. I think with hard work that I can get it back again in a fortnight."

Three hours later Don Lopez returned. "I have arranged it as you desired. It seems the count knows nothing of pistols, and he is quite willing to give you a fortnight to prepare for the encounter."

"Very well, then. I will go this evening to a fencing school, and will put in six hours' work a day, divided into three lessons of two hours each."

"But that would be prodigious, señor!"

"If you feel my muscles you will, I think, admit that they can stand pretty hard work."

Arthur went to the man who was considered to be the first teacher of fencing in Madrid, and arranged to go to him three times a day—at eight in the morning, at two in the afternoon, and at seven in the evening. The master at first said that it would be impossible for him to practise for so long a time.

"Well, at any rate, professor, I will try. It is quite possible that for the first three or four days I shall have to rest a bit sometimes, but I think at the end of the fortnight I shall be able to work the six hours a day without difficulty."

Arthur took off his coat and waistcoat, and turned up his shirt-sleeves.

"By San Martin, you have a wonderful arm!" the professor said.

"We play hard at school in England. All our games demand strength and activity, and it is not wonderful that our muscles are vastly harder and stronger than those of your gentlemen, who would consider it *infra dig.* when boys to engage in any sport that would make them warm."

The professor felt the muscles of his right arm. "Well, señor, if you fence, as your muscles would seem to show, you need only a little teaching to be one of the best swordsmen in Spain. Then, too, your height and age give you great advantage. Well, señor, take the foil and let me see what you know."

"Very good," he said, after a bout of two or three minutes. "You have been well taught. I can see that you are out of practice, and your returns are not as quick as might be. However, if you work as you say, that will soon be put right."

After the lesson, Arthur found his wrist recovering its suppleness, but he was glad to stop before the second bout was finished.

"You will do, señor," the professor said, when he acknowledged that he had had enough. "I suppose you are working in this way for a purpose, and I can tell you that I should be sorry to be your opponent."

Arthur's wrist and arm were stiff the next morning, and he was not sorry to follow his teacher's advice and content himself with an hour and a half at each lesson.

The first week Leon in vain endeavoured to find out from him where he had spent his time. "I used almost always to find you in," he said, "but now, whether it is the morning or the afternoon, I find you away. Of an evening you have often dropped in, but later than usual."

"I am rather busy just now, Leon, and of course go in every morning from ten to one to Colonel Wylde's office, and generally for an hour in the afternoon; but things are so quiet, both up in the north and the east, that he does not consider it necessary for me to start again at present."

"Well, the girls are always saying, 'What has come over Captain Hallett the last few days?'"

"Tell them, please, that nothing has come over me, but that I have some work that keeps me particularly busy. In another ten days I shall have brought it to a conclusion."

Arthur had no doubt that his antagonist had not altogether thrown away his time, and that he too had been practising; but he thought that in all probability this was confined to a little dilletante work lasting perhaps for an hour a day.

At the end of the fortnight the professor announced that never in his experience had he seen so strong an arm and so supple a wrist, and that he believed Arthur could easily hold his own against even the strongest antagonist.

"I myself am considered a good blade," he said, "but during the past two or three days I have with difficulty held my own with you, and indeed you have hit me oftener than I have hit you; so now you have done with me."

"Yes, professor; and I am greatly indebted to you for the time you have spent upon me, and the trouble you have taken."

The professor shrugged his shoulders. "You have paid me well for it, señor; but it has been a real pleasure to me. A teacher is always interested in his pupil, and when he is fortunate enough to have a pupil like you, he does not care what trouble he bestows upon him. Your fencing has been a revelation to me of what your countrymen can do. I speak not of the skill, but of the power to sustain fatigue. When I compare, señor, your earnestness, strength of muscle, and quickness of wrist with the work of the young nobles and cavaliers who come to me and flatter themselves that they are learning to fence, I can well understand why you Englishmen are such great soldiers, and why you spread yourselves over the world and conquer it. Three centuries ago the men of my race were great soldiers. They were strong and hardy, and they conquered well-nigh all Europe, till, unfortunately for themselves, they fell across you, and from that time their downfall began. You fought against us in Holland, you fought with the Huguenot King of Navarre at Ivry, you fought with us on the seas, destroyed our Armada, captured Cadiz, and demolished our mercantile marine, and, as it would seem, broke the spirit of our people; for from that time we have steadily gone down. It makes one sad to think of it."

CHAPTER XVI

ENGAGED

ON the morning of the fifteenth day after Arthur had received Count Silvio's challenge, the two seconds met and arranged for the duel to take place at a distance of a mile from the town. It was to be at seven in the morning, so that there would be no fear of interruption. Each of the gentlemen was provided with a piece of string, the length of the sword of his principal. These were found to be as nearly as possible the same length. It was agreed that the count should bring a surgeon with him, and that no other, save the seconds, should be present at the encounter. Don Lopez went round to Arthur's chambers half an hour before the time to start. Arthur had, the night before, told Roper of what was going to happen, and given him instructions as to the disposal of his horses. "Take anything you like yourself, Roper. What money I have will be in that desk; you may take that to pay for your journey home. You will want it, as we both sent to England the sums we had in the bank."

"I have no fear, captain, that I shall have to take any such step. I feel sure that no Spaniard is a match for you."

"You can't know that, and certainly I have no reason to believe so. If it came to downright hard hitting I fancy I could hold my own against most Spaniards, but in fencing it is a different thing; it is not a question of strength only by a long way."

"Some of the Spaniards are good hardy men, captain, no doubt; but very few of these will be found among the gentry, who pass the day in sleeping, dawdling about, and smoking cigarettes and drinking coffee. Well, I suppose, sir, there is no harm in my going out and taking up a place where I can see what goes on?"

"None at all, Roper; I have no doubt that the count will have a number of his friends to look on. I am sure he expects to run me through without trouble, and he will like to show off his prowess before his friends."

They drove in a carriage to the place fixed upon for the encounter. As Arthur had expected, a score or two of gentlemen had collected near. He spoke to his second, who went up to that of his antagonist and said: "My principal understood that this matter was to be kept private, and that none but ourselves should be informed of it."

This was repeated to the count, who shrugged his shoulders and said: "I mentioned it to a few friends, and no doubt they told others, but it makes no difference whatever."

Arthur pressed his lips tightly together when the answer was repeated to him. "You want your performances to be

seen, eh?" he muttered. "Perhaps you will be sorry you
have got so many witnesses before you have done."

The preliminaries were speedily settled, and the two antagonists removed their coats and waistcoats, and faced each
other. The count began with a few preliminary flourishes,
intended to show off his swordsmanship, and how lightly he
thought of the encounter. He was fully half a head shorter
than his antagonist, and the latter's much longer reach would
have given him a decided advantage had they been equal in
other respects. Arthur stood firmly on guard, contenting
himself with putting aside almost contemptuously the other's
play. He waited till the count steadied down, and began in
earnest. Then, to the astonishment of his antagonist, he
took the offensive. In vain the latter tried to get within
his point; in vain he exerted himself to the utmost, springing in and out; with scarce a movement of his wrist Arthur's
point played in a little menacing circle. There were no fierce
lunges to be turned aside, no openings left to be taken advantage of. Steadily Arthur advanced, and foot by foot
his antagonist had to give way.

In vain the count exerted himself to his utmost. The
perspiration streamed from his face, and his expression
changed from that of half-contemptuous superiority to rage
and uneasiness. Again and again the count felt that his
adversary was but playing with him, and that he avoided
taking advantage of openings that had been left him. His
opponent's face was grave and earnest, but without any other
emotion. Little by little Arthur's advance was accelerated.
In vain the Spaniard attempted to stand his ground against
the menacing point. In spite of his greatest efforts he had
to give way, and was driven backwards across the green sward
on which the encounter was taking place, till he was close to
its boundary. Then there was a sudden wrench, and his
sword was sent flying through the air.

Arthur lowered his point, and said in a quiet, deliberate
voice that could be heard by all the astonished spectators:

"You seem to be a little out of breath, señor; perhaps you would like to wait for three or four minutes before we begin again."

The count, white with rage and shame, walked and picked up his sword.

"Now, señor," Arthur went on, after a pause of two or three minutes, "we will recommence the affair. Hitherto I have but played with you, now I warn you that I shall run you through the shoulder when I get you to the other side of the field."

Again the singular scene began. In vain the count endeavoured to circle round his foe; in vain he tried to arrest his own steady retreat. Move as he would to change his position, Arthur with his long stride and quick spring always kept in front of him. In a quarter of an hour he was driven back across the field; then for the first time Arthur lunged. His antagonist's sword dropped useless by his side as he ran him through the upper part of the arm and shoulder.

"This may perhaps serve as a lesson to you, count, not to pick quarrels gratuitously with strangers of whose force you are unacquainted. Your life has been in my hands a hundred times had I chosen to avail myself of the openings, but I did not wish seriously to injure you. You have brought a number of gentlemen here to-day to witness your triumph: I trust that they have been amused."

So saying, he turned and walked back to the spot where he had left his clothes, put them on, and entered the carriage with his second, beckoning to Roper, who was standing a short distance away, to get up on the box.

"Truly you have astounded me!" Don Lopez said. "I thought that with your height and length of arm you would give him some trouble, but such an exhibition as this was never seen!" and he burst into a fit of laughter. "The count won't be able to show his face in Madrid again for I know not how long. The wound to his body is nothing, but that to his pride is terrible. He will never hear the end of

it. To think that he was driven right across a field as if
he had been a pig under a peasant's goad, without a possibility of stopping; that he should have been disarmed and
played with, is too funny. Of course, the thing will get
about all over Madrid. You will have to be careful, though,
Don Arthur, how you go out after dark, or you may find
yourself with a dagger between your shoulders. It would
scarcely be in human nature for a man to put up with being
made a public laughing-stock without trying to get his revenge, and certainly Don Silvio is not, from what I know of
him, likely to be an exception to the rule."

"Yes; no doubt I shall have to be careful. I suppose
one can buy such a thing as a shirt of link armour in
Madrid?"

"Oh, yes; there are plenty of them to be picked up in the
shops where they keep old weapons and curiosities; a good
one costs money though."

"Money is nothing," Arthur said. "If one gets such a
thing one wants to have as good a one, and at the same time
as light a one, as money can buy. Would you mind getting
one for me, Lopez? I would rather not be seen buying such
a thing myself."

"With pleasure. I will make a tour of all the shops where
they are likely to keep such things, and pick out the best
that I can find for you, and it is hard if I don't manage to
get you one by this evening; although I think you are safe
for a few days, for were you found stabbed now, everyone
would put it down to Don Silvio at once. I should say that
he would hardly attempt such a thing in Madrid. You are
likely to be in much greater danger when you go off to join
the army again."

"Yes, I think that would be the case; but still, I would
rather not risk his beginning at once."

"Quite right; I certainly should not if I were in your
place."

On reaching his apartments Arthur sat down to breakfast

with his friend. Not until the latter had left did Roper make any allusion to the scene he had witnessed.

"Now, Captain Hallett," he said, on returning to the room after letting the visitor out, "what did I tell you it would be? I stayed at a distance and roared with laughter. It was the funniest thing I ever saw—to see him dancing with rage, and you pushing him steadily backwards with scarcely a movement of your sword. It was worse than a fight I once saw in the streets of Liverpool. One of those bullying fellows who stand at the corners of streets and insult passers-by pushed against a quiet-looking chap that was passing him. Well, sir, this happened to be a noted prize-fighter, and the way he gave that fellow pepper was worth walking a good many miles to see. There is no fear of your having to fight another duel while you are out here."

"I think not, Roper; but at the same time I shall have to be careful. When a Spaniard cannot get revenge any other way, sometimes he hires an assassin to put a dagger between his enemy's shoulders."

"Well, sir, I must take to going out with you, and we must not be out after dark."

"I am going to have even a better guard than you would be. I have asked Don Lopez to get me a shirt of mail. People used to wear them a good deal in olden times, and I feel that I shall be all the safer for using one for a bit."

"That will be a good plan, sir; still, at the same time, it might be advisable for me to keep near you. I may as well be doing that as anything else, and if there is to be any sticking with knives, I should like to have a hand in it."

"Very well, Roper; at any rate, you can walk with me when I am going anywhere. Of course, I cannot tell always at what hour I may be returning, and I should not like to keep you waiting about for hours."

"Oh, you could tell me the hour before which you would not be leaving, captain, then I would be at hand at that time. I may as well smoke my pipe there as anywhere else.

The chances are that I should always find someone to talk to."

Three hours later Leon came in.

"What is this you have been doing?" he said excitedly. "I have been to the club, and nothing else is being talked about but a duel between you and Count Silvio de Mora. They say it was the strangest fight ever seen—that you drove him across the meadow, then disarmed him, and told him to get his breath; then drove him back again, and finally, after sparing him fifty times, you ran him through the shoulder."

"These are about the facts of the case," Arthur replied quietly. "I should have been very glad if nothing had been said about the affair, and I arranged that no one but our seconds and the surgeon should be present. Instead of that, the count chose to tell some thirty or forty of his friends; no doubt he thought to make an example of me. The consequence is, as you say, that the affair has got all over the town, to my great annoyance."

"But what was the quarrel about?"

"It was about a private matter, and I would rather that you did not ask me to tell you more; enough that he forced it upon me."

"But, my dear Arthur, it seems to me that this must affect me. Why should the count have fixed a quarrel upon you? If he had forced one upon me, on account of Mercedes throwing him over a year ago, I should not have been surprised; though I don't know why he should have done so, as he appeared to have taken his dismissal in very good part. Why should he quarrel with you?"

"Because it was his fancy, I suppose, Leon."

"Tut, tut!" the other said warmly. "It seems to me that this is a matter that concerns my family, and I must really ask you, my dear Arthur, to tell me frankly how it occurred."

Arthur sat silent for a minute.

"Well, Leon, I may as well ask you a question now which

I should have asked you shortly. I have long loved your sister Mercedes. I have refrained from speaking for three reasons. In the first place, because I am very young. You have chosen to laugh at me when I said so, but in point of fact I am only twenty!"

"Only twenty!" Leon said incredulously; "I have always taken you to be as old as myself."

"And I have told you that I was not so. I repeat I am not yet twenty, and am therefore only a year older than your sister. The second reason I have regarded as more serious: I am an Englishman, and should necessarily take her home if she married me. In the third place, I was not in a position pecuniarily to ask her to be my wife until I was five-and-twenty and came into my estate. The last of these reasons has ceased to exist by my having received from the queens a present of one hundred thousand crowns for the service I rendered them. I had begged them very strongly not to offer me any reward for that service, but Christina said that it was impossible for them to remain under so great an obligation to me. I spite of that I should have still refused, or, if I found that I could not do so, have handed over the money for the benefit of the poor; but the thought that it would at least remove one of the obstacles that stood in the way of my asking you for your sister's hand, decided me in accepting it, as it would enable me to keep her in a position similar to that which she has held at home, until I come into my estate. That estate was worth at my father's death about one thousand English pounds a year. Then there is, of course, a good house and grounds, and the accumulation of the income during the past ten years will have amounted to a sum which would enable me to double the size of the estate. Therefore, I have only the first two difficulties. It is for you to decide whether these are insuperable. So, Leon, I ask you now for the hand of your sister, and I can promise that, if you grant it and she consents, I will do all in my power to make her happy."

Leon rose and grasped Arthur by the hand. "Nothing can give me greater pleasure, my dear fellow, than to grant the request you have made. I shall, of course, be sorry to lose her, but England is not so far from Spain, and I doubt not that you will bring her over to see us sometimes. I and my sisters may even visit you occasionally in England. There is no one to whom I would so gladly see her united, for you have fairly won her. You saved her from death, and I have ever since hoped that some day you would claim her. As to her feelings I can, of course, say nothing, but I am not altogether blind, and it has long been evident to me that she thinks of no one but you. As to money, it is a secondary matter, though I do not say that it is not an advantage that you should have an income of your own, and not owe everything to her. She has, however, a not inadequate portion, as my mother was an only daughter and a wealthy heiress, and her fortune will be divided between my three sisters: her share would amount roughly to some seven or eight thousand crowns a year. There is but one drawback to the match, and that is the difference of religion. You know how bigoted we Spaniards are; we do not allow any Protestant place of worship to exist, save only the private chapel of your ambassador; and the priesthood will move heaven and earth to prevent this marriage taking place. Indeed, it seems to me that the only plan will be for me to take her to England, and for her to be married there. However, the obstacle is not a serious one in my eyes. That you are a Protestant is amply sufficient to show that there are as good men of one religion as of another. Well, will you come with me at once?"

"I will come this evening, Leon. I would rather it had not been settled to-day, when I have just been engaged in shedding blood. However, that was not my fault. Will you be alone this evening?"

"Yes, so far as I know."

"Then I will come in after dinner. I am more nervous

about this than I was before meeting Count Silvio. You see, you have so long made up your mind that I was a man, while I have been thinking, and still feel that I am only a boy."

" Nonsense, Arthur! you stand over six feet. You have the strength of two ordinary Spaniards. You have accomplished marvels and won the gratitude of queens. It is perfectly ridiculous for you to talk in that way. Well, then, I shall expect you this evening. Mercedes and the girls have gone out this morning, and no doubt she will, in the course of her visits, have heard of your prowess to-day, which will be a good introduction, although I do not think she will be surprised in any way, as her confidence in your abilities to do anything you undertake is absolute."

Don Lopez came in late that afternoon. "I have seen quite a perfect coat of mail," he said. "It was made for a bishop of Toledo who had many enemies, and is a hundred and fifty years old. It is very light, and can withstand any dagger thrust. It is dear: the man wants five hundred crowns for it, and declares that he will not take a penny less."

" Thank you, Lopez, that will suit me admirably. I will give you an order for that sum. Will you ask him to send it round to me in the morning?"

Arthur was very nervous when he started that evening for Count Leon's. He still felt in many respects a boy, and in spite of Leon's report, he felt it hardly possible that Donna Mercedes could have come to love him. He dressed himself in his evening suit with unusual care, but did not start till the last moment. He was shown up into the drawing-room as usual. Mercedes and her two sisters were in the room.

" I have to quarrel with you," the former said laughingly. "I hear that you have been cruelly ill-treating a gentleman in whom I had once a great interest;—not only ill-treating him, but turning him into a laughing-stock. Now, señor, I

demand that you tell us what it was about, and why you have
thus assailed a gentleman to whom, as you know, I was once
much attached."

"Were you much attached to him, Donna Mercedes?"

"Well," she said, pouting, "you know I was all but affianced to him."

"By your own wishes, señora?"

"Well, never mind about my own, wishes," she said; "it
is quite sufficient that I was almost affianced to him. Now
I demand from you again a true and complete history how
this came about."

"Well," he said, "you can hardly expect, señora, that I
should go into particulars of this kind before your sisters—
young ladies, who cannot but be horrified by deeds of violence."

Mercedes laughed. "Well, you will tell me some day,
won't you, what it was all about, and why you so ill-treated
him? I hear that he will not be able to show his face for
some time in Madrid."

"I will tell you all that is good for you to learn," he said
in a tone of banter. "I know that you must be grieving
terribly over it."

"Of course I am, dreadfully!" the girl said. "When I
heard how you had been treating him, I almost made up my
mind not to speak to you again. Ah, here is Leon, and looking as serious as a judge."

Leon came up to Mercedes, and to her surprise took her
by the hand.

"Little sister," he said, "I have a very serious duty to
perform. I have had another request for your hand."

The girl turned pale. "You know," she said, "that I do
not intend to marry, Leon; I have told you so over and
over again."

"That may be so, sister, but I believe that ladies change
their minds in these matters not infrequently. The gentleman who is your suitor is not unknown to you. He is of

good blood and honourable position. You will, perhaps, anticipate his name. It is the Cavalero Captain Arthur Hallett, a Knight of Isabella of the first class, and a Companion of the Order of Fernando the Catholic."

The girl's face, which had been set with a mutinous expression, changed suddenly, a deep wave of colour rushed over her face and her head drooped.

"He has my willing consent to the alliance, Mercedes; indeed, I know of no one in the world to whom I could so willingly commit you and your happiness."

"I know, señora," Arthur said, "that I am very unworthy of so great a gift, but at least I can promise to do my best to make you happy."

The girl lifted her head suddenly. "Do not say that you are unworthy," she said. "It is I who should say that. Have you not saved me from death? Have you not saved Spain from being ruined? It is I who feel, above all things, honoured by your love."

Then Leon said, with a slight smile: "I don't think that there is any occasion for me to lay my orders upon you on the subject. Take her, Arthur. I can trust her happiness in your hands with a certainty that my confidence will not be abused;" and he gave her hand to Arthur, who bent down and kissed her.

The two younger girls clapped their hands loudly. "Oh, Arthur!" Inez exclaimed, "I shall never call you Don Arthur again. We are pleased! We always knew that Mercedes was fond of you—anyone could have seen that with half an eye, but we did not know what you felt towards her. We are pleased, I cannot tell you how much! I believe we are more pleased than she is."

"Now, you madcap!" her brother said; "suppose you two come in with me to the next room, and let us leave these two young people alone."

"And did you really doubt that I loved you?" Mercedes said a short time afterwards. "I have been so afraid of showing it too much; but after being carried in your arms all that journey, I knew that I could never marry anyone else. If you had not asked for me before you went away, I should have assuredly gone into a convent."

Half an hour later the others returned to the room, and they held a long conversation together. It was finally agreed, in view of the opposition that would be raised by the Spanish clergy, on the grounds of the difference of religion, that the engagement should be kept quiet for a time, and that things should go on as they were.

"It cannot be many months before this war is over," Leon said, "and you will be returning to England. You will necessarily be away a great deal, and it will avoid much trouble and argument if you assent to the matter being kept quiet."

Both Mercedes and Arthur agreed that it would be better so, as they felt sure that there would be a vehement opposition on the part of the clergy if a member of a noble family contracted a marriage with a heretic.

To Arthur's surprise, when he called next morning Mercedes, who received him alone, said with a flush, "Good-morning, Arthur!" in English. He looked at her with surprise.

"Do you mean to say that you understand English, Mercedes?"

"I have been learning it for the past year," she said in imperfect English, but with a pretty accent. "I loved you, Arthur, after you had saved me, and so I loved everything English; and as I had plenty of time upon my hands I have spent two hours a day ever since in learning it. I had no difficulty in finding a mistress, for several English families settled in the town after the last war."

"And you thought, perhaps, that it would come in useful, Mercedes?"

"I did not quite like to think that," she said, glancing at him; "but it seemed to me that perhaps, as I loved you so much, you might some day come to love me. I never quite thought so, you know, but I could not help sometimes hoping it. Anyhow, sir, it is quite enough for you that, whatever was the reason, I have learned English; and now, when we are together alone you must always talk it with me. I want to get to speak quite perfectly before I go to England and meet your friends."

"You really talk it very fairly now," he said, "and you must not be in the least afraid that anyone will find fault with you."

"I suppose you have heard," Leon said a few days later, "that Don Silvio is still in Madrid. They say he will see no one."

"I shall feel rather glad when he is gone, Leon. He is evidently a revengeful fellow; that is quite clear by the way in which he fixed a quarrel upon me. He won't do anything himself, but I think he is quite capable of hiring a ruffian to put me out of the way. I know that plenty of unprincipled characters are to be found in the city who would willingly do the job for a few dollars."

"I have no doubt about that, and I was intending to speak seriously to you on the subject. Things are still very quiet, but I dare say Colonel Wylde would send you to one or other of the armies if you were to ask him."

"I am not at all disposed to go until I am obliged to; I am enjoying myself a great deal too much for that. But I have taken precautions. Roper comes with me every evening to your house, and meets me at the door when I go away; and, moreover, I have bought a shirt of mail. It is a splendid example of the best sort of work of that kind. I have put it on the table and tried to drive a knife through it, but striking with all my force I simply broke the weapon and did not injure the chain. I put it on now whenever I go out after dark."

"I am very glad to hear it. No amount of strength or bravery can save a man from the hands of an assassin, and a good mail shirt is worth a score of guards, for a man who bides his time will always find a chance sooner or later."

"That is how I look at it, and I can assure you that I am far too happy at the present time to be willing to throw away the smallest chance."

Three days later Don Lopez called at Arthur's rooms.

"I have heard this morning that Don Silvio has gone out of town. Now you will have to look to yourself. So long as he was here I considered that you were safe, for if anything happened to you suspicion would at once fall upon him. Now that he is away, people might suspect as much as they liked, but it would be extremely difficult to bring the matter home to him."

"But I should hardly think he will do anything more in the matter," Arthur said.

"I think quite the contrary," Lopez replied. "If you had simply met him and wounded him, the thing might have passed off quietly. That would have shown that you were the better swordsman, and there would have been an end of it. But you have made him the laughing-stock of the town. It will be a joke against him all his life that he was driven about like a sheep by a man whom he boasted he was going to kill like a dog, and he will never get over it. No one could stand such disgrace with equanimity, but of course it is infinitely worse for a man as proud and as touchy about his family as he is."

"I will look out, but I don't think any precautions will be of much value. If a man wants to stab you, he is sure to find an opportunity sooner or later. However, I have my coat of mail, and I rely more upon that than on any vigilance on my part or on Roper's."

Two days later, when Arthur was returning home from Leon's, two men sprang out from a dark entry and struck at his back. Sharp exclamations broke from them as, instead of their knives burying themselves to the hilt, they struck on a hard substance. Arthur was nearly knocked down by the force of the blows, but springing round, he seized both men by the throat before they could recover from their surprise. Roper, who was walking some ten paces in the rear, rushed up.

" All right, Roper, I have got them! " Arthur cried, and squeezing their throats, he dashed their heads together with all his strength two or three times, with the result that as he released his hold they fell to the ground insensible.

"I think we will walk on, Roper. I must have pretty nearly broken their skulls, to say nothing of half choking them. If we were to give them into custody it would be an endless affair, and I might be kept here for months. They will certainly not repeat the experiment, and whatever attempt Don Silvio may make next, it will not be in the same direction."

The next morning he told Leon of what had happened.

"I don't know whether you did right to let them go, Arthur. There is nothing to prevent this fellow from trying again in some other way."

"Nor would there have been if I had given them into custody. You may be sure that his bribes would be large enough to secure their silence as to who had employed them, and they would simply have declared that they only attacked me to obtain possession of any valuables I might have about me. Don Silvio is rich, and it is a hundred to one that, before the trial came on, the men would have escaped. A hundred pounds would bribe any jailer in Spain. If by accident this failed, he would bribe the judges, so that nothing would ever come out against the villain who set the men on me, and I might be kept dancing attendance on the courts for months."

"That is true enough, Arthur. Still, the matter would be kept hanging over his head, and until it was settled he would be hardly likely to make another attempt upon you. However, we need not discuss it now that you have let the fellows go scot-free."

"I have not let them go scot-free, I can assure you. In the first place I nearly strangled them, and in the second I am by no means sure that I did not fracture their skulls."

"That sort of man has got a very hard skull," Leon answered. "Probably you would have fractured mine if you had dashed it against somebody else's with those muscular arms of yours, but I have doubts whether the head of a professional bravo would not stand even such a blow as that—I won't say with impunity, but at least without any very serious damage."

"Don't say anything to Mercedes about is, it would only fidget her. And I can assure you it does not disquiet me. The mail shirt has indisputably proved that it is knife-proof, and when Don Silvio receives the reports from these two gentlemen he will see that all attempts to dispose of me in that way will be in vain. I give him credit for ingenuity, and it is quite possible he will hit upon some other idea. However, I trust that I shall be able to meet it, whatever it is; and indeed I shall be somewhat interested to see what his next plan may be."

"What do you say, Arthur, to my mentioning this affair at the club, and saying loudly that I have no doubt whatever it is the outcome of your duel with him?"

"My dear Leon, that would simply entail his challenging you, and the man really doesn't fence badly. It was only my superior length of arm and sheer strength that overbore him."

"I could refuse to fight him," Leon said.

"No, I don't think you could, and certainly I should not like you to do so. You and I may feel perfectly convinced that this attack upon me last night was his work, but we have no absolute proof of it. The fact that I beat him in a duel simply shows that I am a much better swordsman than he is, and is no reflection upon his character. So you see, if you were to bring this accusation against him, without having a shadow of real proof, I doubt if you could refuse to meet him. You see, the man has a large circle of friends and relatives, and possesses much influence. You were willing to accept him as a brother-in-law, and although just at present the town has a laugh against him, that would not prevent his friends from rallying round him were you to bring such a terrible accusation against him as that of his setting assassins on me."

"No, I suppose not," Leon said regretfully. "You know, Arthur, I feel more grateful to you than ever, for it is evident now that you not only saved Mercedes from death, but from marriage with a man of whose real character I was altogether ignorant. How grieved I should have been had she been tied to such a man, who would assuredly have shown himself in his true colours sooner or later!"

"Yes, she has certainly had a narrow escape, Leon, though I cannot help thinking that in any case you would have learned more of him before the marriage came off."

Leon shook his head.

"I don't see how I could. He bore a very respectable character, and indeed was thought highly of. That he should have picked a quarrel with you is not altogether unnatural in the circumstances, and really this attempt upon your life is the only thing I have against him. It is a thousand pities now that, instead of treating him as you did, you did not run him through and have done with him."

"I don't know that it has made much difference, Leon. He has, as you say, powerful friends and connections, and whereas, if he had fallen in a duel with yourself or any other noble of his own rank, they would have thought no more of the matter, they would certainly have attempted to avenge his death if I, a foreigner and a heretic, had killed him. The Church counts for a great deal, and I believe he is a very rigid Catholic; therefore the chances are that there would have been a terrible row over it, and I might have had to leave the kingdom, which, in the present circumstances, would be particularly disagreeable to me."

"Well, perhaps you are right," Leon said. "The really unfortunate part of the affair is that he should have taken it into his head to resent the fact that Mercedes did not keep to her resolution of remaining single and perhaps going into a convent."

"But you did not guarantee that she would, Leon?"

"No; but you know, in that letter that you wrote and I signed, we certainly gave him to understand that she broke off the engagement on those terms."

"Yes, that was so. But I imagine that a young lady has the right to change her mind without being called to account for it."

"Yes, that is all very well, but, you see, the gentleman has also some sort of right to resent it. Well, it is useless to say any more about it. You have let the fellows go, and whether for good or evil the matter is concluded as far they are concerned."

CHAPTER XVII

KIDNAPPED

A PRIEST was sitting at a table in a second-class café when a gentleman entered and came up to the table.

"Good-morning, count," the priest said. "I received your note asking me to meet you at this place, and here I am."

"Thanks, father," the other said, as he took a seat beside him and ordered coffee. He waited till it was brought, and then went on: "I wanted to see you about a rather delicate matter that concerns you, and, I may say, the Church."

The priest looked surprised.

"You are, I know," the count went on, "the spiritual adviser of Count Leon de Balen and his family?"

"I can hardly say of the count," the priest said with a

smile, "for, like too many young noblemen of his age, he does not trouble me with his confessions; but of the ladies, yes."

"May I ask if Donna Mercedes comes very often to confession?"

"Well, my son, unless you ask for some very particular reason, that is a question I should not care to answer."

There was a ring of dissatisfaction in the priest's answer that the count was not slow to notice.

"I have a reason for asking," he said. "You know, father, that I was at one time, I will not say actually betrothed, but very nearly so, to Donna Mercedes. She broke off the affair under the plea that she had made up her mind to remain single and to devote herself to good works."

"So she told me," the priest said, "and I highly approved of her determination."

"May I ask, father, if she has repeated that statement to you of late?"

"She has not come to me frequently of late," the priest said in a tone that showed it was a sore point with him.

"I thought so," the count went on. "Well, father, you can hardly help noticing that for some time past a young English adventurer has been frequently at the house."

The priest nodded.

"He is a friend of her brother's. It is a matter that I have regretted, as I have considered that so close an intimacy with a heretic is not seemly; but this cannot affect Donna Mercedes."

"I should say, father, that it does, very seriously. I have information of what takes place in the house, and I can assure you that if not already engaged, it is certain that Donna Mercedes will be betrothed to this adventurer before long."

The priest uttered an angry exclamation.

"It would be a grave scandal, a terrible scandal," he said, "for the daughter of a noble house to be betrothed to a heretic!"

"And a serious loss to the Church too," the count said smoothly. "If this marriage could be prevented, doubtless she would revert to her previous intention of entering a convent; and I need hardly say that she is an heiress, and that her revenues would be better employed in the Church than by this young heretic."

The priest nodded. The fact was too evident to need argument.

"I have done my best to prevent it," the count went on, "by challenging this young upstart to a duel; but, as you may perhaps have heard, he proved himself the better swordsman. I have, therefore, resolved to lay the matter frankly before you, in order that you may, if you choose, put a stop to what, as you say, would be a grievous scandal."

"I do not see how I could do so," the priest said gloomily. "It would be useless for me to speak to her brother, who is most to blame, for he should not have permitted so close an intimacy to arise. Nor do I think that I should succeed with Donna Mercedes herself. She is, I regret to say, of a somewhat headstrong disposition. I have more than once spoken to her about this strange intimacy between her brother and a gentleman who is at once a foreigner and a heretic, but she has always replied that it was a matter on which I should speak to her brother and not to her, as it was he who had brought him to the house. And once when I tried to press the matter she said, in a tone that was not altogether seemly, that he had saved her life, as of course I had heard—though, for my part, I doubt whether Cabrera would have carried his threat into execution—and that she certainly would not take any step to induce her brother to close his doors to his visits."

"No, father, I did not think for a moment that any persuasions would turn this unhappy girl from the course on which she seems to be bent."

"What, then, do you propose? I am willing to take any steps that would put a stop to this deplorable state of things."

" Well, father, you know that, although some laxity has been shown of late years, the laws against infidelity to the Church are still in force."

" That is so," he said. " But this young man is, it appears, an agent of his government; and though we could assuredly use these laws against a native, we could scarcely put them in force against a commissioner of a friendly country."

" That I foresaw," the count said; " but what cannot be done openly can be done privately. There can be little doubt that if this young adventurer were shut up in a cell in a monastery for a few years, Donna Mercedes, when all trace of him was lost, would revert to her original intention and enter a convent, in which case her property would go to the Church."

The priest was silent for some time.

" It is a daring plan," he said, " one of which I certainly could not approve did I see any other way of saving this unfortunate girl from eternal perdition, which would doubtless befall her. Were she to marry this English stranger, no doubt she would in time adopt his religion. I must think it over. It would be a grave step to take, and if it were to be discovered it might cause a serious scandal; at the same time something might be risked for the sake of this young lady's eternal welfare."

" I do not think that the risk would be worth taking into consideration," the count said. " There must be plenty of cells in your monasteries where he could be confined without the smallest fear of discovery. He would, of course, be well treated; and after Donna Mercedes had taken the veil he might even be released on taking an oath never to divulge where he had been, or to make any complaint as to his treatment. He would, doubtless, be glad enough to regain his liberty on those terms.

" When he disappeared suspicion would naturally fall upon me, for it is well known that I have great cause of complaint against him. People would say that I had had him quietly removed—a grievous suspicion to have to bear; but I would do so cheerfully in order to save Donna Mercedes from this young adventurer, whom her brother has so foolishly and incautiously allowed to lead her away. I have no doubt that I shall be watched for a long time; but assuredly no suspicion whatever could fall upon the Church of having come to the lady's rescue."

"Certainly, her marriage to this heretic would be a terrible scandal," the priest said, "and one to be avoided by every possible means. Well, my son, I will think it over, and will lay the matter before higher authorities. Will you meet me here again in a few days' time, when I shall probably be able to give you an answer?"

"Good, father. I feel at any rate that I have only done my duty in endeavouring to save this young lady, whom I sincerely esteem and respect, although there are no longer any relations between us. It appeared to me that it was a matter in which the Church should interfere; and having now laid it before you, I feel that my conscience is relieved, and that I have no further interest in the matter."

"I see, my son, that your opinion is an entirely disinterested one, and that you are acting simply in the interest of this young lady and of the Holy Church."

The count and the priest met again two days later.

"My son, the matter has been decided upon. I have laid it before my bishop, and he agrees with me that it is incumbent on the Church to take every means to prevent this young lady from going to eternal perdition. The monastery in which this young man shall be confined has been settled upon. Perhaps you can tell us the best way in which he can be secured, for he is assuredly a man of exceptional strength and not likely to suffer himself to be carried away without a severe struggle."

"That is so, father. The matter is not without difficulty," the count said. "After nightfall he never goes out without being attended by a pestilent knave, his servant, and the two could not be overcome without a veritable battle. He must, therefore, be taken in the daytime. If you like, father, I will undertake that part of the business, although it is not to be done without some difficulty and danger. He must be enticed by a fictitious message to some quiet house. Here six men will be waiting for him, and as soon as he enters they will fling themselves upon him and overpower him. They will then bind him, and leave him; then, when it is dark, either a carriage, or a stretcher carried by four lay brothers of the monastery, can come for him and carry him off, it makes but little difference to me whither, and I would rather not know, so that I may be able to swear that I have not seen him since the day we met, and that I am wholly ignorant of his whereabouts. If you will be here every day at this hour, I will come and tell you when the bird is caged."

"So be it, my son, and indeed we shall all feel grateful to you for the service you will have rendered the Church."

The next morning Arthur received the following letter:

"Señor Hallett, the writer of this letter has become aware of a plot against you and a certain young lady in whom you have a great interest. If you will call on him at twelve o'clock, he will be awaiting you on the second *étage* of the Number 2 Strada de Barcelona, the first door to the right. He prays you to be silent as to this rendezvous, as his life would be forfeited were it known that he had made this communication to you."

The street was a central one and largely frequented, so no thought entered Arthur's mind that there could be any danger in attending at the rendezvous; and accordingly at a quarter to twelve he left his house, carrying, however, a brace of pistols in his pocket. On arriving at the place indicated, he passed through the open doorway and ascended the stairs to the second floor, then he rang the bell of the door to the right. It was opened by a little old woman.

"Come in, señor," she said; "you are expected."

He entered; she closed the door behind him, and led the way to an inner room. He was about to go in, when there was a rush of footsteps behind him, and four men flung themselves suddenly on to his back, the weight and impetus of the charge throwing him forward on his face. Before he could recover from his surprise and attempt to struggle, a rope was thrown over his head, pulled down to his elbows, and then tightened, and in a minute he was bound and helpless. He was carried into the room and the knots more securely fastened, his wrists being bound tightly behind his back, and his ankles lashed together. Then two of the men left the room, and the others remained sitting with their knives in their hands.

Arthur cursed his own folly in not having let Roper know where he was going; and yet, as he told himself, it was but natural that, having been informed that the plot affected Mercedes, he should have kept the matter to himself. That he had fallen into the power of Count Silvio he did not doubt for a moment; and yet he thought that, unscrupulous and revengeful as he might be, he would hardly venture to put him to death. Every moment he expected him to appear, but the hours went slowly by. He had been gagged as soon as he was bound, and no effort he had made had sufficed to get the gag from his mouth. From time to time he heard footsteps as people went up and down to the floor above, and if he could have freed his mouth he would have shouted, in spite of the knives with which his guards menaced him. At length the light faded and the room presently became dark.

Half an hour after night had fallen, he heard a ring at the bell. One of the guards answered it, and four figures in monks' clothes and with hoods over their heads entered. They brought a stretcher and laid it down beside Arthur, lifted him upon it, and fastened a strap across his shoulders and another across his legs; then they lifted the stretcher and bore him away. He was greatly puzzled by the proceedings. These might be men employed by the count and disguised as monks—he could hardly believe that they were really monks. He was carried for a long time, but as a cloth had been thrown over him, he could form no idea whatever as to the direction in which his bearers were proceeding. When they stopped and knocked at a door, however, he calculated that the journey had occupied at least three hours. They might therefore have come miles from the city, but on the other hand they might have wound about, and so might not be a hundred yards from the place where he was captured. A door opened, and after a pause they moved on again. Then Arthur felt that they were descending some stairs. When they reached the bottom they turned into another door, lowered the stretcher to the ground, and took off the cloth. The ropes that bound Arthur were loosed, a lantern was placed on the floor, and without a word the whole party of monks left the cell and locked the door behind.

Arthur got up at once, picked up the lantern, and examined his prison. It was a cell some ten feet square. At one side was a stone pallet, on which some straw had been thrown, otherwise the floor was perfectly bare. The only window was an opening near the ceiling about a foot long and six inches wide, with two strong bars across it.

"Well," he said to himself, "this certainly looks like a monk's cell, or rather the prison cell of a monastery, and it appears as if I had not fallen into the hands of the count after all. Things are bad enough in all conscience, but even to be in the grip of the Inquisition, which does not, so far as I know, exist now, would be better than to be in the hands of such a scoundrel. Still, it is strange that the Church should have interfered with me. I know how bigoted the clergy are, and how unscrupulous, but I should not have thought that they would have dared to meddle with a British officer. However, I can hardly believe that they will attempt my life; I don't see what good it could do them.

I would give a good deal to know what their game is. Well, I suppose it is useless to bother about it at present. I am so stiff both in the wrists and ankles that I can scarcely stand. At any rate, it is civil of them to leave me a light."

In a quarter of an hour the door opened again, and two monks came in. They put a large jug of water and a dish of fried beans on the floor, and retired without speaking.

"Let me think," Arthur said to himself. "This is Friday, so I suppose it is fast day. I hope this is not a sample of their ordinary fare. However, as I have had nothing since breakfast, it is not to be despised."

He ate a hearty meal, and then lay down on the stone bench, and was soon asleep. When he awoke daylight was shining through the little window, and he got up and looked round again. Certainly the prospect was not a cheering one; the walls were perfectly bare, and broken only by the door and the window. As the cell was twelve feet high, the window was altogether beyond his reach. He would have given a good deal to be able to look out and see whether he was in a town or in the country, and whether or not the window opened into a courtyard. This question was, however, presently settled by the sound of the rumble of distant vehicles. At long intervals one passed the window, and occasionally a foot passenger went by. Arthur therefore concluded that he was in a town, and was equally certain that the window looked into a quiet and little-frequented street, and was probably level with the pavement. This, however, gave him but little clue to the position of the monastery, for there were, he knew, at least a dozen such buildings in the town. Still, it was something to know that he was within reach of human beings.

By standing against the opposite wall, he could now obtain a glimpse through the window. He saw that the wall of the building must be at least two feet thick. Having made what observations he could, he sat down on his bed and waited for what should come next. Presently his breakfast was brought in; it consisted of bread, some fried meat, and, to his satisfaction, some coffee. An hour later the door opened again, and a tall man with a harsh ascetic face entered.

"You perhaps wonder why you are confined here?" he said. "I have come to tell you. You are an obstacle to the designs of the Church. You have seduced the affections of one of her daughters, and in order that she may be saved from perdition, which would be her doom if she were to marry a heretic, it has been thought necessary to seclude you here. Doubtless, in time she will recover from the glamour that you have thrown over her, and will deeply regret her passing aberration; will again become an obedient daughter of the Church, and perhaps find a happy refuge in its cloisters. When this takes place you will be released, but not until then. We do not desire to be harsh with you; you may be supplied with books and other indulgences, but a prisoner you will remain until she enters the walls of a cloister."

"I understand, señor," Arthur said quietly; "and perceive that it is the lady's revenues, and not her soul, which are the main object of your care. Well, señor, you have made me a prisoner, but I have sufficient faith in the young lady's affection to believe that until she is absolutely convinced of my death she will not turn her thoughts towards the cloister, and that therefore you are likely to have me on your hands for a very considerable time. At least, I am grateful to you for your offer of books, and shall be glad if you will furnish me with a selection."

"I may say further," the man said, "that you will be instructed in the tenets of our religion, and that should you see the error of your ways and ask to be received into the bosom of the Church, possibly all further objection to your union with the young lady in question may be removed."

Arthur laughed. "Your opinion of my principles must be a very low one if you can suppose that I shall be tempted to abandon them even with such a bait as you have been good enough to hold out."

"Naturally that is your opinion at present," the monk said coldly; "it may alter after a few months of confinement."

"I fancy not, señor; and I warn you that no more serious offence can be committed than the capture and imprisonment of an officer in the British service."

"I am prepared to take that risk, señor, and you are not likely to be released, whatever happens, until matters are arranged. I will now leave you to yourself."

When the door had opened Arthur observed that a number of monks were grouped in the passage outside, evidently prepared to fall upon him should he offer any violence to their prior, or attempt to make his escape.

When the prior had left, Arthur sat down and thought the matter over. The look-out was certainly not bright. He saw that he had very little chance of making his escape from the monastery. It was no doubt a large building, with any number of passages and corridors, in which, if he could escape from the cell, he would simply be lost, so that long before he could find his way to the gate, he would be overtaken and captured again. One thing, however, he might do. No doubt for a short time the two monks who brought him provisions would be accompanied by others, but when they found that he showed no signs of trying to effect his escape, they would become less vigilant. In that case he might possibly overcome these two men, make his escape to the story above, and drop out a note from the window which might be taken to Leon, who would assuredly obtain his release without delay. He could tear a blank page out of one of the books with which he was to be provided, and write a message upon it. His pencil had not been taken from him, nor his pocket-knife.

The days went on. He had no reason to complain of his treatment; the food was good and wholesome; the monks who attended to him brought a can of water daily, carried away his basin and emptied it, and swept out his cell. A mattress and blankets had been substituted for the straw, a supply of such books as he asked for had been brought to him, and it was evident that his captors desired that he should have nothing to complain of save his loss of liberty.

After ten days he resolved to carry his plan into execution. Tearing out a blank leaf carefully, he wrote upon it:

" I am confined in a monastery. I can give no information as to its position save that it is in the town. Apply to regent for an order to search."

He then signed his name, folded up the slip of paper, and on the outside wrote:

" One hundred dollars will be paid by the Count Leon de Balen to anyone who will bring this note to him."

He then waited for a favourable opportunity.

He had, one day when meat was served to him, abstracted the knife and hidden it in his stocking. The monks, when they removed the tray, did not notice that anything was missing, but he observed that on the following day they carefully felt the mattress. By this he guessed that the loss of the knife had not been discovered till that morning. The monks, fearing that they would be blamed for carelessness, had very likely protested that they had brought it as usual into the kitchen with the tray; and had only for their own satisfaction looked to see if it were hidden there. Arthur had taken it without any definite view of using it; but he thought that if this attempt to obtain succour failed, it might come in useful in any future plan he might devise.

Next day, when the attendant monks were bending to place his basin and tray on the floor, he suddenly rushed at them and hurled them both to the ground. Then he hurried out of the cell.

Four monks were standing in the passage. Running at full speed he dashed at them. Two of them were levelled to the ground; he cast the other two aside, and ran on. At the end of the passage was a staircase. Up this he darted, and found himself in a corridor similar to that below. A number of doors opened from it. He turned the handle of one of these, ran across the room to the window, pushed his hands through the bars, and dropped the note. A moment later he heard a bell ring loudly and sharply. Doubtless one of the men he had overthrown had at once run to it, and was giving the alarm, which would send all the monks to the entrance. He had done what he had to do, so he walked quietly down-stairs again. Five of the monks were huddled in the passage, and at his approach they took to headlong flight. With a laugh Arthur entered his cell and sat down. Presently a terrified face appeared at the door and looked in.

"Come in," Arthur said cheerfully. "I trust I did not hurt any of you. I merely wished to see whether my muscles were in working order. I find that they are quite right, thank you, and having ascertained that, have come back to my cell. You can, if you like, shut the door again, for this room is rather draughty when it is open."

The door was immediately shut, and the bolts shot. Arthur wondered what the next move would be. No one came near him for two hours; then to his surprise he heard a grinding sound against the door, and half a minute later the head of an auger appeared. Another hole was made touching the first, then a fine saw was thrust through. This began to work, and presently a piece was cut out of the door some six inches wide and eighteen inches long. After a pause the piece was fitted in again. Next he heard a sound of screws being driven in, and then he saw that hinges had been fastened to the flap, so that it could be opened and closed from the other side at will. Then he heard two bolts fixed to it. The noise went on for some time, and he knew by the sound that two more bolts had been screwed on to the door itself.

He saw at once that the monks intended in future to pass

his food in to him, instead of entering his cell. This proved to be the case. The flap was opened and his tray handed in, together with a basin of water. "They are determined that the monks shall not be exposed to assault and battery again," he laughed. "I have evidently given them a scare. Now, I have nothing to do but wait and see if anything comes of my note."

A fortnight of anxious waiting passed. His food, books, and water were handed in regularly, but no one entered his cell. He listened anxiously whenever he heard the slightest stir in the monastery that would tell him that search was being made, but no such sound met his ear. At last he came to the conclusion that his note could never have reached Leon's hands. Being but a scrap of paper, it might have escaped the eyes of passers-by and been trodden in the mud, or again, the prior might at once have suspected the reason of his strange conduct and despatched a monk to pick up the note. Several times he wrote the same message on pieces of paper, rolled them up into a small ball, and threw them through the window in the hope that some passer-by might be attracted by the sight of the pellet, and open it to see what was in it.

Till the end of a fortnight he remained patient, spending most of his time in reading; but when he finally determined that the letter had gone astray, he threw aside his books and decided that he must rely upon himself. It was evident that if he was to escape at all, it must be through the wall under the window. He had read of escapes by prisoners, and some of these had been performed in circumstances at least as difficult as those that confronted him, and with means no better than the knife he had in his possession. Much must, of course, depend upon the thickness of the wall and the materials of which it was built. He could see by the window that it must be at least two feet thick, and if constructed of solid blocks of stone there would be no possibility of getting them out, as his knife was but some six inches long in the blade, so that it would be necessary to wear the wall away into dust. Of course, if there were no other way, this is what he must attempt.

But for the precaution that had been taken to prevent his escape, this would not have been possible, for the monks, when they came in, could not have failed to notice the gradual crumbling away of the wall. There was, however, one other chance. As this was a subterranean, or almost subterranean room, there was not likely to be a vault under it; therefore it was probable that the wall was not continued far under the bottom of his cell. It might be one foot, it might be two, but the solid stonework would not go much deeper; it would rest upon a bed of concrete, or possibly of loose rubble. Once through that, he would probably find nothing but earth between him and the pavement above. These pavements were in most of the side streets mere cobble stones. He therefore set to work now to examine the stones forming the floor. They were about two feet square, and after some consideration he determined that the best to operate upon would be that at the foot of his bed, as this would be hidden from the sight of anyone looking through the trap. His greatest difficulty would be to get rid of the materials that must necessarily be removed. Stones he might manage to clear out by throwing them through the window with sufficient force to carry them across the street; earth, he finally concluded, he would have to dispose of in the same way.

In order to do this, however, he would have to reach the window. Of course, if he were certain that the cell would never be entered, he could pile it up against the wall to the right and left of the door, for the hole was too narrow to admit a head. However, this was a risk that he would not like to run. The excavation would occupy many weeks, possibly many months, and it was hardly likely that so long a time would elapse before a visit was made to his cell. After much thinking he concluded that if he took up two of the slabs, and placed one against the wall and the other upon it, he could just reach the window. Then, by fastening the end of a blanket to one of the bars, he could easily pull himself up by it, and throw the mould outside.

This was certain to be slow work, and a few handfuls of soil scattered on the road would not be likely to attract any attention. Examining the floor carefully, he saw that the slabs of stone were by no means even, from which he concluded that they were not laid in cement, probably not even in concrete, but that the ground had been simply smoothed down and the flags laid on it, and perhaps hammered down. The cells had probably not been intended as living rooms, but were used as prisons, perhaps as far back as the days of the Inquisition.

Having once made up his mind and carefully examined the stones, Arthur lay down on the floor and prepared to act. He had just finished his breakfast and handed out the tray as usual, so he would not be disturbed again for at least four hours. He began with his knife to loosen the stone at the foot of his bed, which was on the left-hand side of the cell, and found to his satisfaction that the slabs were laid close together, but not so closely that the knife would not in most places go down between them.

The crevices were filled up with the dust of many years, and it took him till dinner-time to clear this out. He was gratified at finding, however, that while in some places his knife encountered stones when he thrust it deep, at other points he could push it down to the hilt without encountering any obstacle. This showed him that his conjecture was correct. The ground had simply been smoothed down, chips of stone from the building thrown upon it and mixed with the sand, and on this the paving had been laid down. Beyond the fact that his knife went lower than the bottom of the stone, he could not tell how thick the floor was, but he judged that it would probably be three or four inches. It was evident that he could not get this up by the mere leverage of the knife, and he would only break the tool if he attempted it.

This he had expected would be the case, and after the dinner interval he began what he knew would be one of the most tedious parts of the undertaking. It was necessary that he should scrape away part of the stone in order to get his fingers under. His pocket-knife was evidently a better tool for this than the dinner knife he had hitherto used. The slab, so far as he could make out, was a sandstone, but how hard he could not tell. He began by dipping his handkerchief into his basin and letting fall a few drops at the place upon which he intended to operate, namely, next his bed. He started very carefully, giving a sort of rotatory motion to his knife. Gradually the water he had dropped there became a little turbid; this afforded him some encouragement, and he worked steadily on till evening, by which time he had succeeded in removing a piece of the stone an eighth of an inch deep.

After supper he began again, and continued the work far into the night, for he was always furnished with a lamp. At last he had increased the hole to a depth of fully a quarter of an inch, and a width equal to that of his four fingers. Well satisfied with this result, he threw himself on his pallet and slept soundly until the flap was opened and his breakfast tray thrust in. As soon as he had finished his breakfast he set to work again, this time using the knife that had been handed in with his breakfast, and which would not be demanded of him until he returned the tray when he received his dinner. He was glad to make the change, for his hands were blistered badly by the previous day's work, and the smoothness of the dinner knife was a relief to him; besides, he saw that he had already worn away the point of his pocket-knife.

After a fortnight's steady work, he had the satisfaction of feeling the knife go through. In two more days he was able to get his hand in. He now cleared out some of the earth at the bottom, and then putting his hand below the stone, exerted his strength to the utmost, and was delighted to find that it yielded. He laid it down and executed a dance of triumph, which would have astonished the monks had they looked in.

CHAPTER XVIII

ESCAPED

IT was evening when Arthur got up the stone, so he put it into its place again after his delight had a little subsided, rubbed some dust into the crevices, and then flung himself down for a long night's sleep. The next morning after breakfast he set to work to remove the dust round the next stone. When he had done this, he made a hole under it with his fingers even more easily than in the case of the first. He then replaced it, and waited until his dinner had been handed in. Having eaten this, he took up the two stones again, laid one upright against the wall under the window, placed the other on the top of it, then took a running jump on to this, at the same moment stretching his arm as high up above his head as he could. To his delight he found that he was able to grasp one of the bars. He got down, took one of the blankets, and again leaping up, passed an end round the bar and managed to grasp it before he fell backwards.

This pulled the blanket half-way round the bar. He caught hold of both parts when he next sprang up, and was able without difficulty to raise himself until his face was level with the window. The look-out was better than he had expected. In front of him was a street, but on the other side was a piece of waste ground. Nothing could have been handier for his purpose, as the stones and earth thrown on to this would certainly attract no notice. Having taken a good look he lowered himself to the floor, relaid the second stone he had raised, and put the other alongside it so that he could replace it in an instant if he should hear footsteps coming down the passage. Then he took the mattress and bedding off the bench, for he resolved to spread upon the bed all the earth and rubble he got out during the day, as it would be dangerous to throw it out until dark.

After this he set to work with the dinner knife, and it was not long before he had loosened the earth and rubble some inches deep. This he removed, and by night had excavated a hole two feet deep, spreading the rubbish carefully, as he got it out, on the bed. He had not made the hole quite so wide as the stone, in order that this might have a support when it was replaced. Then he hung up one blanket as before, and placed a considerable quantity of the earth in the other blanket and hauled this up to the window, so as to save himself the labour of climbing up afresh with each handful. Listening attentively, so as to be sure that no one was coming along, he flung it with all his force through the window. When he had disposed of all he had brought up he filled the blanket again, and so continued until he had thrown out the whole.

On the following day he not only got out the earth to a greater depth, but was able to push the trench under the adjoining slab, which was in contact with the wall. He got rid of the earth and stones as before. Next morning he worked with renewed vigour, for the result of the day's labour would be to show whether the stone-work was carried down below the level of the floor, or whether the wall rested upon concrete. The third slab came up without difficulty, and digging down by the wall, to his great satisfaction he found that it rested on a foundation of coarse concrete, which would no doubt be troublesome, but by no means impervious. He soon cleared out the earth and rubble to the same level as the other part of the trench, and after spreading it as usual under his mattress, he began the important task of picking out the concrete.

He had not been at work long before he found that in order to get room to use both arms he must widen it out at the end against the wall. This caused a whole day's delay. The cutting of the concrete was toilsome, and it took a week of almost incessant labour to make a passage sufficiently large for him to crawl through. Having ascertained that, as he had expected, the ground beyond this was composed of mixed soil, as that within the wall had been, with fragments of stone, he gave himself a day's rest before proceeding further. It was now six weeks since his imprisonment began, and he felt sure that it would require only three or four days' more work to get to the surface outside.

He wondered what his friends had been doing, and worried greatly about the anxiety that Mercedes would have experienced. This thought indeed had frequently kept him to his work when he would otherwise have desisted, from the fatigue he felt in working in the cramped position which was necessary while getting through the concrete. Roper, too, would be in a terrible way, and Leon would be moving heaven and earth to find some clue to his fate. He wondered what they had been doing, and in what direction they had been searching, for he would have disappeared as suddenly as if the earth had opened and swallowed him, without leaving a single clue.

One thing was certain: suspicion would fall upon Don Silvio. Leon would probably lay the case before the queen regent, and Don Silvio might not impossibly be arrested on the charge of being concerned in his disappearance. He could not help believing that this man was at the bottom of it, for think how he would, no other reason for his seizure presented itself. Ostensibly he had been imprisoned in order that his connection with Mercedes might be broken off, in which case she might enter a convent, to the great advantage

of its revenues. But the knowledge that there was an engagement between them was at present confined to Leon and
his sisters, for it had been agreed that it would be much
better to keep it quiet until the time approached for their
marriage, as Leon felt that the Church would use every
effort to prevent this from taking place.

Mercedes might indeed have spoken of it in confession,
but it was far more likely that Count Silvio, whose jealousy
had been clearly aroused, and who hated him for the result
of the duel, had set the Church authorities to work. It was
not probable that the prior of the monastery had acted on his
own responsibility. It was not a monastery that would
benefit by Mercedes' fortune, and mere zeal would scarcely
have prompted the prior to take so strong a step as to have
him carried off; doubtless, therefore, he was acting under
superior authority. Although the Inquisition had died out,
and heretics could no longer be tortured or brought to the
stake, the Roman Church in Spain was still almost as bigoted as in the olden days, and would assuredly not hesitate
to take steps to prevent what would be considered as the
backsliding of one of its faith. Knowing the enormous influence the priests still exercised, the measure that had been
taken with reference to himself scarcely seemed extraordinary to Arthur, and he resented it rather because he believed
that Don Silvio was at the bottom of it than on account of
the outrage against himself.

After a rest of thirty-six hours, Arthur set to work as
soon as he had eaten his supper. The lamp contained enough
oil to burn all night, and it was only by its light that he was
able to work. Lying on his stomach in the hole he gradually drove the tunnel forward, being obliged frequently to
come out with the earth and rubble as he dug it down. When
he had got two feet beyond the wall he turned on his back
and, placing the lamp on his chest, began to bring down the
earth above him. Luckily the mould was firm and tightly
packed, for while there was thus no fear of sudden falls the

walls stood upright and the earth dug out like putty. He had not the trouble of taking it out; as it fell he merely pushed it back into the open trench.

By morning he could stand upright to his work. As the bottom of the hole was two feet below the floor he was now some four feet above it. The labour had been very great, and although he had worked stripped to the waist he had suffered much from the heat. He rubbed himself with his blanket, as he had done ever since he began the work, for had he washed the appearance of the water would at once have aroused suspicions that he was engaged upon work of this kind. He dressed again, and was ready to receive his breakfast, and after eating this he went soundly to sleep. He could scarce rouse himself sufficiently to get up and take in his dinner when it came, and putting the tray down he at once went off to sleep again. At five o'clock he woke and ate his dinner, and when his supper arrived he put that by till midnight.

He now set to work with renewed vigour, for if all went well he should be free by morning. He put two of the paving stones against the sides of his shaft, and standing upon these was able to bring down the earth rapidly. When he had dug two feet higher he trod the earth that had fallen firmly down, and placing the stones on these, again mounted on them. By twelve o'clock he could no longer reach over-head, and measuring from the level of the floor of the cell, found that the cavity was now seven feet above it. He now pulled out the paving stones, and set to work to dig some holes on each side of the shaft, in which he could place his feet. Having gained another foot by this means he went out, ate his supper, and dressed himself.

He was certain now that he should be out before day-break. Again he set to work. The earth came down fast under the strokes of his knife. At last, about four o'clock in the morning, the blade struck against a stone. This he felt was round, and differed altogether from those he had met with embedded in the earth. Gradually he cleared the space beneath it, and then found that a layer of stones closely packed together formed the ceiling of his shaft. He worked with renewed energy until the whole of the earth beneath was cleared away, then he dug two more foot-holes two feet higher than those he had last rested on. Taking his place in these, he pushed with all his force with both hands. The stones gave way at once, and his hands were in the air. In another minute the rest were cleared off, and putting his hands on the edge of the hole he hauled himself up and was a free man.

In the joy of his heart he set off to run, but presently steadied down into a walk. It was a quarter of an hour before he came upon a church familiar to him, and he was then able to direct his course to his lodgings. He had a key of the outer door, and opening this, he felt his way up the stairs until he reached his door. Another key gave him admittance here. Opening the door of the sitting-room, he felt his way to the mantel. Here were always placed a flint and steel and a bundle of slips of rag dipped in sulphur, for although phosphorus matches were rapidly making their way in England, they were as yet unknown in Madrid. At the first blow of the flint against the steel he heard a movement in the next room, and as the sparks flew on to the tinder by the stroke, he heard Roper exclaim "Who is that?" as he jumped out of bed.

"It is I, Roper!"

There was a perfect shout of joy, and then he heard the honest fellow burst into a fit of hysterical sobbing. A moment later the sulphur ignited the tinder, and he lighted a candle. The door of Roper's bedroom was open, and Arthur saw that he had sunk back on to his bed again with his hands before his face. He went in to him and put his hand upon his shoulder.

"Roper, old friend," he said, "compose yourself. Thank God, I am back again safe and sound!"

"The Lord be praised!" Roper said, as, brushing his tears aside, he stood up and grasped Arthur's hands. "It is almost as if you had come back from the dead, sir. I have kept on saying you would return, though I knew in my heart that I had lost all hope. Why," he said, as they went back to the light, "you are as black as a coal. What has happened to you?"

"It is only honest dirt, Roper. I will go and have a thorough wash, then I will tell you about it;" and he went into his own room, which opened on the other side of the sitting-room. By the time he came back Roper had lighted three more candles, had partly dressed himself, and had got out a bottle of wine and a glass.

"Get out another glass, Roper, and light the fire, then we will sit down and talk it all over. By the way, if you have anything to eat you may as well put it on the table. It is five hours since I have had supper, and I have been doing some hard work since."

Roper hurried away to get the things together while Arthur changed his clothes entirely. Two or three shirts had been handed in each week to him while he was confined in his prison, but he was glad enough of a complete change.

"Now, Roper," he said, as he sat down, "we will eat and talk. In the first place, tell me about my friends."

"The count has been looking for you everywhere, sir. He has had the whole police in search of you. They have got Don Silvio under arrest, but they cannot find out that he was concerned in your disappearance, though nobody has any doubt about it. Miss Mercedes has been ill. She was, I was told, in bed for a month; she is up now, but, as the servants tell me, looking like a ghost. However, I have no doubt she will soon get round, now that you are back.

"The difficulty has been to know where to start looking for you. No one has seen you since you left this house one morning, some two months ago, shortly after breakfast. From that time you had disappeared as if the earth had swallowed you up. I always said, 'The captain will come back if he is alive—bolts and bars won't hold him.' And I really believed so for three or four weeks; but when time went on and there were no signs of you, I began to think that you must have gone under. If you had, I knew it must have been directly you were taken, for before two days had passed Don Silvio had been caught. He was down at his place in the country, and was able to prove that he was there at the date of your capture. Well, they kept him under arrest, thinking that if you did come back you would be able to prove that he had a hand in it somehow."

"I believe he had, Roper, though I may say I have no shadow of proof. Now, I will tell you all about it;" and he went into a full history of his capture, of his imprisonment, of his interview with the prior, and of the manner in which he had made his escape.

"You have done well indeed, sir, to get out of that place as you did! If I had been there, I should never have come out again alive. Lord, how you must have worked! So the priests were at the bottom of it after all?"

"Not quite at the bottom; for I have no doubt whatever that Don Silvio put them up to it. No doubt he said to them: 'Here is a young lady of noble family with a fine income. She wants to throw herself away on a Protestant and a foreigner; if you can manage to keep him away from her, she is pretty sure to go into a convent. She said, when she threw me over a year and a half ago, that it was her intention not to marry, but to lead a religious life; therefore if you get her lover removed now, no doubt she will do so.' You see, there were two motives for getting me shut up—one to avoid the grievous scandal of a Catholic lady of good family marrying a heretic, and the second, that of getting possession of her dowry. Well, thank goodness, I have baulked them! Has Colonel Wylde been here?"

"No, sir; he has been up in the north ever since you disappeared."

"Has there been much fighting there?"

"None at all. Maroto turned traitor and sold Don Carlos. He surrendered on condition of a big grant of money. His army dispersed, and Don Carlos has crossed the frontier."

"And Espartero?"

"He has been made Duke of Vittoria, and is still in the north settling things. In the east there has been fighting, but only small affairs, so you have not lost anything that way."

It was seven o'clock in the morning before Arthur had brought his story to a close, and he now said: "You had better go at once across to Count Leon's—I dare say he will be up by this time. Take him aside quietly, and tell him that I am here, and that I leave it to him to break the news to his sister as he thinks best. When he has done so, I will, of course, go round and see her."

Roper returned in half an hour with the count.

"My dear Arthur! My dear Arthur!" the latter exclaimed, as he ran into the room and embraced his friend. "Thank God that you are back again! I had given up all hope, and had no question at all in my mind that you had been murdered quietly by the orders of Don Silvio, and been buried in some obscure spot where your body would never be found. I could not at first believe what your man told me half an hour ago. I fancy I took him by the shoulders and shook him, and told him he was either mad or a liar. At last I was convinced that he was sane, and we hurried off together. We came too fast for talk, but I gathered from him that you had been confined in a monastery."

"Yes, Leon; and except that I was kept a solitary prisoner in a cell, I had nothing much to complain of. I was frankly told by the prior that I should remain there, however long a time it might be, until Mercedes had taken the veil."

"The rascal!" Leon said wrathfully. "That is just what we feared, or at least something like it, when we agreed that

310 WITH THE BRITISH LEGION

your engagement to her had better be kept private for a time. Not, of course, that I ever dreamt that they would attempt to carry you off, but I knew that they would move heaven and earth to break off the match. Now, please tell me all about it."

Arthur again went through the story, and gave his reasons for believing that Don Silvio was at the bottom of it.

"I regard that as certain," Leon said; "but that does not alter the facts. I shall have to take every care of Mercedes; they may try to suppress her as they have tried to suppress you. I have seen Queen Christina several time, and she is intensely interested in your case. We must go and see her this afternoon, and lay all the facts before her, and I shall ask her to take Mercedes under her protection, which I am sure she will do. Even the Church would not venture to drag her from the palace. As to your affair, it will require a good deal of talking over. Of course, if you report what has happened to your government they will kick up a tremendous row about it, but I don't know that that would be of any advantage either to her or to us."

"No, I can quite understand that, Leon; and it is the last thing I should wish to do. As you say, it will require a lot of thinking about and talking over; but at the first blush it certainly seems to me that, now that I have got away without further damage or injury than being shut up for a couple of months, the best policy is to say nothing about it; but, of course, we shall have to consider whether there will be any repetition of it, and still more, whether your sister is likely to suffer any persecution or to incur any risk of being kidnapped. Of course you have not told her yet that I have turned up again?"

"No. She does not get up till ten o'clock, and I thought it as well not to disturb her; besides, I really knew nothing about it myself beyond the fact that you had reappeared, and even of that I felt scarcely assured until I saw you myself, for I had not entertained a shadow of hope that you

were alive. I will go and break the news to her now. You
may come across in half an hour."

"Very well, but I shall not expect to see her; perhaps
I had better not see her at all to-day. It may be well to
break it to her very gradually. If you were to tell her that
this morning you had obtained a clue, and thought it possible that I had been carried away and shut up in a monastery; then this afternoon you could further say that you
believed you knew which monastery it was in which I was
imprisoned, and that you intended at once to take steps to
obtain my release; then either this evening or to-morrow
morning you could tell her the truth, and take me in
to her."

"I believe that would be the best plan, Arthur. She has
been very ill, and is at present a mere ghost of herself; but
she is of a cheerful disposition, and although she has come
to despair of ever seeing you again, I am sure that she would
eagerly grasp at any shadow of hope, and once she has you
again she will soon pick up."

"In that case I had better not come round to your house,
Leon."

"No, I think not. If any of the servants were to see
you they might, in spite of any orders that I might issue,
make a hash of it in some way or other. I doubt whether
they would be able to help doing so—by their looks if not
by their tongues, for you are a general favourite in the
house; and although no one has ever been told, I should
think that many must have some idea how matters stand
between you and Mercedes. As Colonel Wylde is away, there
can be no reason for your leaving the house, and it is better
that you should not do so, because you would be sure to meet
somebody who would know you; and as your disappearance
has been the talk of the town, they would carry the news
home to their familes, and some of the ladies might take it
across to Mercedes. I will be back again in an hour. I will
come round in my carriage, and then we will drive together

to the palace. To prevent any possibility of someone spreading the news from there, I will give strict orders that whoever calls to-day—no matter who it is—is not to be allowed to see my sister. Of course, I shall not tell either of the girls, their looks would let the secret out before they had been with her for two minutes."

Leon was back in the course of an hour. "I have administered the first dose of hope," he said, "and the effect has been wonderful. Before that she was sitting absolutely listless, taking no interest whatever in anything that went on around her; now she is all flushed and excited. I began by saying that information had reached me that led me to believe that you had been carried to a monastery. I did this very gently, and in a roundabout way, but she leapt to her feet with her eyes blazing, and insisted on knowing what were the grounds of my belief. I was obliged to tell her that I knew for almost a certainty that on the evening of the day on which you disappeared, monks were noticed carrying a litter through the streets. I said that of course this might mean nothing, but that it was certainly singular, and that I had already set a number of men to work to find out where the monks had been last seen, and the direction in which they were proceeding, and that I hoped by this afternoon to get certain news. I promised her that I would let her know directly I did so. I argued that four monks would hardly be carrying a dead man, nor could I see any reason why they should be carrying a living one. I said that a cloth had been thrown over the litter, and that no one could see who or what was beneath it. I left her walking up and down the room in a state of great agitation, and I rather think it would be better to change our plans and let her know the whole truth shortly."

"Perhaps so, Leon. We will sit here for another half-hour, and then you can go in and break the news to her little by little, till at last you can tell her that I am in the house waiting to see her. But I should advise you, as

we go along, to call at your doctor's and take him with
you, in case the shock is too much for her."

"Perhaps that would be advisable," Leon said; "the anxiety and excitement might be worse for her than the sudden
joy would be."

Accordingly they drove back to Leon's, and the count went
into his sister's room, while Arthur went into the drawing-
room, where the two younger girls were sitting. These leapt
up with a scream as he entered, and looked at him as if
doubting the evidence of their senses. He held up his hand.
"It is I myself," he said, "but do not make a noise. Your
brother has gone in to break the news to Mercedes." Convinced that their eyes had not deceived them, the girls ran
forward and embraced him affectionately, pouring out questions as to where he had been, and how it was that he had
returned.

"It is a long story," he said, "and I cannot tell it all
now. I have been shut up to prevent me from marrying
Mercedes, and I have managed to make my way out again;
and as you can see by looking at my hands," and he held
them out, "I have done a lot of hard work in breaking
out."

Both girls uttered exclamations at the blistered state of
his hands.

"They are nothing to what they were after the first four
or five days' work," he said; "they really were bad then.
They have got pretty horny now."

"But who could have wanted to interfere between you
and Mercedes? No one has any right to interfere with her
except Leon."

"There are people who think they have a right to interfere," he said, "and do interfere in most matters in this
country."

"You look very white, Arthur," the elder girl said.

"Yes, I dare say; I have been two months in a cell with
very little light."

"In a cell?" they repeated.

"Yes. There was no great hardship in it. I had books to read and very decent food, so the only thing I had to complain of was my loss of liberty."

He chatted for a few minutes longer, and then the door opened and Leon appeared and beckoned to Arthur to follow him. "She knows that you are in Madrid and free, and that you will be here in a few minutes. You had better leave her to herself for a little while to get calm. Of course, she is greatly shaken, but she stood it better than I had expected when I went in. I found that she believed I had not told her all, and was prepared to find that I had really got some important clue as to your whereabouts. Of course, that made it easier for me to tell her the truth gradually."

They talked for a short time and then Leon went out of the room, and a minute later Mercedes ran in, and with a cry of joy rushed into Arthur's arms. Leon came in ten minutes later, and found her sitting on a sofa with her head on Arthur's shoulder.

"It is almost worth while having been so unhappy, Leon," she said, "to feel such joy as I do now."

"Well, I won't say that, Mercedes; at the same time I admit that it is very joyful to have him back again."

"I know nothing yet," she said, "of what has happened, or what has kept him away from us. I have been too perfectly happy at having him back to think of asking what he has been doing."

"He has been shut up to keep him away from you."

"To keep him away from me?" Mercedes repeated.

"Yes, dear. It seems that it occurred to some of the worthy fathers of the church that it would be a very sinful thing for you to marry a heretic, and also that if this heretic were to disappear, possibly you might take it into your head to enter a convent and bestow your wealth upon the church. Accordingly they seized him and put him into a cell in a monastery, and informed him that he would have to remain there until you had entered a convent. As Arthur entertained quite different views he set to work to escape from his cell, and after six weeks' hard digging underground, he this morning made his way out, and here he is."

"Is it possible," the girl said, standing up with wide open eyes, "that it was the church that took Arthur from me?"

"Yes, dear; some unworthy members of the church."

"Arthur," she said, "when we are married and you take me to England, you shall teach me what your church believes. I will never remain in a church that has treated us so."

"We will talk about that, dear, later on," Arthur said soothingly. "There are bad people and good in every church, and there is no reason for changing because some of them may do wrong things. If some day you really come to think that our religion is the best, I shall be very pleased, but it must not be because some men, in an excess of zeal for their church, have somewhat ill-treated me."

Leon nodded approvingly. "You speak rightly, Arthur. Many evil things have been done in Spain by the priests. I believe myself that the misfortunes that have befallen us are a punishment for the evil deeds done in the name of religion here. But, as you say, it is not because evil deeds are mistakenly done in its name that the religion itself is bad. I myself am no bigot—there are very few educated men in this country who are so—and I fully recognized, when I first saw what Mercedes' feelings were towards you, that if she became your wife it was possible that in time she would adopt your religion. In all their main features there is no great difference between the two creeds, and certainly I should feel no great grief should Mercedes adopt your faith; but I agree with you that it should be the result of conviction, and not merely because she has reason to complain of the action towards you of certain fanatics. Now, we will go in to the girls, who will be dying to know what has taken place."

CHAPTER XIX

MILITARY MOVEMENTS

NOW, girls," Leon said, when Arthur had given a full relation of his adventure, "you must understand that this story must not go beyond ourselves. Whether any steps will be taken in the matter must depend largely upon what the queen regent and her advisers decide. It is a grave matter for the state to embroil itself with the church, and Arthur has already told me that he will be guided entirely by their wishes in the matter. I thank him for his consideration. Angry as I am at what has taken place, I feel that we ourselves could not but suffer were such a grave scandal to get abroad, for whatever might be the results to the people who have been concerned in this, we should undoubtedly be held in some respects accountable for them; and it is certainly a serious matter to quarrel with the church.

" The results might be very far-reaching. If this outrage upon a British officer were known in England, it would produce a most unfavourable impression. The cause of the queen has received warm support there, British soldiers and sailors have been fighting for us; but there is still a strong Carlist party in England, and these would certainly take advantage of this affair to stir up public feeling against us. Therefore, I feel that we are all under a great obligation to Arthur for volunteering to put himself in the hands of the regent, and to consent to allow this business to be hushed up. At any rate, you must preserve absolute silence until we know what is to be done. I am going to drive to the palace now to lay the matter before the regent, and shall be able to tell you more this afternoon. Now, Mercedes, if you will take my advice you will lie down for a bit; you have been ill, you know, and are not yet strong."

"I shall soon be strong again," she said; "still, I shall take your advice, for I do feel shaken, and I want to be bright this afternoon when you come back."

Leon drove with Arthur to the palace, and the former sent in word to the queen regent that he begged to see her in private audience. A quarter of an hour later they were shown into the room where she was sitting. She rose with an exclamation of surprise on seeing Arthur.

"Why, where have you been, Captain Hallett?" she exclaimed. "I began to give up all hope of ever seeing you again."

"It is a somewhat long story, your majesty, but if you will condescend to listen to it I will tell it to you in full. I have come not to demand justice at your hands, but to leave the matter entirely to you, to take any steps or no steps at all, as you may decide."

He then told the story, his narrative being frequently interrupted by exclamations of anger from Christina.

"It is infamous!" she exclaimed, when he brought the story to an end; "most infamous! I thank you most heartily for having come direct to me instead of sending your complaint home. It is a very serious matter. The church is already by no means well disposed towards me, and the priests throughout the country have largely thrown their influence on to the side of my enemies. I have a council this afternoon, and shall bring the matter before them; you have indeed added greatly to the obligation I am already under to you by offering to leave the matter in my hands. Of course, you have a right to large compensation for this illegal imprisonment."

"I can assure you that I desire no compensation at all, your majesty; I have already benefited very largely by your bounty. The only thing I would ask is, that if nothing is done, you will receive Donna Mercedes at your palace and take her under your protection until we are married. Having failed with me, the next attempt will be made upon her, and she would find it a much harder task than I have to free herself from their hands."

" That I will very gladly do, señor; and I don't think that even the church would venture to interfere with a lady under my protection. If it did, it would find me far less forgiving than you are."

The next morning Arthur received a message requesting him to go to the palace.

" Your case was fully discussed yesterday, Captain Hallett," the queen regent said, " and my council are all grateful for your magnanimity in placing yourself in their hands. They are fully sensible of the great wrong that has been inflicted upon you, and of the very serious consequences that might have ensued if you had chosen to place your case in the hands of the British government. I had sent to the prior of the monastery of St. Isidoro, and he was called before the council and ordered to explain his conduct. He did not in any way attempt to deny the facts as stated by you, but declared that he was acting under the orders of the bishop, whereupon an order was sent the latter to leave the country at once and take up his residence at Rome until he shall have received permission to return. The council proposed to pay you ten thousand pounds as an indemnity for the treatment you have received. I told them that I would inform you of their decision, but that you had already expresssed to me your determination not to accept one. They were a little incredulous," she said with a slight smile, " which is not to be wondered at, considering that there was not one of them who would, in similar circumstances, have felt the slightest hesitation in accepting such an offer. However, I told them I would see you to-day and lay the offer before you."

" Which I need hardly say, your majesty, I decline. I own that I am well pleased to hear that the author of this affair has received some punishment. After that, madam, I do not think it will be necessary for Donna Mercedes to avail herself of your kind protection. The issue of this order for the bishop to go into exile will be so strong a mark of your majesty's displeasure that there can, I think, be no fear whatever of any further steps being taken by my enemies. Donna Mercedes has been very ill, and I think she will be more likely to recover her health speedily in the society of her brother and sisters than in the atmosphere of the palace, where, however great your majesty's kindness, there must be a certain amount of stiffness and ceremony."

"I should have been glad to have her with me," Christina said, "but there is no doubt a certain amount of truth in what you say. However, I will have her here frequently, so that it may be understood that she is a special friend of mine, in which case I am sure no one will try to interfere with her."

Colonel Wylde returned that evening, and after hearing the whole story from Arthur, expressed his warm approval of the course he had taken.

"It would have been most damaging to the royal cause," he said, "if this affair had been made public in England; and though I think you would have been more than justified in accepting the amount offered as an indemnity, I can but admire your disinterestedness in refusing it."

"And now, colonel, I am ready to start for any point where you may require my services; I have been idle too long already."

"Well, the war is practically over in the north. That scoundrel Maroto has arranged terms for himself, and for a few of his friends, with Espartero, but has made no conditions whatever for the soldiers who have fought so hard for Don Carlos. However, these have been permitted to return to their homes, and at present Espartero is occupied in settling affairs there and in preparing his army to take the field in the spring against Cabrera. A number of small isolated campaigns are going on in Aragon. We have already three or four commissioners there, but it is perhaps as well that you should proceed there at once, as it is now three months since I have had any reports from you to send in with mine. I have, of course, been obliged to report your disappearance, and shall now mention that you had been pounced upon by some enemies of the queen and held in confinement, but that you had effected your escape."

That evening Arthur heard from Leon that Count Silvio had been released from the close observation he had been subjected to for the past two months. "It is believed," he said, "that he was the instigator of the action against you, but there is no proof whatever that this is so, and there is therefore no excuse for keeping him further under arrest. He has, however, been ordered to retire to his estates, as there is at least the strongest ground for suspecting that he was concerned in the attack upon you by those street ruffians, and his whole conduct has been in the highest degree suspicious."

"I shall be glad to know that he is away, Leon. Of course, I am not sure that he was really concerned in my imprisonment; the priest who is Mercedes' confessor is likely enough to be at the bottom of it."

"I think so too, and have told Mercedes that she had better choose some other confessor."

"I think the two men were set upon me by him; but I am inclined to own that I was in the wrong in the matter of that duel. It was somewhat reasonable that he should have been jealous, and it would have been fair if I had contented myself with running him through the shoulder instead of making him a perfect laughing-stock. I was irritated by his manner, and by the way in which he had brought two or three dozen of his friends to see him run me through. Still, I own that I was wrong, and if the man would come and offer to shake hands I would not refuse to do so."

"Then you are a good deal more forgiving than I should be," Leon said heartily; "and I should like nothing better than to fight him myself. However, I admit that there is something in what you say; certainly he had some ground of complaint against Mercedes. I felt that it was hard upon him when I wrote begging him to break off the engagement. Of course, I have been glad that I did so since I have come to know him better, and feel that Mercedes had a very fortunate escape."

"Don't let her go out unless she is accompanied by one of her sisters as well as her duenna."

"No, I will take care of that; she shall be well looked after, I promise you, and I don't suppose she herself will care for going out except to the palace. It will be well for her to go there pretty often. She is fond of Christina, and she will feel herself that her intimacy there will be a great protection to her."

In Catalonia the Carlists were still very strong. The royal army numbered at least fifty-five thousand men. About seventeen thousand—half of whom were regular troops—garrisoned the permanent forts, and of the remainder twenty-five thousand belonging to the local militia were scattered among no fewer than two hundred and seventeen fortified villages and small towns. These were of no military importance, but if they had not been defended, Cabrera's forces, which were marching about the country, would have swept them bare of their inhabitants, carrying off all the stores they contained, and burning them to the ground. It was therefore necessary to garrison them, not only because this diminished the supply of stores available for the use of the enemy, but because it enabled contributions to be levied for the queen's cause. Undoubtedly the holding of these places answered those purposes, but, upon the other hand, the employment in this manner of practically the whole army in Catalonia completely unfitted it for all operations in the field, and enabled Cabrera to carry on his operations without meeting with any efficient opposition.

In this way he captured place after place, massacring the

greater portion of the inhabitants and striking terror into the others. Arthur had been despatched to join the command of General Van Halen, who was occupied principally in endeavouring to victual Lucena, and in trying in a feeble way to fortify the castle of Onda. The operation progressed slowly, for although the war had been going on for years no tools were available, and it was necessary to send to Cadiz to purchase them. Colonels Lacy and Alderson were with Van Halen when Arthur arrived, and after staying here for a short time he joined the command of General Ayerbe, who was endeavouring to mitigate the Carlist system of atrocities. On this subject Arthur exchanged several letters with Cabrera. General Ayerbe was also endeavouring to prevent the Carlists from carrying out the fortification of Segura, an important place in Aragon, as it lay on the line of march to Teruel and Alcaniz. Parra was lying near, but refused to co-operate with Ayerbe, and Van Halen determined to march on Segura himself and lay siege to it.

Before he arrived, however, Ayerbe, having been reinforced, defeated the Carlists at a place two hours' march from the town, drove them back from their new works, and in his report of the action mentioned that Captain Hallett had rendered material services and had led a small party of cavalry in a brilliant charge which decided the fate of the day. Serrano brought up a battering train from Saragossa. It consisted, however, of only three 16-pounders, a 12-inch mortar, and a 9-inch howitzer, and all the ammunition he could obtain amounted to fifteen hundred shot and one thousand shell. It was a long business to bring up even this feeble train. The weather was inclement in the extreme, and when he arrived in front of Segura—the garrison of which had been very strongly reinforced by Cabrera—he found that his force was wholly insufficient for the attack upon the place, and that the town itself had been burnt by the Carlists to prevent it from affording any shelter to the besiegers.

The surrounding country had been wasted for many miles, and large bodies of Carlists were seen upon some adjoining heights. He therefore consulted with the officers commanding the various armies, and these unanimously declared that it would be madness to attempt a siege in such circumstances. Abandoning the idea, therefore, he embarked upon a series of long and fatiguing marches, by which he caused the Carlists to give up the siege of several places. He did not, however, mitigate the animosity of his rivals, who succeeded in obtaining his recall on the ground of his having abandoned the siege of Segura, which they said might easily have fallen into his hands. Nogueras succeeded him, but was speedily displaced by Ayerbe. He, however, did not long retain the command, which was given to O'Donnell, an active and energetic young officer.

Owing to the absence of any decisive action Arthur remained at head-quarters, receiving orders from Colonel Lacy, who was the principal of the four English commissioners attached to the armies of Catalonia and Aragon. They hailed the appointment of O'Donnell as affording some grounds for hope that at last something like vigour would be shown in the operations of the army, which was at present scattered about the country, employed rather in collecting provisions for their own subsistence than in harassing the enemy.

"If it wasn't that the fighting in the north is finished, and that a few more months will see the end of the whole affair, I should throw up my commission and go home," Arthur said one day to Roper. "This really is sickening, but having gone through so much of it, I should not like to leave until it was all over."

"No, sir; I should like to see the Carlists smashed up altogether before we go. Still, it is dull work. Of course, while we are staying down here in Saragossa we get plenty to eat and drink, but when we are away in the country it is pretty rough work, and a beggar would turn up his nose at the food we have to eat. I should not mind if there was really anything to do, but these Spaniards are so pig-headed that they won't take advice. They have a big army if they would but gather it together and go at the Carlists."

"Yes, it certainly seems like that, Roper; but you must remember that a big army requires a tremendous transport train, for it would have to carry everything with it. At this time of year little food is to be obtained, and in fact the people of these villages and little towns scarcely do any cultivation of the land, for they cannot tell who will reap what they have sown. Then, too, most of the country is mountainous, the roads are everywhere abominable, and even if we had a train sufficient to carry the supplies, it would be so large and cumbrous that its tail would not have left the halting-place when the head arrived at its destination; and you must remember that if we concentrate, the Carlists would do the same. A portion of them would harass us along the whole line of march, while another would make excursions wherever they pleased, for they march light, and could go three miles to every one that we can cover. There is no doubt that this dispersal of our force over so large an extent of country, and among so many towns and villages, is a grievous mistake, but it is very difficult to see what else can be done, for if we gave them no defence these places would all lie at the mercy of the Carlists, and would be obliged in self-preservation to go over to them, thus enormously increasing their recruiting-ground, and enabling them to get stores wherever they marched. If Cabrera would but gather the whole of his force together and allow us to do the same, and risk everything on a pitched battle, the matter would soon be brought to an end. But, as it is, I am afraid we shall have to wait till Espartero arrives before the business can be wound up."

The first step General O'Donnell had to undertake was the relief of General Asnar, who was shut up by the Carlists in Lucena. Having received large reinforcements he started for that place, marching unencumbered by baggage. The enemy's first position near Lucena was easily carried. Five battalions then attacked the enemy's left, which occupied a position that would enable them to take the Christino advance in flank. When this movement was successful, two battalions attacked the right of the Carlist position, while O'Donnell placed himself at the head of the rest of the troops, who advanced with loud cheers to the charge over very rugged ground, and under a very heavy fire. The Carlists would not wait to stand a bayonet charge, and abandoned their ground, leaving the road open to Lucena, where Asnar with his troops had been imprisoned for twenty-two days.

This was a brilliant piece of fighting, and immensely raised the spirits of the royal troops, who found that they were at last commanded by a man, and not by incapable and almost imbecile dummies. On the following day O'Donnell marched to Murviedro, though he had not had more than three hours' continuous rest since he had left Saragossa.

A fortnight later he proceeded to take possession of the heights beyond Arteza, his intention being to besiege Tales, which was important because it commanded the water-supply of the town of Onda. The position of the enemy was a strong one: his right was on a hill called the Pena Negra, and on a round hill on a slope between it and Tales; his centre was upon the Castle of Tales; and his left on precipitous heights. From the last-mentioned the Carlists were driven without loss, after offering but a very slight resistance.

Arthur had been requested by Colonel Alderson—an engineer officer, who was now senior commissioner—to reconnoitre the ground beyond these heights to ascertain whether the place could be better bombarded from the rear. Roper, as usual, rode with him. They had gone some distance when they saw two horsemen approaching at full gallop. As these were apparently unaccompanied, Arthur paid but little attention to them, and rode on until he heard a loud and imperious order to stop. Reining in their horses they awaited the arrival of the two unknown men. They were within fifty yards when Arthur exclaimed, "It is Cabrera himself! Well, I am not sorry to meet him."

Cabrera, as he approached, gave a shout of satisfaction as he recognized Arthur. "Well," he exclaimed, "you have got the better of me twice; this time it will be my turn!"

"That is as it may be," Arthur replied. He saw Cabrera draw a pistol from his holster and he did the same, and the two weapons flashed out together. Arthur felt a stinging pain, as if a red-hot iron had crossed his cheek. Cabrera dropped his pistol, having evidently received a shot in his right arm, but he drew his sword with his left, and rode at Arthur. Both combatants fought with fury—Cabrera animated by a burning desire for vengeance, Arthur by the thought of the importance of killing Cabrera, for he was the spirit of the war, and after his death the Carlist movement would soon come to an end.

The combat was short but desperate. The disadvantage of having to use his left arm greatly hampered Cabrera. In point of skill he would have been in any case inferior to his opponent, but for a time the fury of his assault counterbalanced this. Parrying three or four furious cuts, Arthur delivered a heavy blow on his antagonist's left shoulder, inflicting a severe wound and striking him from his saddle. Cabrera leapt to his feet again. Arthur dismounted and demanded his surrender.

"Never!" the Carlist said. "Cabrera will never be taken alive!"

Roper had by this time disembarrassed himself of his antagonist by running him through the body, and he now rode up. Cabrera was half mad with rage. Both his arms were useless. Just as Arthur was about to throw himself upon him and overpower him, Roper shouted, "Mount, master! mount and ride! Fifty of his fellows are upon us."

Looking round, Arthur saw that a body of men were riding furiously towards them, and were a little over fifty yards away. He hesitated a moment, and then leapt on to his horse, shouting to Cabrera: "Next time, señor, we will finish what we have begun!" and then rode off. Several shots were fired, but leaning low in their saddles they galloped away at full speed, and both being well mounted, were speedily beyond pursuit; and, indeed, most of the Carlists had gathered round their chief.

On regaining their camp Arthur reported what had taken place to Colonel Alderson, who at once took him across to O'Donnell.

"You have done well indeed, Captain Hallett," said the general; "and though it is a grievous pity that you did not kill him, which would have been more to our advantage than the winning of a pitched battle, it will lay him up for a time, and that will be more to us than a reinforcement of ten thousand men. I thank you most heartily, sir, in the name of the government."

Cabrera, indeed, after his wounds were attended to, still gave his orders for the defence of the town, and inspired his troops by his presence. Under his eye they made several desperate sorties against the battery which was being prepared for breaching the wall. The battery was placed and but feebly worked, for throughout the war the Christino operations in the way of sieges were always unskilfully managed, owing to the utter incompetence of their engineers. However, a week after their appearance before the town, fire was opened. The siege was delayed for a time owing to the necessity for sending reinforcements to a body of the queen's troops which had suffered a severe defeat at Chulilla. The battering train was small and indifferent, and several of the guns gave way during the bombardment, which lasted seven days. At the end of that time an assault was ordered.

The engineers obstinately refused to accept Colonel Alderson's advice to make ladders, although it was evident that the breach could not be scaled without them. Resisting very strongly, the enemy's left was at last turned, and the round tower on the right captured. The garrison, however, fought desperately, and made continuous efforts to retake it. All day the battle continued. The breach in the castle was found to be impracticable, but was at last enlarged, and the enemy were compelled to surrender. The day's fighting, however, had cost the queen's troops a loss of at least four hundred killed and wounded, almost all of which might have been spared had Colonel Alderson's advice been taken. Cabrera had left the town before the attack began, being too much injured to take the command himself. The defence, however, had been a gallant one, and although the capture of the place gave great encouragement to the Christinos, the stubbornness of the defence and the loss they had inflicted served to show the Carlists that the conquest of the number of strongly fortified positions they held was beyond their opponents' power.

O'Donnell destroyed the castle and tower, and then retired, as the town could no longer be held by the Carlists for the purpose of harassing the garrison of Onda. He decided now to reduce a number of the Carlists' fortified places and wait for the arrival of Espartero; but the Carlists took the offensive, and their columns moved about with such activity that the army was kept constantly on the march to encounter them and drive them back again into the mountains. It was not till October that Espartero arrived at Saragossa and met O'Donnell there. Then it was decided that, until the arrival of reinforcements which were coming from the north, O'Donnell should continue in command, his force being strengthened by seven battalions of the army of the north. Espartero advanced with the rest of his own force. Their plans, however, were altered by the early setting in of winter. The roads speedily became impassable, provisions were terribly scarce, and the movements of the armies paralysed. All the energies of the commanders were indeed required to maintain the supply of provisions for the troops.

The English commissioners for the most part returned to Madrid. Among these was Arthur, who spent four months there very happily. Nothing had been heard of Don Silvio, who was still living on his estates. It was evident to all that the war would speedily come to a close; bodies of troops from all parts of Spain were moving to the scene of action, and when the season opened Espartero would be at the head of an army against which even Cabrera could not hope to make head. That indefatigable fighter was lying ill at Morella, the result of his wounds, which, although not serious in themselves, had been rendered so by the incessant energy and activity with which he had persisted in moving about. The news of the retirement of Don Carlos had for a long time been kept from the peasantry, but even when it became known it had but little effect upon them. They cared little for Don Carlos; but they almost worshipped Cabrera, and were ready to follow to the death; and when spring came and operations could be resumed, they flocked to his standard again in as large numbers as before.

In February the campaign reopened and Arthur started to rejoin the army. At one of the towns at which they stopped, Roper came in an hour after their arrival and said: "Captain, do you know I feel pretty sure that I have seen Don Silvio. It was only his back, it is true, but I am convinced that it was he. I was walking along when I saw a man who was coming the other way suddenly turn off down a side street. When I got to the end of it I looked down, for I saw by the sudden turn he had taken that he wished to avoid me. By the distance he had gone it seemed to me that he must have been running. He was too far away from me to speak of his identity with any certainty, but I thought, and still think, that it was Don Silvio."

"But what should he be doing here, Roper?"

" That I cannot say, sir. At any rate it seems to me that his presence here just at the moment when we are coming through looks like mischief."

" Well, of course, anyone at Madrid watching me might have found out the day on which we were going to start, and might have sent a message to Don Silvio in time to enable him to ride here before we came along. He may, of course, have brought three or four men with him; he is more likely to have done that than to have trusted to recruiting some fellows here. It is just as well—if it is the man—that you should have recognized him, Roper, for at any rate we shall not be taken by surprise."

" Perhaps, sir, it would be as well to stop a few days here, or to change our route; there are two or three roads by which we might get to Saragossa. They would certainly be farther than the direct one; but it would make little difference whether we arrived there two or three days earlier or later."

" That is true enough, Roper; but if he is watching us here, he could follow us by one road as well as another. We have our pistols and swords, and I should say that we could render a pretty good account of four or five of them."

" I have no doubt we could, captain; still, I would rather not fight against long odds if I could avoid it. You see, sir, since I got that fifteen hundred pounds banked to my credit in England I feel more careful about my life than before. It did not much matter then whether I went down or not; now it seems to me that my life has a distinct value, and I don't want to throw it away."

" Well, I can say the same, Roper. Of course, I always knew I was coming into an estate some day, but I don't know that I thought much about it. Now my life is of great value because it is of value to Donna Mercedes. I don't say anything about the money I have acquired, but certainly for her sake I do hold to life pretty strongly; at the same time I cannot turn back from my duty for an unknown dan-

ger and merely because you think you have recognized Don
Silvio. I have proved that I am a far better swordsman
than he. Since my duel with him I have practised a good
deal with my pistols, and can, I think, account with them for
two or three assailants. You have practised as well, and I
fancy that you ought to be able to settle with two of them
in your four shots. Let us suppose that Don Silvio has
six fellows with him—I should hardly say that he would
bring more. Well, if we can each dispose of two, that
only leaves us with three, counting Don Silvio himself, to
manage."

"Well, captain, that is all right; but if these six men are
lying in ambush and fire together, they may upset our cal-
culations altogether."

"That is certainly so, Roper. But unless we are going
to turn tail and ride back to Madrid on the strength of
your belief that you saw Don Silvio, I do not see how that
is to be helped. Mind, it is I and not you whom Don
Silvio wants to kill. I have got my shirt of mail, and I do
not think that a pistol bullet would go through it; so that
if they direct their fire at me, unless I am shot through
the head I reckon that I shall still be in fighting order after
their first discharge. At any rate, Roper, I do not mean to
turn back."

"Well, if you go on, of course I go on, sir," Roper said
doggedly; "there is no question at all about that."

"I think, Roper, the best thing for us to do would be,
when we have taken our meal, to sally out in different directions with our cloaks on and our caps over our faces. Possibly one or other of us may alight upon him if he is here.
If we meet him, we will talk the matter over again. I don't
want to do anything headstrong; and if we ascertain that
the count is here, we will discuss whether we can make a
detour that will throw him off the scent, though I say hon-
estly I don't think such an attempt would be of any use.
If he has men with him they will certainly be posted on watch

round this hotel, and he will learn all that there is to be learned of our movements; and whatever we do, we shall have to fight for it. If he has more than six men I should say that if we are attacked we had better trust to our horses and not to the strength of our arms, and ride for it. There is nothing cowardly in running away from a greatly superior force, and certainly I shall not hesitate to do so if I see that they are too strong for us."

Accordingly, after dinner they put on their cloaks and sallied out.

"Don't move out of the main street of the town, Roper," Arthur said. "They will not attack us there; but if we were to turn down any side street they might fall upon us suddenly. We had better be back here in an hour's time, and we will then exchange notes."

At the end of that time they met again at the door of the inn.

"I think you are right, Roper. I am sure that one man at least has followed me all the time I have been out."

"I thought so at first, captain; but the fellow I suspected brushed against me roughly before I had been out very long, and then apologized. It struck me that he wanted to look at my face; anyhow, I did not see anything of him afterwards. Don Silvio could not have given them a very accurate description of us; for, as you stand six feet one and I am not more than five feet eight, no one who knew anything about us could very well mistake you."

"I have certainly been followed," said Arthur, "and I feel sure that if I had moved out of the main street I should have been attacked. There were two fellows who kept together, and another who followed close behind. I suspected all three, as they generally kept at about the same distance from me. Well, I have no doubt now that you were right about Don Silvio. I will see if they have got such a thing as a map in the hotel. I don't suppose they have; but at any rate I will ask the landlord to send up some man who knows the roads well to my room, and I will find out as much as I can of the different routes, and then we can decide on what we had best do."

CHAPTER XX

THE END OF A FEUD

THE result of Arthur's enquiries was that the three roads by which he could travel to Saragossa were about equally bad, and that upon all of them there were places along the face of the hills at which attacks might be made.

"I had half a mind," he said to Roper afterwards, "to hire a couple of men as guides, telling them that they had better bring weapons with them. But it is likely enough that one or two of Don Silvio's men may be stationed in the hotel, and you may be sure that they would question anyone who had been up to my room. Don Silvio might afterwards see them and hire their services, and we might be shot in the back when the others opened fire at us from an ambush. So I think we cannot do better than go forward by the main road. If we once get a start of them they may not be able to catch us, for they are certainly not likely to be better mounted than we are; and they cannot go on before us, for then they could not know which road we should take."

Accordingly in the morning, as soon as they had mounted, they took the straight road and travelled fast. They kept a keen look-out at all spots where an ambush was likely to be planted, but everything was quiet, and they reached their destination that evening without adventure.

"It will be more dangerous to-morrow, Roper," Arthur said, as they sat at supper together. "We are fairly started on this road now, and there is no choice open to us as to which route we can take. They will know that, and may start before we do, and choose their position for attacking us."

"Well, I almost hope they will do so, sir. I am not afraid of a fight, but it makes one jumpy keeping always on the look-out, and expecting a shot from every bush we pass."

"I feel that myself, Roper. If we must fight I would rather do so now, and have done with it."

Next morning, feeling that if their enemies had started in front of them, it would be useless to try to evade them, they proceeded at a much slower pace than on the previous day. After riding three hours they came to a spot where the road was cut along the face of an almost perpendicular hill, with a torrent running at its foot. As they began to ascend this, Arthur unbuckled the covers of the holsters, so that the pistols were ready for instant use. He directed Roper to do the same.

"Now," he said, "will you ride on my left, keeping exactly alongside? It is I whom they will fire at, but as this mail shirt of mine will keep out ordinary pistol balls I am not afraid that I shall be hurt. Directly they have fired, they will be sure to jump out from the place where they may be lying; then empty your pistols among them and go at them. There is no place for them to hide here, but there may be farther on. At any rate, do as I tell you. Keep your horse's head in a line with mine."

Holding his rein in his left hand, and keeping his right close on the handle of a pistol, Arthur rode on. Roper had attempted to remonstrate against the order he had given, but Arthur silenced him.

"You must just do as you are ordered, Roper. One or two might shoot at you if you were riding behind me, and then I should be left alone to fight the whole of them. I shall certainly want your help."

They rode along until they came to a spot where the cliff

fell away, leaving a semicircular depression which was filled with low bush.

"They are here, if anywhere," said Arthur. "Get your pistol ready, Roper!"

As they rode along past the place, a number of men sprang up and fired a volley. Arthur felt a sudden and acute pain in the ribs, and was nearly knocked from his horse. Recovering himself with a great effort, he fired twice, and two of the men dropped. A moment later his horse staggered and fell. As it did so he dragged the other pistol out and shot a man who was rushing at him with a clubbed musket. He heard Roper's pistols go off, but was too much engaged with a fourth man who rushed at him, to see what was the result. He had just run his antagonist through, when Don Silvio leapt upon him. Arthur parried the thrust aimed at him, and at once engaged in a furious combat. Don Silvio leapt round him with the agility of a cat, springing in and out, and delivering fierce lunges as he did so. Otherwise there was silence. He was vaguely conscious that Roper was down, but that he had disposed of the last of his antagonists, and that the issue remained solely between himself and the count. He was at a disadvantage with the latter, for while he himself was armed only with the regulation cutting sword, his antagonist had a long, straight, duelling rapier.

For a time he contented himself with standing on his guard, but was several times narrowly touched. At last, seizing his opportunity, he struck at his opponent's rapier with all his force. The blade shivered in the count's hand, but before he could raise his guard again the latter sprung upon him like a wild cat and grasped him by the throat, trying to hurl him over the precipice. Arthur dropped his sword, which was useless to him now, and grasping his antagonist's wrists, tried to drag them from his throat; but rage had given Don Silvio strength, while Arthur himself was almost choking under the pressure. At last, with a

mighty effort, he succeeded, and in turn gained a grip on
the throat of his antagonist. He dragged him to the edge
of the precipice, and, holding one hand on his throat and
with the other grasping him by the middle, raised him from
the ground to hurl him over. Another instant and Don
Silvio's career would have come to an end, but almost in the
act of throwing Arthur paused.

The sight of the count's convulsed face and eyes moved
him from his purpose, and he set him down again on the
road, releasing him as he did so.

"Don Silvio," he said sternly, "I had you at my mercy,
but thoughts came into my mind that caused me to change
my purpose. I feel, as I have all along felt, that I have not
been altogether blameless in this matter. It was natural
that you should have been exasperated by the belief that I
had gained the affections of Donna Mercedes, and that you
should thereupon have forced a duel upon me. I feel that
I was wrong in the way in which I fought you. I might have
contented myself with merely wounding you, whereas I
played with you first and made you the laughing-stock of
the friends you had brought to witness your triumph. Considering that you are a Spaniard and have your ideas of revenge, I can pardon the attempt of those two men, whom, I
doubt not, you bribed to stab me. I do not know what
share you had in getting me into prison, nor do I care to
enquire. I have now again worsted you, and have you at
my mercy; but looking back and seeing that I have been
myself to some extent wrong, I give you your life. Go home,
señor, and retrieve the past. I believe that you were an
honourable gentleman before you were led astray by your
anger at being superseded in the affections of Donna Mercedes. That quarrel has been fought out and come to an
end. Go home and try to forget what has passed. You will
never hear of it from me."

Don Silvio staggered back and stared in bewildered in-
credulity at Arthur, who, turning away, at once went to

Roper's side. The latter was insensible, evidently from the effects of a tremendous blow from the butt-end of a musket delivered by a man who lay dead beside him. Roper had indeed fired and inflicted a mortal wound upon his adversary, who was in the act of striking. The blow had fallen, but it was the last effort of the striker. The two had fallen side by side. Arthur went to his dead horse, pulled out a flask from the wallet, poured some brandy and water between Roper's lips, and rubbed some on his forehead, and soon he had the satisfaction of seeing his follower open his eyes.

"It is all right, Roper," he said, "we have thrashed them all. You have had a nasty knock on the head. Fortunately your crown is pretty thick, and you will be all right again in a few minutes;" then as he saw that Roper was rallying he turned to the count, who was sitting on a fallen rock with his head in his hands. Seven dead bodies lay in the road. The count got up as he approached.

"Englishman," he said in a low voice, "you have indeed proved my conqueror in every way, in fighting and in generosity. I can scarcely even now believe that I am alive, and that you have spared me when I was wholly at your mercy. I do not deserve life at your hands."

"Say no more about it," Arthur said. "I injured you first unconsciously, and then consciously; you have tried to strike back hard, and this is the result. Let all animosity be at an end between us. Go back to your estate, live there quietly for a while, and then let the memory of our duel and all connected with it pass away—such matters are soon forgotten—and return to Madrid. I shall no longer be there. In a few months I shall be back in England. Now," he said in a different tone, "where are these men's horses? They must have ridden here; and as they have killed my favourite, I must provide myself with another."

"They are all round the next turn," Don Silvio said. "I can at least make reparation to you in the matter of the horse, for mine is as good as yours was. I will take one of the others, which indeed are all my own."

"What is to be done with these bodies?"

"There is a man with the horses. I will get him to throw them over into the gorge. It may be months before anyone finds them. We shall lead four of the best of the horses back, and the others can be left for the first comer."

"But the man will be a trouble to you in the future, will he not?"

"No; he is my steward, and devoted to the family. It was he who arranged for the services of these men, at a town twelve miles from my place. He fetched them over and provided them with horses. They will not be missed from their homes, and indeed the town will have some reason to rejoice over their disappearance."

By this time Roper was sufficiently recovered to be able to stand, but he was still a good deal dazed and bewildered. Arthur assisted him to mount, took the saddle and bridle off his own horse, and carrying them with him and leading Roper's horse, he followed the count round the corner. Here was a group of nine horses ready saddled, with a tall old man standing beside them.

"Raphael," the count said, " take the saddle off my horse and put this gentleman's on to it. I have had a heavy lesson, and one that will last me all my life. This gentleman, whose life I strove to take, has spared mine when he had it at his mercy. I must get you to help me to throw into the gorge below the seven bodies of the men who went with me. They have all been killed. Put my saddle on to one of theirs. What do you think we had better do with the others?"

"I would leave them here, señor. I picked out the worst lot on the estate. They are not worth the trouble of taking home; and if I were to lead three or four horses for the five days it will take us to get there, it would be remarked upon. People are sure to come along the road in the course

of the day, and you may be certain that the horses will all
be appropriated before night, and that nothing will be said
about them."

"Very well; perhaps that will be the best way."

The count's horse had by this time been saddled. Arthur
mounted.

"Well, count, I will say good-bye. Our feud has been
a fierce one while it lasted, but it is well over now, and I
think it may have done both of us good."

"I am sure it will do me good," the count said humbly.
"Adieu, may the good fortune you deserve always attend
you!"

Arthur waved his hand, touched his horse with his spur,
and went on with Roper.

"How are you feeling, Roper?"

"I am getting all right, sir, though my head still seems
to hum. I hardly know how it came about. I fired right
at a man close to me. He was in the act of striking at me,
and I thought he would have dropped; but before I had time
to throw up my hand or parry in any way the blow came
down, and I remember nothing else till I found you pouring
brandy down my throat."

"You fired a second too late. I found the man lying dead
beside you, but I suppose the blow was already falling when
you hit him, and it came down on to your head without any
further effort on his part."

"And we killed the whole of them, sir?"

"Yes; I brought down three with my pistols and one with
my sword. You must have accounted for the other three."

"Yes; I fired four times, sir. I know I shot the two first
men, but before I could get my pistol fairly out of the other
holster the third man was on me. I missed him the first time,
but hit him with the second barrel just as he was in the act
of striking me down. He was the only man, I think, who
had a gun, all the others used pistols."

"Now I think of it, Roper, I have a strong suspicion, by

the pain I am feeling, that one or two of my ribs are broken. I felt a very sharp pang for a moment. That mail shirt kept the bullets from penetrating, but it did not keep them from hitting me very hard. I think I will dismount now and strip to the waist, and get you—if you feel up to it—to bandage me tightly. I know you always carry a couple of bandages in your valise."

"Oh, I am well enough for that, sir," Roper said, dismounting. Then leaving his horse he went across to Arthur and assisted him to dismount and to take off his coat and shirt.

"Here are the two bullets, sir, jammed tightly in the coat of mail; one is about an inch above the other. I am afraid two of the ribs are broken. I will make a shift to bandage you up as tightly as I can, and we will stop at the next town, which can only be six or seven miles away, and get a surgeon to attend to you properly. We will walk our horses all the way, it would never do to trot."

When Arthur had dressed again they continued on their journey at a very quiet pace, and arrived two hours later at a town. They put up at the principal inn and sent for a surgeon, who, on examining Arthur, at once found that the two ribs were broken.

"How long shall I be kept here?"

"It will depend how quickly the bones knit. I should say that you ought to stay for at least three weeks; but possibly you may go on before that, provided you take matters quietly. I shall, of course, bandage you up so tightly that they cannot shift unless you give yourself a wrench."

Arthur was detained ten days, but at the end of that time he insisted on proceeding. He was tightly enveloped in broad bandages, and, as he said, felt as if he were in a stiff pair of stays. He promised the surgeon that he would not let his horse go beyond a walk. However, they accomplished the journey to Saragossa at a pretty fair rate, travelling from eight to nine hours a day, making an average of twenty-five miles. By the time they got there Arthur no longer felt any acute pain, and was confident that the bones were healing. However, he resolved to follow the surgeon's advice and not attempt to remove the bandages for another month.

He found Saragossa a scene of great preparations. Espartero had determined not to move, as Oraa had done, with an insufficient siege-train, and during the months of comparative inactivity he had collected a battering train of forty pieces, of which eight were 24-pounders, twelve 16-pounders, ten mortars, and ten howitzers. Each gun was provided with a thousand rounds of ammunition.

Besides the siege-train he had also with him three field batteries armed with heavy guns. Transport had been collected with immense difficulty, for to carry the ammunition alone five hundred carts and two thousand mules were required, besides the waggons of the commissariat train and those for regimental transport. The force that was to accompany these amounted to twenty thousand men, while some eight thousand others were posted on the road and as garrisons in various villages. On the 18th of May the battering train moved forward, and was followed the next day by the main body. The first division advanced to the height of San Marcos, within sight of Morella. The main body with the head-quarters and artillery halted a few miles short of this on the heights above Pobleta.

During the night the weather changed suddenly. A very heavy snow-storm set in, and several men and mules were frozen to death. There was no change on the next day, but on the 23rd the army again advanced, and arrived early in the afternoon within range of the fort of San Pedro. It halted about two thousand yards from the town on its north side. The fort stood on a commanding height and was surrounded by a deep ditch. On its south and west sides it was inaccessible; on its north front it was well covered by a glacis. Its only exposed face was visible from another height, called San Marcos, at a distance of a thousand yards

on the same level on the opposite side of the valley. Owing
to the distance at which San Pedro stood from the city, Cabrera had since the last siege erected another strong redoubt
called La Querola to protect the communications. He had
made a great mistake, however, in not erecting another fortification on the heights facing La Querola. The two would
have protected each other, and their fire crossing the road
between them would have enabled them to hold out, even
against the powerful artillery brought against them, for at
least a fortnight.

Cabrera, however, who was no engineer, instead of covering the approaches with fortifications, had wasted much time
in forming entrenchments in the town which would be of
little or no use after an entry was once made. He himself
was still suffering from the effects of the wounds Arthur had
inflicted upon him, and was unable to undertake the defence
of the place; and when the besieging army drew near he
left the town with some eight thousand men in order to
harass communications, and interfere as far as possible with
the progress of the siege.

Espartero found that it was necessary to take La Querola
before the city itself could be attacked, because it commanded the road by which the siege artillery was brought up.
There was, too, in the valley along which the road ran, an
aqueduct which supplied the city with water, and behind this
a large body of troops could form up without being seen
from the city.

It was also desirable that this should be effected because
the weakest part of the wall was between the castle and the
gate of San Miguel; and were a breach effected there, the
whole of the interior entrenchments would be commanded
from it. The army encamped in front and on the flanks of
San Pedro, the stores and heavy guns being placed on the
height of San Marcos. On the 24th of May the engineers
commenced an approach against the north front of San
Pedro, and the artillery on the opposite height opened fire

upon it. The work of the sappers was arduous; an incessant musketry fire was kept up upon them, and the ground was so rocky that it was very difficult to obtain shelter. Finding, therefore, that the approach could not be made in a regular way, the sappers went forward at a run to within two hundred yards of the fort, and then covered themselves by hurriedly throwing up a stone wall.

Behind this they kept up so rapid and heavy a fire that they silenced that of the defenders, and during the night carried forward the work to within a hundred yards of the wall, and completed a little battery of three 16-pounders, which were to fire at the very small part of the work which was not covered by the glacis. They opened fire at daybreak, but did very little damage. It was otherwise, however, on the eastern side, where the wall was so effectually pounded by the heavy guns on the opposite heights that the whole of the parapet on that face was destroyed, and there was therefore no shelter for the defenders. Some of the light troops seeing this, crept up close to the ditch. The defenders, thinking that an assault was intended, rushed to oppose them, but suffered terribly from the fire from San Marcos.

Again and again they exposed themselves in the most gallant manner, but the fire from the guns was so excellent that they fell in great numbers. At eight o'clock the garrison sounded a parley, and the governor offered to surrender on condition that the survivors should be permitted to retreat to Morella. Espartero refused, and as the garrison could not any longer continue the hopeless defence, the governor surrendered at discretion. In the meantime Espartero had moved some light infantry against La Querola, the newly-raised fort built to keep up the communications between San Pedro and the city. The garrison here showed none of the same spirit that had animated the defenders of San Pedro. Notwithstanding the assistance rendered by a strong sortie from Morella, they resisted the attack for only half an hour and then abandoned the fort, being cut up as they retired by Espartero's cavalry.

Thus the way was opened for an advance of the besiegers to the neighbourhood of the city itself, and the whole army moved forward. A natural ridge, at a distance of from seven to eight hundred yards from the city, covered their movements, and here the batteries were at once commenced. By the 29th all was ready—thirty-five guns were in position —and a tremendous fire was opened against the town. The mortars did not effect the expected damage, for the town was almost entirely composed of stone, and but few houses were set on fire. The destruction wrought by the other guns was, however, very great: the wall between the castle and the gate of San Miguel crumbled rapidly, while the fire from the castle was almost wholly silenced, and a very destructive explosion took place in one of the principal magazines. The northern defences of the castle were almost destroyed, and communication could no longer be held by daylight between it and the town.

At half-past two in the afternoon an officer let himself down by a rope from the western wall and informed Espartero that a meeting of the principal officers of the town had been held, and that it had been determined that the troops in the city should that night endeavour to escape through the besieging army and join Cabrera, who was with the field force and very ill. The garrison of the castle was to remain and cover the escape of their comrades. Espartero at once took precautions to frustrate the attempt to escape. Directing an incessant fire to be kept up by all the guns, he despatched officers to the different divisions to order that the investment, which had not hitherto been complete, should at once be carefully closed, and that at nightfall the troops should draw nearer to the town and occupy in force all the roads, particularly that towards the gate of the Puerta del Estudio, which alone had not been blocked before the siege began. As, however, he was by no means certain that the

information brought by the deserter was true, he directed
the erection of two new batteries at the north-west angle of
the wall, while another battery was erected at the south-west
side of the city, a couple of field batteries being also sent
round there.

At ten o'clock in the evening fire was opened all round
Morella. This seemed to show that the information that
had been received was correct, and that this outburst of
firing was intended to show that the garrison was vigilant
and active. At dawn the troops, ignorant that their scheme
had been betrayed, marched down, headed by the governor.
To their surprise they were encountered by an overwhelming
force, and in the hasty struggle that ensued three hundred
and fifty of the Carlists were made prisoners. The rest of
the column endeavoured to regain the town, but a shell fell on
the draw-bridge and destroyed it. A terrible scene now ensued. A great many of the wives and children of the troops
had marched out with them, believing that the road was perfectly clear. These were pressed back by the retreating
troops. Numbers of men, women, and children were forced
into the moat, which soon became filled with a mass of struggling, suffocating people.

To add to the horror of the scene, those of the garrison
who still remained within the walls, hearing the shouts of the
Christinos—" Viva la Reyna! "—fired miscellaneously, in a
panic, upon friends and foes. At six o'clock in the morning
the officer second in command, and now acting as governor,
sent out to offer to capitulate on the condition that the garrison should be allowed to withdraw to a foreign country.
This was peremptorily refused by Espartero, and at eight
o'clock the place surrendered unconditionally. The remainder of the garrison marched out and piled arms under the
castle, their number exceeding three thousand. In both the
city and the castle the magazines were found stored with provisions sufficient to enable them to hold out for several
months. The defence was, on the whole, quite unworthy of

the traditions of the Carlists—in fact the little garrison of San Pedro alone behaved well.

There could be no doubt that the defenders had been cowed by the overwhelming powers of the siege artillery. They had relied upon being able to repulse any assault that might be made, but were utterly unprepared for a bombardment such as they had to endure. There was no precedent for the collection of so great a force of artillery. At the unsuccessful siege by Oraa only some eight to ten small pieces had been used; these had been badly placed and badly handled, and time had not even been allowed for them to complete the breaches. When, therefore, the walls were swept by the fire of fifty or sixty guns, and the garrison saw their defences in one day crumble before them, they thought only of escape. The lamentable part of the affair was the fearful destruction of life outside the gate.

This was a worthy conclusion of a struggle that had been conducted on both sides with an amount of ferocity, brutality, and bloodshed altogether without precedent in modern warfare; indeed, to find a parallel it is necessary to go back to the wholesale slaughter committed by Alva in the Low Countries.

The English officers, after order was restored, called upon Espartero to congratulate him on his complete success, and two or three of them took leave of him at once, as it was certain that although some guerilla skirmishing might still go on, the war was practically at an end. They then rode back to the hut which had formed their head-quarters during the siege.

The general expression was that of joy that their arduous and thankless work was at an end. They had been, in some cases, for years travelling almost constantly with flying columns, which moved aimlessly through the country, or remained for months together inactive without making an effort to get in touch with the enemy. It was not their business to give advice unless it was asked for: their mis-

sion was to endeavour to humanize the war. And although
at times one or another of the commanders would act with
some little humanity, these were quite exceptional cases, and
as a rule little quarter was given on either side, both insist-
ing that these atrocities were but reprisals for acts of the
other party.

· In vain had the British commissioners urged, in the name
not only of humanity but of good policy, that the customs
of war should be followed, and that their antagonists should
not be excited to madness by the wanton destruction of life,
the wholesale devastation of the country, and the razing to
the ground of villages and homesteads. Both parties admitted the justice of their reasons, both bewailed the necessity for such actions; but both continued to commit them to
the end of the war.   There was, then, a feeling of deep satisfaction among the three or four British officers, at the
capture of Morella and its garrison. As long as that city
remained in the hands of the Carlists, it was a rallying centre for them—a reminder of the signal defeat of the army
that had besieged it. Now it had fallen after a resistance
that could not but be considered as feeble. The Carlists had,
it is true, other strongholds in different parts of the country, but these were comparatively insignificant, and would
doubtless open their gates as soon as detachments of Espartero's army appeared before them.

Indeed, the weakness of the defence of Morella showed
that the spirit of the Carlists was already broken. Had Cabrera remained among them to cheer and encourage them,
the defence would have been much more desperate, though
it could not have been very much more prolonged, for another day or two would have seen the defences so destroyed
that the place would have been untenable; but the fact that
Cabrera was away wounded and sick took all the spirit out
of the defence. The first offer of the governor to surrender
if the garrison were allowed to march out and cross a foreign
frontier, was no doubt the result of an order that Cabrera

had given him before he left, when he found that he was no
longer able to defend the place, and probably foreshadowed
the plan that Cabrera himself thought it likely he would be
compelled to adopt.

Espartero's triumph had been complete. He had, indeed,
proved the saviour of Spain. When he began—one among
half a dozen generals—he found jealousy and jobbery everywhere rampant. Most of the generals thought only of avoiding defeat, and not of gaining victory. So long as the Carlists left them alone they were well content to allow them to
march almost at will through the country. The army, which
was ill-clothed and ill-fed, was wholly deficient in artillery,
and had but a very small body of cavalry. Worst of all, the
government was rotten to the core. Corruption prevailed in
every office, and positions were only secured through favour-
itism, merit counting not at all. Little by little Espartero
changed all this. His honesty, his talent, and dogged perse-
verance triumphed over his adversaries. The people at large
came to regard him as their one hope, and answered his appeal to them by overthrowing the government that had
thwarted him, and making him towards the end of the war
practically Dictator of Spain.

He had all along distinguished himself by the courtesy
with which he had treated the British commissioners. He
had relied a great deal upon the advice of Colonel Wylde,
who was senior of that body, and had himself set, as a rule,
an example of clemency to the captives except when he was
driven by the massacre of prisoners taken by the Carlists to
carry out striking reprisals. Many of the other generals, on
the other hand, kept the commissioners at arm's length, and
would not only give them no information themselves, but
ordered their officers not to do so. It is not difficult to
understand the feeling that actuated them. These officers
were unwelcome at their head-quarters not because they were
there to plead the cause of humanity, but because they furnished the British government with accurate reports of the

movements and conduct of the army, and thus exposed the falsity of their own bombastic reports of their doings.

"For my part, I am heartily glad it is over," Arthur said. "I certainly do not mean to remain to witness the expulsion of Cabrera and the stamping out of the last embers of disaffection. I have had six years of it, and I intend to send in my resignation as soon as I arrive at Madrid. When I came out it was with the intention of serving merely for the term of my enlistment, a couple of years; then I had the good fortune to be transferred to the army when the Legion was broken up, though I still thought that it was but for another year or so. However, I have no reason to regret that I have seen it through. I have been fortunate in all respects—very fortunate in serving under so kind and good a chief as Colonel Wylde."

"What are you thinking of doing if you leave the army?"

"I have a small estate waiting for me at home, which has been little by little piling up capital for me during my absence. I shall be a good deal more fit to take charge of it now, and to settle down, than I should have been if I had never come out here."

"It seems a pity, too," Colonel Lacy said. "You have done very good service, and Colonel Wylde has always reported well of you. You have been a captain now for four years, and you will be sure to get your majority as a reward for your work here."

"Yes, sir; if I had entered the army for the purpose of staying in it, I should have every reason for congratulating myself on my good fortune; but as I did not, I should not value the majority, for which indeed I feel myself much too young. Besides, I should be altogether unfit for it. I learned the work of a subaltern for a year, in a hard, rough school, where there was no occasion to know more than the simplest movements. For the past four years I have not commanded a corporal's guard, and I could no more drill a battalion of British troops on a parade-ground than fly, so I have quite made up my mind to leave, and have indeed only held on for the past two years in the belief that the war would speedily come to an end."

"Well, Hallett, of course you know your own business best; and I am quite sure that if I had a nice little estate waiting for me in England, I should take the same course as you are going to do."

CHAPTER XXI

HOME

THE next day Arthur mounted, and, after saying good-bye to his friends, started for Madrid. He was still wearing his bandages, but as a measure of precaution rather than as a necessity, for the bones had knit well, and Espartero's surgeon had told him that he could safely give them up. Arthur, however, said that he was accustomed to them now, and as they were no great inconvenience, it would be folly to run the smallest risk, and he would therefore keep them on for another month. Roper was in high glee at the thought that he was going to return home.

"When we get to Madrid," Arthur said, "we will both lay aside our uniforms, and you will cease to be my servant. We can return to the position we formerly occupied towards each other, that of good friends, though of course much closer ones than of old. We have gone through many dangers together, and it will only be a matter of regret to me that you should have been in the position of my servant."

"I won't give it up when we get to Madrid, sir. At any rate I shall remain your servant till we embark on board ship for England, after which you will have no more occasion for me, and I shall be proud to become your humble friend. I

suppose, sir," he said with a quiet smile, "you are not thinking of going back to England alone?"

"Not if I can help it," Arthur answered. "Of course
nothing is settled, but I don't fancy that I shall have to go
back alone. If I do I shall return shortly, but I hope to
manage everything satisfactorily before I leave."

Arthur had heard regularly every six months from his
uncle, who had of late said he hoped he would soon leave the
army and return home, and in his last letter, written after
he had come of age, had said: "I may now tell you, my
dear Arthur, that the will of your father contains a secret
clause giving me the power, if I considered you fit to undertake the responsibility, of handing your estates over to you
when you came of age. I must say that it seems to me you
are quite fit to assume that responsibility. Your letters do
not tell me a very great deal about yourself, but it is clear
that, as in these five years you have won your way from being a private to holding a commission as a captain, you
ought certainly to possess a sufficient amount of steadiness
and knowledge of the world to fit you for the not very oner-
ous duties of a country squire. You do not tell us very much
about yourself, and we all consider your letters in that respect very unsatisfactory; but it is evident that you have
seen a great deal of service, and must have cured yourself
of that tendency to wildness that caused us such trouble before you left. In fact we all feel proud of you, holding, as
you do, the appointment as one of the British assistant commissioners.

"I own that it has been a surprise to me, but my wife
declares that she was always sure you would do well, and
I need hardly say that the girls are very fond of parading
their cousin, a captain in the army and royal commissioner
in Spain, among their acquaintances. Of course I do not
urge you to return—that is a question entirely for you to
decide; but I say that, in virtue of the power given to me by
your father, I shall have no hesitation in placing you on

your return in possession of your father's estates and the accumulation of rents during your minority."

Communication was slow, and this letter had only been received by Arthur a few days before his seizure by the monks. It had been a great satisfaction to him, as he would now be able to maintain Mercedes in a position not altogether inferior to that to which she had been accustomed. He had, however, not spoken on the subject even to Leon, preferring to continue to stand on the same basis as before. He travelled by easy stages to Madrid, and was most warmly greeted on his return there by Leon and the girls.

"Rather a curious thing has happened since you have been away," Leon said, when they were chatting together on the first evening after his return. "I have received a letter from Don Silvio. I don't understand it, but it is, as far as it goes, very satisfactory; still I cannot quite make it out. He writes to say that he regrets very deeply his conduct towards us and you, and implores our pardon. He says that henceforth we need fear no annoyance whatever from him, and that he can only hope that some day he may resume his former position as a friend of our family. He says that of course we shall have heard from you the reasons that have brought about this entire change in his sentiments, and that we can easily understand that after your treatment of him he is an entirely changed man. I received this letter a fortnight ago. I really did not know how to answer it, so have waited to get some explanation from you as to the circumstances that have brought about this change in his sentiments, in which I own I have no belief whatever. Indeed I consider that the letter was only written to put us off our guard. Certainly in the letters you have written since you left there has been nothing that would explain the matter, except indeed that you said you had had a trifling affair with some brigands and had got the better of them, though at the cost of a slight wound. Had this anything to do with it?"

"It had, Leon. It was not worth writing about, although the affair was a somewhat sharp one, and I had not intended to say anything about it; but as it has apparently brought about a very satisfactory state of things, I suppose I had better tell it."

He then related how Roper had, as he thought, recognized Don Silvio; how they had discovered that they were really watched; the precautions they had taken against attack; and gave an account of the fight, telling how the seven men who had attacked them had been killed in the encounter. "Don Silvio fought hard," he said carelessly, "but I had him at my mercy. Reflecting, however, that I had injured him by winning the affections of Mercedes, and that I had certainly behaved wrongly in fooling with him in that duel, I let him go."

"You let him go?" Leon said in astonishment. "Do you mean to say that when you had him at your mercy you actually let him go?"

"That is what it came to, I suppose," Arthur admitted. "I had him by the throat at the edge of the precipice, then it occurred to me that the man had good grounds for complaint against me. But for me he might have married Mercedes, and as over and above this I had made him the laughing stock of Madrid, it was natural that he should have endeavoured to get rid of me. I therefore concluded that I ought not to take his life; so I released him and explained this to him, and we parted, I think, very good friends."

Leon gazed at him in astonishment. "By San Paolo, Arthur, but you are an extraordinary man! The idea of sparing that fellow when you had him at your mercy! You astound me!"

"It was good of you, Arthur, wonderfully good!" Mercedes exclaimed, "but just the thing that you would do. I am proud of you! Of course I have always been proud of you, but more now than ever. And do you think he is sincere in this letter he wrote to Leon?"

354 WITH THE BRITISH LEGION

"I do think so. From the way in which he spoke to me I believe that he was thoroughly sincere, and that he felt that he had been in the wrong, and that the feud between us was now at an end. I think, Leon, you can now answer his letter, saying that you have seen me and heard my explanation, and that you are heartily glad that the feud is over and are ready again to receive him as a friend."

"As to that I should be only too glad," Leon said. "Until this thing happened I always esteemed him, as you may suppose by my consenting to give Mercedes to him. He has not injured me, and if you have brought yourself to forgive his attempts upon your life it is little enough for me to shake hands with him again. I will write and tell him so to-morrow morning, and express my willingness that bygones shall be bygones, and that our friendship can be again renewed. And now to return to a still more interesting subject. What are your plans?"

"As I have already told you, I shall to-morrow send in my resignation. The next step must necessarily depend upon you a great deal. It seems to me that it would be exceedingly difficult for Mercedes and myself to be married here. The ceremony could be performed at the British Embassy, but for my part I would much rather that it took place in England; and I should think, Leon, that that would also be most pleasant for you all. Our marriage here would undoubtedly cause a considerable amount of feeling. You would be blamed very strongly for giving your sister to a foreigner and a heretic, and things might be made very unpleasant for you and the girls. My own idea is that the best thing possible would be for us all to travel quietly down to Cadiz, and thence take ship to England. There we could be married comfortably. While preparing for that, I could see that my place was made ready to receive us; then I hope you would stay with us for some time before returning home. In that way you would avoid all trouble here, for whereas a wedding in the face of the public of Madrid would cause no end of scandal, a quiet marriage in England would scarcely be noticed."

Leon was silent for a minute, and then said: "I think a good deal is to be said in favour of your plan. There can be no doubt that the marriage would create much less comment and talk than if it were to take place here. Secondly, I should like to see the new home in which Mercedes is to be established—not to say that I should certainly like to see something more of England; but I don't know about the girls."

"Oh, Leon!" both exclaimed, "you would never leave us behind! Why, of course we should want just as much as you do to be at Mercedes' wedding. You never can really think of leaving us here. What reason could there be why we shouldn't go with you?"

"Well, you see, in the first place you don't speak English."

"Nor do you, Leon, at least not well."

"Well, you know that in point of fact I do speak it pretty fairly. However, it's too important a matter to be settled offhand, girls. Suppose, for example, that one of you took it into your head to marry an English gentleman?"

"Well, Leon," Inez said mischievously, "as it appears to us that you are likely before long to enter the married state yourself, I should have thought that you would be very glad to get us off your hands, even to Englishmen. I am sure if all Englishmen were like Arthur I should have no objection at all. I have always been lamenting that I did not go with you, instead of Mercedes, to our country place, and then perhaps I might have had the chance that Mercedes has had."

They all laughed.

"Well, really, I will think it over, Inez. It might be managed, and the three months' trip would do us all good after the stormy time we have been having here."

"I am sure it would," Arthur said; "so I think, girls, we can consider that settled."

"Well, of course we could not think of going for a month yet," Mercedes said. "You must remember that we shall all have preparations to make."

"But you can get things made in England," Arthur urged.

"No, sir," Mercedes said. "We are not going away without a sufficient supply of clothes. At any rate, we shall want travelling suits, and a lot of other things, though I admit that I should prefer getting some of my dresses in England. I don't want to have everyone staring at me, when I go about, as a foreigner."

"Well, of course you must have time, Mercedes, and I don't think a month is very unreasonable; besides, all sorts of papers will have to be got ready and drawn up."

"Certainly," Leon said. "As Mercedes' guardian and the head of the family, it is my duty to see that everything is done regularly. As far as you are concerned, Arthur, I should be quite content to have no settlements of any kind; but it would be unseemly for a daughter of our house to marry in the haphazard way of a small farmer's daughter."

"I agree with you thoroughly, Leon, but I think it would be better for you to have the settlements drawn up in England. You may calculate that it will be a month after my return before things will be ready, which will give plenty of time for you to have the deeds drawn up there. You see, the laws of your country are not the same as ours."

"I should say they had better be drawn up in both countries," Leon said. "Mercedes' income is a charge upon a Spanish estate, and the people acting as her trustees here would be bound by Spanish law only. I think that when these troubles are all over, and land rises in value again, it would be best that the estates should be sold. Mercedes could then invest her money in England. The other girls' shares would be held in trust for them till they marry."

"That would certainly be a very good plan, Leon. You

will understand, of course, that I wish Mercedes' fortune to
be entirely under her own control."

Arthur spent a very pleasant month in Madrid. He was,
at the regent's request, very frequently at the palace, and
when he informed her that Mercedes was going to England
to be married to him, she presented her with a splendid suite
of diamonds.

"You see, Captain Hallett," she said, "you would not let
me do for you a quarter of what I wished to do; but at
least you cannot interfere between me and Donna Mercedes
de Balen. I wish greatly that you had permanently settled
here. I would have made you a Grand Duke of Spain, and
there would be pleasure in knowing that my daughter would
have one absolutely disinterested and faithful friend. My
own health is not good. I have had a terribly anxious time
for the past eight years. I have been surrounded by men
whom I despise. I have seen how few of them care for the
cause to which they profess to be devoted, and think only
of themselves and their own interests. Fortunately, should
anything happen to me, I shall leave her in Espartero's
hands with a certain knowledge that he will protect and
guard her during her minority."

"I trust sincerely, madam, that there will be no occasion
for him to assume such a charge; but I thoroughly agree
with you that should he have to do so, he will perform it
well and honourably."

Before leaving, Leon and the girls made no formal fare-
well visits to their friends. They knew that if their inten-
tions were announced there would be a storm of opposition,
and that all their friends and the members of the families
with which they were connected would move heaven and
earth to try and dissuade them. Mercedes' engagement had
never been formally announced, and although her attach-
ment for Arthur might be suspected by the intimates of the
family, nothing could be said until their betrothal was made
public.

At last the preparations were all complete, and the deeds drawn up and signed. Leon had made the usual stipulation that while any boys born of the marriage should be brought up in their father's religion, the girls should be brought up in that of their mother.

They journeyed by easy stages—the men on horseback, the girls in the family coach—down to Cadiz, where berths had already been secured on board a ship sailing for England. The voyage was a slow but fair one. After the first day or two none of the party suffered from sea-sickness. Roper had refused to allow a passage to be taken for him aft with the others.

" It is kind of you to wish it, sir, but I should not be comfortable. If you were travelling alone it would be different, but the count and his sisters have only been accustomed to look upon me as your servant. They are always very kind and friendly to me. They know that we have gone through a very great deal together, but I think they would feel—and I am sure I should be—very uncomfortable if I were to sit at table with them on terms of equality."

" Well, it must be as you wish, Roper, but I am quite sure they do not feel it so. They know that I regard you, and always have done so, as a friend; that we have gone through many adventures together, besides the one in which you aided me to save Mercedes from Cabrera. However, it shall be as you like."

The girls and Leon after the first two days thoroughly enjoyed the voyage, which was a novelty to them. On arriving in London the count took private rooms at an hotel, and for two or three days Arthur went about with them, enjoying the sights as much as they did, as he had never before been to London. Then he travelled down to Liverpool by the North-Western Railway—then only recently opened.

He had written briefly to his uncle on his arrival, mentioning the day on which he should come down. When he reached Liverpool, therefore, he drove from the station to his house.

Although he had written home regularly once every three or four months, he had simply mentioned the positions he held, and the scenes he had witnessed, and had said but very little as to his private adventures.

When he drove up to the door his uncle and aunt both came out to meet him. They paused in astonishment. " Is it possible that you are Arthur ? " Mr. Hallett asked.

" Not only possible, but a fact, uncle."

" Well, we are delighted to see you home again, my boy; but we certainly did not expect to see a giant."

" Nor do you, uncle. I am only six feet one, not at all an out-of-the-way height."

" Well, I must kiss you, my dear," his aunt said; " but I almost feel as if I were taking a liberty."

" Nonsense, aunt! I don't think I have changed much since I went away; but of course in six years I have grown a bit bigger. And how are you, girls? How are you both ? "

They went into the house.

" Well, Arthur," his uncle said, looking at him closely, " it may have been only six years since you left us, but by your appearance I should have thought that it was ten."

" I suppose I do look older than I am, uncle. Everyone takes me for three or four years older, but I can tell you it has been a most fortunate thing for me. I should never have been made a captain if they had had an idea that I was only eighteen years old."

" Well, Arthur, I suppose you have quite given up your tendency to get into scrapes," his aunt said.

" I don't think I have, aunt," Arthur laughed. " I have been in a good many of what you might call scrapes since I went away, but as you see, I have come all right through them. The only casualty that I have had is, that I got a couple of ribs broken in a fight with some brigands three months ago. And now I am going to astonish you. I am going to get married."

There was a general exclamation of astonishment. " You are not serious, Arthur ? "

" Never was more serious in my life."

" And is it to a Spanish lady ? "

" Yes, uncle. She is the sister of a count who is a great friend of mine, and I am sure you will say when you see her that she is a most charming young lady. She is a year younger than I am, and is reasonably endowed with the world's goods."

His aunt was the first to rally from her astonishment. " It sounds very nice, Arthur," she said, " and I have no doubt that we shall congratulate you very much when we get to know her; but of course it has come as a little shock to us."

" I expected it would, aunt. I know that English people are prejudiced against foreigners. Of course, I have been living in Spain for six years, and have got over any ideas of that sort."

" But is she a Catholic, Arthur ? " his aunt asked in rather an awed tone.

" All Spanish ladies are Catholics, aunt; but, as this particular one is by no means a bigoted one, we are not likely to quarrel over it. She already speaks English well, and I can assure you that you will find her charming."

" And you say she has a fortune ? "

" Yes, she has about twenty-five thousand pounds in her own right."

" Well, that is comfortable; anyhow, you will not do badly in the money way. Your own estate was worth about one thousand pounds a year, but as it has been accumulating since you were ten years old, and as I have always invested the rents carefully, it will bring you in about as much more."

" That is not bad at all, uncle; and I may add that I have

twenty thousand pounds of my own lying to my order at the Bank of Liverpool."

"Twenty thousand, Arthur! Why, how in the world did you get that?"

"I did a little service to the queen. It really was not worth troubling about, but she and the government between them insisted on making me a present of that sum. I may mention also that I am a member of the first class of the Order of San Fernando and a Knight of Isabella the Catholic. Now, girls, I should like to see you curtsy to me. So you see, uncle, that my running away and joining the British Legion has not turned out so badly."

"No, indeed, Arthur. Of course, you will tell us all about it presently; as yet we can only wonder. I suppose you intend to go back to Spain shortly to fetch your wife home?"

"No, I have no idea of returning to Spain for an indefinite time. Donna Mercedes de Balen—that is her full name, uncle—accompanied me home to England under the protection of her brother, the Count Leon de Balen, whose name I have more than once mentioned in my letters, and with them came their two sisters, Donna Inez and Donna Dolores, two very charming young ladies. They will return home with their brother in three or four months' time. After our marriage takes place they will travel about England."

"You certainly seem to have the whole thing arranged, Arthur, and it appears to me that you are as headstrong as you were when a boy."

"I don't think so, uncle. I have been doing a man's work for six years, and, though I say it myself, have done it fairly well. Now I have finished wandering, and am going to settle down for good."

They talked until a very late hour in the evening. Arthur refused to satisfy their curiosity as to the service he had rendered to the queen, and said nothing about his private adventures. He told them principally about his work in the Legion, and afterwards as an assistant commissioner.

"Now, what is your first business going to be, Arthur?" his uncle asked when they met the next morning.

"The very first thing is to go over to my place. I have no doubt you have had it kept in good order; but it is certain that great changes will be needed before I bring Mercedes home there. I should wish you and aunt and the girls to go over there with me and give me the benefit of your opinions as to the alterations to be made. It will save time if we drive first to some of the best builders and upholsterers in town, and get them to send out men an hour and a half or so after we start, to meet us there. I think," he said, turning to his aunt, "that the wedding will take place in London, and hope that you will all come up and be present."

"You quite take my breath away, Arthur, with your impetuosity."

"Well, aunt, when a thing has to be done it seems to me that the sooner it is done the better. When it is over we shall go away for a fortnight or so, and when we come home the count and his sisters will meet us. The idea is that they shall spend about three weeks with us, and that we shall then travel with them for a month."

"Well, James," Mrs. Hallett said, "it seems to me that the programme is a very good one. The girls have never been up to London, and I have not been up there since we were married. It is nothing of a journey now that the railway is open. I am sure you want a holiday, too; you have not had one for years. Arthur will no doubt get nice lodgings for us, and I am sure we shall enjoy the trip immensely. When is the marriage to come off, Arthur?"

"I should say in about a week or ten days; there is no conceivable reason why we should wait any longer."

"In that case it is only three weeks till your home-coming. You don't suppose that the alterations you propose to make could be carried out in that time?"

"A lot can be done with money, uncle, and I don't care what I spend. At any rate, a portion of the house large

enough to hold our party can be in good order by that time,
and the rest must be finished while we are away."

"I don't know how I can give up my work," Mr. Hallett
began; but Arthur broke in:

"My dear uncle, you need not say that. Your head clerk
can surely manage the business for ten days. If he cannot,
I should advise you to sack him and get another. Now, if
you will give me the address of the builder and upholsterer,
I will drive round and see them and arrange for them to send
men, and will bring the carriage to the door in an hour's
time."

"Well, I cannot go to-day anyhow, Arthur."

"Well, I am sorry for that, uncle, because I should have
liked your opinion. However, in the matter of furnishing
and so on, I know that I can rely upon aunt."

"But I cannot understand," Mr. Hallett said, "why you
didn't get married out there."

"My dear uncle, if you lived in Spain you would very
soon find out the amount of pressure that is used to prevent a young lady of noble family from marrying a Protestant and a stranger. It is simply enormous; and therefore we agreed that it would be infinitely better for us to
come over to England. When a thing is once done, it is
useless to say anything against it. The priests may tear
their hair over what they will consider an act of backsliding on the part of Mercedes, but she won't hear anything of it."

On reaching his house Arthur found that, although it was
in a fair state of repair, a great deal must be done to meet
his requirements. It was a good country house, but not a
large one, and he decided that the dining-room must be enlarged, the drawing-room doubled in size, a boudoir built
adjoining it, and several new bedrooms added. It was
clearly impossible to do all this in three weeks, and it was
decided that the dining-room should be left for the present
as it stood, and the builder promised to put so many hands

to work that the drawing-room and boudoir and rooms over them should be finished in time. The stables were altogether condemned and would have to be rebuilt, and orders were given to have the gardens put in perfect order and planted with flowers before Arthur returned with his wife.

" It is a large order," the builder said, " but as you say that I can put on any number of men, I think I can guarantee to get it finished."

The order for the upholsterer was very large, as the whole house was to be refurnished, and there was much consultation between Mrs. Hallett and the girls as to the patterns, etc. However, they returned in the evening very well satisfied with the work they had done, and next morning Arthur went to town again.

He found that a special licence could be obtained at once, and therefore wrote to his uncle and aunt to come up on the following day by an afternoon train. He met them at the station and drove with them to lodgings he had taken for them in Clarges Street.

" These must be rather expensive rooms," Mr. Hallett said gravely.

" My dear uncle, that makes no difference to you; I am going to pay the piper. While you are here, you will be my guests. I am very flush of money, for I have in my bank six hundred pounds of the money you sent me, for twenty pounds a year in addition to my pay quite sufficed for my wants."

Arthur had secured a room for himself in the same house, and next morning after breakfast took his friends to visit Leon and his sisters. They were mutually pleased with each other, and the girls pronounced Mercedes to be charming, and the other girls almost as nice, though they were unable to get on so well with them, as Arthur had to act as interpreter. After talking for an hour the ladies decided to go shopping together, while Leon, Arthur, and his uncle strolled through the town.

"Well, have you done your shopping to your satisfaction, aunt?" Arthur said when they met again.

"Yes, we have bought loads of things. I am quite frightened to think what your uncle will say when he gets the bill."

"He won't get the bill at all," Arthur said quietly. "You are my guests, and I am going to stand paymaster."

"Oh, but that is impossible, Arthur. We have bought almost everything new. I have reckoned it roughly up, and it will come to over a hundred and twenty pounds."

"If it would come to two hundred and forty it would be all the better," Arthur said. "You don't understand, aunt. This allowance money is burning in my pocket. I have had no means of spending it till now, and I am going to indulge myself. Please say no more about it, but just hand me the bills and I will see them paid. Now, you will really hurt me if you say any more."

Leon and his party came round to dinner, which Arthur had ordered to be sent in from a restaurant in Bond Street.

"How did you and Arthur get to know each other, Mercedes?" one of the girls asked.

"Well, we only knew each other from his knowing our brother up to the time when he saved my life."

"Saved your life! He never told us anything about that."

"That is just like him!" Mercedes said impetuously. "It is too bad of him, everyone ought to know it;" and she gave them a vivid account of the manner in which he had rescued her. After that, she said, "What could I do but marry him? I was engaged to someone else. I did not love him, you know; but is was a proper sort of engagement. The count was a man of good family and a friend of my brother's. He had asked Leon's consent, and Leon had given it, so there was nothing for me to say. But after Arthur had saved my life, of course it was different altogether, and I broke off the engagement. It was more than a year after that before

I became engaged to Arthur. He declares that he never suspected I cared for him, though really I am afraid I showed it very much. Then Arthur had to fight a duel with the count and wounded him, and the count made two attempts on his life, and then you know the Church interfered and shut Arthur up in a dungeon, and he dug his way out in a wonderful way. Have you not heard all this before?"

"No, he never said a word about it in his letters," Mrs. Hallett said.

"Mercedes, you are chattering too much," Arthur said. "You thought a great deal about these things, but there was nothing worth telling."

"I am the best judge of that, sir," Mercedes said, tossing her head. "You go on talking to Leon and my sisters."

"And haven't you heard, Mrs. Hallett," she said, "of the wonderful way in which he rescued the Regent of Spain and the little Queen when they were carried off?"

"Not a word, dear."

"Well then, I shall scold him very much," Mercedes said. "When he has done so many splendid things, why should he not speak of them?"

"I think he might have told us, my dear," Mrs. Hallett said gently, "but I suppose he thought it would look like bragging, and there is nothing Englishmen hate more than that. Men who do great things are the very last to speak of them."

"Ah well, I will tell you some day all about them," Mercedes said, "and then you will not be surprised that I say he is one of the most wonderful men in the world, and why I, and Leon and my sisters, love him so."

The two girls looked at Arthur with wondering eyes. He had always been rather a hero with them in his young days, and they could quite imagine that he would be a brave soldier, but they had never dreamt of his performing such deeds as these.

At the wedding Roper, who had at once on his arrival

gone down to see his family, and who had now come up for the purpose, acted as Arthur's best man. He had vainly endeavoured to excuse himself. Arthur insisted that having for six years been his best friend, he should certainly occupy that place on this important occasion.

In spite of the effort of the builders the house was not ready for habitation at the time fixed on, and it was two months before the whole party returned together from their tour. Roper was by this time installed on a farm on the estate. When Leon returned to Spain he left Inez with her sister, and six months later she married a neighbour of Arthur's, to the great satisfaction of Mercedes; and neither of them has once regretted that she has exchanged the troubles and struggles of her native land for the peace and quiet of England. As to Arthur, he has always said that the day he enlisted in the British Legion was the most fortunate one in his life.

THE END

www.ingramcontent.com/pod-product-compliance
Lightning Source LLC
Chambersburg PA
CBHW072306020726
47501CB00002B/411